A SERPENT IN EDEN

A SERPENT IN EDEN

JAMES OWEN

LITTLE, BROWN

'LE, BROWN

First published in Great Britain in August 2005 by Little, Brown
Reprinted 2005

Map of central Nassau on page xii by Alessia Carrara.

A CIP catalogue record for this book
is available from the British Library.

ISBN 0 316 86121 9

Typeset in Bembo by M Rules
Printed and bound in Great Britain by
Clays Ltd, St Ives plc

Little, Brown
An imprint of
Time Warner Book Group UK
Brettenham House
Lancaster Place
London WC2E 7EN

www.twbg.co.uk

For MariaLuisa

CONTENTS

CAST LIST

Sir Harry Oakes, Bt. – Multimillionaire baronet and murder victim, aged sixty-eight in July 1943

Eunice, Lady Oakes - His wife, aged forty-four

Nancy Oakes – Their eldest child, heiress to the Western hemisphere's largest gold mine, aged nineteen

Count Alfred de Marigny – Her husband, aged thirty-three

Georges, Marquis de Visdelou – De Marigny's best friend, aged thirty-four

Betty Roberts – His girlfriend, aged sixteen

The Duke of Windsor – Formerly King Edward VIII, now Governor of the Bahamas

The Duchess of Windsor – Formerly Mrs Wallis Simpson

(Sir) Harold Christie – Property agent and business partner of Oakes

Axel Wenner-Gren – Swedish tycoon, founder of Electrolux and suspected Nazi agent

Inga Arvad – Former Miss Denmark and suspected mistress of Wenner-Gren

John F. Kennedy – American naval officer and lover of Arvad

Baroness Marie af Trolle – Best friend of Nancy Oakes

Baron Georg af Trolle – Her husband and private secretary to Wenner-Gren

Brenda Frazier – American heiress, socialite and magazine cover-girl, aged twenty-two

Sir Frederick Williams-Taylor – Her grandfather, a banker living in Nassau

Jane, Lady Williams-Taylor – Her grandmother and MI5 agent, queen of Nassau society

Howard Hughes – Admirer of Frazier, former owner of Wenner-Gren's yacht, the world's largest

Ruth Fahnestock – Ex-wife of de Marigny

Lucie-Alice Cahen – First ex-wife of de Marigny

Godfrey Higgs – Barrister defending de Marigny, aged thirty-five

Ernest Callender – Junior to Higgs, aged thirty-four

Sir Oscar Daly – Chief Justice of the Bahamas and trial judge

Eric Hallinan – Attorney-General of the Bahamas, prosecutor of de Marigny, aged forty-three

Alfred Adderley – Nassau's leading barrister and prosecutor of de Marigny, aged fifty

Raymond Schindler – America's most famous private investigator

Leonarde Keeler – Principal exponent of the lie detector and partner of Schindler

Erle Stanley Gardner – Journalist, author and creator of detective Perry Mason

Ernest Hemingway – Friend of de Marigny; a writer

Captain James Barker – Miami policeman and fingerprint expert

Captain Edward Melchen – Head of the Miami Homicide Squad

Lt. Col. Reginald Erskine-Lindop – Commissioner of Police, Nassau

Major Herbert Pemberton – Head of the Bahamas CID

Major Frederick Lancaster – Erskine-Lindop's deputy

Captain Edward Sears – Nassau policeman

Lt. John Douglas – Nassau policeman

Frank Conway – New York Police fingerprint expert
Maurice O'Neil – New Orleans Police fingerprint expert
J. Edgar Hoover – Director of the FBI

Newell Kelly – Oakes's business manager
Walter Foskett – Oakes's lawyer, based in Miami
John Anderson – Banker and employee of Wenner-Gren
Dorothy Clarke – Dinner guest of de Marigny, married to an
    RAF officer
Jean Ainsley – Dinner guest of de Marigny, married to an RAF
    officer
Fred Cerreta – Dinner guest of de Marigny; an American engineer
Effie Heneage – Dinner guest of Oakes
Levi Gibson – Christie's driver and factotum

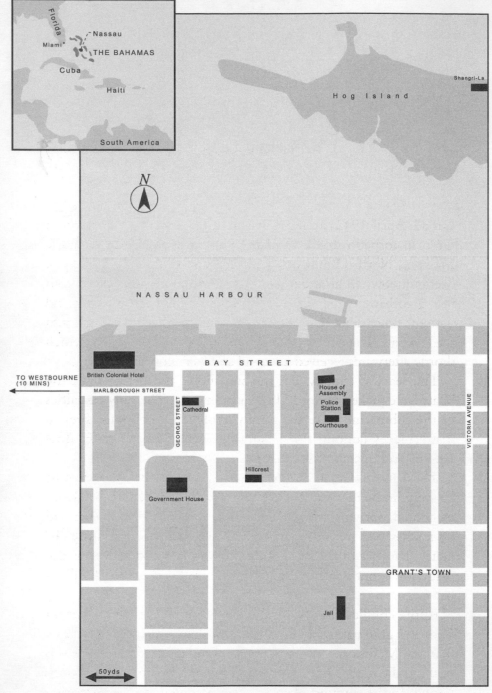

Florida
Miami
Nassau
THE BAHAMAS
Cuba
Haiti
South America

N

Hog Island
Shangri-La

NASSAU HARBOUR

British Colonial Hotel
BAY STREET

TO WESTBOURNE
(10 MINS)

MARLBOROUGH STREET

GEORGE STREET

Cathedral

House of
Assembly
Police
Station
Courthouse

VICTORIA AVENUE

Hillcrest

Government House

GRANT'S TOWN

Jail

50yds

CENTRAL NASSAU, 1943

PREFACE

On 11 April 1942, at about half past three in the afternoon, a German torpedo struck the Blue Funnel liner *Ulysses* off Cape Lookout, North Carolina. My father, who was then six, had just been put down in his cabin for a rest. As water began to pump into the cargo bay, my grandmother scooped up him and his sister and with the other ninety passengers began in orderly fashion to get into the lifeboats. These soon pushed off from the stricken vessel, which shortly afterwards received a second and fatal blow amidships.

The sea was choppy, but the sun shone and before dusk the boats were picked up by a US Navy corvette. The only casualties of the submarine were the family's collection of minor French masterpieces (among them paintings by Courbet and Fantin-Latour) and my aunt's velveteen dog, Pumpkin.

The Owens had left Australia about two weeks previously, heading home to Devon. Three years before, my father had been diagnosed as having tuberculosis and in early 1940 his mother had been advised to move, for the sake of his health, to a less damp climate than that of the West Country. Switzerland had been the first choice, but was ruled out because of the war, so Australia it had been.

As the conflict intensified, the family found themselves cut off from my grandfather in England, and they had spent two years living in Melbourne where it was soon established that there was nothing the matter with my father's lungs. The doctors had been wrong. In the summer of 1942, against advice, my grandmother decided to risk the voyage back to Britain. At the Panama Canal, a fellow passenger with whom she had made friends tried to prevent her from reboarding the boat. Afterwards, he could not be found, and she remains convinced that he was a spy who was signalling their position to the wolf pack.

Following their brief brush with danger, and then a short stay in America, the trio went on to Nassau, in the Bahamas, as the threat from U-boats was too great to risk joining another convoy across the Atlantic. Nassau was the nearest British possession to which my grandfather could transfer sterling for them, and through American relations of his they also had an introduction to the wife of the islands' Governor – the Duchess of Windsor. My grandmother rented a house, Hillcrest, close to the Duke's residence, and there they spent the next eighteen months, far from any other alarms.

That, at any rate, was my impression of their war until a few years ago I belatedly made the effort to actually talk to my grandmother about her time in Nassau. It soon emerged that the Bahamas' isolation had made them a haven for a conspicuous number of people who preferred that they, and their money, should not be unduly troubled by the conflict raging elsewhere, people who enjoyed playing fast and loose with the rules – and with each other. And one episode in her reminiscences soon came to dominate my imagination: the killing there in July 1943 of one of the richest men in the world, Sir Harry Oakes.

My grandmother remembered it vividly. Mostly this was because at a party on the night of his death she happened to have been playing 'Murder in the Dark', but also because she had been to dinner at the Oakeses' and knew some of those involved in the subsequent investigation. The crime had made the headlines everywhere, not just in Britain (where it was the only item to displace war news from the front page of the *Daily Telegraph*) but even in Germany. In America, where there was no rationing of newsprint, the papers ran page after page of coverage for weeks and sent down writers such as Erle Stanley Gardner, the creator of the detective Perry Mason, to cover the story.

Yet sensational as the murder was – and intriguing as it remained by virtue of its not having been solved – in the decades since 1943 it had faded from the public's memory. It had been touched on in histories of the Windsors' time in the Bahamas, and there had been three books about the case, but these seemed to me to have notable defects.

The first two, *The Life and Death of Harry Oakes* by Geoffrey Bocca (1959) and *King's X* by Marshall Houts (1972), appeared to suffer from the handicap of not being able to say what the authors thought for fear of libelling those involved who were still alive. Houts's study also subscribed to a theory of Mafia involvement which, while understandable in the era of *The Godfather*, struck me as based on sources whose veracity was at best unverifiable. The third book, *Who Killed Sir Harry Oakes?* by James Leasor, written about twenty-five years ago, also played the Mafia card, and long parts of it seemed to be constructed as lightly fictionalised fact. What was true, what was imagined remained, to my mind, unclear.

Moreover, none of these writers drew on interviews with those best placed to clear the tangle of rumour and speculation that had grown up around the affair: the people caught up in it. Certainly, one of them, Oakes's son-in-law Count Alfred de Marigny, had written his memoirs at the end of the 1980s. But his account of the crime was necessarily subjective and, as will become plain, his reliability as an autobiographer was not all that it might have been.

Some sixty years on, there was, I realised, a final opportunity to collect together the memories and testimony of the remaining survivors, and with new evidence now available present a fresh and independent account of the case. There was also the chance to preserve a little of a time and place that is starting to float out of reach. What follows, I hope, does justice to that opportunity, and to what Erle Stanley Gardner justifiably called 'the greatest murder mystery of all time'.

The lines at the start of Chapters 1–10 are taken from traditional Bahamian hymns and chants.

ONE

De win' blow east −
De win' blow west −
It blow like jedgement day

It was not yet breakfast time but already Herbert Pemberton was a worried man. As he came up the drive of Westbourne, the lush garden steaming from an overnight drenching, he was turning over in his mind the extraordinary news he had received a few minutes before. Inside his khaki police uniform he was sweating, and it was not because of the heat.

Later he recalled the scene that met him as he arrived at the long, bougainvillea-covered building that was one of the Oakes family's half-dozen homes in and around Nassau. It had just been extended to provide accommodation for the neighbouring country club, which the Oakeses also owned, but what Pemberton now saw was far from tranquil. Fire had run amok in the house. There were scorched spots on the hall stairs, soot smudges on the banister and others on the steps' outside edge. More smoke marked the walls by the bedroom door at the top of the flight.

The door itself was open, and heavily stained on its outer face. Inside, two charred tracts of carpet, like giant stepping stones, pointed the way to a pair of beds shielded from view by a tall screen across whose pattern of Chinese domesticity there now lay a curving black blister. On the nearer bed, face up, was the body of a man said to be worth two hundred million dollars.

His death had not been a good one. A heat that had eaten deep into the heavy wooden frame of the bed had almost wholly consumed his pyjamas. A burn as wide as a hand encircled his chest and abdomen, while others spattered the corpse from head to foot. There was a tangible odour of charred flesh. At some point, the left side of his skull had been shattered, spilling blood across his face.

Pemberton's gaze took in the rest of the room, now a disconcerting mix of the commonplace and the bizarre. Between the two beds stood a table on which were a lamp, reading glasses and a set of false teeth. Above, smoke had crawled high up the walls and flame had destroyed the mosquito net. To one side sat another table, atop which was a large radio. On the other bed was a pair of white trousers and a shirt, and beyond them, on the rough-painted wall of the room, were several reddish marks which resembled handprints. At the foot of the burned bed a small fan whirred quietly, gently ruffling the hundreds of tiny white feathers strewn over the dead man's chest.

Someone had killed Sir Harry Oakes, the richest man in the Bahamas – one of the richest men in the world – and for Major Herbert Pemberton, deputy commissioner of police, it was a bad start to what was going to be a very difficult day.

Pemberton was not alone in the room that morning of 8 July 1943. Indeed, one of the problems with the ensuing investigation would be that before it was sealed off to secure the integrity of any evidence, as many as thirteen people viewed the crime scene. The first of these was the man who had found Oakes's body, Harold Christie.

Then aged forty-seven, Christie was one of the most talked-about men in the Bahamas. Gossip had it that he had made a fortune smuggling whisky to America in the days of Prohibition, twenty years earlier. Certainly he had prospered since by selling land, particularly following the arrival of Harry Oakes and his millions from Canada nearly a decade before. The two had become the closest of friends as they worked on various development schemes, and had seen each other almost every day.

Only the afternoon before, Christie now told Pemberton, they had gone together to get an exit visa for Oakes, who was planning to travel to America later in the week. Permits – Christie shrugged. This war had made everything so unnecessarily complicated.

Afterwards they had played tennis – for though Oakes was twenty years his friend's senior he remained extremely vigorous – and then they had admired some palms that Oakes had planted on the beachfront outside Westbourne. Later that evening Sir Harry had given a small dinner party. Lady Oakes, his wife, was away at their house in Maine, and all their five children were off the island at school or on holiday, including his elder daughter Nancy, who had recently turned nineteen. Her husband, a tall, debonair French Mauritian nobleman named Count Alfred de Marigny, was in town but, as Pemberton knew, he and his father-in-law were rumoured not to be on dining terms.

Following a game of checkers the guests had left, except for Christie, a bachelor, who often spent the night at Westbourne. He had intended to drive the ten minutes or so back into Nassau itself after dinner, but then had changed his mind as he and Oakes had arranged to meet journalists the next morning. They planned to discuss Oakes's scheme to import sheep from Cuba to provide meat for the islands.

Accordingly, when he had woken at about seven o'clock after a night disturbed by tempestuous rain, Christie had gone along the balcony which ran around the house. Not finding Oakes at the breakfast table overlooking the ocean, Christie had knocked on his door. Opening it, he had seen the devastation inside and had tried to revive the older man, but there was nothing to be done. In a state of shock he had telephoned several people for help, including his brother Frank, and then had contacted Colonel Erskine-Lindop, the Commissioner of Police. It was he who had alerted Pemberton, the head of the CID, the force's detective branch.

Erskine-Lindop then had a more delicate call to make. The Duke of Windsor had been the Bahamas' Governor for just under three years, and had been appointed to the remote and rather insignificant colony, many believed, in order to keep the former king (and his wife) safely out of reach of the Nazi regime of which he had been such an incautious admirer in the years before the war. Few were fooled by the brave face that the Windsors had put on the announcement in 1940: one American newspaper declared that the post amounted to being no more than the manager of an expensive winter resort.

One of the Duke's consolations during his time in Nassau, as Erskine-Lindop knew, had been his friendship with Sir Harry. The pair had often played golf together, and they had collaborated on a number of schemes designed to improve the islands' meagre economy and infrastructure. Oakes's death would certainly come as a heavy blow.

What Erskine-Lindop could not have anticipated was how personally the Duke seemed to take the news once he had been woken by his young equerry John Pringle, or that he would decide to take charge himself of the direction of the investigation. Clearly Oakes was an important figure in the islands, and his murder was likely to bring them a little more into the spotlight, but under normal circumstances the search for his killer would have been left to the police.

To the Duke's mind, however, these were not normal circumstances. Because of their consequences, his subsequent decisions have led to much criticism and to his motives being questioned, but that morning at least he appeared to have ample and clear reasons for acting as he did. Foremost in his mind was his memory of the wage riot that had shaken Nassau the previous summer, and the doubts about the Commissioner's abilities that Erskine-Lindop had provoked by failing to quell it before looters had ransacked the capital's main thoroughfare, Bay Street.

His was only a small police force – four officers and 140 constables, with almost half of those spread around the outer islands – and, as was appropriate to the Bahamas' status in the colonial pecking order, its resources were not plentiful. An inspection the year before had found that the police transport pool consisted of three elderly motor cars, one rusting truck and a condemned motorcycle. Then again, it was very rarely called on to do much more than investigate run-of-the-mill assaults and the occasional robbery, and that almost exclusively amongst the black inhabitants who formed the vast majority of the islands' population. Levels of crime had been rising for some years, but, the Chief Justice had commented at the opening of the Quarter Sessions only the day before, these had now declined, and he trusted that it presaged a more law-abiding spirit in the colony. How ironic that hope now seemed.

No, the Duke decided, Erskine-Lindop could not be entrusted with a high-profile and sensitive case such as Oakes's murder. Pemberton might have more than fifteen years' service with the force but he too had no experience of a crime such as this, which might have all sorts of ramifications should the killer not be swiftly caught. Not least, any bungling would further reduce public confidence in the police, and by the public the Duke was thinking chiefly of the conservative lawyers and merchants of Bay Street who after the riot had proved even less inclined to accede to his plans for political and economic reform.

The problem was that it could take weeks for experts from Scotland Yard to arrive. Wartime conditions made travel across the Atlantic difficult, and seats on flights were at a premium. By the time any detectives did make the journey, the trail would have long grown cold. Then the Duke had a bright idea.

London might be four thousand miles away, but Miami was only two hundred. On a visit to that city a short time before, he had been impressed by the local detective assigned to him as an escort, a Captain Edward Melchen. Would it not be sensible to ask the chief of the Miami police department to put Melchen and

the resources of his force at the Duke's disposal as a way of helping Erskine-Lindop in his task? Surely the Americans would be
only too happy to aid their wartime ally, particularly when the
request came from someone of the Duke's standing? He duly
made the call.

To stifle speculation in the press abroad, he then forbade the
cable office to allow any telegrams to be sent, so that word of the
murder should not get out. The only exception was the message
he dispatched to his political masters at the Colonial Office in
London that afternoon: 'Deeply regret to report that Sir Harry
Oakes has met violent death under circumstances which are not
yet known. Hope to obtain expert advice of Chief of Miami
Detectives immediately, to assist local police. Will telegraph
further.'

Its wording set out the facts plainly enough. It was perhaps the
last occasion on which that phrase could be applied to any of the
circumstances surrounding the death of Harry Oakes.

TWO

Once upon a time, a very good time,
De monkey chew tobacco an' 'e spit white lime –

Not for the only time in the case, the Duke's intentions did not achieve the desired result. The decision to close the cable office came too late; word of the killing had already got off the island. At half past seven that morning, Etienne Dupuch, the editor of the *Nassau Daily Tribune* and one of the journalists due to meet Oakes to tour the proposed sheep farm, had telephoned Westbourne to confirm the appointment. A frantic Christie had taken the call and had blurted out the news of Oakes's murder. Straightaway Dupuch had fired off a telegram to the Miami offices of the Associated Press, whose representative he was in the Bahamas.

They duly passed on the story to the British newspapers, who were further intrigued when their cables to Nassau were met with silence. They asked the Miami press to investigate for them, and soon reporters were encamped at the city's airport, preparing to quiz passengers disembarking from the daily Pan American flight from Nassau. The attempt to suppress news of Oakes's death did not stifle rumours, it only encouraged them.

The next day, the story of the baronet's murder was the only item of non-war news to make the front page of the *Daily Telegraph* in London. Amid reports of the German drive on

8   JAMES OWEN

Kursk – 'A Million Men Engaged in Battle' – and the death in an air crash earlier that week of the Polish leader General Sikorski, readers learned of the killing of the multimillionaire 'famous for his gold-mining activities'.

In an era when journalism was considerably more sober, and its practitioners in the Allied nations preoccupied by the struggle with the Axis powers, for Oakes's death to be given the space it was is an indication of the magnitude of the story. Such was the shortage of newsprint that even *The Times* comprised just four pages a day, but both it and the *Telegraph* made room for substantial obituaries of Sir Harry. The *Times*'s readership learned, too, that a pair of American detectives had been summoned to Nassau on a 'secret mission'.

Thursday morning's flight from Miami had carried the two men in question. Captain Edward Melchen, the officer asked for by the Duke, was the head of Miami's Homicide Bureau. A stocky, stout Southerner of fifty whose spectacles were wedged firmly between a large nose and the low brim of his homburg, Melchen had investigated more than five hundred murders in nearly twenty years with the force.

With him, equal in rank but junior in standing, was Captain James Barker, whom the Miami police had also thought to send. A decade younger than Melchen, a head taller, he was blessed with the manly good looks favoured by Hollywood studios of the time, his appearance marred only by a pronounced limp: a motorcycle accident fifteen years before had left one leg more than an inch shorter than the other. It had not stopped the Indiana-born Barker from becoming an acknowledged fingerprint expert. He had made a wide reputation for himself eight years earlier when he had identified by their prints the remains of dozens of former soldiers working on a federal project in the Florida Keys who had drowned during a hurricane.

He was now in charge of all Miami's police laboratories, and while it was true that although they had joined the force at the same time it was Melchen who had advanced further, Barker could comfort himself that he cut the better figure. He was neat, even dapper in a suit, a handkerchief in his breast pocket. Melchen's jacket wrestled with his bulging stomach.

The flight was met by Erskine-Lindop and Pemberton who drove the two detectives over to Westbourne just as it started to rain heavily. It had been a wet couple of days. Though the previous afternoon, Wednesday, had been scorchingly hot – the shops in Nassau had run out of Coca-Cola – on the night of the murder the heat had been the precursor of a tremendous thunderstorm which had saturated the ground with more than an inch of rain.

By the time that Melchen and Barker arrived at Westbourne at two o'clock, the humidity level was approaching one hundred per cent and the temperature was in the high eighties. The pair took a quick look around the house before Barker declared that the conditions meant it was too humid for him to begin dusting for any fingerprints that might have been left by the murderer. The difficulty, it seemed, was that prints are formed mainly from sweat and when the air is very damp they remain moist. If he began brushing, he might simply wipe them away.

Instead, the two detectives began to take statements from those who by now had turned up at the house, drawn by the day's news. It must have rapidly become clear to Erskine-Lindop and Pemberton that – whatever the wording of the Governor's telegram to London – their American counterparts did not see their role as being confined merely to assistance. Whatever might be said in public, as far as Melchen was concerned it had become his investigation.

In fairness to him, it seems likely that that was the basis on which he had been brought into the case. Certainly, from the manner in which Erskine-Lindop now faded into the background it can be assumed that the Duke had told him, and Leslie Quigg, the head of the Miami police, that Melchen was to be given a free hand. Erskine-Lindop may not have been any great loss to the investigation – the Duke would later write that he had 'more or less sat down on the job' since the riot of the year before – and given such an attitude the Duke was not disposed to mind upsetting his feelings.

Yet Erskine-Lindop had almost twenty-five years' experience in colonial policing: if he lacked some of the vigour that the Americans prided themselves on, at least he knew how to do things by the book. His inability to dictate that this should happen in the Oakes investigation would have the gravest consequences. Instead, he and Pemberton had to content themselves with helping Melchen when asked, and with belatedly positioning a pair of constables on guard outside the bedroom. At half past three, the body of its occupant was carried downstairs and taken away to the mortuary.

The story of how a millionaire has made his money is usually as prosaic as the man himself, but there was little that was dull about Harry Oakes. Although he ended his life as a baronet in the British peerage, and had found his fortune in Canada, he was born an American, in Sangerville, Maine, just before Christmas 1874. The town was also the birthplace of Hiram Maxim, the inventor of the machine gun that bore his name.

Oakes's father, William, who came from a family that had been established in the state since the Revolution, had trained as a lawyer but poor health had led to his taking a job in the outdoors instead as a surveyor. His wife Edith worked as a schoolteacher, and was a strong supporter of the temperance movement. Her husband was not overly influenced by her beliefs, and spent much of his time in the local tavern, although all agreed he was the very soul of kindness and consideration. Harry was the third of their five children.

He grew up on the 110-acre Oakes homestead amid the beauties of the Maine countryside, and developed a love for, and an understanding of, the natural world. By the late 1880s his parents had moved a few miles from Sangerville to Foxcroft so that Harry and his brother Louis could attend the town's academy, reputed to be the best in the county. From there Harry went at nineteen to Bowdoin College in Brunswick, the alma mater of Hawthorne and Longfellow, but he gave little sign of possessing their literary talents. Rather, he seemed a quiet, unassuming youth of average ability, bound for a decidedly standard career, perhaps as a doctor since his highest grade in his first year was for hygiene.

Harry did indeed then move on to medical school – probably at Syracuse in New York, although no record of him has survived – but here he abruptly departed from the track laid down for him. In 1898, aged twenty-three, he caught gold fever.

The year before, news of the discovery of gold in the Canadian Yukon had triggered a rush north. Now Oakes too set out for the Klondike, initially to work as a medical assistant at Skagway, in Alaska. His family would not see him again for almost fifteen years.

Harry was, on the face of it, an unlikely gold prospector. He had never been fond of manly sports, and stood just five feet, six inches tall. He soon toughened up, however, living under canvas in freezing conditions, existing on little more than scraps. In Dawson City, he learned the miner's trade, but all the land was already staked: the town was to be only the first stop in a quest that would take him around the world. From Alaska he travelled southwards to the Philippines, working his passage as a purser. Then he panned the Kalgoorlie goldfields of Western Australia before having a spell as a flax farmer and surveyor in New Zealand. Next he returned to America to try his luck in Death Valley, all the while (unlike most prospectors) seeking to increase his geological knowledge and thus his understanding of where gold was most likely to be found. In 1911, now aged thirty-seven, he arrived at the quaintly named Swastika railhead in northern Ontario, midway between Toronto and Hudson Bay.

Eight years earlier, silver had been found to the south at Cobalt while a railway cutting was being dug. In 1906, gold had been discovered at Larder Lake, about thirty miles east of Swastika. In the next two years, more than four thousand claims had been staked there. The stampede north accelerated when in 1910 the vast Hollinger mine was struck to the west at Timmins.

There were riches to be had from this natural treasure trove, but it was an arduous place in which to work, a densely wooded landscape of lakes and streams where in winter the temperature plummeted to seventy degrees below zero and even the moose shivered. Yet under these dismal clumps of poplar and spruce around the town, believed Oakes, ran an extension of the vein found at Larder Lake. He was not alone. Dozens of others had staked or were working claims in the area (among them the future Lord Redesdale, whose daughter Unity Mitford, the future devotee of Adolf Hitler, was, as if by predestination, conceived at Swastika in 1913).

In the years after Oakes had made his fortune, the story was told that he had found his mine by chance. It was said that he had been aboard a train and had been turned off it for not having the money for a ticket. As he stood there in the snow, shaking his fist at the conductor as the engine pulled away, his toe struck a rock. He looked down, and saw a vein of gold glinting through the ice.

It was a tale entirely without foundation, and one that Oakes much resented. It did no justice to almost fifteen years of perseverance and slog, when he had to beg money for claims and credit for food from hardbitten folk in frontier towns who had heard it all before. He had nearly died of exposure in Alaska, and from sunstroke in Death Valley. Through it all he had maintained his confidence in his own abilities, preferring to work alone when he could, keeping a sharp eye out for promising strikes.

It was this combination of persistence, knowledge and preparedness that brought Oakes his chance. Luck had little to do with it. In January 1912, he discovered that a claim made by a man named Burroughs at Kirkland Lake, about six miles from Swastika, was about to lapse. Burroughs had failed to put in the necessary forty days' work on the land. Lacking the funds to stake it himself, he proposed a partnership with four burly brothers, improbably named Tough, who had the contract to slash a road through the bush between Swastika and Larder Lake.

On the evening of 7 January, in weather so cold, legend later had it, that they had to wear five pairs of trousers, Oakes and the Toughs set off to walk through knee-deep snow to Kirkland Lake. As the claim expired at midnight, they restaked it as their own.

Three hours later, another veteran miner, Bill Wright, once a butcher's apprentice in England, arrived at the lake, where some months before he had found traces of gold while hunting rabbits. Finding the others already in possession of Burroughs's ground, he staked that next to it. The two claims would yield two of the richest mines in Canada, Tough-Oakes and Sylvanite, and turn Kirkland Lake into a boom town.

Oakes's instinct had been right. Tests soon showed that the ground held gold, and by 1916 more than one hundred thousand tons of ore was being brought out of Tough-Oakes every month, and it was of an extraordinary richness, up to fifty times the average previously found in the region. Yet Oakes was convinced that there was still more to be had. Even before the first shipment had left the mine, he had staked two fresh claims on the south side of the lake, and then two others. Wright had made four claims to the west of the water, and in 1914, when Oakes incorporated his claims as the (as yet non-existent) Lake Shore Mine, he gave Wright two hundred thousand shares in the company in exchange for them.

As soon as he could, he began selling shares in Tough-Oakes to fund the sinking of new shafts beside the lake. But the work was held up by the outbreak of the First World War, and he needed still more capital. No prospector in Canada had ever managed to retain a mine of his own through to profit, and despite his faith in himself he could not rouse the enthusiasm of Toronto's financiers. So he went across the border to Buffalo, where he finally succeeded in selling half a million shares to investors at 32½ cents each.

Oakes was convinced that a second streak of ore existed on his property. Later it was said that he had a theory that the veins of gold were arranged like the rays of the sun, or that one of the numerous eccentric characters drawn to Kirkland Lake, a reclusive Jewish woman named Roza Brown, had advised him to look under the water itself. Whatever the truth, there was soon nowhere that Oakes had not tried except below the lake, and in 1917 with the help of an engineer he made a flat cross-cut north from the Number One vein.

Suddenly the drill bit tore into rock banded with yellow. The men shrieked and hollered with joy. Oakes had found his bonanza – not a vein but an artery of gold more than forty feet wide and eight thousand feet deep. His skill and tenacity had been repaid a thousandfold.

There was still much to do. Equipment needed to be bought and labour found, all at a time when Canada was haemorrhaging men to the trenches of Flanders and Oakes himself was embroiled in litigation with the Toughs. When the money was finally found for development, and to bring in electric power from Cobalt seventy miles away, the new strike was threatened by water which seeped into it from above, while treacherous quicksand made it hard to work the rock.

Yet Oakes persevered. Soon the ore proved to be so heavy with gold that the mine could afford its own mill, and then its own smelter, which increased the yield to record levels. Lake Shore became the third in what was eventually a chain of seven contiguous gold mines, half of them owned by Oakes or Wright, that stretched for more than two miles.

In the half-century of its existence, Lake Shore would yield eight million, five hundred thousand ounces of gold. By 1929, when it was milling daily one thousand tons of ore, it was producing, on average, eighteen thousand dollars' worth of gold *per day* (now worth about one hundred and ten thousand pounds sterling). The following year, having overtaken Hollinger, it was the largest producer in the western hemisphere, and the third largest in the world (after two South African mines). At its peak in the mid-1930s it was disgorging some two and a half thousand tons of rock every day. Of all the mines in the Americas, only the Homestake in the Black Hills of North Dakota, the basis of the Hearst fortune, ever gave up more gold.

Those investors who had backed Oakes saw not single ships but whole fleets come in. For every dollar that they had put up in 1916 they took out, at the height of their shares' worth, almost two hundred; and no one benefited more than the major shareholder, Oakes himself. Unlike most miners, he had managed to retain half of the company's shares – a million of them. Then, in the early 1930s, he received a piece of luck that stratospherically increased the value of his holdings: the American government raised the price of gold. For decades it had been fixed at $20.67 per ounce. Now, in order to devalue the dollar during the Depression, President Roosevelt increased that mark – almost doubled it – to thirty-five dollars.

By 1943, when Oakes died, it is estimated that Lake Shore had produced about two hundred million dollars' worth (now worth about £1.2 billion) of gold. This was the basis of most reports about the size of Oakes's fortune, but in fact the mine had paid up just over ninety million dollars in dividend profit, half of it to him. Nonetheless, in an era when money went further, and millionaires were fewer, he was comfortably one of the world's wealthiest people. Not as well off as John D. Rockefeller, perhaps about half as flush as the British branch of the Astors, but Oakes was still one of the richest citizens of the Empire that he had joined when in 1915, for business purposes, he had taken Canadian nationality.

He must have felt a long way from his boyhood in Sangerville, Maine. But then, the docile Harry Oakes of those days had gone too. His experiences of fending for himself in the harsh wilderness, of being ripped off, of always being short of money, had forged a gruffer, more autocratic and single-minded man.

As someone whose prosperity was built on hard work, he was not one to tolerate idleness: the fourteen hundred miners at Lake Shore soon learned to go down to the deeper reaches of the shaft when he was about so as not to risk a tongue-lashing. Some of his staff at Kirkland Lake remembered him afterwards as brusque and demanding, and his generosity to the town was compared unfavourably with that of Bill Wright. Others mocked his grandiosity in erecting such a fancy log cabin to serve as his home – it was even heated by steam from the mine – and nicknamed it 'the Château'.

Yet these criticisms, which other writers have turned into the standard portrait of Oakes, only catch half the man. The accusations of parsimony seem unfair given the nature of Kirkland Lake, a town in the middle of nowhere, built with tar paper and timber, which none expected to last beyond the usual short lifetime of a mine – perhaps ten years. Tough-Oakes, in fact, closed down after fifteen. Few people invested in such places for the long-term, and almost no one thought that Lake Shore would be goingstrong after nearly three decades. Even so, in the early years Oakes still built a sports arena, sponsored the ice-hockey team and constructed a nine-hole golf course at the mine – a reminder of his genteel origins.

His younger daughter later characterised him as a man who had no sympathy for those who were looking for a free meal, but his liberality to those in need could be boundless. After his death, the family received dozens of letters from those he had helped, among them former employees. The six mines at Kirkland Lake had provided work for some five thousand men, including Wally Floody, who later dug one of the tunnels for the 'Great Escape' from a German prison camp during the Second World War.

Their life was hard, toiling eight thousand feet underground – much deeper than a coal mine – and so close was each shaft that those in one mine could hear others at work in that next door. Everything revolved around the unforgiving ore. Roads laid on it buckled as moisture crept in from the underground workings. (The road through the town itself was actually paved for a mile of its length with high-yield ore: the construction crew had selected the wrong rock pile.) Yet exhausting and dangerous as the life could be, when there were few jobs to be had in the 1920s and 1930s the miners and their families were profoundly grateful for Harry Oakes. In 1979, his widow was one of the guests of honour at the town's jubilee celebrations.

He had met Eunice McIntyre, a young Australian, in 1923 while travelling by ship to South Africa to discuss mining technology; the vessel was a passenger-carrying freighter rather than a luxury liner, since for all his new wealth Oakes still liked to be careful with his money.

Eunice, the daughter of a civil servant, was heading for

Mauritius, where her sister had married a sugar planter. At twenty-four, she was fully quarter of a century younger than Oakes, and with her good complexion and striking looks she seemed an odd match with the short, middle-aged prospector. Hitherto, romance had not figured much in Harry's life, but now the prospect of a new start opened for him. His tales of gold-mining caught her interest, while she aroused his protective instincts, and they found themselves laughing together often. When they reached Victoria Falls he proposed marriage. Then at Cape Town came the news that her father had died. Oakes was a great comfort to Eunice, and he rearranged his plans so that he could accompany her home to Sydney. They were married there at the end of June, and less than a year later, in May 1924, their first child was born and christened Nancy.

Nancy spent her first years at the Château, where her parents had the plasterwork of her playroom decorated with characters from fairy tales and nursery rhymes. Soon she was joined by Sydney, William Pitt (his grandfather's names), Shirley and Harry Jr.

By the time of his youngest son's arrival, in 1932, Oakes had moved his family slightly closer to civilisation than Kirkland Lake. He had bought a property on the high ground by Niagara Falls, on the Canadian side, that he renamed Oak Hall. During the Depression, he proved to be Niagara's main benefactor, financing employment schemes in the town as well as donating land for a park and what is now the Oakes Garden Theatre. Such civic endowments prove that he was not the miser his detractors have made him out to be.

Nor did he stint on himself, either. Oak Hall – with its Tudor panelling brought from Hampton Court Palace, its chairs on which had sat the signatories to the treaty ending the Boxer Rebellion, and its fashionable 'natatorium' (indoor swimming pool) – cost him half a million dollars to refurbish. Then there was the house at swanky Bar Harbor in Maine, the two in Palm Beach, and a mansion in Sussex (Tottingworth Park, an ugly Victorian confection, just waiting to be turned into a retirement home).

Indeed England, and the cultivation of English society, was becoming more important to Oakes, and in 1935 he bought a house in London at 15A Kensington Palace Gardens, then popularly known as 'Millionaires' Row'. (In 2004, the house became one of the most expensive in Europe when it was sold by its then owner for forty-one million pounds). His neighbours included the Duke of Marlborough, the Marquess of Cholmondeley and Sir Alfred Beit, the diamond heir. The Oakeses had arrived.

Oakes was perhaps less keen than his colonial-born wife on impressing the British with his wealth. He never made any concessions to their dress codes, striding past the nobs in his customary rig of well-worn coat, corduroy breeches and high-laced boots as if for all the world he was off to prospect for gold in Hyde Park. His riches simply meant that he never had to change his behaviour to suit others. Instead he could indulge himself.

Some of the time that entailed behaving like the surly miner he now was; his wife despaired when he stomped across her brand new white carpet in his muddy top-boots. At other moments he could play the part expected of him, one that retained traces of his earlier life and tastes. So in London he commissioned Joe Duveen to buy art for him – a Rembrandt, a Gainsborough, a Constable, two Turners and a Vermeer, the last acquired from J. P. Morgan – and had glasses made to match the silver wallpaper in his dining room. He also began to give money away.

Most notably, in 1938 he donated ninety thousand pounds – about three million pounds in today's money – towards the reconstruction of London's St George's Hospital, then located at Hyde Park Corner (the building is now the Lanesborough Hotel). It was an act of generosity in tune with his principles, but also one calculated to make a splash. The next year he had his reward – 'for public and philanthropic service' – when he was created a baronet in the King's birthday-honours list, the last to be gazetted before the outbreak of war. He might not change his ways to fit in, but he undoubtedly wanted some recognition of what he had achieved. Now, as Sir Harry Oakes, Bt, he had it.

The only thorn in what had become Oakes's bed of roses was his frustration at the amount of tax levied on his Canadian operations. During the 1920s, the government had effectively allowed mine owners to write off half their tax as a way of encouraging investment. But when a Conservative administration was elected in 1930 taxes were raised sharply, especially on profits from mining. Oakes, who had been a conspicuous supporter of the previous Liberal government, felt victimised. By the mid-1930s, he was paying eighty-five per cent of his income in taxation – some three million dollars (now twenty million pounds), making him the largest single contributor to the Canadian revenue – although he was only spending about three months a year in the country. As he entered his sixties, he began, too, to think about limiting his exposure to Canada's heavy death duties.

Two men provided the solution to his worries. The first was his American attorney and adviser Walter Foskett, a short, sleek, self-made lawyer who had founded a highly successful partnership in Palm Beach on the back of the Florida real-estate boom of the Thirties.

The second was Harold Christie.

When Oakes first met Christie, probably in 1933, Christie was not yet forty but he had already had a busy life. Born into a family long established in the Bahamas, he was one of eight children of an eccentric father who made little provision for his offspring's welfare. He had had occasional spells as a successful businessman, but by the time Harold was growing up he had forsaken this for a life of evangelical preaching and writing poetry. The high point of this literary career came when he took third prize in an Empire-wide competition to compose an ode on the coronation of King Edward VII. The practical management of the household devolved to his wife Madge, a veteran of twenty pregnancies.

The sandy-haired Harold was just old enough to serve when the First World War began and he chose to trek north to join the Royal Canadian Air Force. He appears to have taken readily to the opportunities afforded by the wider world outside the Bahamas, and when in 1920 the sale of alcohol was banned in America he began acting as a middleman between the alcohol wholesalers of Nassau and their under-the-counter customers in the United States.

Although many Bahamians knew all too well what Harold's work was during Prohibition, it was not something that he shouted about. While it rapidly made him money, by the time that he met Oakes he was better known in the islands for his more recent activities as a member of its parliament (his constituents included the young Sidney Poitier), as a highly successful estate agent – his business since 1925 – and as the roving representative of the Bahamas.

These last two roles were the twin faces of the idea that drove Christie from the late 1920s onwards, the conviction that the Bahamas – hitherto regarded by the few outsiders who knew of them as sun-blighted scraps of coral – could become a prosperous resort. Sunbathing was just starting to become fashionable, and the islands had no shortage of sand, water and sunshine. Certainly the infrastructure was inadequate, and there were few proper hotels, but Christie realised that investors could soon remedy this. He had two sizeable incentives to offer them: land for development was cheap – and in the Bahamas there was no income tax. All Christie had to do was find his investors.

He was helped in this by the depressed economy of the early 1930s, which drove up taxes in Europe and America and prompted the rich to look for safe havens for their money. The persuasive, patient, amiable Christie toured the European Rivieras, Long Island and Palm Beach with his brochures and patter and was soon selling plots of land to a steady stream of clients. His first big catch, however, was Harry Oakes.

The Bahamas were just what Oakes was looking for. Not only would he not have to pay out on his earnings if he moved there, but in addition the rate of inheritance tax was only two per cent. Moreover, the islands seemed to offer him the opportunity to leave his stamp on a whole country that, unlike the Canadian government, appeared positively pleased to have him as a resident.

Foskett set to work devising a tax-efficient shelter for Oakes's assets. His million shares in the Lake Shore mine were sold to various Bahamian companies formed by Oakes himself. He then bought shares in these corporations, which effectively paid him as a dividend what they received in turn from the mines. Yet since the Lake Shore shares were no longer owned by Oakes but by the holding companies, he was not liable to pay income tax on them in Canada, and once he moved to the Bahamas in 1934 he had to pay the Canadian treasury only a five per cent withholding tax on the mines' earnings. Between 1935 and 1939 the Bahamian corporations gathered in $22,750,000, of which the Canadian revenue was able to take a mere $1.1 million. Oakes's transfer to sunnier climes had saved him eighteen million dollars, equivalent to one hundred million pounds today.

By the time that he and his children were settled in Nassau, Oakes had another reason for shaking off memories of Canada. In January 1935 his sister Gertrude, who had helped to finance his early prospecting and who had later become chief accountant at the mine, was drowned. She had been a passenger on a liner bound for Havana when its steering gear had failed. It had recently become law for steering systems to be rigged so that, like a motor car but unlike a conventional tiller, a turn of the wheel to port or starboard would take the ship in that direction. The emergency steering gear, however, had not been modified, and when an order to turn to starboard was issued the vessel instead shifted to port, and into the path of a fast-moving freighter. Forty-five lives were lost in the subsequent collision, including that of Gertrude Oakes. It was the first in a long line of shadows that would fall across the family.

Pursued by bitter headlines in the Canadian press ('Heart Like Frigidaire to the Land That Gave Him Wealth'), Oakes quickly began to make his presence felt on New Providence, the principal island of the Bahamas and the site of its capital, Nassau. In time, with Christie's aid, he would buy up almost a third of the island, or about ten thousand acres. He began with houses. The first, Caves Point, became his main residence in the Bahamas.

Built for him on a low ridge about eight miles outside Nassau, its square, donjon-like tower overlooked the sea and Lake Killarney behind. Local journalists faithfully recorded all its wonders: the twelve bedrooms; the picture windows on three sides of the living room, which had a white sand beach underneath for the children; the fifty-two thousand gallons of water in the swimming pool.

A smaller home, the Gatehouse, stood at the entrance to the road along the crest to the Caves. To this were later added a town house in Nassau and a penthouse in the city's main hotel, the British Colonial, itself owned by Oakes and supposedly bought on the spur of the moment after he had been refused admittance because of his scruffy clothes. Then, at the water's edge, beyond the golf course, there lay Westbourne.

The house, acquired from Maxine Elliott, a former child star in silent films, was large but not grand, built of white-painted wood on two storeys, with a veranda along the ground floor and a balcony walkway around the dozen bedrooms on the level above. Outside staircases on two sides – to the north, facing the ocean, and to the east – gave access to this. Greenery clambered up the pillars and along the balustrade shaded by the rows of shutters and long roofline, which rose to a single peak over the main entrance.

Inside, it was comfortably furnished without being stuffy. The rooms were plain rather than homely, for the Oakeses thought of it mainly as their 'beach house', an occasional retreat rather than their principal abode. Nonetheless, Sir Harry spent much time here, working diligently to improve the garden and the view onto the sand, now lined by palms. It was cooler down there, too, the wind blowing off the ocean and through the tall casuarinas, and he regularly slept at Westbourne since it was close to Nassau. His room caught the breezes on both sides, and opened out towards the sea.

At the start of 1943, a colonnade had been constructed, linking the house with the neighbouring golf and country club, providing garaging for cars and space above for accommodation. In time, Westbourne was intended to serve as the club's annexe.

The golf course was characteristic of Oakes's developments on the island, created and maintained seemingly without regard to cost and with a single-minded determination to show what could be done. He was a keen amateur player – golf became his bond with the Duke of Windsor, and they were due to play on the day his body was found – and he enjoyed vexing the Governor and other golfing visitors, among them the Crown Prince of Nepal, by using his bulldozer to change holes and bunkers overnight between their rounds. Any sand trap in which his own ball landed would be swiftly eliminated.

Oakes certainly liked to demonstrate who was in control, particularly if it improved his chances of winning. But such teasing shows, too, that he had a sense of humour, albeit a broad one. He was not the killjoy he was later made out to be. For instance, when he was in Palm Beach, his daughter Nancy maintains, he liked a flutter at the casino. He was no high roller, perhaps, but this activity gives the lie to one oft-aired explanation for his murder, namely that he did not approve of gambling and was killed by the American Mafia because he opposed their schemes for building (and controlling) casinos in Nassau.

He had no moral objection to betting, nor did he want to preserve the Bahamas in amber – his construction projects are evidence enough that he wanted the country to develop its potential. Moreover, the Mafia theories are based on a fundamental misapprehension. Oakes would not have tried to block the legalisation of gambling in the Bahamas, because it was already legal. Since 1920 a casino had operated (for tourists only) at the Bahamian Club in Nassau, although it had been suspended for the duration of the war. Its activities were entirely above board – the money that financed its building had been loaned by the colonial administration.

Oakes's other sporting interests included polo, and he duly imported twenty ponies to provide mounts for two teams. But most of his other introductions were less frivolous, relating mainly to the islands' economic development. When he arrived there, the Bahamas were very far from being the modern centre of international finance that they are now. Needy, backwards and remote, they were among the poorer relations of a family – the West Indies – which rated only a very small mention in any list of the British Crown's assets.

The Bahamas comprise more than 3,100 isles, islets, rocks and cays, all floating in the one hundred thousand square miles of shallow water – or *baja mar* – south-east of Florida for which their Spanish discoverers named them. In 1943, only thirty were inhabited, and almost half of the islands' population of sixty-nine thousand lived on just one, New Providence. Most of them struggled to make a living, for the soil in the Bahamas barely covers the coral and they are arid and flat, lacking the mountains, rivers and lush landscapes of the Caribbean further south. The country's highest peak, Mount Alvernia, rises to 210 feet.

Ever since one of the smaller isles, San Salvador, became the first place seen by Columbus in the New World, European settlers had tried, and failed, to reap a profit from the Bahamas. After the Spaniards had chased out the local Arawak Indians, and had been chased out in turn by the British, a colony was established in 1659 by Puritan adventurers at what is now Nassau. Its double-ended harbour made it the natural site for a town, but despite the optimistic name given to the island where it lay, New Providence was an unfortunate choice of home. Unlike neighbouring islands, it suffers much of the year from a stifling heat and an almost asphyxiating humidity. Snow *has* been known to fall on Nassau – once, in 1798.

Every attempt at farming by the newcomers came to naught. But one group of settlers soon realised that there was a rich harvest to be had from the sea: by the early eighteenth century, Nassau had become a nest of pirates. They proclaimed their own republic (one without laws) and appointed Edward Teach – better known as Blackbeard – as their 'magistrate'. For a decade they preyed on French and Spanish treasure fleets until in 1718 the British government dispatched a punitive expedition under Woodes Rogers to tame them. Rogers (who had rescued

Alexander Selkirk, the inspiration for *Robinson Crusoe*, from the island of Juan Fernandez) eventually restored order, and hanged those privateers who refused to repent from trees in the garden of what became the British Colonial Hotel.

Nonetheless, for another century the only profitable industry was wrecking – using lights to lure ships onto the treacherous reefs around Nassau in order to kill their crews and plunder their cargo. By 1773, the colony was bankrupt, and in that state it remained for 150 years. The population grew rapidly when loyalists arrived from New England following the outbreak of the American Revolution, but life for them – and their twelve thousand slaves – was precarious.

All efforts at growing sisal, coconut, pineapple and cotton failed, and early plans to attract tourists from Florida were shattered in 1872 by a fire aboard the *Missouri*, the liner which plied between Miami and Nassau. Eighty-four of its ninety-six passengers burned to death, including two brothers of the American President, Grover Cleveland. Then, almost overnight, in January 1920 the islands' fortunes were transformed.

The catalyst was the passing of the Volstead Act, which banned the sale and consumption of alcohol in the United States. Prohibition had begun, and from every port, harbour and jetty in the islands, yachts, skiffs and motor boats laden with illicit alcohol began to make the short crossing to Florida or the longer run up to 'Rum Row', off the coast of New Jersey. A cargo of a hundred-and-fifty-thousand dollars' worth of whisky might be worth twice as much when sold to the bootleggers, and ten times that amount in the speakeasies of the big cities. The turnover of alcohol passing through the bonded warehouse at Nassau increased by a factor of thirty-five, and some of the smugglers, such as Harold Christie, became rich. William 'The Real' McCoy estimated that he shipped 175,000 cases in four years, making two trips a night and a thousand dollars a time (six thousand pounds today).

Nassau become once more the headquarters of a crew of freebooters. They were able to defy the US Coast Guard at will, for the top speed of its cutters was just fourteen knots, while that of the smugglers' speedboats was four times that. One vessel even belonged to the Bishop of Nassau, although he claimed to have long since sold the *Message of Peace*. When the American authorities brought in the US Navy, the runners turned to seaplanes, making up to five flights a day into the Everglades. Hotels and bars – notably the enticingly named Bucket of Blood – opened in Nassau to soak up the fortunes being made, and men gambled at dice for fifty dollars a throw. New houses sprang up on the former pineapple farm at Cable Beach, while each July saw the high point of the social year: the Bootleggers Ball.

The principal beneficiary of this bonanza, however, was the British Government. Between 1918 and 1922, as tonnage at the port went up tenfold, re-export duty on alcohol at Nassau leaped from £61,827 to £852,573. The money was used to fund much-needed improvements to the islands' communications and infrastructure – the harbour was dredged, electricity brought in and proper plumbing installed. Surplus funds were put towards the reconstruction of the British Colonial following a fire, and the building of a golf course – the precursor of Oakes's – to attract tourists and the Canadian distillers who had started to take advantage of the islands' favourable banking regime. Indeed, it was rum-running that first established the potential of the Bahamas as a tax haven.

With the repeal of Prohibition, however, and the onset of the Depression, by 1943 matters had reverted pretty much to where they had been before, notably for the ninety per cent of the population that was black. Nassau returned to being a quiet place, with a certain provincial charm, built almost entirely of wood and looking as self-consciously British as only a colony can. Its postboxes were red, its cars drove on the left, its wirelesses were tuned to Tommy Handley and *London Letter*; the white population practically lived on Andrews' Liver Salts. On the only high piece of ground, watching over the town, sat the symbol of the Crown's rule, pink-painted Government House.

The covered porches of Bay Street formed the main

thoroughfare between the bulk of the British Colonial – one of the few structures higher than two storeys – and Rawson Square, five minutes' walk away, where the public buildings were. To one side, beyond the trees and the railings, stood the harbour. Fishing boats rode at anchor, their spars singing softly in the warm wind. Horse-drawn jitneys clip-clopped up the street, their progress rarely challenged by the few cars on the island. Bicycles were the principal form of transport; otherwise everyone walked, even the policemen in their white helmets and gleaming brass chinstraps.

Everyone knew everybody else, and their business. The telephone exchange was primitive, and the town's main grapevine. The operators heard every conversation. If you were to ask them to put a call through to Mrs McKinney, as like as not they could tell you that she had nipped out five minutes ago to see her mother, who was feeling poorly. Her Aunt Barbara had told her. Yes, the one with the son who, you know. Such a waste. Little else disturbed the rhythm of parish life. One standby in the local paper was an item that gave the price of fish.

Beyond the prosperous, white-owned grocers' and chemists' shops of Bay Street there lay another Nassau. Roads such as Dog Flea Alley led over the hill to Grant's Town, the black quarter, where the town's native population lived cheek by jowl with their neighbours and their goats. Unlike the rest of the British West Indies, there was no emerging black middle class in the Bahamas, and though the respective statuses of the inhabitants were stratified in many people's eyes by shades of colour there were very few non-whites in public life – this despite the fact that much of Bay Street (including Christie's family) had mixed blood. Although the black population had the vote, many of Nassau's shops and establishments, such as the Savoy cinema, operated a colour bar, and the squalid surroundings of Grant's Town, its world of churchgoing, fetishes and African 'obeah' religions, was off-limits to all but a handful of whites who enjoyed slumming it in black clubs. Their money brought them whatever they wanted, and no questions asked. Even a small household could afford to run to four or five servants.

Once the flood tide of Prohibition cash had stopped washing through Nassau, its Governors realised, like Christie, that the principal hope for improving the lot of most Bahamians lay in exploiting the islands' natural attractions. In the early 1930s, the newly appointed Crown representative, Sir Bede Clifford, began investing government funds in developments calculated to appeal to tourists. These included new hotels, a racecourse, a polo ground and a cable connection to the States. In 1933, there were 10,295 'winter residents', as they were known. By 1937, with the advent of a seaplane service to Miami, their number had more than trebled to 34,000, greater than the permanent population of New Providence itself.

More than half of these visitors were well-off Americans and Canadians – this was not yet the era of global mass travel – and most came for a week or two of sunshine. But above them in social status were those who each year spent the winter season in their houses on Cable Beach or up on Prospect Ridge. The *Nassau Guardian*, the city's conservative newspaper, reverently chronicled the annual arrival of these nabobs: Sir Frederick and Lady Williams-Taylor, grandparents of society darling Brenda Frazier and resident at 'Star Acres'; Sir Herbert Holt, the Canadian magnate, and his sons, the Majors W. R. G. and Herbert Holt; Frederick Sigrist, the brains behind the Sopwith and Hawker aviation firms; Edmund Lynch, he of Merrill Lynch, the owner of an estate on Hog Island on the other side of Nassau's harbour; Anthony J. Drexel and Alfred P. Sloan; John McCutcheon, the *Chicago Tribune* cartoonist, who lived off New Providence on 'Treasure Island'; Arthur Vernay and Suydam Cutting, the botanists and explorers of Tibet; the Hamilton Condons.

This last pair were a very curious addition to the scene, two rich artists of whom he wore make-up (more or less discreetly) and she a monocle and moustache. Such raffish goings-on, however, were almost the norm in Nassau. However stiff the protocol at Government House, however grandly the low-born Lady Williams-Taylor presided over the Emerald Beach Club, however strict the dress code at its American rival The Porcupine (spread over one hundred yards of Paradise Beach), the sun and sand generated a holiday mood in everyone else and if one was careful, almost anything went.

For, despite its exterior correct Englishness, Nassau was a place where people felt off duty. Here, far from London or New York, often far from family, one had room to breathe, to amuse oneself. One former resident characterised it to me as 'a bubble where there was nothing to do but drink, gamble, and run off with other people's wives.'

Here you could make your own rules. Thus, for instance, not thirty miles from Nassau there was an island with a population of two hundred governed on idiosyncratic lines by Joe Carstairs, the 'Queen of Whale Cay', a mannish heiress who had been a champion powerboat racer in the 1920s and whose lovers included Marlene Dietrich.

Then, while there were British visitors of note – the Duke of Kent and Princess Marina on honeymoon, Lady Diana Cooper and one of the Guinness girls, Maureen Dufferin – it was the influx of American glamour that attracted the most attention and made the place feel still more cosmopolitan.

By the late 1930s, Nassau had become a favourite playground for actors, sportsmen and public figures alike. Among those relaxing under the hibiscus were Errol Flynn and Greta Garbo, Irving Berlin and Larry Hart, Gloria Swanson and Douglas Fairbanks. Ellsworth Vines and Fred Perry gave exhibition tennis matches, Walter Hagen and Bobby Jones played golf, President Roosevelt called in on Vincent Astor's yacht.

Some learned water-skiing from an Army officer who had been the first to cross the English Channel in that fashion. Brenda Frazier went as an 'African Princess' to the Emerald Beach Ball. Those excluded from its revels went to the Jungle Club with its phosphorescent lake, or caught Paul Meeres, once of the Folies-Bergère, dressed in his Aztec loincloth and headdress of peacock feathers tipped with bells. It was a world apart.

The outbreak of hostilities naturally reduced visitor numbers,

although those from the States held up well until America came
into the war at the end of 1941. Many were drawn by the
prospect of a sight of the new Governor, the former King-
Emperor, and his Duchess. From the end of 1939, too, the
population of the colony was swelled by evacuees and wealthy
refugees from Europe: young wives sent away with the children
from Britain by their husbands; Jews from France (who found
themselves barred from Nassau's hotels); the Serbian-born
Duchess of Leeds, who had had to hand over her Rolls-Royce to
the SS in Paris; the boys from the Belmont School, Sussex, who
were found accommodation by Sir Harry Oakes.

Many of those who arrived made no secret of the fact that they
were hoping to sit out the war in safety in this balmy haven of
blue mahoe and oleander, content to watch the crabs scuttling
across the pearl-smooth sand. 'They were the most frightful
people,' recalls a member of the Duke of Windsor's circle, 'just
trying to get away to somewhere cushy. No sense of patriotism.'

Nonetheless, many were rich, and that had its advantages. The
same man can remember being egged on by one red-haired harridan
of eighty, all rouge and rum, to pick up a cigarette girl whose charms
he had noticed. 'Go on,' she whispered, leering. 'I'll lend you my car.
And my chauffeur.' It worked: 'I screwed the lass in the pool.' Having
made the acquaintance of Errol Flynn, his later exploits included their
accidentally burning down a whorehouse in Trinidad.

Aside from less exotic flotsam such as my father, his sister and their
mother, the ranks of 'war guests' also accommodated a champion
greyhound, Safe Rock, who was dispatched from Britain with his
keeper, a seventy-two-year-old native of Westmoreland, so that he
might not be unduly troubled by the restricted wartime diet.
'Scientifically kennelled and expertly cared for', wrote the press,
noting the gratifying manner in which the dog had adjusted to his
new quarters. A fatal dose of heart worm from the local mosquitoes
soon followed.

More fortunate than he were three other young British families
whom my grandmother saw much of: Blanche, Lady Boles – whose

husband was to be killed fighting in Italy – and her son; Dulcibel Effie Cathcart-Walker-Heneage, known as Babs ('Baby') Heneage, the party-loving mother of a seven-year-old daughter and young girl twins; and Marcelle Goldsmith, whose boys Teddy and Jimmy (the future environmentalist and tycoon respectively) were boisterous budding tennis players. Their father Frank, a former MP, had been running a luxury hotel in France and, given the family's Jewish origins, had decided to leave just before the Germans reached Paris. Having fought at Gallipoli, he was now too old for military service and in Nassau soon became involved in two of the town's hotels. Jimmy and Effie's daughter, Lynn, often played together; at the age of eight, he swindled her out of her prized stamp collection commemorating the 450th anniversary of Columbus's landing.

Yet aside from these arrivals, by 1942 the Bahamas had been as little touched by the first truly global conflict as any place on either of the two sides. 'The Governor is, on the whole, optimistic,' ran the dry humour of one Colonial Office report, 'that the Bahamas will survive the strain of war.' It was true that when the hurricane season came, in the damp weeks of late summer, tempers could fray in the claustrophobic atmosphere of Nassau. At lunch at one club, a youthful clergyman accused out of the blue a popular Allied consul of sympathising with the Nazis. On the polo ground, an elderly man ran down Britain's performance thus far in the conflict, and was challenged to a fist fight by his equally ancient friend. Otherwise Nassau's inhabitants, and in particular the merchants of Bay Street, were largely oblivious to the struggle.

As my father had discovered, there were German submarines prowling the waters off Florida, but victims of their attacks were still rarities in the islands. Joe Carstairs had picked up forty-seven survivors from a merchantman, and there had been a considerable stir in October 1940 when the only two survivors of a steamer sunk off the Azores had staggered ashore on the Bahamian island of Eleuthera after a voyage of seventy-one days and three thousand miles. Four other men had slipped over the side of their small boat two weeks after the drinking water had run out, but Bob

Tapscott, nineteen, and Roy Widdicombe, twenty-one, had clung on to life, subsisting on flying fish and gulps of rain.

They became local heroes in Nassau, but their story was not to end happily. Widdicombe was drowned when the ship on which he was returning to Britain was sunk a day before it reached Liverpool. Tapscott had refused to sail, but was later killed in a car accident in America. Outside of the cocoon, the world was full of dangers.

There was a handful of Bahamians serving overseas with the North Caribbean Regiment or in the RAF, but aside from the news on the wireless the nearest the war had come to most people was the very limited rationing imposed in July 1943, on the day of Oakes's murder. Petrol had been restricted for some time, and now rationing was extended to include sugar, coffee, salt pork and lard. One's little luxuries, however, were still easy to find: *Motion Picture* magazine for her; Craven 'A' cigarettes for him.

The world conflict itself had reached a lull. The German Army at Stalingrad had surrendered nearly six months earlier and the Afrika Korps had laid down its arms in Tunisia the previous May. The Allies were gathering their strength for the assault on Occupied Europe, a task that would begin with the invasion of Sicily on 10 July, two days after the discovery of Oakes's corpse.

One sign that they were gaining the upper hand came in the form of the greatly increased number of military personnel who started to arrive on the island from 1943 onwards. Previously the garrison had consisted of some veteran Canadian Highlanders, later replaced by a company of the Camerons when noises were made about the possibility of a German snatch-team landed by submarine kidnapping the Duke. When the Camerons were returned to chilly Scotland for commando training, three-quarters of them succumbed to pneumonia.

Following the entry of the United States into the war, however, the Bahamas had acquired a new strategic importance. In return for the loan of fifty elderly destroyers, the American government was granted leases on a number of British bases. One was in the Exumas, south-east of New Providence, while with American help a new landing strip – Windsor Field – was carved out of the limestone coral outside Nassau in preparation for a great expansion of the island's role as an airbase. There were two major reasons for this. First, the skies over the Bahamas were deemed a safer place to learn to fly than those patrolled by the Luftwaffe, and so from the late spring of 1943 the island became home to No. 111 Operational Training Unit, which would eventually teach more than five thousand airmen to fly Liberator and Mitchell bombers.

Secondly, Nassau also became a main staging post for RAF Transport Command, which ferried freight and Canadian- and American-built aircraft to the Mediterranean theatre of operations via Brazil, Ascension Island and West Africa. In 1943 alone, 1,336 aeroplanes travelled this route. Not all the goods they carried were on the manifest. The crews became adept at smuggling first alcohol – often bought from the beach girls in Nassau – and later diamonds. It didn't do to mix the two, however. If you got drunk celebrating your new riches, you might forget to lock the tail wheel on landing. Then the aircraft would skid sickeningly off the runway, ripping open its belly tank on the sharp coral. The base got used to the subsequent fireballs; there was about one a week.

The arrival of what became a permanent contingent of some three thousand airmen in 1943 created new excitement, and new problems. 'RAF all over town, RAF is dressed in brown,' went the calypso. 'Woman lay your body down, you make two shake, you get two pound.'

For war-weary officers and men, for grass widows trying to hide their anxieties, Nassau became even more of a party town: mornings passed luxuriating in the waves; afternoons spent at fish fries under the palms; the nights a whirl of dinners and dances and fund-raisers. One observer compared it to Brussels on the eve of Waterloo (albeit with more mosquitoes), and the smartly uniformed young men were only too eager to invite the likes of my grand-mother up to the control tower to show them how the routes of planes were plotted. Both Blanche Boles and Effie Heneage would go on to marry RAF officers they met in the Bahamas.

Few of Nassau's new residents had been outside Britain before, and for them this paradise of bougainvillea and passion flower, blue skies and humming birds formed too vivid a contrast with the grey familiarities of home. Standards slipped. Lovers changed partners in carefree fashion. The dance went on. 'What a place,' my grandmother remembers. 'One used to say that endless sunshine and living on rum DIDN'T SUIT WHITE PEOPLE!'

Where, because of the evacuees, there had been a noticeable surplus of women, now they were outnumbered and in demand, being chatted up daily in the canteens that they ran for the forces. (The Duchess prided herself on the eggs she cooked for the NCOs.) Liberator pilots, returning from a trip across to Cairo, turned on their landing lights as they came in over their digs, hoping to see who their girlfriend was with. Bars had to close at 10.30 p.m. to prevent the soldiery from becoming too drunk.

The rum-fuelled fun extended as far as the local whores – the two pounds that the calypso urged them to make was two weeks' pay for a labourer. Yet pleasure walked arm in arm with retribution: venereal disease was rife. The black nursemaid who was looking after my father and his sister had so severe a dose that she began to shake all over. This gave my grandmother cause to doubt her suitability as a moral exemplar to her charges, and soon afterwards she duly learned that the girl had been encouraging them to pilfer fruit from the neighbours' gardens.

The unexpected financial opportunities enjoyed by the native women of Nassau did not extend to their menfolk. With employment sorely hit by a blight in the sponge beds, the announcement of the building of the new airfield, with its promise of construction work for several thousand locals, lifted hearts. But soon after building began in May 1942, discontent broke out when the unskilled black labour force realised the huge disparity in pay between their fixed daily rate and that of their American counterparts.

Negotiations achieved nothing. The wage had been set artificially low by the islands' white-dominated Parliament, the House of Assembly, which saw no advantage in increasing it. By the morning of 1 June, the mood had turned ugly, and a thousand-strong mob descended on Bay Street.

The Duke was away in America, but his deputy, the Colonial Secretary Leslie Heape, decided that the police were capable of handling the situation without reinforcements from the Army contingents on the island. Yet such a demonstration was unparalleled in Nassau's history, and Erskine-Lindop, with no experience of anything like this, had just thirty men at his disposal.

By a quarter past nine, the crowd had gathered outside the public buildings where they howled for the heads of the administration and the two main political parties. None would come out to face them, and it was left to the decidedly unimpressive figure of the Attorney-General, Eric Hallinan, the driest of lawyers, to defuse the situation. His mild requests to the protesters that they should disperse were shouted down, and seeing that their demands would not be met the hotter-headed began to cast about for other forms of satisfaction. Their gaze turned back towards Bay Street.

Within a few moments, the crowd – many lent courage by drink, even at this early hour – was rampaging down the road, smashing every window and looting every shop. For half an hour their orgy of destruction went unchecked. Erskine-Lindop, believing that he could not restrain them, simply grouped his men around a statue of Queen Victoria. White passers-by ran for their lives, astonished and frightened by this ferocious display of violence from the blacks – among them women and children – who normally seemed so deferential. Vehicles were abandoned in the street, their doors flung open when their occupants had fled.

Caught up in the midst of the riot was Marcelle Goldsmith. Suddenly, a huge figure jumped onto the bonnet of her car. She saw that it was Red Isaac, a half-black, half-Jewish man who gave tennis lessons to her sons; he was recognisable not least by the distinction of having three nipples. He appeared to be one of the leaders of the horde, and she feared the worst. He had come, however, to rescue her, and guided the car to safety.

At a quarter to ten, Erskine-Lindop was finally instructed to intervene, and he and his constables bravely attempted a baton charge. They were driven back by a hail of stones and Coca-Cola bottles seized from a truck. It was only with the arrival of the Camerons an hour after the looting had started that the crowd was dispersed by the troops firing in the air. The mob retreated to Grant's Town, where they stocked up on alcohol and set fire to the main buildings. The police could do little more than keep blacks out of the white quarter of the city, and in confrontations later that afternoon three men were killed and five wounded by the soldiers. Calm did not return until the following day.

It was this episode, which incensed the 'Conchy Joes', the white property-owning class, that had lost Erskine-Lindop the confidence of the Governor. Despite the arrival of a hundred US Marines to help keep order, Bay Street's confidence took a further battering later in the month when fire broke out one night, quickly spreading among the wooden buildings. The Duke had been putting his feet up on the veranda of Government House after dinner and dashed down to help with the bucket chains. Although the blaze was brought under control by early morning – it was found to be arson: the fire had been started for the insurance by the owner of a clothes shop – the damage had been severe and it contributed to a mood of political unease. Tempers among the black population were not improved either when, as punishment for the riot, the Duke refused permission for the annual Junkanoo carnival to be staged.

Low wages, however, were not the only problem with the airfield project run by Pleasantville Construction, an American firm. There were also rumours of widespread fraud and corruption among the contractors, and in January 1943 it was Harry Oakes who flew to Washington to ask that they be investigated.

For many blacks, his arrival in the Bahamas almost a decade earlier had been a godsend. He had spent lavishly in an attempt to improve the islands' attractiveness to investors and hence the value of his own property. By the early 1940s, he employed more than fifteen hundred people on various building, road-clearing and landscaping schemes on his estates, and he had provided the islands' first bus service for them to travel to and from work. He had given a new wing to the hospital, improved the provision of water to Nassau – always a problem – and started a hotel school at the British Colonial. He also constructed the Bahamas' first airport, Oakes Field, which opened in January 1940, and with Christie he founded an inter-island air service.

With his wealth and clout as an employer, Oakes could have commanded political power in the islands, had he wanted it. But his importance to the Bahamas already gave him access to the Governor, the source of all executive decisions, and though he took a seat in the Legislative Council, the islands' upper chamber, he never played any part in its activities. Unlike its conservative Bay Street members, he lacked vested interests and a position of privilege to defend. Money had not mellowed him, but it had made him – by and large – content.

There was a single fly in the ointment of his ease, and not long after the discovery of Oakes's body it was hovering around Westbourne. Of all the personalities in the case, the most intriguing, talked-about and perhaps misunderstood was Sir Harry's son-in-law, Count Alfred de Marigny.

Even before subsequent events generated still more speculation, the cloud of rumour that hung around Freddie de Marigny was remarkably thick. He was an aristocrat. He was not. He was a gigolo, he was a playboy. He had been twice married, or was it three times? He was rich. He was a gold-digger. He had found buried treasure. He was the Count of Monte Cristo.

As we shall see, sometimes even the man himself was not sure which version of his life was accurate. The key to understanding de Marigny is to appreciate that for him truth was not an absolute: its shape depended on where you were standing. The accounts he gave of his upbringing, wealth and past varied from day to day, from audience to audience. The only thing of which one could be certain was that each story would contradict the last. Taking a deep breath, and steering the best course one can through the shallows of his veracity, the path of his early years appears to have been as follows.

Count Alfred de Marigny was in fact born plain Marie Alfred Fouquereaux in Curepipe, Mauritius, at the end of March 1910. The island, which lies several hundred miles to the east of Madagascar, in the Indian Ocean, had originally been colonised by the French, but it had been a British possession since Napoleonic times. It was still dominated, however, by French culture, language and families, of whom the Fouquereaux, of Norman stock but for centuries the owners of sugar estates on Mauritius, were among the most respected. Young Freddie was therefore born a British citizen, but French was his mother tongue and he spoke English with a strong Gallic accent.

His earliest memories of childhood were of the large house where he was brought up with black servants for playmates. It was a happy existence, surrounded by dogs, chickens and geese, and enlivened by the stories and superstitions that the former slaves had brought from Africa – tales of flying cats and werewolves and moonlight. There was just one thing missing from this idyllic life: his parents.

It is when one begins to examine his various explanations for their absence that one starts to understand how complex de Marigny really was. Any of the versions he gave out would have been dramatic enough for another man, but not only did he have to subscribe to several, each more startling than the previous, it is also impossible to fathom whether any of them were true.

The Count de Marigny published two volumes of memoirs, written more than forty years apart. In the first of these, *More Devil Than Saint*, which came out in 1946, he tells of the marriage between his father, Charles Chrysostomo Fouquereaux, and his mother, Elda Desveaux de Marigny. When Freddie was still a toddler, she fell in love with a man named Lemerle and, deserting her husband and only child, the adulterous pair fled to Paris. The intensely conventional Catholic milieu of Mauritius was scandalised, and Elda was formally excommunicated by papal edict.

As her son, Freddie was ostracised by the other grand Mauritian families and by his fellow pupils at the island's Royal College. His mother's name was never mentioned in the house. His father treated him in a cold and distant manner, and tried to avoid him. He grew up feeling that there was something that set him apart, something that, in time, was converted into a conviction of superiority.

Then, in a scene that would grace any melodrama, at the age of eighteen Freddie met his mother again by sheer chance when playing in a tennis tournament. Their tearful reunion led to a furious argument with his father, after which he decided to take his mother's surname. It was from her side, too, that he took the title of Count that was to prove such a source of fascination. His decisions led to his being disinherited, and from that day on he never saw his father again.

It is an unhappy tale that makes one sympathise with the unjustly treated young Freddie. The problem is that the account differs in almost every respect from that given in his second autobiography, *Conspiracy of Crowns*, written in 1988.

In this, he never becomes aware of his parents' divorce but is told instead as a child that his mother has died. He is brought up not by his father but by his grandmother, his father having gone to live in South Africa. Nor is he educated at the Royal College in Mauritius, but more prestigiously by Jesuits in Normandy.

The inconsistencies do not end there. According to *More Devil Than Saint*, after leaving school he travelled to Paris to study agricultural chemistry, and then went on to London, where he planned to train as a doctor. Instead, in the second volume, he enters Cambridge University rather than Paris, and when he goes to London it is to work in banking, not medicine. He never returns to Mauritius to run a fishing fleet, as he had claimed in the first book, but writes that after making a fortune in zinc trading he became involved in the late 1930s in rescuing Jews from the Nazis. Most blatantly of all, by 1988 he appeared to have forgotten all about his marriage in 1937 to a French girl, Lucie-Alice Cahen.

★

The root of de Marigny's aversion to hard facts was once explained by another crucial influence on his life, his best friend Georges, Marquis de Visdelou. It was quite simple, de Visdelou told a reporter: Freddie's provincial upbringing in Curepipe had left him with an inferiority complex that expressed itself in a compulsion to boast and shock. He was, essentially, a fantasist.

De Visdelou himself was well placed to recognise the type. Eighteen months de Marigny's senior, he and Freddie had been friends since boyhood – they were perhaps distant cousins – and in about 1932 (and of this there is no doubt) they met up again in London. Here Georges, a pale dumpling with a cad's moustache and an abiding interest in cartography, made much play of his title and in October 1936 landed an excellent catch when he married Diana North, the twenty-two-year-old granddaughter of Colonel John T. North, 'The Nitrate King', who had reaped a fortune in Chile from the compound used in fertilisers and gunpowder.

Colonel North had left the modern equivalent of some thirty-five million pounds and the death of Diana's own father, Sir Harry North, in 1921 had made her a considerable heiress. Georges lost no time in moving from his digs in Bayswater to Diana's house in Knightsbridge and, lest there might be any awkward questions, two months after the wedding he changed his name by deed poll (recorded in an announcement in *The Times*) from plain Georges Guimbeau to the Marquis de Visdelou-Bonamour, the title he liked to claim had been left to him by an uncle.

In *More Devil Than Saint*, de Marigny wryly notes de Visdelou's assurances that his marquisate had been officially confirmed by the relevant authority in London. He makes some play, too, of not thinking much of his own title of Count, despite de Visdelou's promptings and despite the fact that it was registered 'in the annals of the Colonial Office'. The arbiter in such matters for British territories, the College of Arms, has not, in fact, ever recognised either title. The most generous interpretation of their authenticity and standing is probably that supplied by de Marigny himself, namely that they were hereditary French courtesy titles local to Mauritius, titles which most people bothered little about.

Nonetheless, it was an *appellation* that Freddie seems to have been prepared to use if it could win him an advantage. He might not flaunt the title, but somehow everyone knew it existed, especially pretty girls. This possible misrepresentation was not the most heinous of sins, but it was an indication that both he and de Visdelou were ready to stretch the truth to breaking point.

Of the two, though de Marigny was the more dynamic it appears to have been de Visdelou who was the stronger personality. Certainly de Marigny seems to have struggled to shake off a man who brought him many troubles, yet with whom he lived for the best part of ten years. Several of those who knew him told me that he found it hard to make other friends and simply followed de Visdelou's lead. 'He is my Hyde side,' he once remarked.

The anecdotes of their years together in London make for entertaining reading – the time they were conned into buying an 'Old Master' that was not, the time they raised funds for Marie Stopes, the advocate of birth control, the time they met the Prince of Wales. Then there were the parties with Barbara Hutton, the Woolworth heiress, and the visits to the Nuremberg rallies. The trouble is, as ever, that it is impossible to judge if any of it is true. Not a single story, hardly a single name appears in both the versions of de Marigny's memoirs.

In the earlier book, de Visdelou is cast as the out-and-out social climber in what are light-hearted adventures, with de Marigny his more naive partner, especially in matters of the heart. With half a century to reflect on his image, by the time of the Count's second book – in which the approach of war becomes the dominant keynote – Georges takes a back seat to the cool-headed Freddie, who bests the Nazis and charms the ladies in a manner reminiscent of the 1930s thriller hero 'The Saint'.

The contradictions come to a head with the two accounts of his marriage to Lucie-Alice in March 1937. In *More Devil Than*

Saint he writes that he was attracted as much as anything by the quality of her mind. De Marigny always regarded himself as something of an intellectual, and he was susceptible to those with good brains, including de Visdelou. On honeymoon in Switzerland, however, he learned of a deep conflict between Lucie-Alice's instincts as a woman and her feminist principles; in particular, she did not want children.

Shortly afterwards the couple sailed for New York aboard the liner *Normandie*. But according to de Marigny he had by then discovered that his bride and the married de Visdelou were lovers, and they parted company as soon as they docked in America. His consolation was that in the meantime he had managed to make friends on board with Ernest Hemingway and his girlfriend, the war reporter Martha Gellhorn. In time, the author would become godfather to one of de Marigny's sons.

Fifty years later, however, Lucie-Alice Cahen has been airbrushed from the picture. (She had, in fact, flown to Florida the day after arriving in New York, and three months later, she and de Marigny were divorced.) Perhaps out of guilt, there is mention in *Conspiracy of Crowns* of a friend called 'Lucie Cohen', but there is no wedding, no Swiss honeymoon and no cuckolding by de Visdelou.

There is an explanation for these variances, but it is not entirely satisfying. Both books were put together with the help of ghostwriters, and the first volume was later disowned by de Marigny, who claimed that it was based on interviews he had given a journalist in Canada when ill and down on his luck after the war. Oddly, in *Conspiracy of Crowns* he even denies that *More Devil Than Saint* exists, mentioning an agreement to write a book that he later cancelled.

More Devil Than Saint consists equally of sub-Chandler prose and elementary mistakes (Erskine-Lindop, for instance, is called simply 'Lindorpt' throughout). However, it includes many facts which can only have come from de Marigny. Moreover, he was clearly a willing collaborator on the second book, which might be viewed as an opportunity to clear up any matters complicated by the first. Instead, it clouds them still further. Aside from errors that may just be the product of an ageing memory or sloppy editing, there are inexplicable omissions – as well as blatant inventions that are all too easy to identify as such.

Thus, for instance, despite her absence from *Conspiracy of Crowns*, Lucie-Alice did exist. In *More Devil Than Saint* de Marigny claims that in 1937 he put her aboard a boat at New York back to France and thereafter never heard of her again. As we shall see, however, she had in fact reappeared six years later at an extremely inconvenient moment for him, and had supplied another explanation entirely for the brevity of their marriage. It was not one, presumably, that he wished to recall in either volume.

Then, too, by contrast with the version given in 1988, de Marigny was indeed educated on Mauritius as he had first maintained, and not by Jesuits in France; in the same interview from 1943 in which de Visdelou identified Freddie's need to boast, he also revealed its origin, that de Marigny had not been sent to school in Normandy like the sons of other rich families. Even seventy years on, that feeling of not having grown up as one of an elite, and the consequent absence of self-confidence, must have still rankled. To the end of his days, it would seem, the Count was never quite comfortable with the truth.

It was this deliberate cultivation of mystery that made him, especially to women, an extremely attractive figure. But it alienated those who were more conventional – and more powerful. Above all, when suspicion began to gather around him, it created doubt in the minds of those closest to Alfred de Marigny as to whether they could really trust his version of events.

Freddie and Lucie-Alice were married in March 1937. Eight months later, he exchanged wedding vows for the second time that year. His wife this time was Ruth Fahnestock Schermerhorn, and where Lucie-Alice had been the daughter of a well-off but undistinguished Parisian factory owner, Ruth was American aristocracy: she was the granddaughter of Abraham Lincoln's personal

stockbroker, the man who had founded the Fahnestock investment firm.

There was only one complication: Ruth already had a husband,
Coster Schermerhorn, and a young daughter. De Marigny, however, if not devastatingly handsome, was well over six feet tall,
green-eyed and immensely engaging. Ruth found him irresistible.

At twenty-nine, she was two years older than Freddie. She was
also blonde, determined and sophisticated, and (as with Georges)
de Marigny found himself powerless to resist a more forceful personality. When he fled New York for Trinidad, she pursued him
with telegrams, telephone calls and three letters a day. When he
refused to come back, she threatened to commit suicide. She was
prepared to sacrifice her marriage, her name, the house on Park
Avenue and the custody of her child for de Marigny, and for him
such passion was extremely attractive.

Deep down, he knew that he was probably making a mistake.
But after the failure of his parents' marriage he does seem to have
genuinely wanted a successful one of his own. His trouble was
that he attracted women easily, and then found them difficult to
reject when his own desire cooled. If he developed a reputation
as a Lothario, it was perhaps not so much that he was a cynical
breaker of hearts as someone who, being still only in his mid-
twenties, lacked the ability to judge quickly whether or not a
woman was right for him.

Ruth was not. She had, de Marigny wrote later, a hard,
demanding side to her nature that he had not seen before she
secured a divorce and they were married in Reno, Nevada, in
November 1937. They celebrated by hurling her old wedding
ring from a bridge into the river below. (Coster, her former husband, subsequently married Ursula Parrott, the author of a once
much-lauded Jazz Age novel, *Ex-Wife*.) Ruth and Freddie honey-
mooned in Tobago, and then settled on Eleuthera, about sixty
miles across the water from Nassau.

De Marigny had visited it while on holiday – he had been staying with Hemingway nearby in Key West – and had been

attracted by the island's beauty, its remoteness and by the pioneering spirit required to make a go of life there. Even in 1939, the
tiny main settlement, Governor's Harbour, had neither electric
light nor a reliable source of fresh water. Already, however, a few
wealthy Europeans had built properties along the coast, notably
the de Marignys' near-neighbour Rosita Forbes, then a very well
known – and well connected – English travel writer.

While de Marigny took to the self-sufficiency required on
Eleuthera, designing a house and planting pineapples, oranges
and grapefruit, Ruth did not, and their marriage soon soured. He
later ascribed this to her jealousy and demanding nature, a verdict
partially supported by Forbes in her memoirs, which note that
Ruth asked of life the improbable and of her husband the impossible. According to de Marigny, Ruth was spoiled and had to
have her own way, with no exceptions.

Still, Forbes makes it clear that the de Marignys' existence on
Eleuthera was not an idyll – she characterises their house as rather
grim – and it cannot have been easy for Ruth to adjust from her
somewhat pampered world to life in a place where the nearest
shop was a twenty-five-mile drive along a bare track. Clearly,
too, de Marigny was not the kind of husband who was prepared
to accommodate himself to his wife's wants or who would
attempt to remedy the cause of her unhappiness. His was not a
mind that saw any value in compromise.

This trait, accompanied by a sharp tongue, would frequently
bring him into conflict with others, including Forbes herself.
Admittedly, Rosita Forbes was, according to her fellow Orientalist
Gertrude Bell, 'a first-class busybody', and a snob too – she had
made much play of her acquaintanceship with the Windsors and
had cultivated the Oakeses as well – and these were characteristics
that riled de Marigny. They fell out over a supply of water that he
had discovered: she coveted it but he wanted to preserve it for
public use. The well-being of the black inhabitants of the islands
was something that de Marigny was, by the standards of the day,
unusually interested in, and he always had notably good and easy

relations with them. It was another attribute that marked him out as an outsider in the Bahamas.

His relationship with Ruth now deteriorated rapidly. The rows came frequently, and while usually followed by reconciliation, each one killed a little of the love they had for each other. Looking back, de Marigny admitted later that he had done nothing to heal the widening rift between them. He could not abide Ruth's jealousy, while for her part she wanted more of his time than he was prepared to give; she was too American, he was very French. After less than two years of marriage, they separated in October 1939.

By de Marigny's account, they agreed to a divorce of convenience principally because Ruth owed tax in America on the trusts that held her stocks and shares. As the wife of a British citizen, the money she had in Nassau to pay this was tied up by restrictions imposed when war with Germany had broken out a few weeks earlier. A divorce would give her control of her finances once more. De Marigny also agreed to let her live at Governor's Harbour for five years and to give her a monthly allowance.

In return, he received ten thousand pounds (three hundred thousand in today's money), certainly no less than he had already had of Ruth's money. He does not trouble to mention this substantial amount in either of his memoirs, but its existence would later be revealed at an awkward moment for him.

It is hard to judge whether, as he confesses in *More Devil Than Saint*, he really had told Ruth that they would remarry after the war, when currency restrictions would have eased. Whether or not this was a subterfuge he used to rid himself of her, what is clear is that, whatever their differences, the split was not final and immediate, and that Ruth still retained much affection for him. For some months after their divorce in 1940 they continued to share a house, and the next year she dedicated a poem to him ('To A de M') in a volume of verse that she published. Its title, *Shoulder The Sky*, was perhaps indicative of her mood.

One suspects that at the root of their mutual dissatisfaction there lay the difference between de Marigny's outer face – the amusing, extrovert public persona with which Ruth had fallen in love – and his more orthodox, disciplined inner self. He undoubtedly liked being noticed, however, and by now his divorces had gained him a reputation in Nassau (to where he moved in 1940) as a womaniser or, as my grandmother succinctly described him, 'an oily piece of work'. As a habitual flirt, with a Frenchman's temperament, this suited him, nor did he particularly mind what people thought of him as a result. He was soon chatting up the actress Madeleine Carroll, the star of *The 39 Steps*, who was in Nassau to shoot *Bahama Passage* (based on an impossibly titled novel, *Dildo Cay*, which by chance begins with the discovery of the body of a rich Bahamian who has had his skull stoved in).

When, at the film's première in the city, Harold Christie tried to escort Carroll to an official reception, he found his way blocked by de Marigny and Georges de Visdelou, who had turned up in Nassau following the collapse of his own marriage. De Marigny briskly told Christie to push off if all he had to offer the actress was a dull party with married men.

De Marigny also chanced his arm with perhaps the most famous glamour girl of the moment, the twenty-year-old American debutante of the year and *Life* magazine cover-star Brenda Frazier who had been courted by Howard Hughes. But on this occasion both Hughes and de Marigny had to give way to de Visdelou, who had surprising success with women, including Frazier with whom he now had a brief but ardent affair.

Such masculine bravado was on the face of it typical of de Marigny, but it was not *au fond* a genuine character trait. He was actually, several people told me, privately a little shocked by the morality – or lack of it – that he found in Nassau. He was, in the Mediterranean manner, rather open about what he thought and did – 'limited, not deep' was how one person described him – and the habitual hypocrisy of the English was not to his taste. Most of all, he believed in hard work and what it brought; he was not the idle wastrel afterwards portrayed by the press. He liked to spend money, but disapproved of drinking and gambling, and was appalled when one acquaintance staked his house at a game of backgammon.

One illustration of the contrast between the two parts of de Marigny's nature was his love of sailing. He had done a little as a boy on Mauritius, but it was not until he came to the Bahamas that he took up the sport seriously, inspired by the World Championships held there in 1938. He bet himself that he would beat Harry Nye, twice runner-up for the world title in the Star class, within two years, and that he would secure an international title of his own within five.

It was yachting's image of money at play that later provided the public perception of de Marigny. Characteristically, he chose to live up to his outer image by provocatively naming his boat *Concubine*. Yet he did not sail just to impress but to win, and (as he later did with bridge) he studied and practised and worked until he could make good on his bet.

Having, at great expense, fitted out five of his friends with the twenty-two-foot-long yachts, he was soon defeating the best that Nassau could put up at the island's regattas. He made his international debut in 1940 and finished last in the World Series. But within a year, coached by the German-Brazilian Walter von Hutschler, he was acknowledged as a top-flight Star skipper and was winning races in Long Island Sound.

Then, in 1942, de Marigny took the much-coveted Bacardi Cup in the waters off Cuba. The competition was second in standing only to the world championships, and he triumphed by defeating Nye, who had been victorious in each of the previous two years.

Remarkably, and somewhat foolhardily, de Marigny committed himself to hours of sailing even though he could not swim. As always, there was a tall story to explain this, something to do with seeing a cousin eaten by a shark which had given him a fear of water. It was a more exciting excuse, at any rate, than simply admitting that he was too bored to endure the mundane business of swimming lessons.

His liking for hard work manifested itself in the form of several ventures he began on the island, among them developing housing, supplying groceries to restaurants and owning a beauty salon. These prospered, and for a time it seemed as if he might be on the straight and narrow. That changed for good, however, at the end of 1941, when he met Nancy Oakes.

Sir Harry's daughter was then seventeen, fourteen years de Marigny's junior, and she had been in love with him almost since he had arrived in Nassau. She had even memorised the number plate of his car. He had seen her around socially several times, but naturally he had thought of her as just the child she was. Now she began to pursue him, and once more he found irresistible a woman's interest in him. Auburn-haired, with a full mouth, high forehead and a slender figure starting to blossom out of girlhood – 'the most beddable thing you ever saw', as one admirer described her to me – Nancy loved to dance, and this became her entrée into de Marigny's circle – and into his heart.

They waltzed and quickstepped with each other for hours at a Christmas ball at the British Colonial, and afterwards they kissed for the first time. In the following days, they went sailing together, water-skied together, and had picnics on deserted beaches up the coast. To begin with, de Marigny was acutely aware that Nancy was a teenager, and he knew that he ought to be staying well out of her way. He told himself that she was just a fun young thing to have around, and that he was certainly not in love with her. Yet when she was not with him, he found that he missed her affection and evident devotion. Soon, despite all his bad experience of marriage, the old dream of making a home, of repairing the damage done by his parents, entered his head.

In his memoirs de Marigny – naturally – emphasises that he was not attracted to Nancy because of her family's wealth. His track record, admittedly, was not good: both his previous wives had been very well off and Ruth had certainly advanced him money. In his favour was his willingness to work and the success that he seemed to be having with his businesses, which appear to have

helped him to live in some style. He writes of how he spent
hours far out at sea, pacing the deck of *Concubine*, arguing with
himself, probing his heart for his motives.

Yet his tales of killings made on zinc in the stock market, that
use of the title – it has the ring about it of the gold-digger, and
whatever the truth it is hard to believe that Nancy's vast inheritance was never a consideration for him. Whether it was the only
one would soon preoccupy all of Nassau.

What definitely appealed to de Marigny was the care that Nancy
showed for him when, unexpectedly, he had to enter hospital in
New York early in May for an operation on a stomach growth.
Though mature for her age Nancy was still at school, in Manhattan,
and came to see him every afternoon. Ruth came to see him every
morning, and soon there were tantrums. She and de Marigny
might have been formally divorced, but evidently his contemplating a union with a young heiress whom he had known for only a
few months was a blow that she could not countenance. Yet crazily,
romantically, recklessly, on 19 May 1942 Freddie and Nancy were
married at a courthouse in the Bronx. She had turned eighteen
and attained her majority, just two days before.

The wedding appears to have been the doing of the impulsive
and strong-willed Nancy, but de Marigny – considerably the older
and theoretically the wiser of the two – did nothing to dissuade
her. The effect on her parents, who had been kept in the dark,
was predictable enough. Her mother was upset, Sir Harry briefly
angry. Then he asked de Marigny how much money he wanted.
Freddie was at least sensible enough to steer clear of that trap and
subsequently signed papers renouncing any claims that he might
have had as her husband on Nancy's assets.

For a period all then went well as the Oakeses tried to make the
best of things. Nancy's younger brothers and sister took to de
Marigny, and Sir Harry offered him a job running one of his
finance companies, the Bahamas Trust. This de Marigny turned
down, preferring not to be under his father-in-law's thumb, but
Oakes seemed to take it in good part. He threw the couple a

belated wedding party, at which he jokingly began auctioning them to the highest bidder, and in midsummer they headed off for a honeymoon in Mexico.

There, almost immediately, Nancy caught typhoid fever and for a time hovered between life and death. De Marigny unhesitatingly gave blood for transfusions, but once the crisis had passed a new horror revealed itself. Nancy had contracted trench mouth, an acute inflammation of the gums that destroys the soft tissue of the mouth and jawbone. Soon she had lost her upper jaw and her teeth, and was plunged once more into a series of life-threatening fevers. Even if she recovered she would face years of reconstructive surgery. For a pretty girl of eighteen, now only able to talk – to make a sort of quack – by pushing her cheeks together, it was a devastating illness.

Though under great strain, de Marigny showed his mettle, caring for Nancy and feeding her with an eyedropper. The bond between them strengthened, but their relations with the Oakeses began to suffer irreparable damage. There were several reasons for the breakdown. As well as harbouring lingering resentment about the secret nature of the wedding, Lady Oakes, Nancy's mother, was by nature rather changeable and difficult. De Marigny claims that she despised him for crying when he was worried about Nancy, and also writes that – being only in her mid-forties herself – Eunice was somewhat jealous of the attention that her daughter was getting from an ardent husband, something that Sir Harry had never been.

It is more easy to verify that relations between de Marigny and his in-laws had been poisoned by a letter that the bitter Ruth had written to the Oakeses and which had come first to their lawyer, Foskett. Its contents are uncertain, but evidence from de Marigny suggests that it made two allegations calculated to enrage the Oakeses. The first was that all de Marigny's money in fact came from her, thus suggesting that he was after more of the same from Nancy. The second claim was that at the time of his marriage to Nancy not only was she pregnant by him but so was Ruth.

The truth of the second accusation is unclear – certainly there were no children born – but in early 1943 it struck a particularly sensitive chord with the Oakeses. Following her recovery from her initial illness, Nancy had indeed fallen pregnant. But fearing for her health and knowing that she would need more operations imminently, her parents, on medical advice, had arranged for her to have an abortion. When he found out, de Marigny's Roman Catholic upbringing asserted itself and a heated row ensued.

Needing a tonsillectomy, Freddie then took a room next to Nancy's in her Palm Beach hospital. The evening that he arrived, at about ten p.m. the telephone by his bed rang. It was Sir Harry, and he was incandescent with rage. De Marigny could barely understand what Oakes was saying he was so angry, something about having heard from a doctor in Mexico that de Marigny had shared a bed with Nancy in the hospital there.

Now Oakes had learned again that, although Nancy was extremely ill and weak, de Marigny could not keep his hands off her. Was he a pervert? Did he not realise that his lust had endangered her life once already? 'Get the hell out of there,' he shouted, 'or I'll come round and kick you out myself.'

In vain, Freddie tried to protest that he was just in the hospital because he needed an operation himself, and had no intention of molesting Nancy. He had in fact thought that taking the room was a good plan because he could be near her. But Oakes was not listening, let alone seeing reason, and he peremptorily ordered de Marigny from the building. He went, but Nancy had overheard the conversation and wept. That night her fever rose. When de Marigny came back the next morning, he told her doctor that Oakes was an old fool and, the surgeon later testified, that he would like to 'crack his head'.

Twenty-four hours later, all had seemingly been forgiven and Freddie and Sir Harry enjoyed a game of billiards together. The tag line from *Bahama Passage*, the Madeleine Carroll film, began, in all its corniness, to seem singularly apposite: 'The two most gorgeous humans you've ever seen – caressed by soft tropic winds – tossed by the tides of love.'

The argument with Oakes was, however, only the first in a series of steadily more vituperative fallings-out. The cause of most of them was the de Marignys' influence on Nancy's oldest brother Sydney, the fifteen-year-old heir to the baronetcy. When Freddie and Nancy returned to Nassau in March 1943, he began to spend considerable amounts of time with them and his parents started to worry that the older pair were trying to turn him against them, and perhaps control his inheritance should anything happen to them.

First, Lady Oakes wrote a letter to Sydney, telling him about Ruth's allegations that de Marigny's money was really hers. Then, on 27 March, a day of rows with Sir Harry about whether the de Marignys should attend a cocktail party given by the Duke at Government House – 'He's not my favourite ex-king' was de Marigny's characteristically blunt excuse – culminated late in the evening when Oakes stormed round to their house and dragged Sydney away.

De Marigny walked with Sir Harry to the car, and people heard them begin to yell at one another in the street. 'You're a sex maniac,' Oakes told de Marigny, who thought his father-in-law was so irate that he would hit him. 'I ought to have both of you whipped.' Then he began threatening to cut Nancy out of his will. 'N-O-T-H-I-N-G,' he spelled out aloud. 'That's what she'll get from me!'

Reconciliation followed the next morning, but the day afterwards – de Marigny's thirty-third birthday – was spoiled by another scene. At four a.m., long after the end of his birthday party, there was a terrible pounding on the door. Outside someone was shouting: 'Open up or I'll break this down!' It was Oakes. When a bemused de Marigny unlocked the door, Sir Harry brushed past him and demanded to be told where Sydney was. Shown the guest room in which his son was sleeping, Oakes suddenly bent down and hauled him out of bed by the foot. 'Get your clothes on and get the hell out of this house!' he bellowed. Then he glared at de Marigny and stormed out. It was the last time that the Count and his father-in-law met.

Relations between the Oakeses and the de Marignys were now completely ruptured, with Nancy firmly taking her husband's side. For her nineteenth birthday in May, her mother sent her a present of money, which she returned. Ten days later, Nancy wrote to her parents, telling them that until they accepted de Marigny as part of the family she was cutting herself off from them. It was a gesture designed to demonstrate her lack of dependence on their wealth but, unwittingly, it was an empty one. Unknown to her, back in February, following the argument about her abortion, the Oakeses had met with Foskett and had significantly altered the terms of their will. Henceforth, if anything happened to their parents the Oakes children would receive a small annual income but would inherit no capital before they were thirty.

At the end of May, with the onset of the summer heat, Nancy left for Vermont, where she was to take a dance course with Martha Graham and build up her strength for forthcoming operations on her face. De Marigny stayed in Nassau, supervising the running of a chicken farm that he had started in order to provide eggs and poultry for the increased numbers of troops now being stationed on the island.

On 7 July, the day of Oakes's murder, de Marigny spent the afternoon racing *Concubine*, competing for the de Visdelou trophy. That evening he gave a dinner party for nine people, including the wives of two RAF officers whom he had met the day before. Around one o'clock, as rain began to fall, he dropped them home. The next morning, Thursday, he rose early to go out to the farm. On his way back into town, at about eleven, he passed a car driven by a friend, John Anderson. He began trying to tell Anderson to memorise some measurements for materials when he realised that Anderson was trying to tell *him* that Harry Oakes was dead.

Until they met the Count de Marigny, what they had heard of his poor relations with his father-in-law had probably not seemed too important to Captains Barker and Melchen. He was not the only man in the world to have that problem, and the obvious suspect at first was Harold Christie, who had told them that he had heard nothing of the ghastly happenings in Oakes's room despite sleeping less than twenty feet away. Yet by the end of that Thursday afternoon, much of which de Marigny spent at Westbourne talking to Christie and Erskine-Lindop, their opinions had started to change. The trigger for this was the post-mortem, which had given them an approximate time-frame for Oakes's death, one that suddenly made them most interested in what de Marigny had had to say about his movements the night before.

Some time after one o'clock, he had driven home his two RAF-wife dinner guests, Jean Ainsley and Dorothy Clarke. They and their husbands were renting one of the cottages owned by Charles Hubbard, a retired director of Woolworths, which lay only about a hundred yards from Westbourne. Having seen the two women home, de Marigny said, he had then driven back alone to Nassau. The timing, and the location, taken with his known antipathy to Oakes, now appeared potentially incriminating.

Once Barker and Melchen had made these connections it was late, and it was not until even later that de Marigny was tracked down to the bar of the Prince George Hotel by Lieutenant John Douglas, a police officer. He explained that de Marigny was wanted back at Westbourne. Having returned there with John Anderson, the man who had told him of Oakes's death, de Marigny was interviewed for the first time by Melchen. Then the American asked him to roll up his sleeves, explaining that since Sir Harry's body had been almost incinerated he was going to inspect him for burnt hairs. De Marigny wrote later that he was startled when he suddenly realised that he was a suspect in the murder. But he remained calm, feeling superior to Melchen and the buttoned-up Erskine-Lindop and Pemberton, who were also in the room.

Using first a lens and then a microscope, Melchen announced

that he could see a considerable quantity of burnt hairs on de Marigny's hands, forearms and eyebrows and in the black beard that he had recently begun to grow. He allowed de Marigny to look through the microscope, and the Count offered a number of explanations: he spent much time in the sun yachting; he had been near a bonfire on his farm the day before; and he had scorched his hand lighting candles at the dinner party. Melchen then asked him what clothes he had been wearing the previous night, and Barker fingerprinted him.

It was past midnight when they all drove over to de Marigny's house on Victoria Avenue, in central Nassau itself. The car containing de Marigny, Anderson and Pemberton arrived first, and there was a further delay when Melchen had to go back to his vehicle after forgetting his magnifying glass. When he went into the house, he was met by Freddie coming out of his bedroom with a neatly pressed jacket and pair of trousers. Melchen's suspicions were immediately aroused. He thought that de Marigny had told him that he had been wearing a suit the night before but these clothes were just a barely matching set in two tones of brown. Furthermore, they did not look as if they had been worn recently.

De Marigny, doubtless with no little condescension, explained to the American that a gentleman's clothes – especially in the tropics – were pressed the day after use by one's valet. Moreover, he would never have owned such a thing as a brown suit. 'Come here,' he then said in his mocking French voice. 'I have something to show you which will amuse you very much.' Pointing out the matador's cape he owned, he handed Melchen a hurricane lamp, saying that he had taken out the electrical fittings in the dining room so that it was lit only by candles.

He demonstrated how he said he had burned himself the night before, reaching down into the lamp's glass chimney. Casually, he then directed the detective's attention to the toolbox of his Lincoln Continental, the car he had used the night before, in case Melchen wanted to inspect it. The detective removed the jack for tests. There was then some excitement when blood spots were found inside the car, although later these were shown to come from chickens.

De Marigny could not, however, produce either his tie or the shirt he had been wearing at dinner the previous evening. He merely gestured to a large laundry basket that contained a dozen white shirts, all made from the same cloth, that were his regular attire. The implication was that it could have been any of those. Seemingly satisfied with their search, the police left him in the company of Lieutenant Douglas who had instructions not to let de Marigny out of his sight, and to bring him to Westbourne first thing the next morning. With Douglas wakeful in an armchair, and de Marigny turning restlessly in bed, the pair passed a very uncomfortable night.

THREE

I spoke to Peter on the sea,
Ev'ry day be Sunday by an' by
He left 'is net an' foller me,
Ev'ry day be Sunday by an' by;
Crying, shine now,
Ev'ry day be Sunday by an' by

Soon after nine the next morning, de Marigny and Douglas and the Americans arrived at Westbourne. The humidity had subsided enough for Barker to begin dusting for prints, while Melchen continued his examination of the murder room and interviewed various witnesses who had assembled downstairs. At one point he called de Marigny up to a bedroom and quizzed him again about Oakes and about his movements on Wednesday night. Barker put his head round the door to check that all was well. Teamwork, they called it. 'Eddie tries to get the man to tell him where he was,' Barker later explained to reporters, 'and I try to prove he wasn't there.' 'And in doing so', interjected Melchen gleefully, 'we prove he *was* there!'

By early afternoon Barker had wrapped up his search for prints, having spent much of the morning scrutinising the Chinese-patterned screen that had been next to Oakes's bed. De Marigny had already left with Douglas, after checking with Erskine-Lindop whether they still needed the missing shirt. 'Don't worry,' he had been told, 'we have your coat and trousers – that's all we want.'

Some words of Melchen's were still throbbing in de Marigny's ears. 'I want to warn you about one thing,' he had growled. 'In this case nobody is too big or too small to be arrested, and even after we've gone we'll come back and keep investigating.' It seemed that Barker was another who did not take too kindly to de Marigny's title. As yet, however, aside from the burnt hairs they did not appear to be able to produce much evidence against him.

Barker told Pemberton that he wanted to process some of the prints he had found, and the police officer suggested that they go to the nearby RAF base, which had a photographic laboratory. They spent most of the afternoon away from Westbourne, and so missed the visit of the Duke of Windsor.

The curious thing was that of all those involved in the investigation it was the Duke who knew the house best. When he and his wife had arrived in Nassau, almost three years before, the Duchess had taken one look at their official residence, termite-ridden Government House, and had declared it uninhabitable. While it was being renovated to her exacting standards, they had borrowed Westbourne from the Oakeses for several months, and had slept in the very room now at the centre of events.

The Duke's star had paled considerably since the 1920s, when as Prince of Wales he had been the toast of the press and the crowds. Now *Time* magazine felt emboldened to call him 'a moth-eaten Prince Charming' accompanied by 'his faded Juliet'.

It was an unsympathetic critique, but the truth was that his decision to abdicate in 1936, and more particularly his behaviour since, had cost him friends in government and wider good opinion. Wallis, his duchess, was still acknowledged to have a great sense of style and the ability to charm in private, and he still had something of his celebrated common touch, but with his renunciation of the throne he also appeared to have given up his sense of responsibility.

If anything, it now behoved him to conduct himself with more discretion so as to spare his brother, the new King George VI, further embarrassment. But the Duke's conviction that he had been unjustly treated by the Royal Family and the Government left little room for consideration of their feelings. Then, too, his 'free' will was actually beholden to the dominant partner in his marriage, as he well knew. Out buying swimming trunks in Nassau, he remarked to an aide: 'I wear the shorts in this family'.

The Mediterranean cruises and frolics in Antibes were one thing, but it was the visit to Germany in October 1937, and the meeting with Hitler – of whose economic policies the Duke had long been an enthusiast – that had most damaged his reputation. When he had made the tour, at a time of international tension, it had seemed merely ill-judged. In retrospect, it actually looked highly foolish, and was the basis of persistent mutterings about where his loyalties really lay. These doubts had not been assuaged by his performance since the war began. A token staff job in Paris had been followed by a hasty flight in July 1940 to Portugal where, it has since emerged, he was the target of German espionage.

As its organiser, Walter Schellenberg, later acknowledged, there was no substantive evidence to suggest that the Duke was pro-Nazi or would ever have agreed to any far-fetched scheme to flit him off to Germany. Like many of his contemporaries, however, he undoubtedly believed at that point in the war that Britain might well be defeated, but unlike others he gave voice to his opinion in company. Disquieting reports of the Duke's table talk began to reach London.

'I had some conversation today with the Duke and Duchess of Windsor, Mr and Mrs George Wood and Major Phillips [Wood and Phillips were the Duke's two equerries],' wrote one observer, David Eccles, to Gladwyn Jebb at the Foreign Office. 'They are very nearly 5th column . . .' Jebb's superior, the Permanent Under-Secretary Sir Alec Cadogan, received similar briefings from Stewart Menzies, the Chief of the Secret Service: 'Source reports that Germans expecting assistance from Duke and Duchess of

Windsor, latter desiring at any price to become Queen. Germans have been negotiating with her since 27 June.'

In those days, uncorroborated intelligence material was treated with caution, but it was clear that the couple were a liability and that a safe place needed to be found to park them. The difficulty was that the Duke refused to return to Britain unless his wife was received by his family and accorded royal status. A post overseas seemed the natural solution, but Dominions such as Canada and Australia did not appear keen to have the former king foisted on them. The Duke's formerly close friend Winston Churchill, now Prime Minister, seized on the suggestion of the Bahamas, and just two days after the Duke arrived in Lisbon its governorship was offered to him.

Churchill knew all about Nassau, having recuperated there in 1932 after he had been knocked down by a taxi in New York. Its lack of importance was clearly a slight to the Duke, but the islands' remote location, far from both Britain and Europe, suited Whitehall's purpose admirably. The Duke demurred at first, but on receipt of a telegram from Churchill – 'At any rate I have done my best' – realised that he had little option but to accept with as much good grace as he could muster. On 17 August 1940, he arrived in Nassau by ship and, hand drenched in sweat, took office by signing his name in the Oath Book.

He and the Duchess stayed first at a house belonging to Frederick Sigrist, the aviation entrepreneur, on Prospect Ridge outside Nassau before moving on to Westbourne. Government House had been hastily rebuilt after a hurricane a decade before and was already in a parlous state. Most reluctantly, the House of Assembly agreed to vote £1,500 towards its modernisation, but the Duchess's taste in rustic French wallpaper (in shades of smoke grey and banana yellow) soon far outstripped that budget. Tactful suggestions dispatched from London did produce one concession, the use of rubber tiles in the passageways.

Another set of tiles soon reappeared in the residence's small swimming pool. Bede Clifford, the former Governor, had once been an aide-de-camp to the Duke, and had celebrated the Duke's accession to the throne by lining the pool with an 'E VIII' pattern. Subsequent events made this redundant, but after the tiles' removal they had been stored in an outhouse and were now put back. Their days in the sun were short-lived, though. The Duchess was not one for swimming – it dried the skin so – and the pool quickly made way for a rock garden.

The Windsors settled into a routine. Wallis busied herself with what war work there was – making bandages and serving in the forces canteen – and gave up her spare time to Spanish lessons and canasta. Now in his mid-forties, the Duke spent the afternoons pottering in the garden (there was the devil to pay if his favourite hoe could not be found) or on the golf course. In both activities he was often accompanied by their terriers, Preezie, Pooky, Detto, Yaki and Bundles. It was not a very strenuous existence, for him or for the dogs. To pass the time, Clifford had enjoyed letting a rat loose in the ballroom and watching his terriers skid helplessly over the polished parquet floor as they tried to give chase.

In the evenings, the couple entertained and occasionally braced themselves for a trip into town. They might drop in to the Royal Victoria Hotel, just along the crest of the hill, where the evenings often started with impromptu musical performances on the terrace, overlooking the coconut palms. There was an Officers' Ball every Friday night, at which the Duke and Duchess were regular guests. Informally dressed in a linen suit, the Duke liked to spend time at the bar, chatting to the men, and sometimes sulking when others were paying too much attention to his wife.

Then they might drift on to the Bahamian, with its handful of tables, artificial moonlight and moth-eaten tapestry of a lion and a unicorn, all too symbolic of the Duke's fall from grace. To lift his spirits, the Duke would take his official car out to the airport and hurtle it down the darkened runway over and over again.

If he was frustrated with his lot, the black population was largely delighted to have him as Governor. There was still much reverence for his great-grandmother, Queen Victoria, who had been the monarch when the emancipation of slaves was proclaimed, and there were somewhat unrealistic expectations of the benefits that the Duke's rule would bring. They were also charmed by the romantic aspect of his history. 'Love, love, love alone,' went the calypso, 'Made King Edward leave the throne.' Not that the song missed the essence of the matter: 'I did not think/ Mrs Simpson was a woman like that/ She wore the tight dress/ To make King Edward fret.'

Although their wives were snobbishly gratified to have a royal Duke in their midst, the merchants of Bay Street were less taken with their new Governor once they realised that, in his executive capacity, he was bent on political and economic reform, a line strongly encouraged by the Colonial Office.

At the apex of the islands' administration there was the Governor and his Council, a group of nine that included career civil servants such as Heape, the Colonial Secretary, and Hallinan, the Attorney-General – both of whom had played undistinguished roles during the riot – as well as half a dozen of Nassau's more prominent politicians. Below this came the Legislative Council, the islands' upper house, a rump body of nine appointees – such as Oakes – that was rarely called on since issues of any consequence (and many that were not, including the importation of a new church bell) were settled by the Governor-in-Council.

The lower chamber, the House of Assembly, was the preserve of the Bay Street Boys, and it was this that became the focus of political opposition to the Duke. Its spirit and practices were a by-word in London for reactionary self-interest and corruption, its ways damned by the Colonial Office as 'government of the people by Bay Street, for Bay Street.' The constituencies, which elected by public rather than secret ballot, were effectively rotten boroughs, and once returned, the five-sixths of the House's twenty-nine members who were white set about ensuring that their domination of the nine-tenths of the population who were black continued, and that nothing – especially taxation – interfered with their ability to make a profit. When war was declared, a bill prohibiting trading with the enemy was not enacted but was referred instead to a select committee.

Unlike reformers back in Britain such as Lord Moyne, who became Secretary of State for the Colonies in 1941, the Duke largely shared Bay Street's preference for which race should be doing the governing. Nevertheless, he was determined to improve the conditions of the island's black inhabitants, who had been hard hit by the rise in the cost of food since the start of the war. In the summer of 1941 he began manoeuvring to get money from the intransigent House of Assembly for public-works schemes and improvements to agriculture in the far-flung Out Islands. He also worked closely on development and employment projects with Oakes, Christie and Axel Wenner-Gren, the Swedish multi-millionaire owner of Electrolux, the vacuum cleaner and refrigerator firm, who had bought the Lynch estate on Hog Island.

This last contact of the Duke's, that with Wenner-Gren, would become an increasingly fraught one, as both the American government and the British (somewhat following the US State Department's lead), believed that the Swede had Nazi sympathies, and might even be an Axis agent. Given the Duke and Duchess's own record in the matter, their friendly relations with Wenner-Gren were a cause of concern to both administrations, although the Americans seemed to have made up their minds almost before the Duke had reached Nassau. A recently released report in the FBI's records, sent to J. Edgar Hoover in September 1940, reads: 'It has been ascertained that for some time the British Government has known that the Duchess of Windsor was exceedingly pro-German in her sympathies and connections and there is strong reason to believe that this is the reason that they refused to permit Edward to marry her and maintain the throne . . . The Duke is in such a state of intoxication most of the time that he is virtually *non compos mentis*.' The source adds that the unlikely figure of Lady Williams-Taylor, Brenda Frazier's grandmother, had been tasked by MI5 with keeping the Windsors and Wenner-Gren apart socially.

She appears to have been no more successful an agent than was the Bureau's man, whose information was not much above the level of high-class gossip. Certainly there is no confirmatory evidence that the Duchess's political inclinations had played a leading part in the Abdication, nor that the Duke was a habitual lush (at any event, my grandmother never saw him drunk – 'a rather tired man with the stuffing knocked out of him' was her verdict). The only exceptions were the drinks he permitted himself after an afternoon's golf. Even when tight, he would insist on driving himself home and, as protocol forbade overtaking of the Governor's car, long queues would form on the approach road to Nassau.

Some of his difficulties were resolved by America's declaration of war. Wenner-Gren found himself blacklisted by the two Allied governments and had to take up residence in Mexico. The decline in tourism from the States dealt a blow to the islands' shaky finances, but this was soon remedied by the announcement of the plans for the new airbase.

The subsequent riot, however, further damaged the Duke's standing with the House of Assembly. It was enraged by his promise to the protesters to raise their pay by a quarter, and then further incensed by the subsequent independent inquiry which criticised Erskine-Lindop for not acting more robustly but which also recommended wholesale political and fiscal reform to deal with underlying grievances. The Duke's awareness that he would have to handle Oakes's murder in a decisive manner if he was not to provoke fresh criticism from the House undoubtedly contributed to his decision to call in Melchen.

Away from politics, the Windsors' principal role was as the islands' figureheads, their leaders of society. It was not a position they enjoyed much, finding Nassau's citizenry dull by comparison with the company they had kept before the war. Rich though the Oakeses might be, their manners and conversation were not up to the standards of the salons kept by Emerald Cunard or Sybil Colefax that the Duchess had known. According to de Marigny, Oakes's dress sense led her to refer to him as 'Charlie Chaplin'. When they could, the Windsors got away from 'Elba', as the Duchess called it, to America, but even these trips caused problems. Their use of Wenner-Gren's yacht to sail to Miami brought unwelcome questions, and by the end of 1941 the US Treasury was asking London where the couple's spending money for these jaunts was coming from, and whether it had gone through the proper exchange controls.

That his finances were a perpetual worry for the Duke is confirmed by my grandmother, who regularly dined at Government House. ('7.45 for 8.15,' reads the stiff card still. 'No decorations.') She and the Governor knew people in common, including Louis Greig, confidant to the Duke's brothers the King and the Duke of Kent. The Duke of Windsor had been hurt by his family's treatment of him, but often bemoaned the fact that he did not have a good photograph of his mother, having buried them all in the garden of his house before leaving France. In deference to my grandmother's Scots blood, he would also insist on playing the bagpipes for her. Since her father was said to be the best amateur piper in Scotland, this was not a test that the Duke came through well. His asking the butler to fetch the royal harmonica was often taken by the ladies as their cue to excuse themselves.

More successful were his abilities as a host. He did not stand on his dignity, especially if he was the focus of attention. He liked to dance the conga and enjoyed a sing-song around the piano, particularly with any American pilots who might be in town. Yet, remembers the youngest of his equerries, John Pringle, he did not stand for *lèse majesté*. When one of the fliers put his arm around the Duke's shoulder, his face froze in shock.

The Duchess, being an American, was less formal still, although she liked it when my grandmother would curtsy to her. ('It was such a silly thing, I couldn't see why I shouldn't.') She was better-looking than photographs suggested, with blue eyes that she knew how to use to disarm the prejudices that people had formed before they met her. She liked to tease my grandmother about her clothes, her trunks having gone down with the *Ulysses*. 'What! Another creation!' she would exclaim about some sack run up in a back street in Nassau, and then hug her Mainbocher dress to herself. The marriage, though, was evidently that of two people who had not expected to be confined with each other. 'Come around,' my grandmother would overhear her saying to her male admirers. 'Times are hard.'

Not everyone got on so well with the Windsors. The argument that de Marigny had had with Sir Harry about his attendance at the cocktail party stemmed from the Mauritian's attitude towards the Duke. In his second volume of memoirs, he claims, unconvincingly, to have met him several times in the 1930s and to have been repelled by his admiration of Germany. There is no mention of this earlier acquaintance in the first book, and a more likely explanation of their antagonism is that deference was not de Marigny's forte, believing as he did that he knew better than those in positions of authority. Once in Nassau, he became embroiled in a running series of feuds with the Governor and his entourage.

There was the row with Rosita Forbes over the water rights, with Government House taking her side. Then de Marigny fell out with Heape, the Colonial Secretary, over a letter that Ruth had written to *Time* criticising the level of conspicuous consumption in Nassau when the rest of the Empire was tightening its belt because of the war. Heape lectured him about the morality of his continuing to share a house with his ex-wife, and was repaid by de Marigny counting off on the fingers of both hands the names of notable married Nassauvians who were having affairs.

This led to an appearance before the Exchange Control Board where Hallinan cast doubt on the motives behind his divorce from Ruth. He told de Marigny that he wanted to know if it was merely a device for getting around exchange regulations. He also wondered how de Marigny was funding his extravagant way of life.

De Marigny pulled a bulging envelope from his pocket. 'Well, it's a bit embarrassing, I suppose,' he said. 'The truth is that there are plenty of women in America who are lonely and unloved, and they like to send me money for the comfort I've given them.'

From the Duke to the Attorney-General, the members of the Board shuddered with horror, and let de Marigny go. In fact, he had only been playing up to his reputation – the envelope contained blank pieces of paper – but his mock explanation had not helped his standing with the authorities, nor had his taking them to task for allowing other prominent Bahamians to flout the rules.

De Marigny continued to offend the more important members of the small community in which he lived. There was an argument with the Duke about the treatment of some prisoners who had escaped from Devil's Island, in French Guiana, now run by a Vichy regime. There was another about a sailing race, about a bottle of cognac he refused to sell to the Duke, about a visa for his Teutonic-sounding yachting coach von Hutschler.

Matters came to a head when de Marigny organised a fundraising dinner at the Prince George hotel for dependents of Bahamian servicemen overseas. He asked the Windsors to be the guests of honour, but was then informed that because of the reputation of the Prince George – there had been a rape there some time before – they were declining the invitation.

Knowing that sales of tickets would be affected, de Marigny rushed round to Government House and began to berate Gray Phillips, the Duke's private secretary (and an accomplished flower arranger).

'Look here, de Marigny,' said the major, 'I can see you're upset, but I'm afraid that His Royal Highness has made his decision, and it's final.'

De Marigny became so angry that he slipped unconsciously into his first language, French. 'His Royal Highness,' he shouted, 'His Royal Highness is now no more than a pimple on the arse of the Empire.' Along the corridor, the door of the Duke's office stood slightly ajar, and French was a language he knew.

The Count takes care in his reminiscences to portray himself if not as a temperate man, then as one whose quick tongue had moral force behind it. In fact, he had behaved foolishly. Quite enough people in Nassau disapproved of his behaviour – the romancing, the insolence, the fact that he had not joined up (his stomach problems meant that he was unfit for military service) – without his gratuitously irritating those whose help he needed, for instance with obtaining a licence for his chicken farm which had not yet been granted. He was only storing up trouble for the future.

★

The Duke went over to Westbourne on Friday after lunch. News of the killing of Sir Harry Oakes had by now made the front pages of the papers in Britain, and he wanted to check on the investigation's progress, hoping that the matter could be resolved as soon as possible. He took Melchen aside and talked to him, and about an hour later he returned to Nassau. At four, Barker came back from the RAF laboratory, and at six o'clock Douglas again fetched the Count from the bar of the Prince George and brought him to Westbourne. At a quarter past six, de Marigny was arrested for the murder of Sir Harry Oakes.

The circumstances surrounding this decision would become the foundation of all the extraordinary events, claims and rumours of the months and years ahead, and they bear some examination.

De Marigny would subsequently allege, first in private and much later in print, that his arrest was the culmination of his vendetta with the Duke, who had encouraged the Americans to pin the blame on him. It is a line that has been adopted by several authors who have taken an interest in the case. For the moment, all that needs to be noted is that, as always, the two versions of his arrest that de Marigny supplies in his memoirs are diametrically opposed.

In *More Devil Than Saint*, written while the Duke of Windsor was alive, de Marigny states that he was at Westbourne when the Governor arrived, and that the Duke gave him two curious stares. Their significance is not made explicit. Perhaps they were those of a man who had been pressuring Melchen into a hasty arrest, perhaps he simply knew that Melchen believed de Marigny to be guilty and would soon take him into custody.

In *Conspiracy of Crowns*, however, written forty years later, de Marigny has changed his tune. He now spells out his belief that the Duke was 'a willing conspirator' in the plot against him. The two curious stares, however, have vanished, for he also writes that in fact he was not at the house that afternoon nor did he observe what the Duke did there.

Almost from the start, the basis for the arrest itself was the

subject of similarly conflicting accounts. It was never made clear
in the testimony later given at de Marigny's trial what reasons
Melchen had given Erskine-Lindop and Pemberton when asking
them to make the arrest. As always, they simply seemed to have
followed his instructions. It seems possible that fingerprint evidence – Barker's field of expertise – was mentioned. Certainly by
the next evening, the *Daily Telegraph* in London was reporting that
the arrest had been made on the basis of hair and fingerprint
analysis, a statement picked up from an interview that the detectives had given to a Miami journalist. When that fingerprint
evidence later became of crucial importance to the trial, Melchen
and Barker would argue that they had been misquoted.
Nonetheless, they must have given Erskine-Lindop at least some
justification for the arrest – they had been in Nassau for little more
than a day. Certainly in other reports that week and at the trial
they confirmed that another suspect, Oakes's stables manager
Harcourt Maura, who had recently been fired, had been eliminated through hair and print examination.

An hour and a half after his arrest, de Marigny was taken to
court to be arraigned. He had requested that Alfred Adderley, the
best-known barrister in Nassau, be telephoned and asked to represent him, but was told that Adderley was not at home. Instead,
the brief formalities were entrusted to Stafford Sands, a fat young
man with a glass eye and an astute grasp of realities who had
already made his mark in Bay Street politics. The magistrate
remanded de Marigny until the following Monday, and he was
escorted to the town's insalubrious jail. As he was locked up for
the night, Nassau began to buzz with talk.

In all the commotion, little notice was taken of the fact that
earlier in the day Oakes's company accountant, Arthur Dew, had
been summarily sacked by Walter Foskett.

De Marigny's cell was not large. It was barely longer and wider
than he was. When the heavy door slammed behind him, he
stood there for a full minute, gazing at the camp bed in one

corner and the lidless bucket in the other. When he lay down on the cot, it was too short for him. Wearily, he tugged the mattress onto the floor and slept on that. The lights stayed on all night, but he was too tired to notice.

He passed the weekend there (during which time the Allies invaded Sicily), and on Monday morning was brought up in court again. At Pemberton's request, de Marigny was remanded for another week while investigations continued. The police held back a crowd of onlookers. He was represented this time by a yachting friend, Godfrey Higgs, a barrister who had handled some paperwork for him before. His experience, though, was in civil cases, and he had hardly conducted a criminal trial since his days as a pupil advocate. The Crown, however, had retained Adderley, who though he was black had risen to become the leading criminal lawyer in the Colony. He had won nine of the ten murder trials in which he had appeared.

In a break in proceedings, de Marigny walked over to talk to Adderley. 'Didn't you get my call?' he said. 'It was you that I wanted to represent me.'

The lawyer looked blank. 'No,' he replied. 'I never got any message.'

It began to occur to de Marigny that he was very isolated. Under British law, there is no bail in murder cases, and his only support of any substance was Nancy, who was still in Vermont, and her first duty now would be to attend her father's funeral.

De Marigny was returned to the prison. Feelings of fear and helplessness began to well up inside him. The smell from the bucket put him off his food, and the brightness of the bulb hurt his eyes. Through the small high window he could see the clouds floating free in the sky. His head began to spin.

He tried forcing himself to get a grip, yanking his hair out so that his mind had to focus on the pain, not on his predicament. He tried push-ups, and then meditation – anything to recover his self-control. For an hour every morning he was allowed to pace around the crowded yard with the other prisoners. Then the door was shut behind him once more. On Tuesday, he started to chalk off the days on the wall of his cell.

There had been one odd episode during the weekend. On Sunday, 11 July, Oakes's body was sent by air to Palm Beach, from whence it was to go to Maine for burial. When the aircraft was already airborne, it was instructed to return to Nassau, where the coffin was opened by Pemberton and the corpse rephotographed. Barker afterwards explained that light had got into his camera and spoiled the film from Westbourne. Later that week, he and Melchen travelled up to the north-east for the funeral.

The Duke of Windsor had been quick to let London know of the pleasing success in the case. Following de Marigny's arrest, he had telegraphed the news to the Colonial Office, giving his reasons for calling in outside help. The local force, he reiterated, 'lacks detective with requisite experience and equipment for investigating the death of a person with such widespread international business interests. I was fortunate in securing the services of Capt E. W. Melchen, head of the Homicidal Bureau, Miami, and Capt James Barker, identification expert.' They had rendered 'most valuable service by their relentless investigations, which have in a large measure resulted in the arrest of the accused.'

London was not slow to appreciate that the Duke wanted credit for his bright idea, but there was an undercurrent of caution in their assessment of his telegram. Having made a little joke about a 'homicidal bureau' being more suitable to the Gestapo, the author of an internal Colonial Office memorandum written on 14 July pointed out that: 'The Governor is at some pains to explain why he took the rather unusual step of calling in men from outside, which I must confess I don't like very much. But in the circumstances, I would not question his judgement.'

Oakes was buried on 15 July 1943 in Dover-Foxcroft, where he had lived as a boy. The ceremony was attended by close friends and immediate family only, including Nancy. Back at the house after the funeral, she saw Melchen and Barker go into the room where her near-hysterical mother was resting. She tried to push her way through the door, but the two detectives refused to let her in. A little later, however, she was called, as her mother was insisting that Nancy should hear what she herself had been told. Nancy had already spoken to Barker on the telephone, and now the detectives outlined in greater detail what had happened to her father.

An intruder, armed with a sharp stick from a pile in the garage, had entered Oakes's room and had attacked him with it. Then he had poured some kind of inflammable liquid, probably insecticide, over the unconscious body and set it alight. Horribly, the flames had revived Sir Harry, who had tried to fight off his assailant, but he had finally been overcome by his agony. The fire had then been relit.

During the struggle, the detectives believed, the Chinese screen by the bed had been knocked over or pushed aside, and on it they had found prints belonging to Nancy's husband, Alfred de Marigny. There was no question that, at the very least, he had been present when her father had been murdered.

It was a grim tale, and one that further deepened her mother's state of shock. Yet it was not one that convinced Nancy. Sixty years later, she recalled Melchen and Barker as a near-comical couple giving what amounted to a pantomime performance. 'Shh!' one of them said. 'You're telling her too much.' Something, she felt, was amiss.

The next day, a memorial service for Oakes was held at Christ Church Cathedral, Nassau. The congregation, which included the Duke and Duchess, heard the Dean say that Bahamians had known Oakes as a benefactor and as a generous employer who had taken his full share in the public life of the colony.

The lesson was taken from St John's Gospel: 'Marvel not at this, for the hour is coming in which all that are in the graves shall hear His voice and shall come forth:

'They that have done good unto the resurrection of life; and they that have done evil, unto the resurrection of damnation.'

FOUR

So hoist up the John B sails,
See how the mains'l set,
Send for de Capt'n ashore,
Lemme go home!

Nancy de Marigny faced a dilemma. For all her certainty that Melchen and Barker were not telling the truth, she really knew very little about her husband of a year, from whom she had already spent much time apart. Might he, in fact, be the killer of her father? Could she really stand by him now that her family believed him guilty, and what would people say if she did not?

In public, at least, she left no room for doubt. On 20 July, five days after the funeral, she returned to Nassau and was reunited with de Marigny in prison. 'In the eyes of many people, I suppose I'm just the hysterical wife trying to save my own pride in defending my husband,' she would later say to reporters. 'But it is much more than that. I have always believed that Freddie could not have done this terrible thing . . . I am the only person who can help Freddie.'

The reality was more complex. Their marriage, with her grave illness, the abortion of a child and the rift with her parents, had not been an easy one. They had been happy to start with, but happiness is the most fleeting of emotions. For Nancy, it had stemmed from the success of her chase, and her defiance of her family, especially of her mother. It seems, however, judging by the accounts of those who knew her and of de Marigny himself, that she soon realised that they wanted different things from their relationship: he dreamed of a stable home and children, but, at eighteen, such things felt like fetters to her just as she was beginning to stretch her wings.

Although Nancy insisted that she had gone to Vermont at the end of May on doctor's orders to escape the summer heat, it seems strange that the couple should have parted so readily, given their difficult year, if all was in order with their marriage. If Nancy did have to go, surely de Marigny could have found someone to mind the farm for him while he went with her.

The truth was that Nancy returned to Nassau primarily out of loyalty rather than from love, and so as not to give satisfaction to those who had told her that she was marrying a gold-digger. Indeed, her friend Marie af Trolle, whose husband, a Swedish nobleman, was Wenner-Gren's private secretary, confirms that at first Nancy had not wanted to return, and that it was only Marie's insistent telegrams that brought her back. Privately, Nancy had doubts about the wisdom of returning. It was a test that she did not wish to face, and one that would force her to choose between a family by whom she felt rejected and a man whom she no longer knew she could trust.

The basis of Nancy's confused emotions lay in her upbringing. After her early childhood in the fancifully plastered bedroom at Kirkland Lake, she had quickly become a seasoned traveller, spending summers in Canada and winters at Palm Beach. At nine, she had been sent to school in Switzerland, where she had made friends with Marie Gudewill, as she then was, a fellow Canadian. She only spent a few months there, and was later educated in England and then in New York, returning to Nassau for the holidays or spending them in Kensington (where she was a member of the local Girl Guides) with her brothers and sister and a gaggle of tutors. Other breaks were spent abroad, and by her mid-teens she had visited places as far apart as Australia, Brazil, Venezuela and Bali, while the outbreak of war found the family in Java.

Nancy had grown up confident beyond her years, with a keen

interest in art and dance which had been encouraged by the rather progressive schools to which she had been sent in England; from Indonesia she brought home distinctly jazzy batik textiles to wear as sarongs. Yet her self-reliance made her headstrong and wilful too and, like many children of self-made parents, she was rather distant from them. Later she blamed this on being sent away to school in Europe, claiming that as a consequence she had seen little of her family. It would have been more honest to say that she was rather ashamed of her father and mother, and all too aware of the gulf in taste and sophistication between the generations.

For all that, Nancy was not particularly worldly, and by comparison with her peers at school her parents had kept her very short of money. One of de Marigny's stratagems for wooing her had been to buy her her first pieces of expensive jewellery.

By the time she was seventeen she had learned to move gracefully, to ski well and had developed an intense gaze that men would find fascinating. She was no respecter of authority either. The first time that John Pringle, the Duke's equerry met her, was when she and Marie af Trolle roared past him in a car while he was drilling a squad of soldiers. He signalled to them to stop, and told the two pretty girls to turn the car around as the road was out of bounds. They promptly told him what he could do with himself, hooted with laughter and sped off in a cloud of dust, waving merrily.

Despite such bravado, however, inside herself Nancy felt trapped. She wondered what her future held for her. She wanted to be a dancer, or maybe an interior designer – she had already helped with the redecoration of the British Colonial – but she was fearful of her mother's plans for her. Though she rather liked her father's rough-and-tumble ways, she found her mother's outlook far too narrow and provincial. The last of many sisters to marry, Eunice Oakes had been transplanted from middle-class Sydney, with its conventional attitudes and expectations, to a life of extraordinary wealth. Thereafter, Nancy felt, her mother never quite knew who she was. 'She should have married someone like a lawyer,' her daughter told me. It did not help that the Oakeses' relationship had rather cooled, and that they now spent most of their time in different countries.

Then Nancy had met Freddie, and for the first time had completely lost her heart to someone. It is sometimes difficult to remember that she was still a schoolgirl, lacking in experience and self-knowledge. De Marigny seemed to offer her all she wanted just then in life, not so much security as fun, someone to adore, and an escape from her parents. Their marriage had been propelled by a heady rush of love, borne on a flood tide of waltzes and kisses and lazy afternoons on deck, but above all it was a characteristically impulsive bid by Nancy for independence. It had freed her from her parents' house, and from their strictures – her brother Sydney, for instance, had to comply with their mother's order not to come to Nassau from Canada after the murder – but the price had been the break with them. That with her mother, who was perhaps rather jealous of her and also looked down on de Marigny for his Catholicism, was particularly severe.

Coupled with de Marigny's alienation of Government House and Bay Street, this meant that the pair now found themselves with very few allies, and alone together. Nancy soon convinced herself of Freddie's innocence, but of where her heart lay she was less sure.

Freddie himself had started seeking comfort in religion, and was doggedly working his way through a Bible he had been brought by a prison chaplain. Nancy took a more short-term approach, and two days after her return to Nassau she invited ten journalists from the world's press to interview her in the house in Victoria Avenue. Attired in a plain white dress, she answered their questions with the poise of a countess.

'One thing that is more or less unpredictable is human nature,' she pronounced. 'I cannot say that I have made a study of it, but from my knowledge of Freddie during the year since our marriage, this situation seems fantastic to me.' Smiling sweetly, Nancy denied that there had been strained relations with her family, and said that there had been no public announcement of her marriage beforehand only because her parents understood that it was something she regarded as a private affair. She joked, too, that the beard de Marigny had grown while she was away did make him look rather villainous.

Whatever she might be feeling inside about the state of her relationship with him, in public she was determined to put on a brave show. The press lapped it up, and so did the photographers afterwards.

Her wish not to air all of the family's laundry was understandable, and she demonstrated a shrewd grasp of what the press wanted and how to get them on her side. 'Nancy Oakes de Marigny,' thundered the newsreels in the following weeks, 'nineteen-year-old daughter of the victim, loyal wife of the accused.'

By then, she and de Marigny had found another ally, his barrister Godfrey Higgs. The son of a fairly well-to-do sponge merchant, Higgs was then thirty-five, although he looked older than his years. He had spent most of his life in Nassau, but his parents' influence and a spell at a minor public school in Somerset had made him a very English Bahamian, with a conservative cast to his retentive mind. His father was more of a traditionalist yet; he still put on a top hat before he called on his own parents.

At first Godfrey had hoped to become a doctor, but family circumstances had dictated that he could not afford to go to university and instead must go out to work. He was therefore indentured to a barrister – no formal qualifications then being needed for the profession – and was duly admitted to the Nassau Bar in his early twenties. Gradually he began to make his way, both in the law and in politics, helped by his marriage to a rich American wife, Suzanne, who funded his love of sailing.

By 1943, he had become the leader of the government party in the House of Assembly, and sat in the Governor's Executive Council as its youngest member. At the bar, too, he had built up a flourishing business, although most of it was corporate work –

such as an action between the Coca-Cola and Pepsi-Cola concessions on the island – and his was largely a paper practice, confined mainly to legal advice rather than concerned with handling trials in court.

In his early days as de Marigny's counsel he tried, in his affable, soft-spoken way, to give the impression of calm and confidence to the press, urging them to quash silly rumours, such as that his client was to plead insanity. Only an unbroken succession of cigarettes betrayed any strain; Stafford Sands had advised him not to take the case, lest it ruin his reputation professionally – and socially.

It was not that the de Marignys lacked other friends – more than twenty had come to Freddie's birthday party in March – but they tended to be the younger, more rackety set who could be of little help. Older contacts, such as Christie and Erskine-Lindop (who had been born on Mauritius and had been at Freddie's party), had their own agendas now, while the few others of that generation who took de Marigny's side tended to be peripheral figures.

Rosita Forbes wrote in her memoirs that she could imagine much of Freddie but not the premeditated battering of his father-in-law's head, yet her influence counted for little in Nassau. A former Governor of Mauritius, Sir Hesketh Bell, now retired to New Providence (and living in the same lodgings as my grandmother's friend, Lady Boles), knew de Marigny's relatives and took his part as well.

By and large, however, the Count's arrest allowed respectable society to vent its disapproval of him, his wife and his circle. Marie af Trolle was asked to leave her sewing group by Lady Boles because she was a friend of de Marigny's; according to Marie, that reduced those in the group who could sew properly to just one, Marcelle Goldsmith. More vindictively still, the Duchess of Windsor asked Group Captain Waite, the Commanding Officer of the airmen on the island, to stop Nancy from working in the forces canteen because she was a bad influence. Petty as all this was, the de Marignys were paying for their earlier insults.

The Duchess's husband allowed his private feelings about de

Marigny to spill over into his correspondence with the Colonial
Office about the affair. Its circumstances, he told the Secretary of
State (Moyne having been succeeded by Oliver Stanley) 'are
sordid beyond description and I will be glad when the trial is over
and done with . . .

'What is unfortunate is that, whether de Marigny is guilty or
not, local opinion is sharply divided for and against him . . . The
older and more conservative elements and the whole negro population suspect de Marigny's guilt,' he judged, before airing his
own assessment of the Mauritian.

'De Marigny, who is a despicable character and has the worst
possible record, morally and financially, since his adolescence, has
insidiously bought his way with his ex-wife's money into the lead-
ership of a quite influential, fast and depraved set of the younger
generation, born of bootlegging days, and for whom they have an
admiration bordering on hero-worship. This unsavoury group of
people would therefore like to see de Marigny escape the rope at
all costs, whether guilty or innocent – but if the coloured people
are ever given the slightest reason to suspect the jury, then the consequences may be grave.' The case, he added, had unfortunately
attracted 'sensational publicity' in the American press.

The tenor of the letter strikes one as somewhat hysterical, and
reveals more about the Duke's prejudices than about the truth of
the situation. Though most of the white inhabitants did believe de
Marigny guilty, the native population was more divided, as many
admired him for having good relations with his black employees.
Equally, the likelihood of de Marigny's friends bribing the jury
was almost as remote as the spectre of the race riot that the Duke
raised in his letter.

It is the Duke of Windsor's open dislike of de Marigny that has
since provided the basis for the scapegoat theories of the case. Yet
there would seem to have to be deeper motives for such an action
than a few cross words and jibes about pimples, especially since it
was slights against the Duchess more than those against himself
that the Duke really minded. Those motives, it has been claimed,

lie in the Duke's secret and scandalous ties to Harry Oakes and Axel Wenner-Gren.

The Swede had been the subject of gossip since the moment he had first arrived in Nassau in the late 1930s aboard his yacht *The Southern Cross*, 320 feet long and the largest in the world, which he had bought from Howard Hughes. He had taken a liking to the climate and in 1938, following Edmund Lynch's death, he had acquired his estate on Hog Island – Shangri-La. (The name, taken from James Hilton's book *Lost Horizon* (1933), was a fashionable one of the day because of its escapist connotations: it was also the original name of the American presidential retreat Camp David.) There he extended Lynch's mansion and built remarkable terraced gardens modelled on those at Versailles. Among the guests who sunned themselves amid the statuary were his fellow Swede Greta Garbo and Marlene Dietrich. Like Oakes, he had come a long way from his origins.

He had been born in 1881, the son of a retired small-town timber merchant who had saved enough to put his son through university in Germany (then a prime cultural influence on Sweden) and later through business school in Berlin. Wenner-Gren had afterwards taken a job with a light-bulb company, A. D. Lux, which had allowed him to travel to America to observe business methods.

After pulling off the coup of securing the contract to flood-light the opening ceremony for the Panama Canal, he had returned to Europe, where in Vienna he saw the prototype for an industrial-sized vacuum cleaner. Realising that it could be adapted for homes, he persuaded Lux to buy up the patent, and to pay him for sales of the machine in company stock. By the mid-1920s he had virtually cornered the world market in cleaners and owned the business, which he renamed ElectroLux.

The firm had still greater success when it began to develop refrigerators, and by the late 1930s Wenner-Gren was the largest private employer in Sweden, with interests in newspapers, banking and wood pulp, of which he was the world's leading producer. He had also bought up the holdings of the disgraced safety-match tycoon Ivar Kreuger, and had stakes in the armaments manufacturers Bofors and Saab. These in turn brought him into contact with Krupps, the German munitions maker, then busily rearming the *Wehrmacht*.

It was links such as these that came to provide much of the ammunition for those who later claimed that Wenner-Gren was covertly working for the Nazis. The principal source for this suggestion was the several meetings that he had had with Hermann Goering in 1939 in the vainglorious belief that he could use his influence to prevent the outbreak of war. The Swede had also managed to see President Roosevelt and the then Prime Minister Neville Chamberlain, but it was his good standing with the *Reichsmarschall* that stuck in the public's memory. Rumours about him only redoubled when *The Southern Cross* was involved in one of the first incidents of the war, the sinking of the passenger liner *Athenia*.

This ship had left Glasgow for Montreal with fourteen hundred people on board, including three hundred Americans, two days before the outbreak of hostilities between Britain and Germany. At about nine p.m. on the first evening after the declaration of war, 3 September, she was sunk without warning by a U-boat and 112 lives were lost, including those of twenty-eight neutrals. Wenner-Gren's yacht was in the area at the time and came to the *Athenia*'s aid, rescuing several hundred of the passengers. *The Southern Cross*'s presence, however, seemed to some suspicious, and stories spread that she had been directing the German submarine's operations.

In its files, the American State Department had already marked down the globe-trotting Wenner-Gren as 'an international personage of the type found in the novels of E. Phillips Oppenheim', the popular spy writer. During the next couple of years, they began to monitor the Swede's movements, and their dossier on him was soon brimming with information.

There was the German education, of course, and then it turned out that his brother owned a bakelite factory in Germany and was still living there. Somewhat more substantial grounds for suspicion was a letter sent to Wenner-Gren from Rio de Janeiro at the start of August 1940 which was intercepted by the FBI. Written in German, it mentions the arrival of a 'new and interesting family with which we assume you will at once become friendly . . . in the house of that family is held sympathetic understanding for totalitarian ideas.'

The reference to the imminent arrival of the Windsors is clear, and was taken by the Americans to be instructions for the pro-Nazi Wenner-Gren to make contact with the like-minded Duke. In fact, the tone of the letter suggests that it was unsolicited rather than a reply to earlier correspondence from Wenner-Gren. While it might have been an attempt by a German agent to put pressure on Wenner-Gren, it does not provide any confirmation of his own beliefs or actions. Nonetheless, given what the Americans already thought were the Duke's views on Germany, it was enough to make them monitor his mail and telephone calls once he arrived in Nassau, and to increase their watch on Wenner-Gren.

By the end of 1941, they were following a new trail. One of Wenner-Gren's interests was ethnography, and towards the end of that year he sent a Hungarian adventurer named Paul Fejos to Peru as the leader of an anthropological expedition for his Viking Foundation. Fejos had had a previous existence as a Hollywood film director and had few scientific qualifications, which inevitably led the FBI to wonder if the venture had some other purpose – later there were rumours of wireless equipment being cached in the hills – but of more immediate interest to them was Fejos's wife, Inga Arvad.

Then in her late twenties, and breathlessly described in her Department of Justice file as 'a woman of exceptional physical attractions', Arvad was a Danish-born former beauty queen turned journalist who before the war had interviewed many of the leading Nazis, including Hitler and Goering. The Führer, it seems, was particularly taken by her. In 1940, by now divorced from her first husband and married to Fejos, she had moved to Washington and had landed a job as a writer with the *Times-Herald* newspaper, for whom she interviewed politicians. While her husband was in South America, she had also found herself a lover, a young naval officer named John Fitzgerald Kennedy.

The importance of Jack Kennedy's family in American politics, as well as his own military work, was enough for the FBI, on Hoover's instructions, to begin round-the-clock surveillance on Arvad. Agents broke into her apartment and found a signed photograph of Hitler. They trailed the lovers (as did a pair of private detectives employed by the jealous Fejos), and in February 1942 when Kennedy returned to Charleston, where he was stationed, they bugged his room and recorded their lovemaking sessions.

The tapes revealed little of interest except to those of a prurient disposition: the twenty-four-year-old Jack, apparently, was a man of both considerable appetite and stamina, and he and the bosomy Inga had 'sexual intercourse on numerous occasions'. So smitten was he with her – an emotional entanglement was a new experience for someone who usually regarded women as playthings – that he even talked to a priest about the consequences should he, a Catholic, marry a divorcée.

Though the Bureau's operations had uncovered no evidence of Arvad having Nazi sympathies, the romance itself appeared to them to reinforce their suspicions that she was a German agent using her charms to worm secrets out of well-placed men in Washington. These she would then report to her paymaster, Wenner-Gren.

For, the Bureau had discovered, between July 1940 and January 1942 Arvad had received more than eight thousand dollars (now worth fifty thousand pounds) from the Swede. When questioned in 1945, she stated plausibly that the money had been simply advance payments to her husband for his work and expenditure in Peru, and certainly for a spy she had not tried to cover her tracks very carefully. At the end of January 1942, Harold Christie was interviewed by the Bureau about Wenner-Gren, in the course of which conversation he volunteered the information that Arvad was about to 'divorce [Fejos] and marry Ambassador Kennedy's son'. The affair had already been hinted at by gossip columnists including Walter Winchell, and it came to an end soon afterwards.

By then, however, following Pearl Harbor, Wenner-Gren had already been placed on the American government's proclaimed list, barring him from the country and freezing his assets there. In London, the Ministry of Economic Warfare (MEW) noted that it had no proof itself – embassy reports from Stockholm said that he was regarded in Sweden as 'a pompous ass, but not guilty of any worse offence than extravagance, attempted social climbing and tax dodging' – yet since it was their policy to follow their ally's lead in such matters, Wenner-Gren was duly placed on the British list and his businesses in Nassau were impounded. He himself was then in Mexico, where he was forced to spend much of the rest of the war.

The Swede's travels, and the extensive building and draining work on Hog, had given rise to all manner of stories consistent with the FBI's suspicions. One voyage by *The Southern Cross* in 1940, tracked by the Americans, had consumed a surprising amount of oil, leading them to think that it may have been re-fuelling submarines, and this remained the main rumour about Wenner-Gren. A gossipy letter from Nassau in 1942, recorded by the censors, claimed that his speedboat had been seen going out late at night without lights, and that oil had been spotted in the water. ('The authorities are so awful here,' concluded the writer, 'that if a person is murdered, unless the murderer is standing on the spot he isn't caught.') A thorough search of Hog by Major Nash, MI5's officer in Nassau, failed however to turn up any hidden submarine pens.

The truth, as the MEW admitted candidly towards the end of the war, was that (as with Inga Arvad) there was no real evidence that Wenner-Gren had any sympathy for the Nazi regime. He had in fact been 'the victim of a series of rather unfortunate coincidences.'

Had they dug harder, they might have established this earlier. The theory that Wenner-Gren was connected to the sinking of the *Athenia* is scotched by Marie af Trolle, whose husband was on the bridge of *The Southern Cross* when the liner's distress signal was received. Far from wanting to establish an alibi, Wenner-Gren, it appears, gave orders not to stop, as he was terrified of submarines and was convinced that the yacht would be the next target. It was the vessel's captain who decided to pick up survivors, and when Wenner-Gren's wife Marguerite – a dipsomaniac with near-nymphomaniac tendencies – threw a fit because the curtains in the sitting room were being used to dry off those rescued from the water, the captain promptly had her locked in her cabin.

Clinching proof that Wenner-Gren was no Nazi might be thought to have arrived a little later, when the British Embassy in Stockholm learned that Wenner-Gren was also on the Germans' own secret proclaimed list. Nonetheless, he remained on that of the Allies until September 1946.

The true reason for this, however, had nothing at all to do with any Teutonic leanings, and its ramifications have everything to do with the Duke's alleged involvement in de Marigny's arrest.

Fifteen years after the war ended, the State Department admitted unofficially to the FBI that it had actually targeted Wenner-Gren so as to put paid to a plan he was hatching in Mexico with Maximino Camacho, the brother of the country's president, to control the export of key materials such as iron ore. Wenner-Gren had already assembled backers who included J. Paul Getty, the oil baron. Washington's source was the interpreter at Wenner-Gren's meetings with Camacho, and what worried them was not so much the notion of an Axis agent controlling Mexico's economy as that if the scheme succeeded it would prevent American businessmen from doing the same. So Wenner-Gren was blacklisted, the Camachos duly took fright, and the proposed cartel collapsed.

Yet there was more to the Swede's operations in Mexico than just this. When he was quizzed by the FBI in 1945 about his pre-war meetings with Goering, he also told them of his involvement in Banco Continental, a bank in Mexico City that he had planned to form with several others – including Harry Oakes. The plan had been that each of the investors should put up $325,000 in pesos (worth £2.5 million today), although in the event Oakes had been unable to get his money out of Nassau due to exchange controls and Wenner-Gren had put in a double share.

But it has been alleged, not least by de Marigny himself, that there was someone else who availed himself of Banco Continental: the Duke of Windsor. The theory goes that Wenner-Gren used his yacht to take $2.5 million (now worth fifteen million pounds) of the Governor's money out of the restricted sterling area for investment in Mexico. He performed the same service for Oakes, who, it is said, was thinking of moving his operations to Central America. Any such prohibited financial manoeuvres would have been highly compromising had they been discovered, so when Oakes was murdered, lest his accounts be too carefully investigated the Duke called in Melchen and ensured that the finger of suspicion was quickly pointed at de Marigny.

As will become apparent later, the basis for this hypothesis is paper-thin. For now, all that needs to be noted is that it runs counter to everything that is known about the Windsors' finances at the time. The Duke may have stooped to a little laundering through Oakes or Wenner-Gren to get dollars for his trips to the States, but there was certainly not several million dollars to hand for investment at a time when the Duke's only realisable asset was a ranch in Canada. Nor is it likely that either Oakes or Wenner-Gren would have advanced such a large loan to the Duke, whose future income was obviously uncertain; after the war, the Windsors depended heavily on the largesse of others.

In the course of their investigations into Wenner-Gren, the Bureau discovered one other notable fact. On 10 July, the day after de Marigny's arrest, Melchen and Barker had visited the US censorship station in Miami, which routinely monitored all mail, telegrams and telephone calls into and out of Nassau (including the Duke's request to the police for help). They told the officer in charge that they wanted to locate a particular message that they believed would establish the motive for Oakes's murder.

Because the request was not relevant to the war effort, the censor refused to make his files available, but afterwards searched them for his own satisfaction. He did not find the message alluded to – if there was one to be found – but he did notice something else, which was that de Marigny had several times been in touch by telegram with John Anderson. This was the acquaintance who had told him of Oakes's death and who, after Wenner-Gren was blacklisted, was one of the three government-appointed trustees of the Swede's affairs in Nassau.

De Marigny, it turned out, already had his own file at the Bureau, since his contacts with the German-Brazilian von Hutschler were thought suspect, as was his friendship with an Indian, Edanji Dinsha, thought to be of 'questionable responsibility' and for whom he had been investing money in the Bahamas. When the censorship office later interrogated Anderson about de Marigny's connections with Wenner-Gren, Anderson became very nervous, leading the interviewer to think that the trio were tied together in some way.

Having taken an interest in the subject, the district cable censor made a note of another thing about Anderson – the amount of time he spent away from Nassau. In the two years up to the end of 1943, he had been absent from the colony for some two hundred days.

Then in his late thirties, the Canadian-born Anderson had been tempted away from his accountancy practice in 1936 by the chance to run the Bahamas General Trust (BGT), which had been set up by two of Canada's leading financiers, Max Aitken (afterwards Lord Beaverbrook) and Sir Herbert Holt. The following year he had moved on to the Bank of the Bahamas, owned by Wenner-Gren.

The FBI came to believe that he had then become the Swede's bagman, the frequent go-between from Nassau to Mexico who kept Wenner-Gren's affairs ticking over. The question was: what was in the bag?

While at BGT, Anderson had been considered clever, but his seniors had soon noticed that he ignored their instructions and had 'get-rich-quick ideas' and plans of his own. Early in 1943, he had travelled to Mexico City from Texas but then, cable traffic records showed, he had 'disappeared for almost a month'. Even his office in

Nassau did not seem to know where he was, judging by their frantic attempts to locate him by telegram. There was a hint that he was
in Costa Rica, but what he was up to, and for whom, no one knew.

'He is a handsome individual,' concluded an official who later
interviewed him, 'with a shifty eye, and all the earmarks of a
conman.'

On Monday, 19 July, ten days after de Marigny's arrest, the pre-
liminary review of the case against him began in Nassau's
Magistrates Court. It was presided over by Frank Field, who doubled as the coroner and whose task it was to decide if the evidence
against the Count was strong enough to warrant his being sent for
trial by the Supreme Court, which dealt with serious charges
such as murder.

The local appetite for news of the affair, already keen, was
further whetted by remarks made by Melchen and Barker to
reporters as they arrived back in Nassau for the hearings. Melchen
announced that the fire in the bedroom had been set so as to
make Oakes's death seem accidental, but it had been extinguished
by the humidity. 'When the first energy of the fire was exhausted,
and it had to rely on the inflammable qualities of the material,' he
explained, 'it went out because the material was so damp. This is
what enabled us to make our case.'

Appearing for the Crown in front of Field was Adderley, who at
fifty was almost fifteen years senior to Higgs. Despite their colour,
his family had a record of public service in Nassau – his grandfather, Aladdin, had owned large estates on New Providence – and
he had received an education at an English public school and then
at Cambridge. His chief success to date had been his defence a few
years earlier of a Philadelphia lawyer who had kidnapped his young
son from the beach at Fort Montagu where his ex-wife, a member
of the Du Pont family, had been holidaying with her new husband.
In one of his rare forays into court, Higgs had appeared for the
prosecution, and had lost.

The first evidence heard by Field was medical and was given by

Hugh Quackenbush, the doctor who had examined Oakes's body at Westbourne. He estimated that death had occurred between two and a half to five hours before he arrived – in other words, between 2.45 and 5.15 a.m. – but the extent of the burns made it difficult to give a more precise time-frame.

The injuries suffered by Oakes were then described in greater detail by Lawrence Fitzmaurice, the acting Chief Medical Officer of the Bahamas, who had carried out the post-mortem. Although the burns were appalling – especially on the left side of the body, where they had been severe enough to cause the fingers to contract into a claw – what had actually killed Sir Harry had been four wounds to his head, shaped in a long diamond pattern above his left ear. The indents were triangular, with their apices facing forwards, and they had caused multiple fractures of the skull.

The most prominent of the wounds had penetrated to a depth of more than 1½ inches and, said Fitzmaurice, had been made by a hard, blunt instrument with a defined edge. He had found no foreign substances in the brain, such as a bullet, although a dark, viscid substance in the stomach (which turned out to be wine) had been sent for analysis. He preferred a time of death between 1.30 and 3.30 a.m. – a considerable variation from Quackenbush's estimate – and it was this which the police took as their frame of reference, and which made them suspicious of de Marigny's post-dinner drive.

In court, it is the task of an expert witness such as a doctor to appear convincing but, as is often the case, here that expertise was given more weight than it merited. Neither Quackenbush nor Fitzmaurice were actually trained pathologists, and much of what they had to say should have been treated with caution. In particular, their joint assertion that the formation of heat blisters on the skin showed that Oakes had been alive when burned – because their presence demonstrated circulation of the blood – influenced thinking about the sequence of events in the bedroom, and bred speculation that Sir Harry had been tortured before being killed. Yet their evidence was simply wrong: blisters draw on liquid in the tissues, and so can continue to form some time after the heart has stopped beating.

Although this point was not challenged by Higgs, his willingness to contest scientific evidence, using his own research into the subject, was to become a central feature of his conduct of the case. Indeed, the most notable characteristic of the hearing in the Magistrates Court was his decision, prompted by de Marigny, to cross-examine witnesses from the outset. Normally the defence would not have revealed its hand at this stage by asking questions that would give the prosecution an idea of the line it might take at any trial. Instead, it would content itself with learning what the Crown's argument was and hope that the magistrate would pick the necessary holes in it. Yet from the start Higgs followed an aggressive, almost personally hostile line of inquiry intended to sink the case before it reached the Supreme Court.

Part of his palpable anger may have been due to frustration at the prosecution's delaying strategy. After the medical evidence had been given, Adderley told Field that they were not intending to introduce any more testimony in the near future, and asked for a week's adjournment. De Marigny was returned to his cell. When the hearing resumed on the following Monday, a fuming Higgs claimed that the Crown was deliberately trying to slow down proceedings. Their thinking, he said, was to postpone calling Melchen and Barker until the last moment, so that should there be a trial soon afterwards it would leave the defence as little time as possible to prepare.

Adderley denied this, at which Higgs pointed to an interview that the two Americans had given the week before to the *Miami Herald* in which they had explained that this was precisely the Crown's approach. Melchen had added that nonetheless they intended to be as fair as possible to de Marigny – 'strictly Marquess of Queensberry rules'.

Devious as these tactics seemed, the broader truth was that the prosecution was still trying to nail down some aspects of its case. On 23 July, before the resumption, Pemberton and Melchen had travelled to New York to visit the serological laboratory run by Alexander Wiener, an eminent forensic expert and a protégé of Karl Landsteiner, the discoverer of blood grouping.

Their consultation of Wiener raised the hackles of a party that no one knew was interested in Oakes's murder: J. Edgar Hoover. Jealous of the standing of his organisation, Hoover asked the Bureau's agent in Miami to explain why Melchen had chosen to use a private laboratory rather than that of the FBI in Washington. Although the organisation could not intervene officially in the case once it had been given to the Miami force, Hoover still wanted to extract some kudos from it if possible, and he also wanted the local detectives to acknowledge the Bureau's supremacy.

With persistence, some of the FBI's files of the time can now be consulted, including Agent Kitchin's reply. It makes for interesting reading. Melchen, it seems, felt that the Bureau's laboratory had taken all the credit for the solving of an earlier crime – a quadruple murder – that he had worked on, and so he was reluctant to turn to them again. This time, he was going to go his own way.

Moreover, the agent mentioned, in that earlier case Melchen had overruled Barker's furious protests in order to send the evidence to the Bureau. Perhaps the relationship between them was not as harmonious as presented.

Though it took no formal part in the investigation of Oakes's killing, the Bureau's records on it are extensive, stemming from their historic interest in several of the concerned parties, such as de Marigny, as well as from the censor's monitoring of Nassau's communications. They also received screeds of anonymous tip-offs and crank correspondence about the case, as well as other information that seemed worth following up.

One such item came from a former New York prizefighter named Alfred Greenwood, once a sparring partner of Jack Dempsey's. Greenwood told an agent at the end of July that he had known Oakes in Canada, and that the millionaire had at the time been heavily involved in the illegal smuggling of Chinese workers south into the United States. He now had his own theories about why Sir Harry had been killed.

Hoover saw no harm in the ex-boxer being interviewed, but when an agent went to do so he discovered that Greenwood had been found dead in his room a few days after airing his thoughts. He was fifty-one, and was said to have died of 'natural causes'. Probably there was nothing in it; it was just something that seemed to happen around the Oakes murder.

In the Magistrates Court meanwhile, several important points had emerged. The first came from Mabel Ellis, the maid at Westbourne who had prepared Oakes's room on the night of his death. She revealed that, on his instructions, none of the windows or doors of the house were ever locked. This was a man who felt safe, not one who was expecting danger.

Then came the testimony of the two RAF wives who had attended de Marigny's dinner party, the dark-haired, slightly chubby Dorothy Clarke and Jean Ainsley, a taller blonde. Nancy, dressed in a wide-brimmed straw hat held in place by a white scarf, and de Marigny, in brown coat and trousers, white and tan shoes and a garish blue and red tie, watched their evidence intently. When Ainsley described him as having worn a tie at dinner that was 'rather loud', de Marigny caught his wife's eye across the courtroom and grinned. A broad smile lit up her face, then she hid her blushes behind her fan.

The two women confirmed de Marigny's presence near Westbourne when dropping them home, and the time, about 1.20 a.m. – de Marigny had drawn their attention to the fact that Clarke's watch was fast by twenty minutes. Even so, that was right at the outer limit of the accepted time-frame for the murder, and, Clarke mentioned, de Marigny had not brought a hat or a raincoat with him, as if he did not intend to be outside for long on a wet night.

There was a brief adjournment, during which Nancy and Marie af Trolle ate an ice cream outside the courtroom, seemingly oblivious

to the small crowd that stopped to watch them. Then the next witness was called, a Constable Parker, who said that early on the
Thursday morning de Marigny had come into the police station to
ask about a licence for his car. Parker recalled that he had been
struck by his wild-eyed expression and his lips, which had appeared
swollen. The hearing was then adjourned for a further week. So
far, it appeared that neither side had landed a meaningful punch.

By the time that the court met again, on 3 August, Higgs had
decided that he needed to share the workload of research and
advocacy with another barrister, or junior, and Ernest Callender
was retained. Then thirty-four, Callender was of mixed race, his
mother being of French extraction while his father, himself a
senior barrister and King's Counsel, was originally from British
Guiana. Like Higgs, Callender had gone straight to the Bar from
school, and like him too had originally wanted to pursue another
line of work, on the stage; he still sang well, and played the
ukulele. Having turned to the law, he had established a promising
reputation in criminal trials, especially in cross-examination, and
it was for this that Higgs recommended him to de Marigny.

On Callender's first day in court, the prosecution case moved
up a gear with the appearance on the stand of Captain Barker. He
began by outlining his impressive-sounding credentials, which
included attendance at the National Police Academy, run by the
FBI, and membership of the nine-hundred-strong International
Association for Identification, of which he was now one of the
five directors. He had given evidence, he said, in hundreds of trials
in Florida.

After recounting his work on the initial day of the investigation,
which included the discovery of the burnt hair on de Marigny,
Barker related how on the Friday morning he had resumed his
search for fingerprints on the six-foot-high, cream-coloured
Chinese screen, which was now produced in court. The afternoon before, when he had decided that the humidity was too
high to brush it safely, he and Pemberton had folded the screen
and had placed it in the hallway outside the bedroom. Now he

raised some six or eight prints from it. Among them were those of Pemberton and Quackenbush, which he discounted.

'And,' asked Adderley, 'was that all you found?'

'No,' said Barker. 'There was another print.'

'And were you able to recognise that?'

'Yes,' came the reply. 'It corresponded to the little right finger of Alfred de Marigny.' And with a flourish, Barker walked over to the screen and marked the relevant spot with a blue pencil.

It was a dramatic moment – the revelation for the first time in public of the keystone of the case against de Marigny – and it must have given Higgs pause for thought. Yet his client kept up an air of not appearing unduly concerned, smiling and whispering something to the barrister. Occasionally he looked across court and exchanged smiles with Nancy, who was looking pretty in a straw hat.

When Higgs came to cross-examine Barker, he established three other salient facts: the detective had found prints on only two objects in the room, the screen and a drinking glass by the bed; any print in the house would deteriorate within three or four days in such a climate, and so could not have been left by de Marigny some time before (he said he had not been at Westbourne for two years); and Barker had discovered the finger-print between eleven a.m. and one p.m. on 9 July.

The next day it was Melchen's turn in the witness box. He too started with his qualifications, which included the investigation each year of between fifty and sixty-five murders in Miami. He then told the court that, while Barker had concentrated on look-ing for prints, he had handled the physical examination of the bedroom and its environs, together with the analysis of the burnt and bloodied materials. At two spots on the carpet, one near the bed and the other near the wardrobe, he had smelled an odour of kerosene or petroleum, and thought that the propellant used for the fire might have been Fly-Ded, the insecticide contained in the spray gun in Oakes's room. He theorised, too, that the baronet, his pyjamas on fire, had reached the hallway, where one of the walls bore a man-shaped smudge, before he had been overtaken by his attacker and dragged back into the bedroom. The Americans were beginning to depict de Marigny as the perpetrator of a peculiarly brutal murder.

While Barker was working on the screen, said Melchen, de Marigny had not been allowed upstairs, so excluding the possibility that he might have accidentally touched it then. Between about three and four o'clock on the Friday afternoon – in other words after Barker had found the print – he had interviewed the Count in a bedroom off the hallway. De Marigny had told him about the arguments he had had with Sir Harry, and about the letter that Ruth had sent the family, which he thought Foskett had shown to Lady Oakes to help effect a breach between her and him.

During this evidence, de Marigny seemed to exhibit considerable calm about his fate, consistently leaning over the rail to chat *sotto voce* with Adderley, whom he kept quietly in stitches with his banter.

It was an impressive – an aristocratic – display of sang-froid. It masked the Count's true emotions. When each day's session ended he was taken back to his cell, and once more he found himself alone. It was then that the dream returned, and every night it was the same. As he woke, drenched in sweat, he could still feel the rope tight around his neck, his lungs gasping, his feet kicking wildly in the air.

The hearings continued until the following Saturday, with Melchen's evidence being followed by that of a New York Police fingerprint specialist, Frank Conway, who confirmed Barker's identification of de Marigny's print. Next came Harold Christie, who a few days before had had to deal with a second death, that of the family matriarch, his mother Madge. Large crowds gathered in the square outside the courthouse to watch his arrival, but were driven under the porches of the Post Office by a squally rain shower.

Christie's testimony added a little more detail to what had already come out in the press about the night of the murder. After the guests had left, he told the court, he and Oakes had talked for about a quarter of an hour in his host's room. He had then read a magazine for a while, and had gone to sleep at about midnight. Twice he had been woken, once by mosquitoes and once by a heavy downpour, but otherwise he had heard nothing.

The day before his appearance in the box, Christie had given an interview to journalists in which he had described finding Sir Harry's corpse as 'the greatest shock of his life'. He now repeated what he had told them, that on first seeing Oakes he had thought that he might yet be alive, and had attempted to revive him by propping his head up on a pillow, wiping his face with a wet towel, and holding a glass of water to his lips.

It was on this pathetic, almost bleakly comic scene of Christie cradling the burned and battered body of a dead man that Higgs turned his fire. Christie had been called to give evidence about his discovery of the murder, but his presence on the stand now allowed the defence to imply, if not to suggest explicitly, that he might know more than he was saying.

Christie, however, proved a steady witness. The day after the murder, when he had been under suspicion and de Marigny still free, he had been shunned by Bay Street. My grandmother had already been invited to take tea with him, and when she had arrived at the appointed time, disdaining social embarrassment in favour of the duties of friendship, he had been almost more grateful than words could say.

Following the Count's arrest, Christie had lost his pariah status and now, feeling the ground firm under his feet, he was unafraid in court to own up when he could not remember certain details. Higgs had to be content with extracting one or two pieces of information on which he could work later, such as the revelation that Christie had asked his driver to bring his car round to Westbourne during the dinner party, although he was intending to stay the night. He said that he and Oakes had planned to use it the following day for the tour of the sheep farm.

More worrying for Higgs than his inability to rattle this witness was Christie's having supplied the court with a potentially incriminating motive for de Marigny. About two weeks before the murder, the Count had asked him to sell his property on

Eleuthera as he said he had considerable expenses to meet. The prosecution had first tied de Marigny to the crime scene, and now had supplied a reason for the killing: lack of money, to be remedied by Nancy's inheritance.

The stop-start hearings continued the following week with Bert Pemberton, the head of the CID. It was his forty-seventh birthday, and it was to be an unhappy experience for him.

Adderley began by asking how he had protected the integrity of the screen. The prosecution wanted to quell what was emerging as one of de Marigny's lines of defence, that he might have touched it at some time when he was in the house after learning of the murder. Pemberton said that the screen had been moved to allow the removal of Oakes's body, and then the hallway in which it was placed had been guarded by three constables in rotation. De Marigny had been told not to come upstairs. The next day, he had seen the Mauritian around Westbourne in the morning, but not anywhere near the bedroom where Barker was at work. All seemed clear enough.

Higgs, however, took another tack, designed to undermine Pemberton's authority as a witness: 'Could you tell the court who was in charge of this investigation?'

Pemberton looked surprised. It was almost as if he had not thought about the matter before. 'I suppose,' he said, after a little, 'that, as the head of the CID, I was.'

This presented Higgs with an open goal.

'Did Captains Melchen and Barker consult you about the removal of Sir Harry's body?'

' No,' admitted Pemberton, 'they didn't.'

'And can you say which day it was sent for burial?'

He could not.

'And was it your idea to remove Sir Harry's body from the coffin and re-photograph it?'

'No,' Pemberton had to say. 'I understand it was the wish of Captain Barker.'

'And one more thing, Major. You will remember that there were two bloodstained towels found near the body. No doubt they might be vital pieces of evidence. Can you tell me where they are now?'

Pemberton looked lost. He could remember no such towels. His evident discomfort drew no sympathy from Higgs.

'Are you sure, Major Pemberton, that you really were in charge of the investigation?'

Higgs's implication was clear. Pemberton's word had counted for little during those two days at Westbourne, and any of his instructions to de Marigny or about the screen could have been countermanded or ignored by the two Americans. It was only their testimony that the magistrate should take note of.

Pemberton did, however, clear up one matter. Some authors have since criticised the police for not taking a statement from a watchman said to have been on duty in the grounds of Westbourne on the night of the murder. Christie had said that there was one at the adjoining Country Club, and one at the house who also tended the sheep. Pemberton told the court that two watchmen had been at the Country Club that night, pre-sumably both of those mentioned by Christie. Perhaps they had seen something peculiar and were just keeping their mouths shut, but at least the police had interviewed them, and for their part the defence never thought it worthwhile getting them into court.

The next morning, Friday the thirteenth, the three constables were wheeled on to support Pemberton's version of events. All corroborated what the officer had said about the screen, and two said further, as Melchen had done, that de Marigny had not come upstairs until about half past three on the Friday afternoon, a few hours before he was arrested. Even then, he had not come within twelve feet of the screen.

In the next session, Higgs returned to the attack. First, how-ever, Field heard from Newell Kelly, the tall, bespectacled manager of Oakes's property interests in Nassau and now, with Foskett, one of the trustees of his estate. He was among the few people close to his former employer to have an alibi for 8 July, having been away from New Providence on a fishing trip.

He added a little more colour to the picture of bad relations between de Marigny and his father-in-law, telling the court that on three occasions the accused had said to him how angry he was at being abused and maltreated by Oakes, such as when he had come to drag Sydney away from the house. If Oakes didn't watch out, he had threatened, pointing to his outsize shoe, 'he would use his big foot on him.'

Then Pemberton had a confession to make. Returning to the stand, he said that, whereas earlier he had testified that he had not seen the bloodied towels in Oakes's room and did not know what had happened to them, now he did recall having seen one on the bed that day. Astonishingly, he had in fact had it sent to him for analysis when he had been in Miami on 22 July, and had afterwards taken it home with him, where he had kept it wrapped up in his bathroom with other exhibits. He had only found it again that morning. He had then also discovered the second towel mentioned. It was in Christie's room at Westbourne, where it had lain undisturbed for more than a month.

Addressing Pemberton in a dismissively icy tone, Higgs asked if he did not make notes during an investigation. 'Yes,' pleaded Pemberton, 'but you must realise that I was not the only person investigating this case.' But had he made notes about the towels? No, he admitted, he had not.

At best, his behaviour amounted to gross incompetence, reminiscent of the figure that de Marigny could remember crawling drunkenly around the floor of a bar, begging to have his shiny black police cap back. At worst, it was something more sinister. The towel that he had now located in Christie's room, he had to agree, did not match Melchen's description of it being heavily streaked by smoke and blood.

Following Pemberton's cross-examination, Field proposed a resumption the day after next, but Adderley said the prosecution would not be ready for another week. At this point Higgs lost his temper, and what the local newspaper called a 'spirited verbal duel' ensued, through which could be heard the magistrate's Irish-Barbadian tones struggling to keep the peace. He eventually granted the adjournment, at which a grinning de Marigny put his arm around both lawyers and declared: 'Next time, I shall offer a trophy!'

By 24 August, the end of the hearings – which had begun almost five weeks before – was in sight, but there were still several significant witnesses to be heard. The first was de Marigny's bank manager, who strengthened the prosecution's hand by testifying that in the year since his marriage to Nancy the Count had spent some six thousand pounds (worth £190,000 today), about three-quarters of what he had in the bank. In addition, about half of that sum had come from Nancy herself.

Moreover, his current account was now empty – some fifty-seven pounds overdrawn – while his business account was just five pounds in credit. This, however, it was pointed out, was not an unusual state of affairs for de Marigny, whose balances see-sawed (and in the last few weeks he would also have had legal bills to pay).

The next witness was Lieutenant Douglas, the officer who had spent the uncomfortable night in de Marigny's chair. His evidence began rather promisingly for the prosecution. He had been ordered to keep de Marigny under close supervision, and the next morning they had driven over to Westbourne together. In the car, de Marigny had begun to talk about his strained relations with his father-in-law.

'I know what you mean,' Douglas had said, trying to be friendly, 'but that doesn't mean you want the worst to happen to someone.'

'That guy, Sir Harry,' de Marigny had replied, 'the old bastard should have been killed anyway.'

They had arrived at the house a little early, and had walked down onto the beach. There the Count had asked whether, under English law, a man could be convicted on circumstantial evidence, or if the murder weapon was not found. Douglas told him not to fret, but in the courtroom doubtless Adderley was feeling well pleased with this damning-sounding testimony.

When leading evidence from his own witness (as opposed to cross-examining one favourable to the other side), a barrister only likes to put questions to which he already knows the answers, so avoiding surprises for which he is unprepared. Thus when Adderley then asked Douglas if he had had de Marigny in his sight all that morning, he can only have been expecting the innocuous answer 'Yes.' It was not what he got.

Something had been pricking Douglas's conscience. Perhaps it was the drink that de Marigny says he had turned to, perhaps it was his Scots Presbyterian upbringing as a son of the manse, perhaps it was thoughts of his father, who was just days from death. No, he told Adderley, between midday and one o'clock de Marigny had gone upstairs with Melchen, and had remained there for about three-quarters of an hour.

Adderley was flummoxed. The officer's evidence was clearly in conflict with the statements that Melchen himself and the constables had given about the timing of de Marigny's interview – after 3.30 p.m. – and if it were believed it meant that de Marigny could claim to have touched the screen before Barker had finished examining it. He would have a route of escape. Worse still, if Melchen was wrong about this – or had lied – what value did the rest of his evidence have?

The last batch of witnesses to testify began with Walter Foskett. On 10 February, he said, de Marigny had come to his office in Palm Beach to ask for his help in improving relations with the Oakeses. Foskett had refused, saying that he disapproved of de Marigny's having married Nancy without her parents' knowledge. He also mentioned to the Mauritian the existence of the letter from Ruth to Lady Oakes, whose contents de Marigny then hotly denied. Five days later, Sir Harry and his wife changed the provisions of their will.

The catalyst for this, said Lady Oakes when she gave evidence, was the argument that they had had with de Marigny about Nancy's abortion. (She had not yet read Ruth's letter.) The implication was that they thought that the pregnancy showed she was irresponsible, and that her husband had too much of a hold over her. Her account of the rupture in the family made public for the first time what had long been gossiped about, and gave the lie to the version that Nancy had earlier spun to the press. The break with her daughter appeared to have added an extra depth to her grief, and every time Lady Oakes mentioned Nancy's name in court she seemed to have to stifle a sob.

The penultimate person called, the twenty-seventh summoned by the prosecution, was John Anderson. Given that he and de Marigny were on friendly enough terms – so friendly, indeed, that eighteen months earlier the Count had loaned him one thousand pounds (worth thirty-five thousand today), which he had yet to repay – the tenor of his evidence was to be curiously harmful to his cause.

He began in a helpful enough way, saying that when he had told de Marigny of his father-in-law's death, Freddie's reaction had been one of incredulity. Then, however, he stated that later that same afternoon, de Marigny had told him that he had several drums of gasoline at Victoria Avenue that he wanted to dispose of.

Adderley did not miss the import of this: 'Was this after he had told you that Sir Harry had been burnt?'

It was. Anderson had suggested that de Marigny get a truck in to shift the petrol. Then, as a conscientious citizen, he had gone to the police to tell them about the fuel.

Worse was to follow. 'Have you had any other dealings with the accused in recent months?' Adderley asked.

'Yes. Some months ago he solicited my help in another matter. He told me that his former wife Ruth was claiming one hundred and thirty thousand dollars from him.'

It was a vast sum – about one million pounds today – and it was not one that de Marigny had to hand. He had asked Anderson to help keep the suit from getting to court, and Anderson had approved a loan of two thousand pounds (seventy thousand in today's terms) by the BGT, although only ten per cent of this had so far been advanced.

A dire shortage of money – an angry father-in-law changing his will – threats against 'the old bastard' – that incriminating finger-print: things were starting to look very bleak indeed for de Marigny.

Compared to these points against him, a mix-up about some towels and the times of an interview seemed to be very small beer. When Adderley told Field that that concluded the prosecution's presentation, it was no doubt with a sense of a job well done.

Higgs, however, had one surprise to spring. Again departing from conventional tactics in the lower court, he produced a witness of his own. Ulrich Oberwarth was that very rare bird in the Bahamas, a Jew, one of the few refugees from Nazi Germany who had been accepted into the Colony, and that only because he was a doctor. As well as working at the hospital, he had been the medical officer at the prison, and on de Marigny's first morning there he had examined him.

He had found not a single sign of burning. No singes, no scalds, no brilliant hairs. Not a trace of fire. In cross-examination, he admitted to Adderley, however, that he had made his inspec-tion with the naked eye, when a lens would have been more sure. He also admitted that he knew de Marigny socially a little.

This friendship was perhaps what had impelled Oberwarth to take it upon himself to double-check what he had heard about the investigation so far. More certainly, though he denied it in court, it must have been the reason why he was suddenly transferred to other duties outside the prison. Soon afterwards, he began to think it a good idea to apply for other jobs, and by the end of the war he had settled in Canada.

At 11.40 a.m. on 31 August, Field told de Marigny to stand up.

'From the evidence,' he said, ' I am satisfied that a prima facie case has been made against you, and I order you to stand trial.'

De Marigny's face remained expressionless, although later he shared a cigarette with Higgs as he waited to be taken back to the cramped, confining cell. He would have to endure more than another month of late-summer sweltering there before the

Quarter Sessions opened on 6 October. The Crown had five weeks to strengthen its case. Higgs had five weeks to work out how to save de Marigny's life. A rope had already been ordered from the chandler for the hanging.

Public opinion was broadly satisfied by the outcome of the hearings. All at Government House, all of Bay Street and most of the white population – the pool from which the trial jury would now be drawn – were sure of de Marigny's guilt. Not that it was needed when the murderer was as plain as this, but the police, aided by the American detectives, had clearly done a thorough job.

They had not, however, followed up quite every piece of information that they had been given. On the night of the killing, Marie af Trolle and her husband Georg had been woken by a knocking on the door of their house at Cable Beach, not far from Westbourne. It was Newell Kelly's chauffeur, needing to borrow a monkey wrench to change a tyre in the rain. He had brought the tool back soon enough, but with Kelly away on his fishing trip, what was his station wagon doing out in the small hours? The af Trolles reported the nocturnal visit to the police, but they heard no more about it.

FIVE

It's me, it's me, O Lawd
Standin' in the need of prayer

Two weeks after de Marigny was committed for trial, there was
some unexpected news. Erskine-Lindop, it was announced, had
been promoted to Deputy Commissioner of the larger Trinidad
police force and would be leaving Nassau in a few days to go on
leave and then take up his new post. It was a change that glad-
dened hearts in Bay Street, especially as he was to be succeeded by
his second-in-command, Major Lancaster, who had a reputation
as a martinet keen on maintaining good order. As yet, no one
seemed to have appreciated that the appointment also meant that
Erskine-Lindop would not be on the island when the Oakes case
came to court.

One person who had realised the value of being away then was
the Duke, and in mid-September he and the Duchess set off for
America for what would prove to be a break of almost two
months, although their time in the States was not without an
agenda. 'I have not much doubt,' wrote Lord Halifax, the British
Ambassador in Washington, to Oliver Stanley, the Colonial
Secretary, after their visit, 'that it is in both their minds to groom
themselves for future occupation of this Embassy.'

The Duke would later be criticised for his absence during the

trial, but in fact he had been encouraged to stay away from it by
the Colonial Office. 'In view of the sordid circumstances of which
you have told me,' Stanley had written in reply to the Governor's
outline of recent events, 'you are wise to be away from the colony
when the accused . . . will appear before the Supreme Court.'

Higgs, meanwhile, had been away on a trip of his own, study-
ing fingerprinting in New York, and when he returned he began
in earnest to assemble the material that he would need for de
Marigny's defence. To help him gather this, he had persuaded
Nancy to hire a battery of technical experts.

The first of these had already arrived a month before and had
busily set about his work, which was largely to be seen going
busily about his work. Raymond Schindler was, at sixty, the most
famous private detective in America, a status he had achieved by
mastering the arts of both crime solution and self-promotion.

A stout, silver-haired man, with a passing resemblance to Alfred
Hitchcock, he had grown up in Wisconsin as the son of a priest
turned insurance salesman. When young, he too had dreamed of
making a fortune in the goldfields and had worked for a year in a
mine in California. Falling back on his father's later trade, he had
stumbled into detective work while investigating false insurance
claims made in the wake of the San Francisco earthquake. By the
time of the Great War he had his own firm, and by the mid-1920s
he was the detective of choice for cases of high-society blackmail
and missing jewels. His principal client was Anna Gould, the
daughter of the unscrupulous railway magnate Jay Gould, on
whose estate he lived in a guest cottage that had its own bowling
alley and indoor swimming pool.

His taste for the high life extended to New York's nightclubs.
He had his own table at '21' and at the Stork Club, for he liked
the limelight and he adored celebrities. But these places were
also where he did business, cultivating the gossips who could provide him with the inside information he needed, although in his
publicity he made more of his pioneering use of the dictograph –
the wire-tap – to acquire evidence. His hobbies, somewhat

surprisingly, were ballroom dancing (he had built a tree house-cum-dance floor in the branches of a giant oak next to his house) and opera; it was Schindler who organised the first American trip to the Oberammergau passion play.

With his nose for a case that could only enhance his reputation, Schindler accepted with alacrity Nancy's request for his assistance. But he imposed one condition: if he found any evidence that pointed to de Marigny's guilt, he would turn it over to the prosecution. Nancy agreed. She, too, she said, would want to know if he had proof that her husband was guilty.

She put Schindler up with the af Trolles, and in the last week of August he got to work. His presence was a gift for the press, and he in turn wasted no time in providing them with copy designed to sow doubt as to the certainty of de Marigny's guilt and to win public sympathy for the Count's wife. 'Believe me,' he told journalists soon after arriving, 'she is a very determined lady.' Within a few days, newspapers were obligingly reporting that he had discovered that the prosecution had information which they had not disclosed to the defence because it did not fit their theory of the case. He had found it at Westbourne.

Schindler had a taste for melodrama. 'Imagine the setting,' he told one reporter. 'That lonely old house' – in fact it had been built only a decade before, but facts were often secondary considerations for Schindler – 'with the lightning flashing and the thunder roaring, the rain coming down and the waves breaking.

'Sometime during the night a man goes into the room and murders Sir Harry. Then he goes round burning spots all over the house – spots that have a connection with the crime: a wall here, a drapery there. He stays around the house, mind you. That certainly isn't the action of a normal person. The average man, after he had committed the crime, would have gotten out as fast as he could.' That was vintage Schindler – a broad slice of ham garnished with a pertinent point or two.

'I spent three days in the death room, trying to visualise what had taken place there,' he said to the New York press after the case. Again, it was a striking image, but not a very accurate one. He had, in fact, managed to gain access to Westbourne only briefly. There he had examined Oakes's bed but what had interested him more was that he had come across two constables in the act of washing down the walls of the room, erasing the mysterious smudged prints.

'What are you doing?' he had said in some surprise. 'Isn't this evidence?'

'No, sir, it's not,' came the answer. 'We were told to clean up this place, and that's what we're doing.'

'But these handprints are highly relevant to the case!'

'No, sir. The American gentlemen have already taken everything relevant. We was told that Mr de Marigny has long fingers. These here are short ones. Like we said, it's not relevant.'

It was Schindler's introduction to the mindset of those in charge of the case, and the first confirmation of Nancy's insistence to him that all was not well with its conduct.

Schindler was heartened by what he had learned, and having passed the story on to Higgs (though not to the press), he sought Nancy's permission to bring in a colleague with whom he often worked. This was Professor Leonarde Keeler, an altogether different kind of detective. He had been well known in police circles almost since he was at high school, when he had been taken on by the criminologist John Larson as his protégé. He had gone on to run Chicago's crime-detection laboratory, based at Northwestern University, where he had made his name by refining and becoming the foremost exponent of the use of the polygraph, or lie detector.

Still only in his late thirties, Keeler had recently moved into private practice, and the Oakes murder was to be one of his first important cases. Following his arrival, he and Schindler locked themselves away, making experiments on the twin of the Chinese screen, which had been in Oakes's bathroom at Westbourne. Schindler took care to leak the news that the results were most encouraging.

★

Ray Schindler did not come cheap. His fees, not including expenses, amounted to more than two thousand dollars (twelve thousand pounds in today's money) a week. Then there was Keeler to pay, not to mention Higgs and Callender. The sums required were going to put an inordinate strain on the de Marignys' finances, already weakened by medical bills and by the rift with Nancy's parents, for though the public might think of her as an heiress, she knew her funds to be very limited. In mounting desperation, she turned for help to her mother. Unbeknown to either, their ensuing correspondence was intercepted and copied by the FBI.

On 22 July, shortly after she had seen her husband in prison for the first time, Nancy cabled her mother at The Willows, Lady Oakes's seaside house in Maine. In the telegram, Nancy wrote that she was certain of de Marigny's innocence and wanted the true circumstances of the murder made known. Her mother, it seems, had said that she would give her any money she needed, and now that she'd had to hire Schindler Nancy intended to redeem that promise. Otherwise, she wrote, she would be driven back on the generosity of others.

This can have had little effect, since three days later Nancy sent another telegram in which she repeated her appeal for aid, without which she feared de Marigny would be wrongly convicted and the murderer would escape. She might have suspected someone in particular, but naturally she did not name them in the cable. Ratcheting up the pressure somewhat, she threatened to go to the press and tell them of her desperation if money was not forthcoming. This threat did produce a reaction, a two-line telegram from Lady Oakes the following day which stated that she would wait to see what happened in the Magistrates Court (due to begin its proceedings that morning) before making any decision.

The next cable in the sequence was sent on 2 August to Nancy by Paul Zahl. Then working at the Haskins Laboratories in New York, Zahl was an Illinois-born research scientist in his early thirties who had claimed some public attention a few years earlier by his discovery when barely out of Harvard of a 'lost tribe' in the Amazon.

Like Schindler, Zahl was the son of a clergyman, and had rebelled against his strict evangelical upbringing. An ingrained puritan streak meant he put in long hours in his laboratory, but he dedicated himself in equal measure to New York's nightclubs, where his dashing comportment and wanderlust found no shortage of female admirers. After meeting Nancy, he had appointed himself her 'big brother', and she had consulted him when she wanted to find experts to go over the prosecution's evidence. The bespectacled Zahl had sprung to her defence. He had something of a romantic bent to him, and helping a girl in trouble was no doubt more appealing to him than his work on bacterial toxins. As will become clear later, his motives were not perhaps exclusively chivalrous.

It was Zahl who had initially suggested that Nancy should bring in Schindler, and with Lady Oakes stonewalling he was sent up to Maine to try to persuade her to open her purse. He was bluntly rebuffed. Nancy's mother refused even to see him – she was incommunicado for medical reasons, he was told. He duly telegraphed his lack of success to Nancy in Nassau.

The cable appears to have arrived while she was writing to her mother. That letter provides a vivid insight into their difficult relationship, and into Nancy's somewhat overwrought state of mind at the time. In it she oscillates between an almost childish tone – one that looks hopefully for an affection from her mother that was lacking – and equally childish reproofs. For all her poise in public, Nancy was at heart a rather lost girl of nineteen.

Towards the end of the letter, which deals mainly with the conditions that de Marigny was enduring in prison and her plans to drive up to see her mother in Maine, Nancy abruptly states that she has received a telegram from Zahl, and then veers into a desperate series of pleas – some underlined four times – begging her mother to talk to him and hinting at mysterious dangers that threaten the family.

'My God,' she writes, carried away by fear, 'do you want us all to go the same way? You must *divine* the seriousness of this thing *not only us* [*sic*] but our country. You must see Dr Zahl. Have you any feeling of self-preservation? God, you must.'

The meaning of her warnings is unclear, but it seems that they were born more of fear than of actual knowledge that the murderer might strike again, and are as much an appeal to her mother to save the family's good name as to be on her guard against a specific menace. Yet against the glacial reserve of Lady Oakes, they had all the melting power of a glow-worm.

On 1 October de Marigny's trial was fixed for the eighteenth of the month, and on 3 October Harry Oakes's will was published. It did not deal with the disposal of the great bulk of his wealth, notably his mining shares, just his personal property, which amounted to almost £3,672,000 (worth £110 million today). His widow received a third of the estate, his children the remainder – but not until they reached thirty years of age.

This was the change that the Oakeses had made with Foskett's help as the result of their worries about de Marigny's influence on their two eldest children. For another eleven years, Nancy would be limited to an annual handout of twelve thousand dollars (seventy-five thousand pounds in today's terms), by no means a negligible sum but hardly riches such as would impress a husband who had spent three times that amount in a year. Nor would it much ameliorate her current financial predicament; it would pay Schindler for little more than a month. Moreover, Oakes's fortune would henceforth be administered by three trustees: Lady Oakes, Newell Kelly and Foskett himself.

A week later, the magistrates reconvened to hear a new witness. Thomas Lavelle, a neighbour of the de Marignys, would be away during the trial, so had been ordered to give his testimony now. For some time he had been running his mouth off about having heard the argument between de Marigny and Oakes on the night when Sydney had been hustled away from the house on Victoria Avenue. Sir Harry had called the Mauritian a 'sex maniac' and had been in a 'mad state of mind'. Lavelle had not volunteered

Sir Harry Oakes in
1940 at The Caves, one
of his half-dozen homes
in and around Nassau.
(Nassau Magazine)

Oakes (second left) with the Tough brothers, prospecting at Kirkland Lake in 1911.
(The Museum of Northern History at the Sir Harry Oakes Chateau)

Nancy Oakes (seated)
and Marie af Trolle
in Havana, 1944.
(Marie Gudewill)

Bay Street, Nassau, in 1943, looking towards the Br   Colonial Hotel.
(Bahamas Department of Archives)

Count Alfred de Marigny (centre) leaving for court with Lt Douglas (left); note the caddish co-respondent shoes. *(Ralph Morse/Time Life Pictures/Getty Images)*

The genial public face of the Bahamas: Harold Christie. *(Ralph Morse/Time Life Pictures/Getty Images)*

It Girl: Brenda Frazier at
her grandparents' house,
Star Acres, outside Nassau.

(Nassau Magazine)

The Duke of Windsor with his staff in the garden at Government House.

(Jonathan Ramsay)

The Chinese screen on which Barker said he found de Marigny's fingerprint. *(Louis Williams/Archive Photos)*

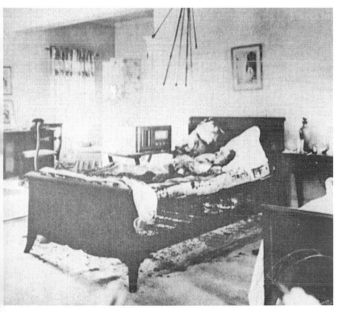

Oakes's burned and battered body in the bedroom at Westbourne. *(Louis Williams/Archive Photos)*

Exhibit J. *(Corbis)*

Westbourne: Oakes's bedroom was above and to the right of the entrance.
(Nassau Magazine)

De Marigny's yacht *Concubine*. *(Nassau Magazine)*

Nancy Oakes returns to Nassau
after learning of her father's murder.
(Nancy von Hoyningen-Huene)

Hallinan, Daly, Higgs and Callender study a plan of the de Marignys' house. *(Ralph Morse/Time Life Pictures/Getty Images)*

De Marigny snatches a quick smoke.
(Ralph Morse/Time Life Pictures/Getty Images)

Effie Heneage and her daughters.
(Nicola Heneage)

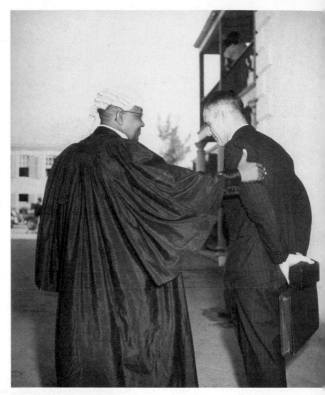

Alfred Adderley and
Captain James Barker.
(Ralph Morse/Time Life
Pictures/Getty Images)

De Visdelou with the blonde Betty Roberts and
Ray Schindler. *(Ralph Morse/Time Life Pictures/Getty Images)*

The monument to Sir Harry at
Oakes Field, Nassau. *(James Owen*

this information when Pemberton had interviewed him, but he had since been brought to book by Frederick Lancaster, Erskine-Lindop's successor.

There was little new in this for the watching journalists since it served only to confirm the strained relationship between de Marigny and his father-in-law. What was new was that Freddie was seen to have reverted to being clean-shaven, having grown a beard and moustache when he had been getting up early to go to the farm. Now he had removed them, albeit with the Crown's permission, given that the state of his facial and head hair was part of their case against him.

The press, pushed for copy, agreed that a beardless de Marigny looked younger and more debonair, especially as he had also changed the way he parted his hair. Less cheerful news, according to de Marigny's memoirs, arrived a day or two later. His friend Basil McKinney had found a couple of caretakers who were willing to tell Higgs about an unknown boat that had docked at Lyford Cay, on the western end of the island, on the night of the murder. It was then a remote spot, marked for development by Christie and home only to bird life, grassy swamps and a few holiday cottages (one of them rented by my grandmother). But before the men could talk one was found drowned, the other hanged.

This episode has been the foundation of much of the speculation about Oakes's death, with several authors – and their unnamed sources – stating that the mystery boat belonged to the Mafia, and even that Oakes was killed aboard it. De Marigny himself subscribes to another solution, and one can only reiterate that there is no verifiable foundation for such a theory. More substantially, there are in fact no newspaper reports at the time of the two murders alleged by de Marigny. A gatekeeper at Lyford Cay was found dead, but he was elderly and had had a stroke.

The defence may have been clutching at every straw, but the prosecution was also still feeling the need to reinforce its case. On

15 October, three days before the trial began, Hallinan asked Melchen to get the FBI to check its files for information on de Marigny as he had had a tip-off that the Count had previously been investigated by the Bureau for trafficking drugs. His source was probably police records from Mauritius, where the Crown had been making enquiries about de Marigny's background.

The request to the Bureau was made through 'Pump', the code for the wartime exchange of secret information between the British and the Americans. Despite this, and despite the fact that only two weeks earlier Hoover had hosted an official visit by the Duke and Duchess, the FBI was not in an accommodating mood. 'After the run-around we got on this case,' wrote one official, remembering Melchen's use of a rival laboratory, 'I don't think we ought to do a thing, particularly in view of the request coming through Captain Melchen.'

A senior member of Hoover's directorate, Edward Tamm, suggested that it be booted over to the Narcotics Bureau, part of the US Treasury, and Hallinan was politely instructed to contact them instead. The FBI did not feel the need, either, to tell him that a few weeks earlier it had been contacted by a man who had chatted to Oakes while the two had waited for a flight shortly before his death. Sir Harry, he said, had told him that de Marigny was a fortune hunter who had married Nancy for her inheritance, and he believed that his son-in-law would 'hasten events' if given the opportunity.

With the approach of the trial, Nassau began to chatter with renewed vigour. The chief (and scandalous) allegation concerned the exact nature of the ménage at Victoria Avenue, where lived de Marigny, Nancy, de Visdelou and – much of the time – the latter's girlfriend, a sixteen-year-old platinum blonde named Betty Roberts.

Almost any contact with the quartet could be hazardous to one's reputation. When John Pringle, the Duke's young equerry, went round to the house several evenings in succession, there was gossip that he and Nancy were having an affair. They were not, he insisted to me. Now that Freddie was in prison, and Georges had moved out to a hotel, his concern had been that she had no one to protect her. All they had done was drink Brandy Alexanders and listened to gramophone records.

In an attempt to keep the scale, and the tenor, of the press attention from her husband, Nancy now banded together with Suzanne Higgs and Marie af Trolle. Marie, who had blonde waist-length hair, a mother said to be worth fifty million dollars (£275 million in today's money) and a husband twenty years her senior, was not short of admirers. When Sir Alison Russell, a very retired colonial judge, came to Nassau to write a report on the wage riot, Marie was placed next to him at dinner, and was startled to find his bony hand fondling her knee under the table.

'I always like to pin my napkin to a lady's frock,' Sir Alison said by way of explanation. 'Then I don't have to keep looking for it later.'

Marie and Nancy made a pretty pair, and embarked on a campaign to keep up Freddie de Marigny's morale. Suzanne smuggled in chocolates, while his butler brought him a bottle of wine, disguised as a pot of tea.

Nassau's courthouse stood – and still stands – at the centre of the town's public buildings, flanked by the main police station and directly behind the islands' parliament. The morning of 18 October 1943 dawned cloudy and muggy, and by half past eight an orderly queue had begun to wind its way from the court's neo-classical porch past the war memorial on the green outside and around the square itself. At nine o'clock, there was a rush to fill the five benches in the courtroom that had been allocated to spectators. At half past ten, the court crier thumped his staff on the floor and the Chief Justice of the Bahamas, Sir Oscar Daly, resplendent in scarlet robes and white wig, descended from his chamber to open the trial of Alfred de Marigny.

The high-ceilinged courtroom was not large and the central players in the drama that was about to be presented sat close

together. To the left of Daly's desk there was a wooden cagelike
structure, built up several feet above the floor and barred on three
sides – the dock. In it sat de Marigny, conservatively dressed for
once in a lightweight grey suit and blue tie. From time to time he
winced and gingerly felt his spine; he had been suffering from a
painful carbuncle brought on by stress and by sleeping on his
prison mattress. When he leaned forward to relieve the discomfort
the bars of the dock imprinted deep furrows on his forehead.

Facing him across the room was a long pew for the jury, as yet
to be selected, and next to it the dark wooden witness box with
its waist-high rail. In front of Daly was a desk for the barristers in
their wigs and black gowns. Already the court crier was busy
puffing insecticide around their feet and those of the judge.

Perhaps eighty or so people were packed closely onto wooden
benches behind, while crammed up against the walls were those
without seats, a mixture of constables in their helmets and brass-
buttoned white jackets and other spectators, mostly black or
drawn from the poorer whites of Nassau. Though the town's elite
talked of little else, it would not be done for them to be seen gaw-
ping at the spectacle in Court No. 1. Through the windows
poured a torrent of light, illuminating the room's white mouldings
and pale blue paint. Outside, a still paler sky looked down on
green vines and patches of red tiles. Inside, all was quiet.

There was one other group of onlookers in court. There was
said to be more press interest in the case than in any since the
kidnap of the Lindbergh baby a decade earlier. Given the sensational ingredients of the crime – a murdered millionaire, a dashing
aristocrat in the dock, a beautiful heiress and all the pomp of the
British legal system – such attention was not surprising, not least
because for many readers the affair had provided a welcome diver-
sion from the war. The newspapers helpfully provided them with
a guide to the pronunciation of 'de Marigny' – 'It rhymes with
"Marry me".'

All the major news media had arranged for their Nassau corres-
pondents to file copy, or had sent out their star reporters with

instructions to go big on local colour. There was Ruth Reynolds for the *New York Daily News*, Elizabeth Townshend for the *New York Post* and Jeanne Bellamy for the *Miami Herald*, while the brothers Dupuch, Etienne and Eugene, were covering the story not just for their own paper, the *Nassau Daily Tribune*, but also for the *New York Times*, Reuters, the *Daily Telegraph and Morning Post* (as it then was), and the *Daily Express*. *Time* magazine was running regular features on the case. A table had to be made specially to accommodate the number of journalists in court, and the hotels of Nassau gleefully doubled their prices.

The *New York Journal-American*, owned by William Randolph Hearst, prided itself on its full treatment of such scandals, and had gone one better than its competitors by hiring someone used to writing about sudden death, Erle Stanley Gardner. Although then still a practising lawyer in California, for more than ten years Gardner's pulp novels, some of them featuring his creation Perry Mason, had been growing in popularity. During the course of the trial, his fictional detective was to find a much larger audience with the broadcast on CBS of the first radio serial of Mason's adventures.

Gardner, then fifty-four, had been given a free hand by the paper, and frequently wrote up to four pages a day on the trial. He knew what the public wanted. When, early in the proceedings, the press were shown around Westbourne, Gardner noticed the game of Chinese checkers that Oakes had been playing with his dinner guests.

'Well, Colonel,' he said breezily to the newly promoted Lancaster, 'there's the board, just as it was on that fateful evening.'

'I'm sorry to spoil your story,' came the rejoinder, 'but the police have actually been playing checkers here for the last four months.'

'Don't let it worry you, Colonel,' was Gardner's ironic response. 'Facts will never spoil a Hearst story'.

The first matter for Chief Justice Daly's attention was the empanelling of the jury. Because of the high profile of the case, the twelve jurors were to be drawn at random from a larger than usual list of thirty-six names, including some who were normally spared jury service, such as members of the House of Assembly. All those on the list were men, however, and all of them were white. As if he was drawing teams for the FA Cup, the court crier rattled the numbered balls in a box, and one after another pulled out an initial twelve. Various excuses were given, and challenges were made by the barristers of both sides against those that they felt might have prejudices one way or the other. Rapidly, the number available for service dwindled to twelve. After yet another potential juror had been excused for bladder trouble, the defence withdrew their original challenge against one man and finally the panel was complete.

They did not form a representative selection of Nassau's population. Rather, they were an embodiment of its most rigidly respectable face. One was a sponge farmer, another owned the bakery, a third was an accountant. Then there was the clerk of a tobacco firm, the proprietor of a stocking shop, and the man who ran the Government Ice Department. Most of them bore Bahamian names still redolent of a Puritan ancestry: Seighbert Russell, Hullen Farrington, Jerome Bethel – the last had been born into a strictly religious sect at the settlement of Spanish Wells.

All were married, all went to church on Sunday, all knew each other well. The foreman, James Sands, was the town's leading grocer, and the uncle of Stafford Sands, the one-eyed lawyer. His father, who had been prominent in island politics, had once had a business with Higgs's uncle, ferrying tourists over to Hog and selling them oranges on a stick to eat.

The make-up of the jury, then, was much as Higgs had expected. He knew that it would be a hard task to convince them of de Marigny's innocence, given the battering that his client's private life would take from the Crown. He would have to put his faith in the judge to hold the ring.

Clad in his wig, Oscar Daly may have seemed to American

reporters at first to epitomise their conception of a British judge, but conventional as his life had been it was also one of wide experience. Then sixty-three, he had been educated in France, Germany and at Trinity College, Dublin, before being called first to the Irish Bar and then to that of Kenya. He had returned to England to fight in the Great War, and had taken part in the battles at Ypres and on the Somme before becoming Intelligence Officer for his division. After the war he had gone back to Kenya, where he had built up a lucrative practice and had been appointed King's Counsel before accepting a transfer to the Bahamas as Chief Justice in 1939. He was knighted in 1942.

There were some other perks to the job, including a house on Prospect Ridge, but any prestige was only local and as the move also considerably reduced his earnings one can conclude that the judiciary must have been an office for which he had a high regard and whose work he took seriously. His efficient, impartial presence was much needed in Nassau. His predecessor, Sir Richard Tute, had stayed too long in the job, and as the Colonial Office struggled to find someone to replace him he became more and more deaf, and his judgements more and more perverse. It was fortunate for de Marigny that it was not Tute who was presiding over this trial.

At half past eleven, Alfred Adderley prepared to outline the Crown's case to the jury. The prosecution team was actually led by the Attorney-General, Hallinan, a tall, thin-faced Irishman with a toothbrush moustache and the air of a pernickety school handyman. Scrupulously polite, to the point of punctiliousness, he had already crossed swords with de Marigny over his behaviour in Nassau and Ruth's letter to *Time*, but his taking charge of the case was due more to its gravity, and to Oakes's prominence, than to any personal animosity towards the Mauritian.

His post as Attorney-General, however, was largely a political one and since his courtwork was a little rusty he deferred to Adderley's powers of oratory. For Higgs's part, he was glad to hear that Adderley would be Hallinan's junior, for it meant that the law officer would have to make the closing speech, and Higgs knew that Adderley was by far the better persuader of a Nassau jury.

'At the outset,' said Adderley in his gravest tones, 'I must impress upon you the seriousness of this occasion and the terrible nature of the case which is to crave your time and painful attention over many days in this court.'

At more than sixty years' remove, Adderley's style sounds grandiloquent, even theatrical, and must have seemed so even to those who heard it. Yet its flavour was not unfamiliar; it was the language of the King James version of the Bible on which his audience had been raised, and they associated such orotund phrases with solemn occasions. Peppering his speech with allusions to the Old Testament and lines from Shakespeare, Adderley set out the main points of the prosecution's case.

Much of this had already been heard in the Magistrates Court, and Adderley condensed it into three different motives for the murder: 'for revenge, for satisfaction, and for gain.' The killing was a crime of hate – the lack of robbery and the burning of the body pointed to that. De Marigny was on the worst of terms with Sir Harry and had threatened to get even with him with his 'big foot'. The Mauritian was in dire straits financially, continued Adderley, and faced ruinous claims from his former wife. His hatred could only be slaked, and his debts wiped out, by getting his hands on Nancy's fortune.

'Murder is murder, and a life is a life,' ran Adderley's sonorous thunder, 'but this murder is, as Shakespeare, the immortal Bard, says in one of his Sonnets 'as black as hell and as dark as night', in its foul conception a deed which could only originate in a depraved, strange and sadistic mind.

'A mind indeed,' he continued, with a sly reference to de Marigny, 'a mind which is foreign to the usual mind which comes before this Court, with a complete disregard for humanity in so vile a murder which besmirched the name and peace of this tranquil land.'

It sounded magnificent, and Gardner lapped it up. In his commentary on the first day's proceedings, he described Adderley's delivery as 'masterly . . . as able a courtroom speech as I have ever heard.'

So that they should not come as dramatic revelations to the jury, Adderley conceded from the start two points in the defence's favour. The first was that the Crown could not prove conclusively what liquid had been used to set the bedroom alight. The second, and more significant, was that a police officer, Captain Sears, had come forward to say that at about midnight on the night of the murder he had seen Harold Christie being driven in a car through the centre of Nassau. Christie, of course, had stated that he had been asleep at Westbourne all the time.

The accuracy of Sears's identification was clearly going to be of great importance, but Adderley swiftly moved on to the opportunity that de Marigny had had to kill Oakes – his admission to being near the house after his party – and the evidence that supported the police's assertion that he was culpable. There were the burnt hairs, the absence of his shirt, the conversations with Lt Douglas that hinted at too much knowledge. Then there was his fingerprint – 'without doubt the only absolute and infallible method of identification.'

'The criminal's hand,' Adderley pronounced, 'is his greatest enemy.' In a corner of the courtroom, covered with a sheet, stood the Chinese screen, a mute witness waiting to reveal its secrets.

There were, said the barrister, fourteen separate pieces of evidence that each pointed to de Marigny's guilt, and he listed them. Some were only circumstantial, but at issue was whether they could be twined together to make a noose for the Count's neck. 'Return a verdict of guilty without fear or favour,' he concluded, 'knowing that you will be doing the thing which will satisfy your God, your conscience and the demands of British Justice.'

And with that uplifting admonition ringing in its ears, the court was adjourned and the jury taken on a tour of Westbourne.

★

The first witness called the next morning was the housemaid Mabel Ellis. She revealed three new points of interest. First, she had only worked at Westbourne for a few weeks, although she had been employed there previously when it had been rented to one of the managers of Pleasantville, the American firm building the air-base. Secondly, she had dusted the screen on 7 July, the day of the murder, so any prints on it would almost certainly be new, and thirdly she was sure that when she had left that evening at ten-fifteen, while the dinner party was still in progress, Mr Christie's car had been parked at the front of the house. The importance of this became clear once Christie himself took the stand.

The trial would illustrate very clearly the hothouse nature of Nassau society. Those on both sides knew each other very well and were bound by ties both professional and personal. Higgs and Adderley were senior politicians, Christie and de Marigny were on good terms, Higgs and Christie both sat on the Duke's Executive Council with Hallinan. Nonetheless, for Higgs nothing was more important than his duty to his client, especially since he was now convinced of his innocence. His three principal targets in court would inevitably be Barker, Melchen and Christie, the last person to have seen Oakes alive. Accordingly it was against Christie's version of that night's events that Higgs now directed all his forensic skill.

From the moment he entered the box, Christie – the confi-dent, persuasive salesman – seemed a tired and uncertain man, very different from the almost unshakeable witness he had been in the lower tribunal. A large crowd had gathered on the lawn out-side the court, and through the open windows came to them the sound of Higgs on the attack.

Having made the customary feints of the advocate – a few questions about times and places to establish that Christie's memory might not be faultless – Higgs began to thrust repeatedly at one spot, sometimes drifting into another line of questioning only to again press home his assault. The focus of his questions was the car that Christie had asked his driver, Gibson, to bring down to Westbourne.

Christie claimed that he had told Gibson to park it several hundred feet away from the house, near the Country Club. Mabel Ellis, of course, had said that when she left the vehicle had been outside the front door, as it had been the night before when Christie had stayed there. Christie said she was mistaken. He had instructed Gibson to conceal the car, a station wagon, because he feared that after dinner the guests might want lifts into town. Since petrol was rationed and he and Oakes might have needed to use the car the following morning to tour the farm, he had wanted to keep it out of sight.

Higgs's questions began to make Christie visibly nervous, and he started to sweat, dabbing at his forehead with a handkerchief. No, he insisted, it had been a spontaneous decision to telephone Gibson, as he had not been planning to stay the night at Westbourne, had not even been planning to eat there before Oakes suggested it. De Marigny, he went on, was lying if he said that Christie had turned down an invitation to his supper party on the grounds that he would be dining with Oakes. Thus far, Christie had kept his end up, but Higgs's scheme of insinuation was becoming only too clear to him; Higgs meant to divert the spotlight from de Marigny's movements that night to Christie's own.

Higgs could not openly accuse Christie of knowing more about the murder than he was saying – it was not Christie who was on trial – but he hoped to suggest to the jury by his line of questioning that Christie had had the car brought down because he wanted to use it later that night to go somewhere in secret, and he had erred by letting Mabel Ellis see it. Finally, towards the end of the afternoon, Higgs put the question directly to Christie. Had he left Westbourne that night? Christie denied that he had.

Yet Sears – who had known Christie since boyhood – had seen him in a car in the centre of town?

'If Captain Sears said he saw me out that night, I would say that he was very seriously mistaken, and should be more careful in his observations.' To Christie's relief, shortly afterwards the court adjourned for the day.

The next morning, Higgs concentrated on another area of Christie's testimony: his behaviour on finding his friend's body. He had given a very detailed description of this, but some of his actions certainly appeared odd. Why, for instance, had he gone back into his own room after his gruesome discovery to check if there was anyone hiding there, or if there were any signs of fire? Was it really the 'logical thing' to do, as he claimed, if he had just come from sleeping there?

Then there was Christie's statement that he had believed Oakes was still alive when he first saw him. Higgs picked up a photograph of the corpse lying burned and bloody in the bed, and showed it to the jury.

'Does this,' he said witheringly, 'look like someone who is alive?' Then Higgs tried a different tack. Christie had said that he had found Oakes on his back, and had cleaned his face with a wet towel. Higgs pointed to the picture of the baronet's face, spattered with blood, his hair thick with gore. He asked Christie if this was a face that had been wiped. Christie maintained that it was, but his replies were coming louder and louder now, and there were pauses between them (Gardner even began timing them).

If he had expected some signs of friendship from Higgs, he was receiving none, and his tension was palpable. Higgs pressed him. Had he wiped the face? If so, which side of the towel had he used? 'For God's sake, Higgs' – it burst from Christie almost as a scream – 'be reasonable!'

Patiently, methodically, Higgs circled his quarry. Now he pointed to a narrow line of blood that ran over Oakes's cheek and across the bridge of his nose. Had not Christie said that he had found him on his back? If that was true, how could that blood have flowed upwards, against gravity, from the colossal wound by Oakes's ear? The implication was evident, and startling. Someone had moved Oakes's body after he had been killed. But who, and why? And had Christie really found him where he claimed?

Higgs had one more blow to deliver. Christie had said that he had still been wearing his pyjamas when he went into Oakes's room at about seven o'clock. Yet if he really was expecting to go out early with Oakes to the farm, why had he not bothered to dress?

The suggestion hung in the air like a scimitar above Christie's head: did he already know that no one would be going anywhere that morning? There was a silence, a long silence which Gardner timed at thirty-seven seconds. Finally he mumbled something about them not having planned to go out until ten a.m.

Christie's hesitation must have impressed itself on the jury. A confused, even grieving friend was one thing but, as Gardner agreed in his column the next day, Christie's evidence had not seemed wholly convincing.

Yet the curious thing was that Higgs's last question was what barristers call a 'bad point', a superficially promising but mistaken line of thinking. Christie actually had the perfect defence against it, because he was telling the truth. He and Oakes really had not planned to leave until mid-morning, and so he could have dressed later. Dupuch had even telephoned at breakfast time to confirm the appointment for later on. But like a batsman worn down by too many fast deliveries, it was the poorly bowled long hop that had found Christie out and made him lose his head.

In the days afterwards, it was put about that Christie's evasions had been forced on him by an ulterior motive, but an honourable one: he had been shielding a woman. That woman, it was fairly common knowledge, was my grandmother's friend Effie Heneage.

A long-legged beauty, who had danced on the stage (and been a lion tamer's assistant), Effie thought she had made a great match when she married her stage-door Johnnie, who had a castle in Scotland and a house near Ascot large enough to be requisitioned by the US forces. But she discovered on honeymoon that Heneage drank – he would be dead before he was forty – and the war gave Effie the excuse to take the girls and leave him behind. In Nassau, she had become Christie's mistress.

She had come down to Westbourne that evening to watch the

tennis and have a drink with Oakes and Christie – they had had Tom Collinses, a mixture of gin and sour and soda that was the cocktail of the moment – and had stayed for dinner.

Naturally, Effie had gone home afterwards, but Christie, it was said, had arranged to come over later, and it was for this that he needed his car brought from town. Following the murder, he faced an invidious choice: confess where he had really been, which would give him an alibi but would also expose Effie and her children to shame – or protect her even at the cost of bringing suspicion on himself. As a gentleman, he had taken the latter course.

If this version of events were true, it would explain much, such as Christie's concealment of the car, his not having heard the noises of Oakes being murdered, his searching his own bedroom for intruders and, it was said, the sighting by Sears. The question was whether it had been Christie's only reason for being out that night, or whether he had had some other pressing motive for leaving Westbourne.

Christie had spent less than a day on the stand, and had only been cross-examined by Higgs for two and a half hours spread across two sessions. By comparison with what was to follow, it was not long, but it had almost broken him. Sagging at the waist, gripping the rail for support, he was asked a final question before he stepped down. It came from the jury. Had the electric fan been on in the room when he entered, and had it been scattering the feathers found on the bed?

Christie's answer was straightforward enough. It had been on, but no feathers were being blown about. It was a reply that should have put paid to one of the more persistent, and lurid, theories attached to the case.

At the time it was bandied about, and it has since been suggested by several other writers, that Oakes's murder was either a ritual killing – perhaps by some voodoo priest with whose wife Oakes had been fooling – or was intended by the assassin to be taken as such. The evidence was the presence of the feathers on

Oakes's torso and nowhere else in the room. Since they had not been consumed by the fire, it is argued, they must have deliberately been added afterwards. Indeed, they had adhered to the fluids seeping from the corpse and had had to be hosed off.

The real explanation, however, is that the feathers had come from one of the pillows whose outer covering had finally burned away in the heat of the flames, as commonly happens in house fires. Evidence that one of the pillows was damaged was given later. The breeze from the fan, as Christie testified, was not strong enough to distribute them and so they settled where they fell, perhaps protected from the heat below by Oakes's body; it seems likely, as Higgs intimated, that he had been turned over at least once.

More pertinently still, if the feathers had been scattered as a warning that would suggest that the murderer wanted the cadaver to be found, and had waited around until the flames had died down before adding his finishing touch. Yet the spraying of inflammable liquid around the room – on the cupboards and carpets by the door – would seem to point to an attempt to destroy the house by fire, not to a plan to have the body discovered. Christie's testimony should have persuaded the press to renounce the voodoo theory, but that was not their style. Sensation at short notice was their speciality.

SIX

Pray, leader, pray,
Why don't you pray?
Oh! The pretty bright star shall be your guide,
Turn back an' pray

Higgs had won a small victory by his dazzling of Christie, but bucked as Nancy and de Marigny were, he and Callender knew that more important battles were to come. However, before they got to Melchen and Barker – and to de Marigny's own evidence – there were a large number of other people to deal with. It is human nature to be the more convinced of someone's guilt the more witnesses there are, so for now their prime task was to prove to the jury that all the evidence that they were hearing was circumstantial. It did not tie de Marigny to the scene: only the fingerprint could do that.

The appearance of Madeline Gale Kelly on the stand was Callender's first opportunity to show his ability. Newell Kelly's wife was American, and had originally come out to Nassau to work as a singer at the British Colonial. She had then taken up interior design. Among her commissions had been the decoration of the hotel, a task in which Nancy had helped, but Mrs Kelly had been in fading health for some time. Just stepping from her car at Oakes's funeral she had broken a bone in her foot.

The Kellys had a cottage right inside the entrance to Westbourne. Her husband, Madeline Kelly said in her evidence, had left Nassau on a fishing trip the day before the murder, but she had her mother living with her. During the night of 7 July, she had got up three times to close the windows and to check that the back door was locked: the gathering storm had clearly made her nervous. The next morning, after seeing Oakes's body, she had observed de Marigny's arrival at the house. Even before going in he had asked for a glass of water and said he was going to be sick, behaviour that struck her as theatrical.

Callender was unable to shake her from this, for Madeline Kelly denied that de Marigny had asked for the water *after* hearing the details of the murder (he had not been allowed by Pemberton to go up to the room itself). Yet her cross-examination did yield one point in the defence's favour. As soon as she saw Oakes, she said, she knew he was dead. Christie's evidence was undermined still further.

It was then the turn of two guests at Oakes's dinner, Charles Hubbard, the owner of the cottages near Westbourne, and Effie Heneage herself. They both corroborated Christie's testimony, saying that it was only after the meal that they had discovered he would be staying the night, and accordingly it was Hubbard who had taken Effie home. Given the whispers already circulating, Higgs probably did not feel the need to ask Effie again, as he had in the Magistrates Court, whether she had seen anyone later that evening – besides her children's nanny. After leaving court, she went straight home and lay down, shattered. For some reason, Christie had been behaving most unpleasantly to her in the last few weeks. She had tried to keep the trial from the children, but her eldest daughter Lynn, who was then nine, remembers sneaking into the kitchen to read the newspapers with the servants.

By now, halfway through its first week, the trial had eased into a routine. The barristers had become familiar figures to the jury as they took it in turns to lead the witnesses through their evidence or to cross-examine them, giving their partner an opportunity to refresh his memory about the next to come (or, in Adderley's case, perhaps to reflect on the latest horse-racing results). The dominant figure in court, however, was Daly. Quaint as may have seemed his use of a pen and inkstand and a thick, suede-bound ledger to record the evidence, he was an alert umpire.

If one of the lawyers tried something that he considered unfair, Daly was quick to intervene, and he had no qualms about taking his time to clear up a point he had not grasped, even to the extent of questioning someone himself. One witness used the word 'expeditious', and Hallinan suggested that he meant to say 'expedient', only to receive a blank look from him.

'Do you mean speedy or desirable?' Daly asked.

'Speedy,' the witness replied.

'Then he does mean expeditious,' Daly informed Hallinen. Daly cut a dignified but avuncular figure in his tortoiseshell glasses, yet he knew, too, where to draw the line. When the jury, who were sequestered in a hotel and guarded to make sure that they talked to no outsiders, asked to have a barber sent in, Daly refused, saying that he himself had taken the precaution of getting his hair cut the day before the trial. The jurors would have to do their best to give each other a trim.

At noon every day a siren sounded outside. Daly rose, allowing the spectators a short break to attend the wartime prayer service on the green. Row after row of hats and scarves filed out: women had to have their heads covered in court. When they returned, woe betide any interlopers who had taken the opportunity to occupy their places on the benches.

The next to give evidence were the two doctors, Quackenbush and Fitzmaurice. They described again the horrific burns that Oakes had suffered, particularly to his left side; presumably that was where most of the inflammable liquid had been sprayed, and it is worth noting that it was not more evenly distributed. Both concluded that he had been struck in his bed before being set alight while unconscious but not yet dead.

Oakes had been killed, according to Fitzmaurice, by a combination of shock, haemorrhaging of the brain, and a fractured skull. He believed that the body had not been moved, while Quackenbush thought that the line of blood suggested that it had. Perhaps of more interest was something that Hubbard had said. He and Quackenbush had entered the room together, and on seeing Oakes's head the doctor had remarked that the wound might be self-inflicted. When taken through his evidence by Hallinan, he accepted that it was impossible for four such wounds to be caused by suicide, and indeed it was not a theory explored by the police. But it was one to which Quackenbush himself would later return.

That night, the jurors went to see a film – *Above Suspicion*, with Joan Crawford, which was doubtless thought highly suitable. One of their number, however, demurred. Jerome Bethel objected to movies on religious grounds, so because the jury were compelled to stay together like a wise monkey he sat through the whole showing with his hands over his eyes.

Dorothy Clarke had changed her tune. In the Magistrates Court, de Marigny's petite, black-haired dinner invitee had testified only about the time at which her host had dropped her and Jean Ainsley home in the early hours of Thursday. Now, under cross-examination from Higgs, she had something to add. On the Friday morning, she and Ainsley had been summoned to Westbourne. At some time between eleven a.m. and midday she had seen de Marigny going upstairs with one of the American detectives. About forty-five minutes later, she had heard Betty Roberts ask the Count if he had been sleeping. 'No,' came the reply, 'I've been upstairs with Captain Melchen.'

Suddenly, the defence's principal triumph in the lower court – the contradiction by Douglas of Melchen's testimony – had convincing corroboration. De Marigny was being offered an avenue of escape, that he had touched the screen in the hallway before Barker had finished working at one p.m., and Hallinan wanted to know why. Clarke was a prosecution witness, and yet he had heard nothing of this before. Had she been in touch with the defence behind his back?

Clarke admitted that she had. She had heard around town what Melchen had said in court about the time of the interview, and she had gone to see Higgs. Neither he nor she had told the prosecution. Higgs, it seems, fuming at the Crown's delaying tactics beforehand, had decided to play dirty. Daly agreed with Hallinan that it would have been better if he had been informed, but Higgs was not obliged to do so. His behaviour was bad form, but it was entirely legitimate

Now Hallinan had a problem to ponder. He was due to call Ainsley soon, but could he risk putting her on the stand? His technical problem was that since she was his witness, unless he was given special permission by Daly he would not be allowed to ask her any questions querying her evidence – that was Higgs's job, in theory. Her testimony helped to place de Marigny near Westbourne, yet if he called her she might recant as her friend had done, say something damaging, and he would be unable to do much about it.

While the Attorney-General was thinking furiously, Adderley began what seemed to be the simple enough task of leading Constable Parker's evidence-in-chief. At the first hearings, Parker had said that early on the morning of Thursday 8 July, de Marigny had come into the police station to ask about a licence for his truck, and that he, Parker, had been struck by his wild demeanour and bulging lips.

When Callender came to cross-examine Parker, he decided to employ one of the oldest weapons in the barrister's arsenal.

'You would agree, wouldn't you, Constable, that it's one of your duties to be observant?'

The incautious Parker duly assented.

'And would you say that you know my learned friend, Mr Higgs, well by sight?'

The policeman vouched that he did, and at this Higgs, in a manoeuvre that was clearly pre-arranged, covered his eyes.

'So, Constable, you say you know Mr Higgs, and that you are observant. Can you please tell the court what colour his eyes are?'

It was a low trick, and not one that Parker could counter. If he answered correctly, it did not prove that he was telling the truth about de Marigny. If he got it wrong, it would inevitably diminish his credibility as a witness.

Parker gambled. 'They are blue.'

Higgs took his hand away. His eyes were hazel.

As a ploy, it was revealing of Callender's skill in criminal advocacy. It was a question that sounded as if it should be easy for an observant person to answer. But in practice the colour of an acquaintance's eyes is not something that most men (unlike most women) will remember.

The bespectacled Leonard Huggins, born in Trinidad but of Chinese descent, had replaced Dr Oberwarth as the medical officer at the prison. He had also examined the contents of Oakes's stomach and, he now told the court, he had found no trace of any of the common poisons. More importantly for the defence, when quizzed by Higgs he backed up what Oberwarth had said earlier. Six days after the murder, Huggins too had examined de Marigny's arms for burnt hairs, and had seen no sign of them, although he conceded to Hallinan when questioned that his inspection had been with the naked eye, not with a microscope as best practice prescribed.

Then it was Jean Ainsley's turn to enter the box. As she did so, Hallinan announced that he would not call her evidence. In effect, she had become a witness for the defence. He would be able to attack the answers she now gave to Higgs, but he would be limited only to what she mentioned.

Ainsley began by repeating how she and Clarke had met de Marigny for the first time at the Prince George Hotel on 6 July. He had invited them to dinner the next evening (their husbands being away on duty), and there she had noticed him trying to light a rather short candle. 'I may burn myself,' he had said. The next morning, she too recalled him going upstairs with someone at about eleven a.m. And yes, she had told the prosecution about the candle, but they had not raised the subject when she gave evidence in the lower court.

Faced with all this, Hallinan decided merely to get Ainsley to confirm de Marigny's presence near Westbourne. No doubt he hoped that the two women's obvious partisanship for de Marigny would lead the jury to discount their evidence, and he quickly brought on the next witness.

The foreign press sat up when Herbert Pemberton's name was called. The weather made people feel drowsy, and the mosquitoes were still biting. 'Do something about those blighters,' Daly had told a court official. 'They're swarming under my desk.' Yet Pemberton's testimony was going to be interesting. In particular, wondered the reporters, would he repeat his bumbling perform-ance of August? They readied their pens.

Hallinan's chief concern was to rectify the impression of incom-petence that Pemberton had given last time. Thus, once the police officer had described again the scene in the room – the orderly bedside table contrasting vividly with the signs of conflagration – the Attorney-General moved to deal with the bloodstained towels that Pemberton had mislaid. Pemberton said that he had never had any intention of hiding them. He had simply been tired when he gave evidence, had forgotten about them, and in truth had not considered them important, presumably because he thought they had been bloodied after the murder when Christie had used them to wipe Oakes's face and his own hands.

When Higgs began his cross-examination, he immediately attempted to re-establish his influence over Pemberton. At bottom, he knew perfectly well that the issue of Pemberton's competence was a side matter, as were the towels, and that all that really counted was the evidence of Barker and Melchen. Yet it was a chance to damage the prosecution's standing in the eyes of the jury, and accordingly he seized it.

'Would you please tell us,' said Higgs mildly, 'when you first saw the alleged fingerprint of the accused on the screen?'

'Captain Barker did not show it to me,' replied Pemberton.

Higgs feigned surprise. 'Excuse me. Can you repeat that? Is it correct that you never in fact saw the print *in situ*?'

'Yes, I never saw the fingerprint on the screen.'

'Not even when you and Captain Barker went to the RAF base together to develop the photographs?'

'No.'

'I see,' said Higgs. 'Most interesting.'

Next, he returned to an earlier theme. He asked Pemberton if he had noticed the state of Christie's bed. Did it appear to have been slept in? Pemberton said that it seemed to him very little ruffled, although he could see that someone had lain there as there was an indentation on the pillow.

Finally, Higgs delivered a few more kicks at the Major's reputation. The strange waist-high marks on the walls of the room, Pemberton confessed, had never been analysed, and perhaps a dozen people had traipsed in and out, contaminating the scene. Then, when he had searched de Marigny's chicken farm and dug up its lavatory – looking for the murder weapon – he had done so without a search warrant. Equally, when he had gone to Victoria Avenue to take away de Marigny's typewriter for some checks, he had not got permission from the defence, and furthermore he had then taken the candlesticks without consent either. In short, he had made a pig's ear of his responsibilities. Whatever criticisms might later be made of the Duke's decision to call in the Americans, he had judged correctly that the local police lacked the experience for such a case.

A month before Oakes's murder, the MI5 officer in Nassau, Major Nash, had reported to London that the local police force was too small, and had too few white officers, to carry out all its duties properly. The service's Director-General, Sir David Petrie, an old India hand, had concurred ruefully ('You know how things are in the West Indies') and had passed Nash's letter on to the Colonial Office. There, one official had mused about whether Nassau's CID – Pemberton's department – was up to scratch: 'If it [Nassau] has one, of which I am not absolutely sure, it must be primitive in the extreme.'

Now those apprehensions had been confirmed. To cap matters, Pemberton admitted to Hallinan in court that the department's only fingerprint camera had been out of commission at the time of the investigation, hampering Barker's attempts to take photographs. He said, too, that the Americans had not asked him to examine under a microscope the burnt hairs found on de Marigny. Only Erskine-Lindop had done that. And he, of course, was now at the other end of the Caribbean, in Trinidad, and would not be called as a witness. With that thought in mind, the court adjourned for the day.

Before it met again the following morning, Saturday 23 October, Nassau started to absorb a new scandal: Harold Christie was a fugitive from American justice, and had been for twenty years. His past had finally caught up with him.

In 1923, the newspapers reported, Christie had been charged with illegally transferring a schooner from the American to the British registry of ships, in order to make it easier to smuggle alcohol into the States. He had been indicted in Boston, but had fled and was still wanted by the authorities.

Even if Christie's days as a rum-runner were known about by the older residents of Nassau, and remembered with a wink and a tot, this was still a sensational story, and for once much of it was true. The FBI's files show that in the early 1920s Christie was regarded as a major player in the battle of the bottles and was one of the Bureau's main targets.

'Christie is one of the big guns in the rum-running game,' wrote one agent to Hoover. 'It would be a big thing for Prohibition to land him.' He was leading a Pimpernel-like existence, frequently visiting the States in disguise or under an alias, and though snares were laid for him he eluded them all. Considerable effort – the files are several hundred pages thick – went into trying to catch him, and a certain amount of time was even spent trying to identify if he had black blood.

An Agent Browne added his ha'p'orth of wisdom: if Christie had crinkly hair and prominent lips – a 'characteristic of the Negro race' – it could be accounted for, as in black people, by the 'excessive heat and sunshine' which prevailed in the Bahamas. Browne also noted that Christie closely resembled his brother Percy and should not be mistaken for him. The Bureau, in fact, had already confused the two: the photograph of Harold Christie in their files is actually of Percy. Perhaps not surprisingly, they failed to catch Christie, and in desperation pinned the boat charge on him.

Good gossip though it was, it had a tame ending. It soon emerged that the case had been dropped in 1928 because it was a non-extraditable offence – and besides, the war against alcohol had by then been lost. Christie had agreed to pay a small fine the following year, and that had been that.

What is more interesting is why this had all surfaced now, during the trial. It was, of course, not a coincidence. In a letter dated 23 October from one of Hoover's assistants, D. M. Ladd, to the Director he reports that the day before he had had a visit from Paul Zahl and a Dan Vaccarelli. They had told him that there was an indictment outstanding against Christie, and had asked if the Bureau would therefore take steps to arrest him. Ladd was quickly able to tell them that the warrant had lapsed, but nonetheless the story was leaked to the press, who were only given the more exciting half of its history.

Although Ladd seems to have been unaware of it, Vaccarelli was actually a former agent of the Bureau, and more pertinently he had worked on the case against Christie in the 1920s. Doubtless he had made contact with Zahl or Schindler to tell them of the warrant once he had seen Christie's name in the papers.

In the weeks and years that followed her father's murder, Nancy Oakes repeatedly and publicly dismissed allegations that Christie knew more than he was telling about that night's events. Indeed, she once told me: 'Harold Christie had nothing to do with my father's death.' Yet the truth is that from the start she suspected him, and so set Zahl on his trail. Hence the visit to the Bureau, and hence the decision to use the press to damage Christie's public image.

★

Not surprisingly, more attention was paid by Nassau to this revelation of Christie's criminal record than to another, less prominent
item of news. A couple of days before, the House Military Affairs
Committee – one of Congress's standing supervisory bodies – had
filed in Washington its report into the building of the new airfield
at Nassau. Its findings made salutary reading. It had discovered
widespread corruption and inefficiency at the project, with backhanders and pilfering a daily occurrence. Free haircuts, for
example, were being given by three barbers who were on salaries
of $175 per week (now worth one thousand pounds); they were
subsequently fired, and rehired at ten dollars a week. And the
British Colonial Hotel, which had been leased from Oakes by
Pleasantville, the contractor, as accommodation for its employees,
was somehow being operated at a loss of seven hundred thousand
dollars (now worth four million pounds) a year, all of which had
been charged to, and paid by, the United States government.

John Douglas had been the defence's principal asset at the prelimi-
nary hearing. Now he calmly repeated what he had said there, that
de Marigny had gone upstairs with Melchen at about noon. It was
all the more galling for Adderley that, as Douglas was the prosecution's witness, it was he, Adderley, who had to elicit this evidence.
He did have the satisfaction of hearing Douglas recount again de
Marigny's conversation in which he had said that Oakes 'should have
been killed anyhow'. But it was the contradiction of Melchen that
was the more important statement, and the jury would have been
impressed by the even-handedness of Douglas's testimony. It helped
both sides, and thus could be trusted. If de Marigny were to be
acquitted, he would owe much to Douglas's memory, and honesty.

The next day, Christie began a damage-limitation operation. In
an interview with Jeanne Bellamy of the *Miami Herald*, he said he
felt that he was being deliberately 'smeared' by gossip. He said that
rumours that he had been protecting a woman when he gave evidence were unfounded, and feared that the fallout from the case
would hurt his ability to promote the Bahamas abroad.

'You may as well bury me as take my life's work away from me. Nassau is my hobby and livelihood.' Christie tried, too, subtly to quell any idea that he might have been involved in Oakes's death. 'In addition to being one of my best friends, he was also my best client,' he told Bellamy. 'He purchased more property from me than any other six persons.' If money was all that was at stake, certainly he had no reason to kill Oakes.

There was no reason either, thought Jerome Bethel, for the jury to spend the day having a beach party. It was a Sunday, the Lord's Day. Yet since the jurors had to stay together, rather than deprive them of their low-minded fun he went with them, and spent the afternoon under a palm tree, reading his Bible.

So far, lively as the trial had been, the struggle between the two sides had been no more than a series of skirmishes. When, on the Monday morning, the Crown called Edward Melchen, the defence prepared itself for full-scale warfare.

Melchen, Adderley knew, had appeared in courts in America scores of times, but for all his robust, jowly bonhomie the additional formality of a British court, with its bewigged barristers and deference to 'Your Honour', might fluster him. Then, too, Melchen might not be prepared for the latitude which a British judge would give counsel in cross-examination, rather more than was then customary in the States. Adderley would have to deal with the timing of de Marigny's interview upstairs, but before he got to that he wanted to settle his witness and establish him in the jury's mind as an authoritative, professional expert. He began by asking him about his search of Westbourne.

Melchen said that after arriving at the house he had looked for footprints and tyre marks, but there had been too many people going in and out and he had seen none. The room itself showed signs of fire, especially to the north side of the bed and the left side of the body, facing the sea. Though he did not say so, perhaps he concluded that the killer had come up the stairs from the beach. It was possible, too, that the murderer had left this way, as there was blood on the inside and outside handles of that door, although that might have been left later by Christie.

From the evidence, he believed that there had been two seats of the fire, the bed itself and near the cupboard by the door into the hallway, where some liquid with a petroleum base had been thrown. The scorching had been caused by gases rising from the fire. He could replicate the blaze, he said, with half a gallon of gasoline, kerosene or Fly-Ded, the insect repellent.

A flit gun containing this had been found in the room, and the maid had said that it should have been about half full, whereas in fact it was only about a quarter so. In court, Melchen admitted that, though he had once favoured Fly-Ded, he did not know what liquid had been used to start the fire, but there was speculation at the time – and since – that the sprayer had been turned into some kind of blowtorch. Again, this theory ignores all the facts.

Aside from needing to be pumped continually, which would hardly have made it a convenient source of flame, it was missing less than half a pint, when Melchen estimated that eight times that amount of fluid had been used. Probably Oakes had sprayed the room after Mabel had gone, and Melchen had used it for tests too. Moreover, any such improvised use of the flit gun would suggest that the burning of the room was a decision made on the spur of the moment whereas, as will become clear, that was not the case.

Melchen and Barker had done some experiments with different inflammable liquids – Barker had burned his hands when testing gasoline – and had found that the shade of the lamp by Oakes's bed was flame-resistant, which was perhaps why the fire had not taken there. Melchen had noticed three pillows on the bed, among them one almost clean which Christie had put under Oakes's head and another which had burned and burst – the source of the feathers. He had also examined Oakes's face. He never saw the eyeballs, but the eyes were closed. Schindler would later claim that a flame had been deliberately played over the lids, adding heat to the voodoo rumours, but Melchen would have seen and mentioned any such scorching.

Continuing his evidence, Melchen said that when de Marigny had been examined by him and Barker for burnt hairs on the Thursday evening, Erskine-Lindop had also looked at the hairs concerned through the microscope. He had then asked the Count to account for his movements the night before, and he had claimed that after dropping his guests off he had returned home at about 1.45 a.m. This much had become well known, but now Melchen revealed something else that was to be central to the trial.

After going to bed, de Marigny had told him, he had heard de Visdelou leaving his apartment on the other side of the house at about 2.30 a.m. He had heard the Chevrolet truck start: Georges was taking Betty home to her mother's. The Marquis had returned half an hour later and de Marigny had called to Georges to come into the room and take his cat away because it was making too much noise. He had done so, and they had spoken briefly.

'The cat that miaowed too much' – it was a gift of a title for Erle Stanley Gardner. De Marigny's full alibi was now revealed for the first time. Fitzmaurice's post-mortem had placed the murder at some time between 1.30 and 3.30 a.m. Yet here was de Marigny home at 1.45 a.m., there at 2.30 a.m. when his friend went out, and seen at 3.00 a.m. by de Visdelou when the cat was acting up. To drive fifteen minutes from his house to Westbourne, check that he was unobserved, steal into the bedroom, kill Oakes, set the place on fire and then drive home – it was the work of an hour at least. He would not have had the time to do it, if he was telling the truth.

So far, Melchen had performed solidly on the stand. Now Adderley came to the crunch. At what time the following day had he taken de Marigny upstairs to talk to him? At noon, admitted Melchen. In the Magistrates Court he had said it was between three and four p.m., but now he thought it was nearer noon. It was a reverse for the prosecution, but they recovered a little ground with what de Marigny had then told Melchen in the bedroom: Oakes was very bitter about the Count's marriage to Nancy, would not listen to reason, and consequently he had come to hate the 'stupid old fool'.

Adderley had done a good job, and now he and Hallinan crossed their fingers that Callender would not be able to land any telling blows. Still, the sticky point about the interview would no longer come as a surprise to the jury, and otherwise Melchen was bearing up well.

When Ernest Callender got to his feet, his heart would have been racing. His experience might have enabled him to appear calm enough, but this was the most important test he had faced in his young career, and he had been preparing for it for weeks.

His strategy had to be to discredit Melchen as a truthful witness, to chip away at any support he could give to Barker's evidence. His plan was to conduct a detailed comparison of what Melchen had said in the two courts, highlighting discrepancies so as to make the jury doubt his word and showing what he had failed to investigate, thus undermining his standing as a professional.

Yet as the hours wore on, Callender was failing to make much headway. He put his suggestions to Melchen, but the officer batted them away in a reasonable manner. Yes, this might have happened that way, he could not say for sure, probably it was not important. Callender extracted one or two points of interest: Melchen had only examined de Marigny's arms in three or four places, he thought that the marks on the walls did look like handprints, and he had heard about but not seen a green thread found on the screen (de Marigny had been wearing brown at dinner) – but these were all Barker's department, and so he had left them to him. Worse for the defence, he thought that Christie's bed had been slept in.

Daly told Callender several times to stop wasting the court's time over minor differences in the witness's evidence, and Hallinan relaxed a little. The only moment when Melchen appeared flustered was when he returned to court after the lunch break: he had narrowly avoided being run over by a fire engine.

★

It was an innocuous question that got him.

'Captain Melchen, when did you learn that the print on the screen belonged to de Marigny?'

For the first time, the American looked discomposed. 'Well,' he said, 'I knew on 9 July [the day of the arrest] that a fingerprint was being photographed.'

Callender sensed an evasion. 'And you were told it was de Marigny's?'

Melchen seemed uneasy. His pudgy hands squeezed the brass rail of the witness box.

'No.'

'No? When exactly were you told?'

Melchen gave up the struggle. 'I didn't know whose print it was until 19 or 20 July.'

Callender's heart must have almost stopped with surprise. He asked the detective to repeat what he had said.

'When the accused was arrested on 9 July, I did not know that his fingerprint had been found on the screen.'

Callender had no idea where this was going – it had never come up in evidence before – but he pursued it like a huntsman who has seen a fox break cover. Given his line of questioning, which soon brought him to what the detectives had said to Lady Oakes at the funeral, he might have taken his cue from something that Nancy had observed, but even so he could not have expected the torrent of revelation that now burst from Melchen.

'So when de Marigny was arrested for the murder,' reiterated Callender, 'you were not aware of the main clue to his alleged guilt? When, then, did you know of this piece of evidence?'

Melchen looked yet more ill at ease: he believed that it had been on 15 July, the day of the funeral, when Barker had told Lady Oakes about it. It was not until 19 July that he knew exactly which finger it was: the little one on the left hand.

Callender played up his astonishment for all it was worth.

'Have I got this right, Captain Melchen? You mean to say that you had been working with Captain Barker since 8 July, you had gone back to Miami with him, you spent three days travelling to Maine with him, and yet he never once mentioned this most vital piece of evidence?'

'That is so.'

'Not until almost a week after the defendant was arrested?'

'No,' confirmed Melchen.

'Naturally, you discussed the case during the journey to Maine?'

'We did.'

'And in all that time Captain Barker said nothing about his finding de Marigny's mark? Isn't that rather strange?'

Melchen said nothing. The next voice he heard was that of Daly.

'Captain Melchen, you didn't answer the question. Isn't it strange that Captain Barker did not tell you about the fingerprint of the accused found on the screen?' Wearily, Melchen agreed that it was.

Now Callender had the whip hand. Turning to the detective's interview of de Marigny, he asked Melchen to explain his change of heart about its timing. Melchen replied that his memory had been at fault, and he had corrected his statement when he had been shown Douglas's notebook a few days previously. He had not been trying to prove that de Marigny was not upstairs before the print was found. It was simply a mistake.

Callender's sarcasm lashed the air.

'What a mistake! And what a coincidence that both you and the constables should make the same mistake!'

It had been Callender's day, and no mistake.

The jury had been put up in the small Rozelda Hotel, within walking distance of the courthouse. It offered self-contained flats as well as rooms, and the twelve men were divided between two of each. A pair of constables made sure that no one strayed in or out, passing the time by playing cards on the porch. One could eat out on the patio under vines, and Nancy had taken to having her lunch there until Schindler pointed out that she might be thought to be trying to influence the jury, who also ate there in a group. Now, without a husband for company, she spent most nights with the af Trolles.

Besides the jury, of an evening Melchen and Barker could be found at the hotel, often sitting together with Conway, the fingerprint expert whom Hallinan had brought from New York, and Charles O'Malley, a graphologist whose evidence had not been needed. A dozen or so of the foreign press were usually gathered around the big table in the dining room, discussing the day's events as they ate their chicken. The Rozelda was known for its chicken. It came from de Marigny's farm.

One evening, Georges de Visdelou dropped in, a rather hangdog figure without Freddie de Marigny to follow around. He had a couple of cocktails with Ray Schindler and as the gin flowed – and as the jokes became a little less amusing – a challenge was issued. De Visdelou prided himself on his ability as a dancer, and people said that he and Betty Roberts made a lovely couple on the dance floor. Now the portly Schindler – this boiled egg on legs – had the nerve to claim that he could show Betty a better time in the rumba. As the reporters crowded round, encouraging Schindler, a time was set for a showdown at the Prince George Hotel, on the waterfront.

At the appointed hour, de Visdelou and Betty took to the floor, as did Schindler and his partner. The locals looked at the mob who had turned up to watch, and turned down their mouths in icy disgust. But as the band set the tempo, those who had come to laugh at Schindler gazed at one another in surprise.

Few knew that (like the similarly stout Lew Grade) Schindler had been a champion dancer in his youth, and now he matched de Visdelou stride for elegant stride, sashay for sashay, wiggle for wiggle. At the end, the spectators burst into applause, and a show of hands was taken – a tie!

Honour was satisfied, although conservative Nassau was not. Some of the young crowd had even arrived at the hotel in shirtsleeves. 'We would no more think of walking down Bay Street without our jackets,' one resident assured the press the next morning, 'than we would without our trousers on.'

A chastened Melchen had returned to the stand. By now he had been there for more than eleven hours, most of it under cross-examination, and he had wilted visibly. Yet something, or someone, had been bolstering his will overnight. While Sir Oscar was reading back to him his record of Melchen's testimony from the day before, the detective announced that he wanted to change what he had said. He had been 'a little confused yesterday'. Daly asked if he was not used to giving evidence, and Melchen said he was, but not at such length, and he had gotten tired.

Now Melchen tried to clarify his story. He had just remembered that when Barker and Pemberton had gone to the RAF base, they had said they were going to process a print that they thought belonged to de Marigny. Yes, that was how it was, although they hadn't told him why they believed this. Then at the funeral Barker had told Lady Oakes that he was still working on a print thought to belong to de Marigny.

Daly frowned. 'That is very different from what you said yesterday. Tell me – now that you are not tired – have you talked to Barker about this since yesterday?' Melchen denied that he had: he had only spoken to Hallinan, albeit in Barker's presence.

Melchen had not really helped his cause much, and he had irritated the judge to boot. But he had one more point to add, in response to a question put to him by Daly. When he had gone upstairs with de Marigny, Corporal Knowles had been standing in the doorway of Oakes's room, just across from the screen, and Corporal Tynes had been on duty when they went back down. It was impossible that de Marigny could have touched the screen then. Of this Melchen was certain.

In his column, Gardner told his readers that Callender's inquisition of Melchen had been 'a shining example of the possibilities of cross-examination.' Yet flattened as Melchen had been,

inexplicable as was Barker's earlier silence about the print, the bal‑
ance of power in the case still lay with the prosecution.

All Melchen's confusion, all Callender's triumphs, would not
matter one jot if the jury believed that the print on the screen
belonged to de Marigny, left there by him on the night of the
murder. His fate would be decided by the duel between Higgs
and Barker.

SEVEN

Brudder for yo' soul's sake,
Come out de' wilderness,
Come out de' wilderness,
Come out de' wilderness

Jim Barker looked like heroes are meant to. He was tall, broad, handsome and fearless, and his evidence was going to nail Count de Marigny. Gardner, himself an attorney, thought him one of the most impressive witnesses he had seen in twenty years, a man 'very much at home with himself'.

Barker began by telling the court of his hurried dash to catch the noon flight to Nassau after the Duke of Windsor's call, which had mentioned only the death, and possible suicide, of a prominent citizen. The detective had hastily assembled his kit – film, camera, two microscopes – driven home and packed, and then raced the fourteen miles to the airport. The plane had been held for him.

On arriving at Westbourne, Barker had quickly assessed that the Chinese screen might be fertile ground for prints, as in a darkened room it would have presented an obstacle to any attacker approaching the bed beyond. Having decided that it was too damp to dust for fingerprints that day, he had concentrated on the fire, and having found no burnt hairs on Christie he saw them that night on de Marigny. The next morning he had resumed his search for prints, and had taken between fifty and seventy from the screen, although only a few were legible.

All had been lifted with Scotch tape, that is to say that tape had been applied to where a powdered impression had been raised on the screen and the fingerprint had then been lifted clean off and placed on white card. This method preserved the prints against evaporation, and made comparison easy. Right at the end, however, Barker had run out of tape and so had had to lift the last three with some specially prepared adhesive white rubber, similar to a tyre patch. When he had been using this, he had been working at the top of the end panel on the right-hand side of the screen.

That afternoon, looking through his haul, he had noticed an impression which looked similar to one of de Marigny's prints. The Count had been fingerprinted the previous day. Barker had gone to the RAF laboratory to enlarge it. De Marigny was arrested that evening, 9 July. Barker had returned to Miami the next day and had locked the evidence away. After he came back from Oakes's funeral, on 19 July, he had examined it again, and this time had also seen that one of the rubber lifts was that of the little finger of de Marigny's right hand. Case closed.

Hallinan asked him to clarify just one thing. In his testimony, Melchen had mentioned a print of the little finger of de Marigny's *left* hand, not the right. What was the reason for this? It was simple, said Barker. The impression that he had noticed on 9 July had been of the left hand, while that he had spotted on 19 July was of the right. He had, in fact, found two of de Marigny's fingerprints on the screen. It was just that he hadn't realised this on 9 July because the rubber lift, unlike the Scotch tape one, was opaque and thus he was in effect looking at the print in reverse. Once he had recognised it, he had seen that it was a clearer print than the other, which was why he was relying on it in court.

It all made sense. Barker's story explained everything. De Marigny's arrest had all along been on the basis of a print that

Barker had identified that second day; Melchen had just got in a muddle over there being two dabs and over which of them he had been told about. The Crown had double proof, in fact, of de Marigny's guilt. Well pleased with how things had gone, Hallinan moved formally to admit into evidence Exhibit J, the damning print.

And Higgs countered. Entirely unexpectedly, as the Attorney-General was making his request Higgs rose and asked Daly to rule the exhibit inadmissible. While listening to Barker, he had been thinking fast.

Higgs had gathered, he said, from the detective's testimony in the Magistrates Court that the photograph of the print that Hallinan proposed to submit was that of a print on the screen. Now he learned that it was not on the screen at all, but on a piece of rubber. Quoting legal textbooks, he maintained that it was normal for a print once dusted to be photographed in place, showing where and on what it had been found. Ideally, that object too would then be produced in court, and only if said object was immovable should the print actually be lifted off so that it could be exhibited. Once there was no trace of a print on the object, the defence could always allege that it had never been there in the first place. Producing a print on its own, with no supporting photograph, said Higgs, was like just producing someone's signature as proof that they had signed a particular document.

Higgs had clearly been doing his homework. But Barker's evidence had also forced on him an important change of tack. Hitherto, the defence's efforts had been concentrated on showing that de Marigny could have accidentally touched the screen when going upstairs on 9 July. Now they must deal with another possibility: that the print had never been on the screen at all, but had been taken from somewhere else.

Faced with the prospect of not being able to use his central piece of evidence, Hallinan too had been thinking quickly. There was no dispute, he said, that this was the original fingerprint. It had simply been transferred from one background to another, like an old painting put on a new canvas. The validity of the print itself remained, whatever the background. If the defence wished to allege that it had been found elsewhere, then that allegation might have some bearing on the weight that the jury should allow the print as evidence, not on whether the print itself should be admitted in the first place. It was for the jury to decide the worth of the evidence concerned and so they must be allowed to see it.

De Marigny was alert now, tense, watching Daly. The judge turned to Barker. Was he, Daly, correct in thinking that all traces of the print had been removed from the screen? He was. Then why had the detective not photographed it first?

Barker shrugged, and said that he needed a particular camera – not the one he had brought with him – for that kind of work. Hallinan helped him out, explaining that, as Barker had already said, he had had to pack in a hurry without knowing what the job might entail. But, continued Daly, could he not have telegraphed Miami and asked them to send him the camera on the next flight? Barker shrugged again, appeared a little flustered, and said he supposed that he could have done that.

Sir Oscar looked displeased. He would much rather have been out for one of his nice walks just then. Judges do not like to have to make rulings on the hoof, unguided by precedent and previous rulings, but since neither side had produced anything to show conclusively what was acceptable in such cases, he was going to have to decide for himself. The exhibit stayed in. If the jury wanted, they could discount it. Hallinan was relieved. De Marigny looked glum.

It was a setback for Higgs, but not a fatal one. He knew that he had some more shots in his locker, and he trusted to the preparation he had done. Above all, the longer he cross-examined Barker, the more he would understand his nature, and hence his weak points.

Higgs started with the last matter that Hallinan had dealt with when leading the American's evidence. When Barker had appeared in the Magistrates Court, he had marked with a blue pencil the area from where he had taken the rubber lift. It was the most heavily smoked part of the screen. Now he had told the jury that he was not prepared to say it had come from there, but he was sure that it had come from the top part of the panel. Higgs asked him to look again at the screen, and as it was shown to him something inside Barker popped.

'I wish to inform the court,' the detective declaimed dramatically, 'that the blue line I now see was not made by me. There has been an effort to trace a blue line over the black line that I made on 1 August in the presence of the Attorney-General. *That blue line is not my work.*'

Higgs goggled with astonishment. Daly stepped down from his chair, and he and Hallinan huddled round the screen. There was a silence. Then, just as abruptly, Barker retracted his statement.

'I wish to withdraw what I said about the alteration,' he said meekly. 'I find my initials where the blue line is.'

Barker had made both lines, the black and the blue, the first in early August and the second two days later in the lower court. But more importantly, Higgs had found his weakness. Barker seemed cool enough on the outside – all spruce handkerchief and slicked-back hair – but inside he was boiling: the man was a pressure cooker. Turn the heat up, and he just might explode.

Higgs could not know it, but Barker's entire career had been pock-marked by episodes of recklessness and hot-headedness. Something had been driving him on all his life: to get out of small-town Indiana, to get up after the motorcycle accident that had nearly ended his career, to get all the way to the FBI. That was his ultimate goal, and nobody was going to stop him.

By the mid-1930s Barker had a reputation for aggression and zeal – perhaps too much of both. His successes in Miami had already led the Bureau to consider him for its training course, but it had noted that he had a 'determination to do things without the benefit of advice' and that he would 'act on impulse to the exclusion of his better judgement'. When he had applied for the course, something had even impelled him to shave four years off his age on the entry form. Barker wanted badly to be noticed, and to be noticed soon.

Having established that until 1 August there had been nothing to mark the location of the fingerprint, Higgs now asked Barker why he was now not prepared to say where the print came from, when in the earlier hearing he had been so certain. Barker replied that it was because he could no longer find any traces of powder on the screen.

'And isn't that precisely why you should bring the object into court?' said Higgs coolly. It was exactly the point he had made before about the risk of lifting leaving no traces. Barker's importance to the prosecution was as an expert on fingerprints. Now his claims to expertise were being dismantled. And Higgs had not yet finished with this issue.

Why, he wanted to know, had Barker come to Nassau at the end of September? Was it not because two days earlier Pemberton had witnessed Keeler making experiments on the duplicate screen, and had realised that the print could not have come from the place marked by Barker, Area No. 5? Was that not why the Crown had sent for him?

'That is highly coincidental,' said Barker.

'It *is* highly coincidental,' Higgs riposted.

Barker stood his ground. He had only realised a few days before the trial that the print probably did not come from Area No. 5. As a result, all he was prepared to say now was that it came from somewhere in the top six inches of the panel.

Higgs appealed to Daly. The defence had understandably based its experiments on showing that the print could not have come from the marked area. Now Barker had moved the goalposts, and they needed more time to study the screen. Daly agreed they could have it if they needed it. In the meantime, Higgs returned to his relentless scrutiny of Barker's methods.

First, he examined the detective's experience of fingerprinting. There was no doubt that Barker had effected a great expansion of his department's activities, but it still came as a surprise when he admitted that he had been made its superintendent in 1930 after only five months there as a clerk. And his tenure had not been continuous. In 1939, he had been ordered back to the beat for twelve months – for insubordination.

Next, the barrister wanted to know if Barker had ever before used a lifted print as evidence. He claimed that he had.

'Could you tell me the name of just one such case?'

Barker looked as if he was making an effort at recall, then shook his head. 'I cannot.'

'Oh, come now, Captain Barker. Not one?'

Higgs was starting to enjoy himself, Barker was not. In quick succession the detective was forced to agree that he could have left the print on the screen (which, as the jury could see for themselves, was not an immovable object) and that he had not tried to find a suitable camera to photograph the print when he realised that the one he had brought with him had the wrong focal length. In short, Higgs implied, Barker had been careful to do nothing that would show where Exhibit J had been found.

With every question, the defence's thinking was becoming clear: Barker had decided that de Marigny was his man, and that he was going to find his fingerprint on the screen. Higgs now needed to show that Barker had therefore not looked anywhere else, nor at anyone else, for his culprit. He had already admitted to not examining the marks on the walls because he thought them of no value, and to having obliterated any prints on the door handles when he powdered them. Had he, however, dusted the thermos on the night table? No – he had only processed what he thought an attacker might have touched. The lampshade? Or the stair rail? For heaven's sake – the foot of Sir Harry's bed? Barker denied that it had a footboard. The photograph that Higgs passed to the jury told a different story.

How about other people who had been into the room – he

would want to eliminate their prints if he found them. Had he rolled fingerprints of Mrs Heneage? Mrs Kelly? Colonel Lindop? Mr Hallinan? Captain Melchen? Mabel Ellis? What — none of them? And what about Harold Christie, who had admitted touching a glass in the room?

'I didn't get a print,' said Barker. 'It might have been smudged.'

'And you didn't find a single print of Sir Harry's?'

'No.'

Higgs let it sink in. 'Although Sir Harry and Mr Christie had lived in the house together for days, you say you didn't find a single one of their prints?'

'No.'

Barker was toppling. Higgs had yet to land a knockout blow, but he had his opponent's measure. There was just one more thing he wanted before the court adjourned. Having asked the foreman of the jury to touch the screen, he asked Barker to demonstrate how he would lift the print. The detective did it perfectly.

Systematically, question by question, Barker was being backed into a corner, and the strain was telling. This morning, Higgs had been asking him about the burnt hairs that he, Barker, had seen on de Marigny's forearms. Barker told him that he had found signs of burning at the back of the arm by the elbow.

'Did you examine the inside of the accused's forearm?'

'I did,' said Barker authoritatively. 'But there was little, if any, hair there.'

Higgs made a valiant effort to control the joy in his voice, and invited Barker to look again at de Marigny's arms. He went over to the dock, and the Count rolled up his sleeves. Daly joined them. There was another long silence.

'On examining his arms' — the words came reluctantly from Barker's mouth — 'I'd say that he had more than the usual amount of hair on his forearms. There is hair on the inside of his forearms.'

It was a great moment for Higgs, the kind that a criminal barrister might have once or twice in a career. He had worn Barker down: the American detective had rashly overextended himself, and he had fallen headlong into a pit of his own making, destroying his credibility as an observant, truthful witness. A key piece of the detectives' evidence – their discovery of the burnt hair – was suddenly flawed. As OJ Simpson would one day demonstrate, the glove could not be made to fit.

More concessions were now wrung from Barker as Higgs asked him why he thought de Marigny's arms might have been burnt. Did Barker believe that the Count had taken off his coat, for surely any jacket or shirt would have protected those arms? And was the fact that de Marigny had not produced his shirt not in his favour – he could have given them any one, since they were all white, and they would not have been any the wiser. And speaking of producing, what had happened to the clippings of de Marigny's hair that the detectives had taken? Barker said that they had been entrusted to Melchen.

There was the noise of a chair being shoved back, and someone pushed their way through the crowd and out of the doors. Schindler silently eased his bulk after them. On the grass outside, all five and a half feet of Eddie Melchen was retching and gasping for breath.

'I'll fix him, Ray,' he raged, 'I'll fix that son of a bitch!'

Hitherto Higgs's questions had dealt mainly with Barker's presentation of the fingerprint and his methods of work; he had helpfully demonstrated on the foreman that he was quite capable of lifting a print competently if he wanted to. The time had come, felt Higgs, for an assault on the central allegation itself, namely that the Captain had found de Marigny's fingerprint where he said he had.

First, Higgs asked him if a lift would normally pick up any background irregularities as well as a fingerprint. Barker agreed that it would. Higgs pointed to the screen, and asked why, if he had found it there, none of the floral pattern that ran close to its edge showed on Exhibit J.

Barker had his answer ready: 'It was taken from a place on which there were no patterns.'

The net had been thrown over his shoulders. Now Higgs jerked it closed. 'Could you show me?' A piece of paper one inch by three was cut out and handed to Barker. It was the size of the rubber lift he had used. Moving his way around the edge of the screen he began trying ever more carefully to fit it onto the screen without touching the pattern. He tried it this way. He tried it that. The room was quiet, and too warm. Nowhere in the top six inches of the screen – the area from which he claimed the print had come – was free of the wretched scrollwork. Unless . . .

'It cannot be done,' said Barker, with one of his practised smiles. 'But I think I might have done it this way.' And he slid the front of the paper onto the screen so that half of it remained hanging over the edge.

Higgs voiced aloud what everyone was thinking. 'Wouldn't it have been much simpler to have extended it forward and lifted part of the background?'

Barker was on his back in the dust of the arena. The noise in his ears was like a far-off sea. From the emperor's box came the quietus.

'Yes, Captain Barker. What Mr Higgs wants to know is: why were you so careful to exclude any of the background?'

By the next morning, Barker had completed sixteen hours in the witness box, nine of them under cross-examination. Between them, he and Melchen had taken up all but an hour of the week in court. And Higgs was not yet done.

His questions showed the jury that he was unhappy with Barker's claim that he had not recognised the fingerprint on the white rubber lift until so late in the day. Was it likely that someone as practised as Barker would have made such an elementary error as not to realise that the print had been reversed? And the story of the second print, not produced in court. It was too pat, too convenient. The defence knew that Barker had mentioned print evidence at least three times before 19 July, when he said he had first recognised the rubber lift – in a press interview with Jeanne Bellamy, in a phone call to Nancy, and to Lady Oakes at the funeral. Having the earlier print let him off the hook.

If it existed. Higgs loaded his final salvo. 'Wasn't the accused's latent print, Exhibit J, in fact obtained from some object during his interview in the north-west bedroom at Westbourne?' It was the first open accusation that the evidence had been faked.

Barker denied it. Higgs handed him a sheet of contact prints. They were enlargements of the photograph of Exhibit J.

'Do you see those two circles on the right?' he asked. 'How do you account for those?'

Barker suggested that they might be globules of moisture, and claimed that they would not have been broken by dusting or lifting. Otherwise, he had to admit that there was nothing on the screen that seemed to correspond to the circles in the picture.

'Is that another coincidence, Captain Barker?'

'I have to believe it is.'

Higgs nerved himself. 'This is the most outstanding case in which your expert assistance has been required, is it not?'

'Well,' said Barker, grinning, 'it's developed into that.'

'And I suggest that in your desire for personal gain and notoriety you have swept away truth and fabricated evidence!' With that contemptuous dismissal, Higgs abruptly sat down.

'I,' said Barker, with some dignity, 'I emphatically deny that.'

Atop the screen, a banana bird began to twitter. Having glided in through the window, it began to pirouette daintily, nabbing an insect before hopping lightly onto the coat of arms behind Daly. From there it jumped onto the fan above the judge's head, a streak of yellow chirruping cheerfully as it swept round and round before swooping out to the blue beyond.

De Marigny seemed hardly able to contain his delight at how things were going. To his natural cockiness had been added an exuberance born of having cheated death – surely the jury wasn't going to hang him after Higgs's demolition of Barker? – and in the dock he was now the picture of animation. He waved at friends, winked at a pretty girl reporter, and whenever Exhibit J was mentioned held up his right little finger. Then, as casually as he could, he leaned back, propped his feet up on the bars and began to chew a matchstick.

Such studied cool barely disguised de Marigny's nervousness. During Barker's evidence, he had been clasping his hands in front of him, almost as if praying that the jury would see the light. For all his bravado perhaps even now he sensed that for some people it was impossible to believe that a policeman might lie. One of them was Gardner, who would later tell his readers what he thought had really happened: it was Barker who had been framed.

While the detective had been at the funeral in Maine, Gardner's theory went, someone had obtained de Marigny's print and had placed it in Barker's office, so that when he saw it there on 19 July he genuinely did think that he had found it. It would have made a good solution to one of Perry Mason's mysteries, but it fails to account for the other print that Barker said he had already recognised before heading north. The FBI had less faith than Gardner in police officers' integrity. On 28 October a number of senior agents found a memo in their in-tray, attached to a copy of a newspaper report about Higgs's cross-examination.

'We ought to see that Miami Office and we here give Melchen and Barker a wide berth in the future,' read the note. It was signed 'H'.

Frank Conway had an Irishman's skin, and it was not used to the sun. Pink-faced, his blue eyes blinking behind his spectacles, he outlined his record of seventeen years' service as a fingerprint expert with the New York Police Department. His task was to shore up Barker's evidence.

His first success, formality though it was, was to have Higgs admit that the defence would not contest the identity of the print. There was no question that it came from de Marigny; it was just its provenance that they doubted. Then Conway outlined the advantages of lifting a print. It was his own practice, he said, never to examine a fingerprint on the object itself. It might get smeared, and it was awkward to keep turning away and comparing it with those of suspects. It would be much better to work from a photograph, or if no proper camera were available, as in this case, then a lifted print was preferable to none.

The prosecution was recouping some ground, and Adderley made haste to capitalise on this. Would the pattern on the screen necessarily show on a lift? No, said Conway, not if the scrollwork itself was not powdered. Nor when a print was lifted would it always leave a mark.

It was Callender's turn to man the breach. He first got Conway to take a print from the screen, and the expert agreed that the pattern would show if there was dirt or smoke there. Then a more loaded question: had Captain Barker asked him before the trial to suggest where the print might have come from?

'I think I told him that if it came from Area 5, it would have to be from the exact spot where "5" was written.' It was precisely where Barker had tried to show that the lift could be put without touching the pattern. Callender invited him to try to fit the piece of rubber there himself

'And if it did come from that spot,' continued Callender calmly, 'wouldn't the scrollwork show?'

'I thought you were speaking about just the print. It is impossible for the lift to fit there without touching the scrollwork.'

'Then, it would have raised some of the pattern?'

Conway acknowledged his defeat. 'Yes, especially if the screen was dirty.'

Callender had one more matter to deal with, and invited Conway to look at the circles on the image of the print. By now, the tall, lean New Yorker had abandoned all pretence of being able to help Barker. He had already, he said, examined the screen two weeks before for the origin of these marks. He could not see anything which might have caused them.

That afternoon, the camera crew from Movietone News were invited to film the defence team. They recorded Schindler, Keeler and Nancy – who as a future witness had not been allowed to attend court – scrutinising photographs of the prints and making a great show of trying to fit lifts onto the screen that they had taken from the bathroom. The footage shows Nancy, in particular, glowing under the admiring eye of the lens. It was not just in court that the battle for the de Marignys' reputation could be fought.

The jury was becoming restless. Influenza had done the rounds and its effects made them miss the comforts of home. One night, when asked what they would like for supper, the answer came back: 'Six blonde hostesses.' Hallinan told them, however, that the prosecution's case was drawing to its finish.

In the Magistrates Court, Melchen's evidence about the timing of the interview with de Marigny had been backed up by Corporals Knowles and Tynes. Melchen had since been forced to change his testimony, and now the hapless policemen were obliged to follow suit.

Tynes might have looked smart in his uniform with its white coat, navy trousers and red piping, but otherwise he did not cut an impressive figure. First he told the court that he had not seen Barker go into the bedroom where de Marigny and Melchen were – the defence had hinted that the American fingerprint expert had put his head round the door to check that Melchen had got de Marigny to touch something – but then Tynes had to admit that he had been in Oakes's room all the while, and so could not see what Barker was doing. He also agreed that he had made a mistake as to the time when de Marigny had been taken upstairs.

His colleague Cleophas Knowles fared worse yet. He too confessed to his earlier error about the timing. Higgs let him know what he thought of all this – 'Another error!' And when had he realised that he had erred? He thought it had been the same day, after reading Lt Douglas's statement in the paper. Higgs pounced. Douglas had not given evidence until fully eleven days after him! What a memory!

Higgs was not to have such an easy ride with John Anderson. 'Small, chubby and common,' was how Marie af Trolle remembered him. She might have added 'devious', too. Wenner-Gren's aide had already damaged de Marigny's cause when he had previously testified that Ruth had asked him to return one hundred and thirty thousand dollars of her money. Now he revealed that less than a month before Oakes's death he had helped de Marigny draw up a financial statement in which he acknowledged that he had received some twenty-five thousand pounds (£750,000 in today's money) from her since their divorce in 1940.

De Marigny knew that he was in a bind. Moreover, Anderson continued, the Mauritian had told him that he had spent his last penny, having sold everything except for the property on Eleuthera where Ruth was actually living.

Anderson had asked him what were his prospects of inheriting Oakes's money. De Marigny had told him that the old man was rapidly drinking himself to death. Was it wishful thinking? And had the wish been the father to the thought?

Higgs protested that again the defence had been taken by surprise by this news about de Marigny's acceptance of his indebtedness to Ruth. Daly brushed it aside, but Higgs did manage to cast doubt on one part of Anderson's evidence. When being led by Hallinan, Anderson had said that while driving back into Nassau from Westbourne on the day when the body was found, de Marigny had told him he had some black market drums of gasoline at Victoria Avenue and had asked how he could get rid of them. Since gasoline might have been the fuel for the fire, the jury's ears had pricked up at this. Now Higgs suggested that the drums had in fact only been delivered that lunchtime, while Anderson was there, and moreover they had been bought by de Visdelou.

Anderson denied it. Yet there was no denying that it was he who had told the police about the gas in the first place. What is more, his implication of de Marigny in the murder in this way was not an isolated incident. It was part of a pattern.

A few days before, on the same day that he saw Zahl and Vaccarelli, Agent Ladd of the FBI had had another visitor, and he had been talking to de Marigny's defence team. This man – even now, more than sixty years later, the Bureau will not release his name – told Ladd that he understood that the FBI now knew that Christie had a criminal record in the United States, but he was not calling in connection with the Oakes murder itself.

For he was also aware, the man went on, that Christie had paid several visits to the FBI to intercede for the blacklisted Wenner-Gren. He himself, however, had come as an intermediary for someone else, namely Wenner-Gren's assistant John Anderson.

Anderson, it seemed, was a worried man. He was concerned, runs Ladd's memorandum of the meeting, 'that he might be left "holding the bag" in the wake of Wenner-Gren's troubles.' He wanted to put his role on the record. The Bureau had for some time wondered what was in the bag: now he was going to tell them.

Wenner-Gren and Christie, the man claimed, had brought the Duke of Windsor into a plot to divert illegally millions of dollars to Mexico for exploitation after the war. Anderson had tried to warn them of the risks, but had failed, and had been rebuffed when he tried to alert the British authorities.

So here, then, is the foundation for the theory, later advocated by de Marigny and others, that the Duke, Oakes, Wenner-Gren and Christie were all complicit in a financial scandal that Sir Harry's murder threatened to expose. They had needed something – someone – to throw investigators off the scent and had chosen Freddie de Marigny.

As a tip-off, it was certainly one that the Bureau took seriously enough to recommend that agents should interview Anderson after the trial was over. At first glance, too, it is not apparent why he would not be telling the truth.

Without Anderson's own testimony, any assessment of his

motives must necessarily be speculative. As to the substance of his claims, however, one can point to a complete absence of corroborating evidence. He never seems to have provided any afterwards, and even at the time of the approach to the FBI his intermediary said that Anderson did not know where the records of the transaction were kept, or if there were any.

Equally, when the Bureau went through Wenner-Gren's finances after the war, they found no trace of any such scheme, and they would not have been shy about revealing anything compromising involving two people they regarded as Nazi sympathisers, the Swede and the Duke. Moreover, as has been mentioned before, the Duke simply did not have access to that sort of money.

Evidence of wrongdoing does not always survive. Yet to put one's trust in Anderson's otherwise unsubstantiated claims is to fail to take account of what is known about him – a man distrusted by his superiors, a man on the make, a man with an agenda.

If Anderson's proxy approach to the Bureau had been the only example of such behaviour, it might plausibly be said to have signalled a change of heart, an act of repentance. But it did not. Anderson was someone who systematically got others into trouble. He had already been in touch with the FBI about some businessmen whose associations he thought might be suspect, and later he would let slip to the British details of one of Wenner-Gren's bank transfers. Then there was his volunteering the information about the petrol to the Nassau police, and the consequent implication of de Marigny in the murder. And, in July 1942, there had been the curious episode of Mr Tropea.

That month, the British Embassy in Washington reported that it had learned that it was possible to obtain illegally dollars for sterling through the staff of Pleasantville, the airfield contractors. Their informant was a man named Tropea, a minor employee of the firm, who said he had been approached by Anderson who was seemingly under the impression that Tropea was one of the company's senior executives. He had asked if Tropea could change some money for him. Tropea had asked how much. Ten million pounds, said Anderson coolly. He could let Tropea have it at a favourable rate.

The US Treasury thought that this was money belonging to Wenner-Gren which Anderson was trying to launder, as it may well have been. What is striking, given the sums involved – some three hundred million pounds in today's money – is that Anderson had blundered so incautiously when it came to establishing Tropea's identity. Or was this, in fact, just another example of his trying to get someone else – in this case Wenner-Gren – to take the fall for something in which he had participated?

It would not be his fault, Anderson could always say to the FBI, if they failed to find proof of what he had told them about his master, Sir Harry Oakes and the Duke. And if he was deliberately misdirecting the authorities, what activity of his own was he trying so hard to conceal?

It was an obvious manoeuvre, but effective on the jury for all that. Lady Oakes, the grieving widow, would be the last important witness for the prosecution's case. Dressed in black, stifling an occasional sob as she cooled herself with a palmetto fan, she made a dignified figure, if a small one; as a concession to her loss, she was allowed to sit in the witness box, but so short was she that a pile of cushions was needed before her face could be seen above its rail.

She and Sir Harry had tried to make the best of a bad situation, she said, after they had learned of Nancy's elopement with the accused. She corrected herself. 'Alfred, I mean Alfred – I hate that word, the "accused".' The other children had liked him – he had taken them sailing – and he had been very attentive to Nancy. When she had fallen ill, he had unhesitatingly given blood transfusions, and had offered four thousand pounds (one hundred and twenty thousand today] towards the medical expenses.

Lady Oakes had refused it, however. She thought it was not his money, but Ruth's. Nonetheless, this had not been the cause of the breach between them. That had been Nancy's subsequent pregnancy, and the two operations needed to terminate it.

'And I had given Alfred instructions before leaving Mexico to take such good care of Nancy,' Lady Oakes told the court firmly. 'All this suffering was so unnecessary.'

From this episode had sprung the Oakeses' conviction that de Marigny was irresponsible and careless, interested solely in his wife's money and not in her welfare. They had been reinforced in their beliefs by Ruth's accusatory letter, the letters that de Marigny had sent them in response to this, and one that he had written to young Sydney which stated that he felt the Oakeses were treating him as an outcast. It was signed 'Big Brother'.

'I think it's the most diabolical letter that anyone could have written to a child of fifteen about a parent,' was Eunice Oakes's opinion. She left no one in the courtroom in any doubt of how things now lay between her and her daughter, and what had been her response to that – the alteration of her and Sir Harry's wills 'to protect the children from themselves'. When he afterwards gave evidence, Foskett used exactly the same phrase.

After her mother's arrival in Nassau ten days before, Nancy had gone to the airport to meet her. Lady Oakes had left instead by a side door, and the two had not spoken since. It was now clear what would be her mother's answer to her daughter's telegrams begging for help. She thought that de Marigny was guilty of the murder of her husband, and that Nancy was beneath contempt for standing by him.

What the jury was thinking, at the end of the Crown's evidence, no one could be sure. But one thing was certain. So far, everyone except the man himself had had their say about Alfred de Marigny. Now, finally, it was his turn.

EIGHT

You see my fader? Oh yes!
Tell 'im fo' me! Oh yes!
I'll ride my horse on de battlefiel'
I'se gwine to heaven in de mawnin'

By electing to give evidence, de Marigny was taking a gamble.
The law did not compel him to take the stand in his own defence,
and if he did so he would expose himself to cross-examination by
the prosecution. Then, too, his foreignness – his accent, manner-
isms and attitudes – would be all be the more apparent to such a
conservative jury. Yet Higgs would have told the Count that if he
did not testify then all the work that they had done so far might
be undermined by renewed suspicions that he had something to
hide. By putting him in the witness box, Higgs could better control how he was perceived.

He was pushing at an open door. De Marigny the champion
sailor, the silk-tongued flirt with a heart full of righteous anger
was not short of confidence. After four months sweating, cursing
and brooding in jail he wanted nothing more than to take on his
accusers in public. All his loneliness, his fears, his pain at being
apart from Nancy spurred him on: he was ready, all right.

Excitement about the day's proceedings drew an even larger
crowd than usual. The queue for places began when the morning

was still fresh, and all the seats were filled early. Several people chose to bring their own chairs, and by the time that Daly entered even the aisles were packed. In some spots, two people perched on the same seat, fending off a third. Those who had thought ahead had brought sandwiches and a thermos for the lunchtime adjournment; those who had not, eager to keep their place, went without. And those (including the jury) who felt they had to get something to eat found themselves swept back by the tide that poured in to seize the vantage points vacated. Eventually the police intervened to restore a semblance of order.

De Marigny made an imposing figure on the stand. Its raised level, added to his natural height, meant that he dominated the court. His now thin frame leaned forward as he gripped the rail of the box. Instinctively, the room leaned forward to hear what he had to say.

Speaking in a slow, deliberate manner, the Count started by relating the history of his wooing of Nancy, who earlier that day had visited the prison to wish him luck. That had meant much to him. At the time of their marriage, he said, he had had assets of some thirteen thousand pounds (about four hundred thousand today), more than half of it in cash, making him by the standards of the time an independently wealthy man. It had been a love match, not a fortune hunt.

When relations between himself and Sir Harry had become strained after Nancy's pregnancy, de Marigny continued, it had been Oakes who had been hot-tempered and moody, never him. He had told Newell Kelly that he would take his 'big foot' to his father-in-law, but he had meant it as a joke and had said it in a light-hearted way.

On the afternoon before the murder, he had raced *Concubine* and then had dressed for his dinner party. Higgs asked him what he had worn – a creamish shantung shirt, as he always did. Doubtless Higgs had told him that today was not the day to change his routine. The jury could plainly see such a shirt as he gave evidence.

And a tie? 'I have so many ties that I don't know which one I wore,' said de Marigny, smirking. In a deft piece of theatre

Schindler stood up behind Higgs and spread twenty-three of them, in harlequin shades, all over the table. 'Yes,' said de Marigny. 'Those are some of them.'

Later the Count had set up the tables for dinner, and while lighting the candles in two hurricane shades – to the right with his right hand, and to the left with his left since he was ambidextrous – he had burnt himself when the match flared up.

Now Higgs came to a critical part of de Marigny's testimony. The party had broken up at about 12.30 a.m. although de Visdelou and his girlfriend Betty had left earlier because the Marquis had a bad cold. De Marigny had taken the two RAF wives home just after one a.m., and had offered his friend Freddie Cerreta a lift at the same time, but Cerreta had declined it. De Marigny had used his green Lincoln car and had come straight back from the cottages.

On arriving home, he told the court, he had moved the Chevrolet he used on the farm, which was blocking the entrance to the garage, and had parked the Lincoln inside, next to de Visdelou's car. Then he had gone up the outside stairs to the Marquis's flat and had asked if de Visdelou wanted him to take Betty home too. But Georges had said that he would do it himself later.

All the servants were still in the house, washing up after the dinner, and de Marigny had gone to bed at about 1.45 a.m. At about three a.m. he had been woken up by a fight between Grisou the cat and his bull-terrier pup. Grisou had fled into the Count's room and had made a noise by jumping up onto the windowsill, disturbing the Venetian blind. Then he had heard the sound of the Chevrolet starting up – Georges was giving Betty her ride back to her mother's house, not far away on Shirley Street. De Marigny knew that de Visdelou liked to have the cat in his room, and when Georges came back about fifteen minutes later he had called out to him and the Marquis had come into de Marigny's room to collect Grisou. Early the next morning, de Marigny had picked up the keys to the Chevy from a dozing de Visdelou and had driven over to the farm to count his chickens.

Higgs then moved on to the circumstances of de Marigny's arrest. First, the Count stated that the gasoline had definitely not been delivered until that lunchtime, after the murder had been discovered – it could not have been the fuel for the fire. Then he recalled the search for burnt hairs that Melchen and Barker had made that evening. He remembered, he said, how they had complained that the light in the room was poor – there was just a standing lamp on the table – and when they claimed to have found singed hairs he was not invited to look at them through a lens.

Higgs asked de Marigny about Melchen's belief that he had produced a jacket and a pair of trousers in matching shades of brown, rather than the brown suit that he had initially told him he had been wearing. De Marigny's reply was that of the born dandy: 'I have never,' he said dismissively, 'owned a brown suit in my life.' That at least had the feeling of truth about it.

The next day, Melchen had taken de Marigny upstairs at Westbourne at about 11.15 a.m. to interview him. He had asked him questions about people in Nassau and his early life, and in between had tried to shake him with sudden accusations – 'What would you say if I said that you were seen coming in here last night?' and 'Didn't you want to get quits with Sir Harry?' It was, said de Marigny, 'regular police stuff.'

The American detective had offered the Count several cigarettes from a packet of Lucky Strikes, and had asked him to pour him a glass of water from a pitcher on the table next to them. Some time after this, Barker had looked in and asked if all was well. Yes, Melchen had replied, all was well. That evening, de Marigny had been arrested.

Higgs concluded by getting the Count to rebut Anderson's suggestion that he was down to his last penny and desperate for money. De Marigny's bank accounts gave a false impression of his affairs, he maintained, because a few weeks before the murder he had transferred £7,708 (£230,000 in today's money) to de Visdelou in connection with some business he had with Christie. Then, what with the property he owned, including the farm, and the sums he was owed – not least by Anderson – he had another eleven thousand pounds (worth £335,000 today) in assets. Money was the least of his worries, was the defence's line, and not suffi-cient motive for him to have killed Oakes.

The day reached its climax at a quarter to four. Higgs addressed his client one more time. 'Did you go to Westbourne on the night of 7 July?'

De Marigny edged still closer to the front of the witness box: 'I did not.'

'Did you kill Sir Harry Oakes?'

Drawing himself up to his full height, de Marigny let his answer ring around the courtroom – 'No, sir!'

A hundred people let out the breath they had been holding in, and the press began to scramble for the door. That night, Nassau's cable office reported that it had transmitted 18,750 words of copy about de Marigny's testimony, more than double the number devoted to the Duke of Windsor's arrival in 1940.

It was the first time that most people in the room had observed at first hand the de Marigny of legend, and the verdict on him the next morning was more positive than he might have expected. He had seemed more French than many had thought him to be but on show had been his sober, responsible side, the loving husband rather than the light-hearted *boulevardier*. He had made a favourable impression. Then again, so far he had not been asked any awkward questions.

Hallinan posed the first of them. He stood and looked at de Marigny. 'What was your father's name?' It was Alfred Fouquereaux, came the reply. (Not, in fact, the name given on his birth certificate, which was Charles Fouquereaux, but his father may have been known as Alfred.)

'And where did you get the name de Marigny?' The Mauritian explained that it had been his mother's surname, and that he had taken it at her request after their meeting on the tennis court when he was eighteen. Hallinan was not satisfied, and suggested that Fouquereaux was a bourgeois name and that de Marigny had merely adopted the other to allow him to use the accompanying title. De Marigny denied it, but the bogus Count, the social-climbing gigolo, was being once more paraded in front of the jury.

It was then that the Crown entered into evidence a deed poll dated 21 May 1937 recording de Marigny's change of name. Little was made of it by Hallinan, but what is clear is that however he might have introduced himself in the decade concerned it was not until almost ten years after he had met his mother again that de Marigny formally took her surname.

His decision to do so may have been influenced by de Visdelou's own change of name (from ignoble Guimbeau) a few months before, and like his friend he might have been prompted to do so to impress his new wife – Lucie-Alice Cahen, the woman he later airbrushed out of *A Conspiracy of Crowns*. By the time the deed was stamped, however, the pair had already parted.

Lucie-Alice had since been waiting for her revenge, and now that de Marigny was in trouble she took it. In an interview with American reporters, she gave a very different picture of the Count from the one he was trying to fashion in court. Their life together had been very short, and emotionally brutal. Following their wedding in Paris in March 1937, they had sailed for New York on honeymoon (they had not gone to Switzerland, as he later claimed), but, she recalled, 'my husband's attitude had changed overnight.' He spent all his time on board ship flirting with other women, and she felt humiliated.

'I don't know how I lived through those six days,' she said. De Marigny told Lucie-Alice that he had married her on impulse, but now realised his mistake and was in love with another woman. De Marigny was 'a creature of his whims and was of an extremely vacillating and changeable disposition.' When she cried, his temper only became worse.

The day after the boat docked, Lucie-Alice flew down to Miami, and ninety days later, having established residence, she was granted a divorce. (The judge was the same one who would later finalise de Marigny's divorce from Ruth.) They had been married, in effect, for a week. She returned to France; de Marigny did not return her dowry.

The Count is a cad: this was more like the popular conception of Nancy's husband. Yet, though it made for good reading, it is unclear how much truth there was in it. No doubt Lucie-Alice had felt scorned and hurt by de Marigny, but in *More Devil Than Saint* he gives a different reason for their split, namely her affair with de Visdelou. Perhaps likeliest of all is the version I had from Marie Gudewill: Lucie-Alice had married de Marigny to escape her family, but she had been under the impression that he was rich. He had had the same mistaken idea about her. During the voyage, each had discovered that the other was broke. They had laughed about it, and had agreed to part.

Perhaps Lucie-Alice regretted their break-up more than de Marigny did, perhaps there was another motive – a new husband, an angry father – that now compelled her to play the injured party. Whatever the answer, the episode tends to confirm the idea suggested by the deed poll, that the de Marigny of those days was a man drawn to money. By the time that the document went through, in May 1937, he no longer had any need to regularise his change of name, for his wife had gone. But then, there were rich women in America too, and an aristocrat's title might serve him even better in the New World than it had in the Old.

De Marigny's ex-wives were not yet finished with him. In court, Hallinan continued to harp on the state of the defendant's finances, and he now came to Ruth's pressing the Count for the repayment of her loans to him. The demand was brought on by her jealousy of Nancy.

'Didn't you say this in a letter?' Hallinan asked. "'When I told Ruth I had married Nancy, she said 'What about the money?''"

De Marigny looked uncomfortable. He must have given some promise, some encouragement to Ruth – the prospect of remarriage after the war perhaps – which had now been stripped from her. He was soon to look unhappier still, for the Attorney-General was into his stride.

'And in a letter to Ruth's lawyer, did you say: "Today I have nothing. I have spent my last cent"?'

'Yes.'

'But at the time you had £1,500 in de Visdelou's account?' De Marigny had to admit that it was true. In fact, he acknowledged that he had more than that, considering the money he was owed by others. But in the letter to the lawyer he had not owned up to this – on the advice of Anderson.

Daly interrupted him, and asked him to repeat what he had said. De Marigny squirmed. 'It was a statement all fabricated. Some of the figures are correct, but some are not correct. On the advice of Mr Anderson, I sent this to him to send a copy to Ruth, though I knew some of the items were not correct.'

Hallinan had achieved his purpose. De Marigny might or might not have more money than it seemed, but he had certainly been sufficiently worried by the financial implications of Ruth's change of heart to have to resort to trickery. Worse, he had been shown to be someone who had no qualms about lying

Only rarely will cross-examination destroy the evidence of a witness. Its prime usefulness to a barrister is as an opportunity to insinuate notions into a jury's mind which, even if not borne out by what they hear, can still act in the advocate's favour. Accordingly, Hallinan now proceeded to trail innuendo after innuendo in front of the court.

When had de Marigny stopped living with Ruth – on his oath! Had he not been with her while he was romancing Nancy? Had he not deliberately waited until just after Nancy's eighteenth birthday before he married her? Was Sir Harry happy that his daughter was living in the same house as a couple – de Visdelou and Betty Roberts – who were not man and wife? His meaning was clear: de Marigny had the morals of an alley cat, and so did his friends.

Then Hallinan moved on to a more substantial point. De Marigny had claimed in his evidence that he had invited Christie to be one of his guests that evening, but Christie had told him that he was already due to dine with Oakes and stay the night at the house. In his testimony, Christie had denied that he had spoken to the Mauritian, and had maintained that the meal with Oakes had been a spontaneous decision.

Hallinan needed to tread carefully here. He wanted to suggest that de Marigny did not in fact know that Christie was at Westbourne, otherwise clearly it was less likely that he would have gone to the house to commit murder. At the same time, he could not afford for de Marigny to discredit Christie any further, so he did not dwell long on the matter. In so doing, he might just have missed something important.

Anderson had said beforehand that after telling de Marigny of Oakes's death they had set out to try to discover more news, but the Count had told him he did not know at which of Oakes's several houses his father-in-law was staying. Such an absence of knowledge would obviously reinforce his claim to innocence, and Anderson had duly testified that it was only when they saw the police cars outside Westbourne that they had decided to go in.

Yet here, by contrast, was de Marigny saying that Christie had informed him that he was spending the evening with Oakes *at Westbourne*. The incompatibility with his statement the very next morning to Anderson about Oakes's whereabouts is obvious. The Crown would later content itself with alleging that de Marigny had been feigning ignorance when he spoke to Anderson, but it is a mystery why they did not explore the matter further in court – and why Higgs allowed such a potentially dangerous inconsistency to form part of his defence in the first place.

The contest between de Marigny and Hallinan had settled into a rhythm of brief, quick darts by the barrister and sharp parries by the Count. *En garde*. An attack in tierce.

'When he searched your house, Captain Melchen says you brought out clothes to show him not from the laundry room but clean ones from your bedroom.'

Riposte. 'I think Melchen lies.'

'After you came back from seeing the ladies home, you went to ask de Visdelou if you could take Miss Roberts home. Was he dressed?' Low, in septime.

'He just stuck his head through the door.'

'Isn't it strange you should only see his head?'

'I just don't remember – it's obvious.'

'It is obvious.' Stop thrust. 'You don't want to tell us if he was dressed or not.'

Hallinan had been pressing him hard, but de Marigny knew that he must eventually come to his interview with Melchen. He waited for his opportunity.

'When you were in the north-west bedroom, tell us how you were sitting.'

'On the left of me was a dressing table with a glass top. There was a tray with two glasses and a glass pitcher of water. He asked for some water. I lifted the pitcher, while remaining seated, filled two glasses, gave Melchen one and took one for myself.' Now Hallinan lunged too far.

'I take it that, being ambidextrous, you poured with your left hand.'

'Yes. I probably poured with my left hand, and handed him the glass with my right.' It was not a question the Crown had needed to ask, and it had allowed de Marigny to ram home the defence's explanation of how Barker had taken his print. Hallinan had ceded the initiative to his opponent.

'You say Mr Christie must be lying when he says you did not invite him to dinner.'

'I'd say he was mistaken.'

'And Mrs Kelly is also mistaken when she says you said you were going to be ill before you entered Westbourne?'

'Definitely so.'

'And Constable Parker is definitely mistaken when he says he saw you looking strange at seven-thirty that morning?'

'No – he lied.'

Laughter welled up in the courtroom. It had been de Marigny's bout. He had regained his bounce, and even felt able the next morning, as his evidence was being read back to him by Daly, to admit that he had misled the jury when he had said previously that he had never received twenty-five thousand pounds from Ruth, when in fact he had had it. He had even managed to turn telling a lie to his advantage.

Gardner opined that in general the Count came across as a straightforward witness. He – and the jury – might have thought differently had they known that all the while de Marigny had thousands of dollars tucked away in New York, money whose existence he had kept secret from Nancy, Ruth and the court.

Before the Count stepped down from the box, Sands, the foreman, asked him to demonstrate lighting the candles in the hurricane shades. De Marigny struck a match, but it was blown out by the fan overhead. This was turned off and, holding the spill between his index and middle fingers, he reached down into the glass chimney. He pulled his hand back sharply, and wrung his fingers.

His luck had held again – just as he said he had done at the dinner party, he had burnt himself, this time under the eyes of the jury. The wind stood fair for him. The press was in agreement: de Marigny would probably be acquitted, unless something unexpected emerged.

The atmosphere in court that morning was rather flat. The *tricoteuses* had not had their victim, but the mob had been satisfied. For the first time, there were empty spaces on the benches behind Higgs. For the first time, too, he felt an easing of the pressure on him, and he and Callender dealt briskly with a brace of other witnesses who had been at de Marigny's dinner. 'Is he excitable?' asked Daly of one. 'Well, in the French way', came the answer, which provoked more laughter.

Daly was then told that de Marigny had lit his brandy after dinner, which also perplexed the Chief Justice, used only to Christmas puddings being treated in this manner. 'It may be a

French custom,' offered Higgs, which drew yet another round of giggles. There was something positively end-of-term in the air.

The balding, dark-jowled Freddie Cerreta was an engineer who had been working for Pleasantville at the airfield. It was he who had introduced Jean Ainsley and Dorothy and Captain Clarke to de Marigny at the Prince George Hotel, and he had come to the party the following night. He bore out de Marigny's testimony that the Count had offered him a lift to the British Colonial when taking the two women home, but that he had declined it. As Higgs pointed out, if de Marigny had been planning murder he was unlikely to have asked Cerreta to come along, as it meant he would have to make an extra trip back to Westbourne after dropping him at the hotel, Ainsley and Clarke naturally having been escorted home first.

Flirtatious company though that pair may have made, they could not compete with the Lolita-like charms of Betty Roberts. Her blue eyes, straw-coloured hair and bright red lipstick were those of an over-made-up doll, and as she twisted self-consciously in the box on her high heels, her youth was all too apparent. After going upstairs from the party at 11.30 p.m. with the coughing de Visdelou, she said, she had fallen asleep on the sofa. The Marquis had decorously retired to his room. She had heard him and de Marigny talking in French at about 1.30 a.m. and then she had woken again at 2.40 a.m. De Visdelou had taken her home in the Chevrolet, which she'd noticed had been moved from the driveway.

Adderley believed that there were some boundaries that should not be crossed. Sixteen-year-old girls consorting with married men more than twice their age was one of them, for all that de Visdelou had revealed a few days earlier that he was being divorced in England by his wife and was intending to wed Betty. Summoning up his most reproving tones, Adderley began to take her to task.

'Did you tell Captain Melchen that you went upstairs because you were somewhat intoxicated?'

'I don't recall it, but I may have.'

'I suggest to you that you then went to sleep and did not wake any more until two o'clock.'

The voice was girlish, but firm. 'I deny that.'

'You say you were sleeping on a couch in the sitting room.'

'Yes.'

'And Georges was sick – undressed – in bed.'

The squeal of outrage could be heard halfway to Cable Beach. 'He was *not* undressed, I beg your pardon!' Adderley hastily retreated. These modern girls, he really didn't know what had got into them.

A few minutes before midnight on 7 July, Captain Edward Sears drove out of Nassau's Central Police Station on patrol. There had been a sharp squall a while earlier, and there was still a little drizzle in the air. He cruised down Bay Street towards the British Colonial and turned left into George Street, which looks up towards Government House. Coming towards him was a station wagon, heading for the harbour, and as it passed him the man in the passenger seat was illuminated by the street light above. It was Harold Christie.

Sears's identification of Christie, in a car that had approached from the direction of Westbourne, was one of Higgs's strongest cards, and presented a problem for the prosecution. Hallinan dutifully tried to shake the former sponge merchant – how fast had the vehicles been travelling, had Sears been talking to the other policeman in the patrol car at the time? – but he had little success.

Sears admitted that he had not been able to track down the station wagon. But since he had known Christie since they'd been schoolboys, the accuracy of his identification has to be accepted. Although (assuming that both cars were right-hand drive), Sears would have had to look across the other driver to see the passenger, Christie would have been no more than eight feet away, with the cars travelling at a combined speed of less than forty m.p.h., and Sears got a look at a three-quarters profile of Christie's face.

It has been suggested that Sears may have seen Christie's brother Frank, who resembled him closely, and who, like Harold, also drove a station wagon. Yet, aside from the fact that Sears knew both men well, there remains the obstacle to this version of events that Frank Christie never came forward to claim that it had been him who was out that night.

Another explanation was offered to me by Levi Gibson, the chauffeur who had brought Christie's station wagon down to Westbourne earlier that evening. He told me that Sears, out of loyalty to Christie, was trying to give him an alibi for the night's events. But in that case surely it would have been more helpful for Sears to have said nothing about it, or to have admitted that his identification was wrong. Gibson also says that Sears tried to persuade the police sergeant who was with him at the time to confirm the sighting, but he would not do so. But, in any event he was not called to rebut Sears's statement.

For the watching Gardner, Sears was a 'quiet, forceful man, with a keen sense of his responsibilities.' He was no liar. Contrary to his own evidence, Christie *did* leave Westbourne that night. Gibson believes otherwise, because when he went to pick up Christie's car the next morning, to collect Foskett from the airport, he found that the ground underneath it was still dry while elsewhere it was saturated. But then, Christie was not the only person in Nassau who owned a station wagon.

Georges de Visdelou had known de Marigny for seventeen years. They had lived together, lent each other money, and even shared lovers. That one of these women had been de Marigny's wife at the time was of a part with their peculiar symbiotic – or was it parasitical? – relationship. Now Georges, he of the marcelled hair and damp fingers, held his best friend's life in his hands.

As the fingerprint was for the Crown, so were Georges's talks with Freddie de Marigny early on that Thursday morning both the strongest and potentially the weakest parts of the defence's case. After the staff had left for the night, only de Visdelou could vouch for de Marigny's presence in the house, and now the strength of that evidence would be tested.

'A sartorial symphony in brown', as one paper put it, the Marquis looked nervous as he took the stand. Led by Higgs, he largely confirmed de Marigny's version of events. On his return from taking Betty Roberts home, Georges had parked the Chevrolet in front of the garage and pocketed the keys; thereafter de Marigny could not have used either it or the Lincoln whose exit it was blocking. Then Georges had gone into the kitchen for a glass of water. De Marigny had called out to him to come and get Grisou, and he had slid open the screen door from the dining room onto the porch to let the cat out.

Higgs sat down, and Adderley rose. He, by contrast, appeared confident. Was it true to say, he began, that, from what Georges had told the court, he had not, in fact, gone *into* de Marigny's room to collect the cat?

'I possibly did, but I cannot recollect,' said de Visdelou. For the first time, a note somewhere between vagueness and worry had entered his voice.

'In fact,' continued Adderley relentlessly, 'did you not tell Major Pemberton, and also sign a statement on 11 July using these words: "Actually, I did not see de Marigny from midnight to ten a.m. the following morning."'

Higgs and Callender looked up sharply, appalled. This was the first that they had heard of any such statement, or of Georges not corroborating Freddie's alibi. Adderley, however, had already moved on.

'And did you not also say in your statement that, while at Westbourne on 9 July, de Marigny reminded you that he had shouted to you about the cat but,' and Adderley paused for emphasis, 'but that you had no recollection until he reminded you, nor could you remember taking it at all.'

With a dull thud, Adderley laid the statement on the desk in front of him. It was the sound of the scaffold opening beneath de Marigny's feet.

NINE

Oh don' you let the Devil fool you,
Oh don' you let the Devil fool you,
Oh don' you let the Devil fool you,
He make you t'ink dat yo' all right!

As Higgs flicked rapidly through the document, de Visdelou dug himself still further into the mire. He was in a funk now, shell-shocked, almost visibly quailing under the impact of each question.

'I don't remember anything in that statement,' he stammered. 'I am French, and very emotional. My best friend had just been arrested and my mind was very vague.' He seemed similarly wit-less now, protesting that after the murder he had been quizzed by too many people, from too many angles: it had been a week before his nerves had recovered.

Adderley's verbal jab cut through Georges's upraised hands again. 'Do you recollect whether *anything* you said in the signed statement is true?'

'Yes,' said an exasperated Sir Oscar, 'it seems that you gave Major Pemberton very accurate information on relations between you and the accused several years ago, but when it comes to two or three days before, you are vague. Can you explain that? Why did you make a mistake about the incidents of Thursday morning?'

The implication was self-evident. Was de Visdelou lying? Had de Marigny really been in his room?

Whether it was from guilt, confusion, or apprehension of what he was doing to his friend's cause, Georges now seemed almost hypnotised. All he could offer to Daly's interrogation were weak acknowledgements of their force – 'Yes, yes, I said that.' The judge tried to sum up his evidence.

'You said in your earlier signed statement that you did not see the accused between midnight and ten a.m. But now you say he called you for the cat.'

'That is how I recollect it,' replied de Visdelou, dully. An uncharted reef was ripping through the hull of de Marigny's alibi.

Higgs, though, looked calmer than he had a few moments before. 'My learned friend Mr Adderley put several passages to you from your statement,' he said, trying with his voice to coax de Visdelou out of his trance. 'But on page four' – and he turned to make sure that Daly caught the significance of this – 'did you not say: "I and my friend left and went upstairs. About 1.30 a.m., de Marigny came to my apartment door and *asked me if he could take my friend home*." You did say that, didn't you?'

Higgs was seething at the trick that Adderley had tried to pull. Now it was the other's turn to be covered in confusion. Daly rounded on him.

'Mr Adderley, I got the impression that he said in his statement that he knew nothing about this, that he did not see the defendant that night?'

Adderley knitted the air with his fingers. 'It was simply the question of his having actually *seen* the accused, Your Honour. Whether he *heard* him is another matter.' Semantics was not one of Daly's hobbies, and his pursed lips indicated his disapproval. Higgs recognised that the situation had been salvaged, and even de Visdelou seemed to have come to life again. Higgs hustled him off the stand.

The Crown's barrister had made a grave mistake. Not only had he annoyed the judge, but his piece of sharp practice had rebounded against the prosecution's case. The embarrassment caused by its uncovering had blotted out the fact that de Visdelou had at first told the police only that he had seen de Marigny at 1.30 a.m. and not later as well. Had he merely been confused and vague, as vague as he had been in not mentioning to Higgs the statement that he had given to Pemberton? Or was a fat grey cat in fact the only solid thing in de Marigny's story?

When the prosecution had engaged Frank Conway, Higgs had found a fingerprint expert of his own, Maurice O'Neil. Like Conway, he was a policeman, having been supervisor of the New Orleans identification bureau for almost twenty years. He had made his name in the intriguingly entitled 'Goat Castle case', where his evidence had cleared an eccentric couple suspected of murdering their neighbour, and by now he was a past president of the International Association for Identification. One of this organisation's other directors was James Barker.

It is interesting to speculate what O'Neil's prior opinion of Barker might have been. From the testimony he subsequently gave it seems clear that O'Neil had supplied Higgs with much of the ammunition that the barrister had used against O'Neil's fellow detective.

O'Neil began by saying that he had never heard of a case in which a court had accepted a lifted print as evidence: the proper method was to use enlarged photographs of the fingerprint in place. He had examined Exhibit J, the print of de Marigny's little finger, and had found three circles in the pattern – one large and two small. They were definitely part of the background of the object from which the print had been taken, and he could see nothing on the screen that could have caused them.

It was time, thought Higgs, for some surprises of his own. Casually, he asked O'Neil if he happened to have anything with him that could have produced such a background. Savouring the moment, O'Neil reached into his jacket pocket and slowly withdrew an object. Then, like a conjuror at a children's party, he flourished it in front of the court. It was a drinking glass with a design of red circles.

Hallinan was on his feet in a trice, protesting. 'If the defence were going to introduce that glass, I should have had the opportunity of asking the accused whether the glasses allegedly used in the north-west bedroom did have such a design.'

Daly was taken aback. 'But the defence are not suggesting that the print was taken from a glass.' He was correct, in so much as Higgs had never done so explicitly. Hallinan, however, knew how things lay. 'Oh yes,' he said bitterly, 'that suggestion has been made all along.'

'No, we didn't suggest that,' said Higgs. He had merely put it to Barker that it came from 'some object' in the bedroom. Still, there was no harm in letting the jury have the subtext again. 'Captain Melchen was also asked about ashtrays and other objects in the room.'

And with that, Higgs asked O'Neil if he had anything else that could be used to demonstrate the pattern of circles. On cue, the detective felt in his other pocket and pulled out a glass cigarette case.

Given that the jury then asked to see a fingerprint being lifted from this the Attorney-General could undoubtedly see how their minds were turning. But he still needed to cross-examine O'Neil. It proved to be hard going. When he suggested to O'Neil that Conway had been correct to say that without the right camera Barker had been justified in lifting the print, O'Neil asked why Barker hadn't merely placed the screen on a table and compared the mark directly with the impressions he had taken.

'Yes.' Daly nodded. 'I wondered why that couldn't have been done.'

'Is that the method employed in New York?' replied Hallinan, flailing a little.

'It should be.'

As Hallinan came increasingly to realise how bad was the hand that Barker had dealt him, with each question a little more desperation entered his voice.

'Isn't there a danger of a powdered print being destroyed if the humidity is great?'

'No, not if properly protected.'

'But suppose the damp gets to it?'

O'Neil was immovable. 'The climate is humid in New Orleans too, but I've kept objects with latent prints for years.'

Hallinan was pleading now. 'Isn't there a risk in an *extremely* humid climate?'

'No.'

Daly slid another card towards Hallinan. It was an unwanted Jack.

'Have you ever heard of a latent print becoming illegible after being powdered, owing to the climate?'

'Never.'

Even a barrister with little court experience knows that when his opponent resorts to facetiousness it means that he has lost faith in the effectiveness of his questions. When Higgs heard Hallinan's next one, his heart must have given a little flutter of joy.

'One big circle, and two small ones, and another smaller than the others,' said Hallinan. 'You say that indicates a background of an industrial design. Do you go in for surrealism?'

The bank had lost, and all that remained was for Higgs, in re-examination, to collect his winnings.

'You say that you're not prepared to say whether a lift *was* taken from that area to the left. Are you prepared to say whether or not a lift *could* have come from there?'

O'Neil glanced across the room at the Chinese patterns, and then down at the white rubber patch that he had been handed.

'That,' he pronounced with an air of finality, 'that positively could not have come from that screen.'

Charles Rolle was de Marigny's butler and valet. As befitted a gentleman's gentleman he was fastidious and exacting in his care of his master. He knew how the Count liked his breakfast – two poached eggs on toast, dry but never burnt.

On the night of the dinner party, Rolle had been on duty with another butler and the cook. The last guests had left at about one a.m. He had been in the kitchen when de Marigny returned, and could see the length of the driveway. The Count had moved the Chevrolet around the back and then, three or four minutes later, had come into the house through the living room. 'Good night, Charles,' he had said. Rolle and the cook had left at about 2.30 a.m., having waited until the rain stopped before setting off on foot. The next morning Rolle arrived at Victoria Avenue at about eight o'clock and pressed de Marigny's clothes.

If Rolle's evidence was truthful, it virtually eliminated de Marigny as a suspect. It placed him in the house from about 1.45 a.m. until 2.30 a.m. – he could hardly have left without the staff seeing or hearing him – giving him a window of only half an hour or so to get to Westbourne and back before de Visdelou came to claim his cat.

In cross-examination, however, Rolle's powers of observation proved suspect. Adderley pointed out that he had told the police that de Marigny had been wearing a blue shirt, a light blue coat and canary yellow trousers at dinner. Moreover, the only source he had for the time he had left the house was what the cook, Edith Smith, had said to him as they went.

Four other of de Marigny's servants then testified. Smith said that when de Marigny returned, another helper had been lying drunk in the garage; perhaps that explains what the Count was doing for three or four minutes there. The housemaid testified that she saw nothing unusual the next morning about the clothes her master had worn, while de Marigny's farm manager and his chauffeur told the court that the Count had recently been near a large bonfire while scalding chickens.

Hallinan and Daly, however, both pointed out to the jury that de Marigny's staff were perhaps not impartial witnesses. The housemaid and the chauffeur were also married to each other, and de Marigny had lent them money for a house. Loyalty from servants to an employer was all very well, but like everything in Nassau, it had to know its place.

★

Thus far, one of the central figures in the drama had been con-fined to the wings. As a future witness, Nancy had been forbidden to enter the courtroom while other evidence was being heard lest it influence her own. Under strain, kept apart from de Marigny, it had been an exhausting few months for her.

Whatever her feelings were now for the man she had married – whether his new vulnerability had rekindled a love that had seemed to be fading or whether the pressure on her had finally doused it – Nancy had maintained a brave front, both for her sake and for his. She gave no hint of how her emotions lay. But it was clear that she had been unhappy at not being able to play a more active part in clearing away the shadow that loomed over both of them. Now at last she was called to centre stage, and she made the most of her entrance.

When her name was announced by the crier, Nancy paused briefly on the threshold of the court, hesitating. The crowd took in her neat figure, set off by a black dress with little white polka dots, a white beret and gloves. She threw back at them a look of defiance, and glancing neither right nor left walked straight to the witness box, her head held high, her gaze directed a foot above the assembled mob. As a performance, it was all the more impres-sive since she was running a fever temperature. Higgs had been so concerned about her that he had only given her ten minutes' notice that she was to be called. When she began to speak her voice was almost inaudible.

Nancy looked just once at her husband, who was weeping quietly into a handkerchief, and gave her evidence looking into the lofty open well of the court, as if appealing to some higher power. Her fingers made a cat's cradle from invisible strands of hope and worry.

Nancy's testimony was principally about her failing relations with her family, and went over ground which had already been well-trodden. Higgs, however, was not so much interested in this as with presenting the Count and Countess as a happy, normal couple – certainly not as people motivated by greed. He also wanted to establish in the jury's mind the image of Sir Harry's daughter stricken by grief for her father but showing her faith in her husband's innocence.

Nancy gave Higgs everything that he could have wanted. When she came to relate what Barker had told her at the funeral – that 'there was no question who the guilty party was' – she began to sway in the box, and clutched at the rail. Sands, the jury foreman, gallantly rushed up with a high stool for her to sit on.

After she had recovered her composure, Nancy testified that de Marigny had never asked her for money – indeed, had offered after the marriage to sign a document waiving his claim to anything that Nancy might inherit – and that it had been she who, by choice, had paid the hospital bills and the purchase price of the land for the farm. She had never heard her husband make a threat against her father.

Hallinan's stance was rather different. If Nancy was not prepared to stand apart from her husband, then they must be condemned jointly as a heartless pair. His evidence came from a letter that she had written her mother just before leaving Nassau in May. Now he read it to the court.

Nancy had told Lady Oakes that she was returning her birthday present of two thousand pounds of war bonds as it felt more like an act of charity to poor relations than a loving gift from parents. Since the de Marignys had returned from Mexico, the Oakeses' attitude to Freddie had changed markedly, and if they preferred to believe a third party rather than their own flesh and blood, she would be forced to choose between her family and her husband.

That third party was Walter Foskett who, Nancy wrote, had been deliberately misguiding their judgement. She could now see the truth in gossip and stories that she had heard about him before, and if her parents could not overcome their prejudice against de Marigny and treat him with respect, for her part she could never again feel love and respect for them, nor accept any of the material advantages that parents normally gave their children. 'I pray God,' the letter ended, 'that you may see the truth and justice of these statements.'

'That's a pretty hard letter for a girl to write to her mother, don't you think?' said Hallinan.

'Not if you were feeling as I was.'

Nancy denied that she had wanted to sever relations irrevocably with her parents. She hoped only to provoke them into talking to her, and she had been vexed at the manner in which the money had arrived: a routine letter from the bank without any accompanying personal note from her mother.

The wording of her letter appears to bear out Nancy's claim. Certainly it might have been written in girlish anger, but it is an appeal to her parents to change their minds, not an immutable resolution. Her father's death had denied them the chance of reconciliation. It had also put paid to the notion of returning the bonds; in Nancy's changed circumstances, they had come in very useful for paying Schindler.

The jury had just one question for her. Had she or de Marigny known that her parents had altered the terms of their will in February, after the row about her pregnancy? She said that she and her husband had suspected something of the sort, but had not been certain. In fact, Nancy said, she had never been aware of the contents of any will until after her father's death. And with that, the last witness for the defence stepped down from the box.

Higgs's closing speech to the jury was a model of its kind. He began by reminding them of their heavy responsibility, one that he himself had felt keenly throughout the trial. A man had been murdered, and the life of another was at stake. There could be no half measures here. Either they would decide that Alfred de Marigny should go free, or they would condemn him to be taken away and hanged by the neck until dead. They must make that choice solely on the basis of what they had heard in court, ignoring what else they might know about de Marigny's past life and conduct.

The case, Higgs maintained, had been a singular one in several ways, and the strangest feature of all was that of more than thirty witnesses called by the prosecution, just two – Melchen and Barker – had given testimony that directly supported the Crown's contention that Oakes had been killed by his son-in-law.

Immediately, Higgs had focused the jury's attention on one small, weak area of the prosecution case, a case that all along had derived much of its strength from the sheer mass of circumstantial evidence against de Marigny. Now Higgs had moved to negate that advantage. He recapitulated what the other witnesses had said, but only as a way of dismissing them from serious consideration and emphasising that it was just the testimony of the two Americans that counted. Pemberton had given lengthy evidence, but he had seen neither the print nor the burnt hairs. Conway, the fingerprint expert, could not testify as to where the lift of the crucial print came from, and so was of no consequence. Constable Parker had an overactive imagination. Newell Kelly had heard the accused threaten to kick Oakes, that was all. The entire case depended solely on the reliability of the word of Captains Barker and Melchen.

It was their evidence – the print, the hairs and the absence of his shirt – that tied Alfred de Marigny to the crime scene. Yet, said Higgs, as calmly as he could, how could one trust what Barker said? In the Magistrates Court he had suggested that the photographs of the print had been taken when it was on the screen, and he had marked the place where it had been.

Now the detective had changed his story entirely, and could not say where any of the fifty or more lifts he had taken had come from. He had tried and failed to fit a piece of paper into the only spot where the scrollwork would not show, and had eventually done so only by carefully letting much of it overhang the edge.

Equally astonishing was the revelation of when Barker had found the print, and his story of initially being confused by its being reversed. Barker was not confused, Higgs held, merely trying to cover up for Melchen's admission that he had not been told of the print until more than a week later. As for Melchen, it had been he who had lured de Marigny into the bedroom to obtain the impression in the first place, and then had lied, as had the constables, about the timing of the interview. However, in fairness to both detectives, continued Higgs (making it clear that he meant no such thing), the possibility must be considered that they had found by mistake a print left by de Marigny somewhere in the house on an earlier visit.

Higgs dealt equally briskly with the hairs and the shirt. The prosecution case, he summarised, was fashioned from 'irrelevant evidence and the deliberate falsehoods of policemen.' By contrast, he invited the jury to consider the transparent testimony given by the witnesses for the defence. Was it logical that de Marigny would offer Cerreta a lift home if he was planning to stop on the way and murder Sir Harry? Was it logical to think that after committing this foul deed he would go up to the flat and offer to take Betty home? Was it logical that she, de Visdelou and the servants would all run the risk of lying for him?

No, what made the defence's evidence so compelling – so logical – was that it did not tally in every detail. If the two Mauritians had agreed to fabricate an alibi, de Visdelou would never have told the police that he could not remember fetching the cat until de Marigny had reminded him. Moreover, if de Marigny had killed Oakes, his only motives could have been hatred and money. Yet after Oakes's outbursts in March, they had never met again. If de Marigny had been roused to violent hatred, why had he waited until July to strike? And if he needed the money – which he denied – why had such an intelligent man murdered in such a clumsy fashion?

'After hearing all the evidence,' concluded Higgs, 'if there is left in your minds any reasonable doubt that the accused committed this crime, you must acquit him of the charge. I merely remind you of this, gentlemen, because it is the law of our land, and not because I feel that the defence has to fall back on reasonable doubt to obtain an acquittal.'

'On the contrary, gentlemen, I feel that the evidence which has been placed before you proves conclusively that Alfred de Marigny never killed Sir Harry Oakes and I believe, gentlemen, you can return only one verdict – and that a unanimous one of Not Guilty.'

It had been a fine speech, worthy of the grave burden that Higgs had shouldered for so long now. As he sat down, after almost three hours on his feet, he had reason to feel that he had met the challenge well. Juries are always hard to gauge, and often they can surprise even seasoned advocates with their verdicts, but all in all Higgs believed that things had gone well.

At any rate, they had gone better than the evening before when he had rehearsed the speech with Callender as his jury. As he reached the end, he had looked up from his notes to see what his junior had made of it. Ernest had been stretched out in a chair, fast asleep.

Absorbing as Nassau found the trial, Bay Street's newspaper of choice, the *Nassau Guardian*, still made room for the things that counted, the monitoring of the comings and goings of the winter residents and the better-connected 'war guests'. At the end of October, it now informed its readers, Lady Boles had received a cable from Mrs Arthur Owen letting her know that she and her two children had arrived safely in England.

With the U-boat menace in the Atlantic diminished, my grandmother had left the island earlier in the month and this time, after an uneventful passage, had reached home. From some-where, the Duchess had managed to find her a purseful of dollars for the journey, and as thanks my grandmother had left a parting gift – some Georgian wineglasses – for the Windsors to find when they returned from America. The thank-you note, embossed in yellow with a coronet above a design of two Ws entwined, arrived from Wallis Windsor in January 1944.

'It is indeed nice to have something really good in Government House,' she wrote gratefully, saying that she was glad to hear that the family had finally been reunited. 'And may we meet,' she added, 'in the days of Peace.'

Hallinan was merely looking forward to the end of what had been a very taxing trial. First, however, he was going to try his very best to persuade the jury to convict Alfred de Marigny of Oakes's murder. The evidence surrounding the fingerprint was clearly fraught with problems, so his method was to begin instead with all the other elements that made up the Crown's case, patiently rebuilding its strength in the jury's mind.

The point, he said, that he wanted them to remember above all was that de Marigny was a man who lived extravagantly. In eighteen months of marriage to Ruth, he had worked his way through ten thousand pounds (three hundred thousand in today's money), and by May 1942 his now ex-wife was threatening to sue him for the return of one hundred and thirty thousand dollars, the equivalent today of almost a million pounds. De Marigny needed money fast, and Nancy was to provide it: the crazy, hasty, 'romantic' wedding that month was no coincidence.

Soon, however, continued Hallinan, de Marigny had realised that he was losing the goodwill of his father-in-law – such as it was – and relations between them continued to deteriorate. Things were slipping, and Oakes was the cause. With him out of the way, de Marigny could work on Lady Oakes through his domination of Nancy and her brother Sydney. 'Then,' concluded Hallinan with an uncharacteristic oratorical flourish, 'the whole Oakes fortune would lie at his feet.'

Suddenly there was a commotion in court as Nancy jumped up and pushed her way noisily and angrily through the throng to the door. 'I could not bear to sit there and hear him say such filthy things,' she told reporters the next day, riled in particular at the suggestion that Freddie must have forced her to write the letter breaking off relations with her parents. Nancy de Marigny knew her own mind.

Her electrifying gesture of support for him sparked a resurgence

of hope in de Marigny's heart. Only a few months earlier Nancy
and he had seemed to be drifting apart, under pressure from her
family and with Nancy anxious about her health. Yet since she
had returned to Nassau he had come to rely on her more and
more. She had been the rock on which he had built his defence,
the focus of all his dreams for the future, the one thing that had
kept him sane.

Every morning she had come to his cell with the poached
eggs and toast that Charles had made and had wished him luck for
the day. At night, it had been her whom he saw when he did
finally sleep. With little to do but examine his conscience, and
with only the Bible for company, de Marigny's love for his wife
had begun to burn with a new intensity.

The next morning, 11 November, Hallinan told the jury that he
did not propose to speculate about what exactly had happened in
Oakes's bedroom. It was enough to know that the baronet had
been brutally slain. Instead he would turn to 'the involved question of the fingerprints'.

The value of Barker's evidence, as was obvious, turned on the
detective's integrity. Barker, Hallinan said, had an almost unblemished record with the Miami Police Department yet the defence
was prepared to throw mud at him. If Barker had decided to fabricate evidence, he must have done so from the outset. What
motive could he have had for that? And if he had decided to go
down that road there were much easier ways of falsifying clues.
Why, for instance, had he not simply marked a spot on the screen
and said on the first day that he had found a fingerprint there,
instead of waiting until 19 July, so creating problems for himself?

Barker was an honest and experienced policeman, and the
defence's objections to his methods were groundless. Given the
conditions, it was permissible for him to have lifted the print to
preserve it, and if he had not fingerprinted others who had been
in the room it had been because Pemberton had told him that
they had not touched anything. The defence were no longer

claiming that de Marigny had accidentally touched the screen, and their theory about the glass did not hold water: when Melchen had taken it from the Count's right hand, he would have smudged any prints on it.

Hallinan's speech was long, but it was effective. It had neatly avoided mentioning such problems as Barker failing to divulge the existence of the print to Melchen, and Hallinan had left the jury with an easy way of resolving their doubts.

'A case such as this, built on circumstantial evidence, is like a portrait,' he told them. It was impossible to look at just a single feature and identify the man – perhaps one might think that the artist had not got every detail quite right – but taken together they formed a clear image, a picture of the murderer of Harry Oakes.

Adderley's rhetoric might have worked up a jury's emotions more than had Hallinan's precise, desiccated presentation, yet the law officer had not been above appealing to their prejudices. Look at the type of people de Marigny associates with, he had implied, look who supports what he says: a dubious foreign 'Marquis', his teenage mistress and some black servants. Is it this lot you believe? Or is it people like us?

'The United Nations,' began Daly, in words that carry a faint echo today, 'is now fighting a war for liberty, and one of the most cherished principles of liberty is that no man should be condemned in the Empire except by a verdict of his fellows.' Every judge runs his courtroom in a different way. All act as referees between two competing sides, but some like to blow the whistle, and to steer the direction of the game, more than others. Sir Oscar Daly was an interventionist.

'Think of me just as a thirteenth juror,' he said mildly to the jury, 'someone who is here solely to advise on the law and help you discuss the case.' It must be up to them to decide the verdict, he went on – before showing them exactly what he thought that verdict should be.

Daly's recapitulation of the evidence was a tour de force that

lasted four and a half hours and amply demonstrated his command
of the case. Only rarely did he have to refer to his five hundred pages
of notes, a feat of memory that impressed the watching journalists.
He began by emphasising that the jury must disregard any rumours
that they might have heard prior to the trial and, more surprisingly,
he stated that they should treat with caution much of the expert evidence that they had heard in the past three and a half weeks.

Prosecution witnesses, Daly said pointedly, often inclined their
testimony towards the Crown's case, and the jury had to consider
if the police had been trying to make the facts fit their theories. In
the row in front of him, Adderley and Hallinan must have started
to feel rather low.

Not that Higgs was to be spared. There was no evidence, however, said Daly, taking off his glasses and peering down at the
defence barristers, that police evidence had been deliberately fabricated. That was not to say they had not made mistakes – but that
was entirely a different matter.

De Marigny's heart was positively palpitating by this stage.
What did this judge mean? Did he think he was guilty, or innocent? As Daly got into his stride it soon became plain which it
was, and the Count settled back in his seat and began to chew
contentedly on a matchstick.

To Daly's way of thinking, the police had made a number of
grave errors, which cast doubt on their testimony. The prosecution must show beyond a doubt that the fingerprint had been
found where they said it was found and when. Yet Barker had not
marked the position of the print, nor sent for a camera to have it
photographed. That he had not done so was incomprehensible.

'Another extraordinary mistake that Captain Barker made,' the
judge continued, 'was that in the Magistrates Court he opined
that the print came from Area No. 5 on the screen, and it was not
until he consulted with Mr Conway a few days before the trial
that he found it could not have come from there. That was a very
grievous error.'

By now, Daly's delivery was becoming more and more angry. He

tossed his head and pushed back his wig as he set out Barker's failings. He was unable to understand why there had been such a long
interval between the American detective's lifting of the print on 9
July and his identification of it on 19 July. He had explained that it
was because it was reversed, but any expert would know that – even
the jury did by now. Then, too, they would recall the dramatic
moment when the detective had alleged that someone had traced
over his line on the screen, a claim he had had to retract moments
later. Was he someone who jumped to hasty conclusions?

It was unfortunate, too, that Erskine-Lindop had not been called
to corroborate the evidence about the burnt hairs. Instead, the
Crown was asking them to trust Captain Barker's memory, yet he
had made that incredible statement that de Marigny had smooth
forearms when the briefest of glances had showed the opposite to
be true. 'Wouldn't you think he would be more careful?'

Just then, with Daly summing up favourably for the defence,
and the jury drinking in his words, a tremendous eruption of
coughing and retching broke the hush. De Marigny had choked
on his matchstick. Higgs gave him a withering stare, and his
embarrassed client tried to avoid his gaze.

The jury were men of the world, concluded Daly, and they
understood that the relationship between de Visdelou and Betty
Roberts was perhaps not as platonic as the couple maintained.
That might explain some of the odd atmosphere in that room that
night and the Marquis's statements. They had seen too that de
Marigny was no fool when he gave evidence. Was it likely that he
would have told Melchen that he had hated Oakes if he really was
guilty? But, of course, that was for the jury to decide. Perhaps the
Court was a consummate actor, as the Crown claimed.

Whatever they did decide, Daly hoped that their verdict would
be unanimous. If in their opinion the accused was guilty beyond
a reasonable doubt, they must not shrink from their duty in sending him to the gallows, but all twelve must be agreed. Otherwise
it was their duty to acquit him, and a majority of two-thirds
would be acceptable for a Not Guilty verdict.

At 5.27 p.m. the jury was sent to an upper room to decide the fate of Freddie de Marigny.

Not a soul moved from their chairs. The jury might be out for hours, but the spectators would wait for them. Outside, a crowd began to grow by the minute, and soon a line of policemen was needed to hold back the hundreds gathering on the green. Night fell on Nassau.

Inside the courthouse, the press readied their telegrams for dispatch. It was an easy task. Each reporter had two prepared: one read GUILTY, the other NOT REPEAT NOT GUILTY.

Finally the tension became too much for de Marigny, and he was escorted out of court and across the way to the Central Police Station. There he paced the floor, working his way through cigarette after cigarette, occasionally glancing across nervously at the lights in the jury room. What were those twelve men saying over there, as they held his life in their hands? Surely Higgs's work – and Daly's words to them – had done enough to save him, to overcome their prejudices? Surely it had. But what if . . . what if . . .? A cold wind blew through the square, rustling the leaves of the giant silk cotton tree.

On the floor above, Nancy was giving an interview to a journalist. 'Freddie is not a stupid person,' she was insisting, 'and the crime was stupid and clumsy.' She ascribed the rift between herself and her parents to her having not seen much of them when she was being educated abroad. 'Now everything in my life has been knocked for a loop. I'm only hoping for the best.'

Suddenly a cry came up – 'The jury's back in!' It was 7.20 p.m. They had been out less than two hours. What did it mean? Was that good, or bad?

Nancy walked slowly across to the courthouse and, pale-faced, took her seat. A moment later, Freddie was marched back in under guard. He looked quickly around the room, but failed to see his wife.

Daly entered and sat down. Somewhere in his desk was the

square of black cloth that he would place on his head if he now had to pronounce the death sentence. The Registrar faced the jury box, and de Marigny rose to his feet. His flesh prickled with sweat and his stomach fell away. He was not afraid to die, but he was afraid that he might feel faint if the verdict went against him. All seemed very quiet.

'Gentlemen, are you agreed on a verdict?'

'We are.'

'How say you?'

'Not Guilty.'

There was an instant of silence, then pandemonium. As women leaped up, cheering, Freddie smiled and this time he saw Nancy. Her eyes were closed, and she was swaying back and forth.

'Order! Order!' shouted the judge. 'Order! Order!' shouted the police, with just as little effect. Striving to make himself heard, Daly told de Marigny that he was discharged. The Count stepped down from the box and threw his arms around Nancy as she rushed to meet him. A wave of noise began to flood into the room.

As the doors were thrown open, and the de Marignys, arm in arm, stepped out into the crowd, the hubbub rose to a new pitch of intensity. The night was illuminated by the flash of a score of cameras as the press trampled on each other in their scrimmage for photographs. Onlookers, mainly black and hundreds strong, began to sing 'For He's A Jolly Good Fellow', and heaved de Marigny onto their shoulders. An elderly woman pawed at his arm while police and soldiers tried vainly to stem the tumult.

American troops, RAF personnel and smiling Nassauvians milled hither and thither in a maelstrom of singing, shouting and backslapping. Finally Freddie and Nancy were propelled into a car, which sped off towards their house. Slowly, the spectators in the square and those in the courtroom drifted away into the dark. Underfoot, crushed and forgotten, were two dozen telegram forms bearing the word GUILTY.

★

In all the commotion, it was not until five minutes after the de Marignys' exit that the jury foreman was able to tell Daly that they wanted to add two riders to their verdict, which had been 9–3 in de Marigny's favour. The first was to record their dissatisfaction that Erskine-Lindop had not been summoned from Trinidad to give evidence.

The second was to recommend that Alfred de Marigny should immediately be deported from the Colony.

TEN

De talles' tree in Paradise –
De Christian call it de tree ob life
All my trials, Lord, soon be over!
I'm on me jerney 'ome

In Victoria Avenue a crowd of several hundred was gathered to welcome home the couple in triumph. Their house had been bedecked with flowers, and the butler Charles was already opening champagne. At the bar in the Prince George, de Visdelou was pouring drinks for all comers, but the numbers of those around their cottage rather alarmed the de Marignys. Having escaped death, for a moment the Count reverted to bravado, tossing a few soundbites to waiting reporters – 'I was tried ten per cent for the murder of Sir Harry, and ninety per cent for marrying his daughter' and 'I enjoyed the trial. It got me out of jail every day.' Nancy was more circumspect: 'I am too happy to speak,' she said, before they thought better of lingering and drove off for a quiet dinner with the Higgses and af Trolles.

The next morning, the *Nassau Guardian* was spitting fire in all directions. It lambasted the 'utter failure of the heads of the Police Department from the first moment to realise their responsibility in this matter,' seething that the prosecution had been 'badly let down by the lack of definite and satisfactory evidence.' There was no doubt what it thought the verdict should have been, had the jurors witnessed fewer blunders in court.

Its less conservative rival, the *Tribune*, left another question hanging in the air: 'Who made the first and biggest error that led to the greatest fiasco in a criminal trial held in this Colony?' Overt criticism of the Duke of Windsor would have been a little too bold even for the *Tribune,* but he could expect to hear echoes of *sotto voce* comments about his decision to call in Melchen and Barker when he finally returned from America.

The international press had already moved on. In New York, another society murder case had broken. Wayne Lonergan, a Canadian, was accused of killing his young wife Patricia, heiress to a brewery fortune. The pair had moved on the fringes of Brenda Frazier's set – nights at El Morocco, early mornings at '21' – but had latterly been estranged. Patricia's lover had been the first suspect, a handsome, twice-divorced Count with a now familiar-sounding name – Gabellini. The twist was that before his marriage to Patricia, Lonergan had been her father's boyfriend.

The evening after his acquittal, de Marigny and his friends were in a party mood despite having heard about the deportation recommendation. Among the guests was Leonarde Keeler, the lie-detector expert, who had been unable to convince the judge to let him demonstrate his kit in court. It did not take much persuasion for him now to rig up his polygraph and show how it worked, using a few of the women present and cards picked from a pack.

'I want to take it,' said de Marigny suddenly. Nancy looked across at him. 'No, no, it's all right,' he told her. 'I've always wanted to take it.' Schindler and Keeler were secretly delighted, and soon cuffs and cables were fastened to the Count's chest, arm and pulse. The Mauritian grinned up at Keeler from his armchair: 'Ask me anything you like about the case – just don't ask me about my past.'

The room grew very still.

'Is your name Alfred de Marigny?' said Keeler.

'Yes.'

The recording pens did not waver.

'Do you live in Nassau?'

'Yes.'

No movement.

'Did you kill Sir Harry Oakes?'

De Marigny looked at his wife.

'No.'

The paper rolled smoothly on.

'Have you eaten something today?'

'Yes.'

'Did you touch the Chinese screen?'

'No.'

His answers had triggered no abnormal response. For Schindler and Keeler, it was final confirmation of de Marigny's innocence.

In prison, de Marigny had rediscovered his faith, and the morning after the verdict he and Nancy had attended Mass. Now he wanted to take a step further with her, and the following Saturday the priest with whom he had talked so often in his cell, Father Bonaventure, waited for them to arrive at his chapel. None of de Marigny's three marriages had been witnessed by the Roman Catholic church, an omission he had decided he wished to rectify. 'We seek to do Christ's work in welcoming back lost sheep,' the good Father had told reporters the day before, but now he waited an hour – and in vain – for his flock to appear.

De Marigny later gave out that the ceremony had had to be called off at the last moment because he had realised that Nancy had not yet reached twenty-one, the age in the Bahamas when she could marry without her parents' permission. The reality was that her husband's plans had taken her by surprise. Nancy had been so focused on the trial itself, on the events leading up to the verdict, that she had not really considered her future – their future – and how her heart stood. Now she wanted time to think.

The last few months had proved to be a watershed for de Marigny's Countess. It had been the first time in her life that she had found herself at the centre of events, and she had blossomed. Without her parents to restrain her, and without a husband beside her, Nancy had discovered that she relished the attentions of the press, and those of the intelligent men in whose company she found herself all day. She had married while still a girl, and was only now realising how attractive almost every other man seemed to find her. And she had seen so little of her husband these past few months. First she had been in New England, then he had been in prison every night, and in court – where she could not go – during the day. She had so few real friends on the island, and the nights had been lonely.

It was no surprise, really, that Nancy's heart had strayed, and at least three times, I was told, she had found others to console her. Among her admirers had been Paul Zahl, the scientist who had recruited Schindler, and a few months after the trial he wrote to her fondly, and flirtatiously.

While Zahl was in part making contact in the hope of discussing some issues relating to her father's death, the letter also suggests that his friendship with Nancy had not been entirely platonic. He certainly seems to have wished that they were still together, and expresses his hope that she does not think too unkindly of him. The trouble was that Nancy was not sure any longer *what* she thought.

At about the same time as Father Bonaventure was waiting by the altar, the Executive Council of the Bahamas had met in special session. There was one item of business on the agenda: whether to deport de Marigny from the Colony.

That ExCo was even considering such a step is little short of extraordinary. Much as the *Nassau Guardian* might have thundered that the jury's rider was 'endorsed by a large majority of the thinking public', it carried absolutely no weight in law at all. Even more arbitrary was the decision by the Council to add de Visdelou's name to that of de Marigny.

What had prompted such behaviour? In a word – embarrassment.

Hardly had the Not Guilty verdict been returned than Heape, the
acting Governor, began sending a flurry of telegrams to London.
'Am strongly of opinion that deportation order should be made,' he
wrote on 12 November. Two days later, he told the Colonial Office
that the newspapers were out for blood, that the general opinion
was that the Count was guilty, that the verdict had been inevitable,
given how things had transpired in court – but that 'nothing
matters if we can get de Marigny and Guimbeau out of the
Colony.'

To his superiors, Heape insisted that 'retention of these men
will create discord in the community and demonstrate the impo-
tence of local government.' In fact, all it would achieve would be to
intensify still further the blushes of the Governor when he returned
later that week, and it was this that the Duke of Windsor – who
was undoubtedly instructing Heape all the while from America –
was trying to forestall.

London, however, had weightier matters to attend to, and it
told Nassau with no little asperity there was no chance of an RAF
Transport Command aircraft being laid on to take the pair to
Mauritius, as Heape had requested.

Nonetheless, Heape pressed on. At the meeting on 15
November at which Higgs, Hallinan and Christie were present, the
majority of the Council voted that both men should be deported.
Higgs and Herbert McKinney, however, 'wished it to be recorded
that while it was desirable that Mr de Marigny leave the Colony, he
should be permitted to leave of his own accord and that no deportation order should be made.' As ever, de Marigny had provoked
strong feeling, and deep divisions, in Nassau society.

The timing of the meeting, while the Duke was still absent, was
no coincidence, allowing as it did the decision to be taken without
him being seen to participate. Yet once he had returned, he was not
shy of revealing in private his feelings about de Marigny and his
friend. When a letter from de Visdelou arrived, asking for six
weeks' grace to put his affairs in order, the chilly official response
was that the Governor-in-Council required him to leave immedi-

ately. And in a remarkable outburst to London on 25 November, that quite equalled for character assassination his pre-trial comments to Stanley about de Marigny, the Duke let fly the following assessment of the stone in Nassau's shoe:

> His matrimonial history shows him to be an unscrupulous adventurer. Twice divorced and three times married since 1937. Despoiled second wife of £25,000 and then married daughter of millionaire. Has evil reputation for immoral conduct with young girls. Is gambler and spendthrift. Suspected drug addict. Suspected of being concerned in the unnatural death of his godfather Ernest Bronard. Evaded Finance Control Regulations by obtaining divorce from second wife. Convicted of offences of being in unlawful possession of gasolene [sic] and of gasolene rationing orders. Engaged in two businesses in violation of Immigrants Act. Jury upon acquitting de Marigny of murdering his millionaire father-in-law unanimously recommended immediate deportation.

Even allowing for the frustration that the Duke was feeling at de Marigny's continued presence on the island, this litany of wickedness demonstrates a most unmajestic pettiness. Very few of the graver allegations could be substantiated, although it was true that earlier that week both the Count and de Visdelou had been fined for having bought the drums of black-market petrol.

Some would have it that such a display of nervous tension was proof of the Duke's complicity in a conspiracy against de Marigny, and that hence it was now all the more important that the Mauritian should be removed from the Colony. It is far more likely, however, that the Duke had simply descended to the level of his charges and caught Bay Street's prevailing disease: prejudice.

Yet there is perhaps one accusation that carries a little more weight, if only because both my grandmother and others I talked to remember it being persistently attached to the names of both de

Marigny and de Visdelou before Oakes's murder. It is that they were, to use the modern phrase, date rapists and that – to show that nothing is new – they used drugs to help them in this less than wholesome pursuit.

Twice it was mentioned to me that both men were reputed to use Mickey Finns to drug girls' drinks and leave them helpless, and there was a story in common circulation that one of their victims had been left pregnant. Certainly no charges were ever brought, and it may only have been the kind of rumour that went with the two men's undoubted attractiveness, and attentiveness, to women. But the fact that many believed it may help to answer three questions: why the jury asked that de Marigny should be deported, why the otherwise seemingly blameless de Visdelou was added to the list, and what the Duke meant by 'immoral conduct with young girls'.

He may just have been referring to de Marigny's wooing of the seventeen-year-old Nancy, or to a gross rumour that the Count himself mentions that de Marigny kept a brothel in Nassau stocked with under-age girls with whom he would blackmail businessmen. But perhaps the phrase was more revelatory than the Duke knew. He himself had been an unscrupulous womaniser in his youth, and indeed was even then suffering the consequences of an earlier bout of philandering.

The FBI files show that in late 1943 he was being bothered by letters from one Rhoda Van Bibber Tanner Doubleday, a demanding American woman who had divorced well and who, after 'running around quite a bit' with the then Prince of Wales, had convinced herself that he had agreed to make her his queen before he fell under the spell of Wallis Simpson. Worried that he was going to be blackmailed, the Duke had sought the aid of the Bureau, who had agreed to look into the matter.

Little more was heard of Mrs Doubleday. Since the days of their acquaintance, however, the Duke had moved on to more intimate, voyeuristic pleasures. Bert Cambridge was a noted jazz musician in Nassau, and also one of its few black politicians. In later life he liked to reminisce to anyone who cared to listen about the afternoons when he had been summoned to the Governor's residence, not in his political capacity but in his musical one – to accompany the striptease artistes who gave private performances for the Duke.

The Duchess, Cambridge remembered, took it all in her stride; there was not, perhaps, much other entertainment to be had in the Bahamas.

Loath as he was to turn and run, de Marigny had quickly realised that there was no future for him now in Nassau. Such was the prevailing animosity towards him that his businesses stood no chance of flourishing, and he saw that it would be wiser to cut his losses and make a fresh start with Nancy elsewhere. She too seemed willing to leave her past behind, and three weeks after the trial, in early December 1943, the couple took a yacht across to Havana. There they became house guests at the *finca* of the Count's friend Ernest Hemingway.

They had not, however, escaped their troubles. While de Marigny enjoyed his days of shooting with the writer, and developed a passion for the sport of *pelota*, Nancy found Hemingway embittered and overbearing. She got on rather better with Martha Gellhorn, with whom she became good friends, and got on far too well with Hemingway's son Jack, with whom she went on to have an affair.

The de Marignys' marriage was beginning to unravel. Whatever the root of their difficulties, which probably predated the trial, it was compounded by money worries. The costs of de Marigny's defence had been extremely high – he put them at ten thousand pounds (three hundred thousand today) – and he had been forced to sell almost all he had to pay the likes of Schindler, Keeler and Higgs, to whom he had even sold *Concubine*. Afterwards, he and Nancy would dispute who had paid for what, but by then Nancy had problems of her own. Nearly all her assets were in sterling and in the Bahamas, from where it was extremely difficult to extract them during wartime. Nancy, reduced to selling her furniture to pay for medical treatment, was used to being comfortable and secure, not a gypsy without money in her pocket.

In an attempt to improve their financial position, and to justify himself to the world, de Marigny signed a contract for a book about the trial. Shortly afterwards, he claimed, there were two attempts on his life. In the second, a bullet was fired at him from the street through a window, hitting a pan of hot chocolate that he was stirring. He thought it wiser to return his advance.

Whatever the truth of this, there was no doubt that the Oakes case had not gone cold. When Zahl wrote to Nancy in Cuba in April 1944, he revealed that he, at least, was still taking an active interest in its solution. With Dan Vaccarelli, the ex-FBI agent, whose motives arose 'from his former dealings and his disdain for the Nassau crowd, including the Christie element', he had steadily been making inquiries and, he believed, progress.

'What I'm trying to say, and the reason for my cable, is that we think we know who the perpetrator is. Naturally, I won't put the man's name down on paper; and furthermore he is not known to you personally. Suffice it to say that the suspect is a native, now on one of the outer islands, and in committing the crime was in some-one's hire, whose identity we also know.'

The use of Christie's name is clearly an indication of who Zahl thought that person was. It was on Christie's trail, after all, that he and Vaccarelli had been when they had gone to see Agent Ladd at the FBI the year before. There was, however, someone else whom Zahl wrote that he would like 'to have a few drinks with . . . although I do not implicate him': Walter Foskett.

Christie, meanwhile, was also busy with the Bureau, fingering someone else. In May 1944 he travelled to New York to hire a private investigator to re-examine the crime and to determine who the culprit was. He had lunch with Brenda Frazier's husband, John 'Shipwreck' Kelly, a former college football star who he knew also acted as a trawler of gossip for the FBI. He told Kelly that Nassau – by which he meant himself – thought it bad for the tourist business that the death had not been solved, and that there would be avail-able a fund of ten to fifteen thousand pounds (£300–450,000 today) to help clear it up. Christie told Kelly, too, who he thought had murdered Oakes: Alfred de Marigny.

As Kelly subsequently reported to the Bureau, what was so funny was that when he had been in Cuba a little while before, de Marigny had vouchsafed to him his own thoughts about the identity of the killer: Harold Christie.

Ray Schindler was not finished with the matter either. In July 1944 he wrote to the Duke of Windsor, offering to investigate the mystery for free. He received a dusty answer: 'In the event of the re-opening of the case . . . proceedings would be conducted by official and not private investigators.' It is in any case a moot point how much Schindler might have achieved beyond keeping his name and generous dimensions before the public eye. For all his vaunted reputation, he had unearthed, at prodigious cost, almost nothing that could have helped de Marigny. If he had a skill, it was in public relations, and as self-appointed master of ceremonies he had certainly managed to get the press on Nancy's side. But aside from seeing the handprints being washed down at Westbourne he had shone little light on the mystery itself.

Though Zahl felt that Higgs had been 'in a bad way' before Schindler's arrival, and that the detective had 'contributed just enough to push the case over its critical hump', he was scathing about the man's forensic skills. 'He failed utterly in the faith we had in his being able to pull a rabbit out of the bag,' he commented to Nancy. 'As a matter of fact, you probably know that practically all the dope which Schindler had was material I had gathered and in good faith turned over to the Schindler agency.'

Keeler had been of more help, conducting experiments on the duplicate of the screen, although, Zahl reflected, 'I don't think Marie helped much by interjecting a personal note (i.e. Keeler) while the trial was in full sway, and while goings-on were under closest scrutiny by the world's press.' It was not just elderly judges who had fallen for the charms of the girls of Nassau.

It had been Barker's skills, rather than those of Schindler, on which the trial had turned, and at the end of August 1944 they were scrutinised once more in the former frontier town of Deadwood, South Dakota. The occasion was the annual meeting of the International Association for Identification, whose board of directors now called Barker to account. He freely admitted that he had made mistakes, but insisted that the latent print of de Marigny had come from the screen. The five-strong panel also heard from O'Neil and Keeler.

Their verdict was merely that Barker had 'departed from the best approved methods' and accordingly should be strongly reprimanded. The board's thinking was relayed to the FBI by one of its members, the Bureau's own Quinn Tamm. The key, he said, had been Daly's insistence that there was no evidence of deliberate fabrication by Barker.

'My personal reaction . . . was simply this,' he wrote in his report: 'Barker was not competent to conduct an investigation of the type to which he was assigned. The case was too big for him. He very definitely bungled the whole investigation through faulty techniques . . . I feel that he probably had a solution to the case within the scope of his investigation and that he failed to appreciate the value of the material he was developing . . . I feel he did develop the latent fingerprint in the Oakes residence.'

Although de Marigny had been found innocent, few people, it seemed, believed that he really was. Soon he found himself at the very bottom of society's heap. Having argued once too often with Nancy, he had taken passage as a deckhand on a steamer bound for Canada, and in the spring of 1945 he was given permission to enter the country – but only for thirty days. America had already made it clear that he was not welcome there. Shortly afterwards, he woke up in a Montreal hospital suffering from hypoglycaemia.

It was from his sickbed that de Marigny's first memoir, *More Devil Than Saint*, emerged. It was in Montreal, too, that he and Nancy parted for good. By then she was involved with a Danish pilot in the RAF named Hans Edsberg, and she and her husband mutually agreed that whatever had once bound them together had long since dissolved. He writes that she had coarsened; perhaps she felt that he had been in love with someone she no longer was.

Their romance had always had something of a fairy tale about it: a charming Prince; a Princess trapped in the ogre's castle; a pot of gold at the foot of the rainbow. Now it had reached the most unhappy of endings.

By this time those who had made the Bahamas their wartime sanctuary had begun to leave the islands. This outflow included the Windsors. The Governor resigned his post in March 1945, and shortly before VE Day he and Wallis waved goodbye (and good riddance) to their little-loved home of the last four years. By July they were on more welcome ground, as guests at a lunch given by Hugh Fulton, an intimate of the new American President, Harry Truman.

Fulton had been chief counsel to the anti-corruption committee which had investigated Nassau's new airfield and, the FBI learned, he was most anxious during the meal to talk to the Duke about a particular someone who had died unexpectedly not long before he was due to give evidence – Harry Oakes.

And then gradually, as the years passed, the events of the summer of 1943 and the name of Oakes himself began to fade from memory.

For some few years afterwards the case regularly resurfaced in the headlines. First there were the cranks. In 1950, a California shoe clerk named George Boyle confessed to the murder, saying that he had committed it on a fishing trip while drunk. A little later that year, a cook on a Nassau-registered yacht by the name of Majava told police that two women were involved in blackmailing the killer, whom he hinted was Christie. Some months on, a taxi driver called Nicholas Musgrave was sent to prison for writing threatening letters to Lady Oakes demanding forty thousand pounds.

When Musgrave died in jail several years later, his death was inevitably labelled 'mysterious' by the press. The Oakes case had already begun to attract that kind of aura, largely because of the murder, also in 1950, of Bettie Renner, a Washington-based lawyer who had once worked as a secretary for the FBI. When her half-naked body was found outside Nassau, the newspapers claimed that she had been investigating the Oakes killing. They had no evidence for this, but it made for a better story than the rape and murder of a tourist. Thereafter, the death of anyone remotely connected to the case was proof of the curse attached to it.

Nearly a decade later, the affair was once more revived when a Nassau politician, George Stevenson, said that he was prepared to name the guilty party, 'a close friend who had drunk with him a few hours before.' Stevenson claimed that he had fresh evidence from Schindler, but nothing further was heard of this. Christie, meanwhile, let it be known that he would sue anyone who linked his name to Oakes's death.

For at long last the Bahamas was beginning to boom, and all Christie's salesmanship was starting to pay off; he certainly could not afford to have his name sullied at this juncture. After the war, high taxes in Europe had encouraged more of the wealthy to move their money to the Bahamas. By the mid-1950s, second-home owners and tourists were also starting to arrive in quantity – and then Fidel Castro came to power in Cuba. With the imposition on Americans of an embargo on travel to their erstwhile favourite playground, visitors to nearby Nassau increased tenfold, and then tenfold again. In 1950, the islands attracted thirty-two thousand tourists; by 1968, more than a million; and by 2000 they were playing host annually to some four million sun-seekers, who collectively spent $1.5 billion and generated ninety per cent of the country's revenue.

The landscape, and the value of the land itself, was also transformed. Seafront properties such as Westbourne were torn down and replaced by hotels, and in 1961 the Oakes family trust sold 3,200 acres at Cable Beach for development as houses and shops. Nancy said that she had wanted to build on it herself, but the offer was simply too good and she was overruled. Besides, all that cheap land that her father had bought was now the Oakeses' prime asset;

five years previously the worked-out Lake Shore mine had been sold.

At the heart of everything was Harold Christie. The ocean of money that now washed into Nassau must have reminded him of the good times during Prohibition, although increasingly the Bahamas would come to be associated with the smuggling of some-thing deadlier and even more profitable than rum – cocaine. The deals being cut, and the fortunes to be made, ensured that politics and corruption were soon synonymous in Nassau, one of the chief offenders being Stafford Sands, the one-eyed lawyer who had rep-resented de Marigny on the night of his arrest. Control of Eden had become very lucrative indeed.

Yet Christie remained untainted, ever the beaming public face of the islands. In winter, he travelled to London with his brochures, setting up his office in a suite at Claridge's. The rest of the year, as chairman of the Development Board, he kept an eye on construc-tion projects, notably the luxury gated community being built on land he had sold at Lyford Cay, home to the very rich in need of the very private, among them Sir Sean Connery, Arthur Hailey, and Christie himself.

In 1959, at the age of sixty-two, to the surprise of all, the eter-nal bachelor took a bride. He had met Virginia Johnson, a divorcee twenty years his junior, when she had decorated his house. Further contentment followed in 1964 when he was knighted, for services to the Bahamas. Nine years later, the nation that he more than anyone else had helped to stand on its own feet won independence from Britain.

Two months after the Bahamas' flag was raised for the first time, Christie died in Frankfurt while there on business. He was seventy-seven. He died rich, satisfied and admired by all. Just one shadow had troubled the bright evening of his life, as Diana Mosley recalled after both of them had been the guests of Lord Beaverbrook in the South of France. Beaverbrook had been among those enticed to move to Nassau by Christie's patter, but he was not above teasing the Bahamian. 'Come on, Harold,' he said, as they sat down to dinner. 'Tell us how you murdered Harry Oakes.' It was a joke that drew from Christie a very tired smile.

While waiting for the Allies' justice, Hermann Goering had some unexpected visitors in his cell. They were two agents from the FBI, and they wanted to talk about Wenner-Gren. They had been told by the Swede's former secretary, Elof Ostman, that the tycoon had spent much of the war caching large sums of money in South America for the *Reichsmarschall*, a story that seemed to confirm all their suspicions about him.

Goering, however, poured cold water on the tale, saying plausibly that he had never known Wenner-Gren well and frankly regarded him as nothing more than an opportunist. Confirmation soon arrived from America that Ostman had been put up to his story by a disgruntled former lawyer of Wenner-Gren's. Though the Bureau subsequently grilled the Swede, and went carefully through his Mexican and Panamanian bank accounts, beyond a little false fronting they could find no evidence of money laundering nor of anything else to substantiate the rumours about him – including Anderson's story of the millions salted away for the Duke of Windsor.

Wenner-Gren was finally taken off the proclaimed list in 1946, and proof that his reputation had been rehabilitated to some extent came when Truman's daughter stayed at his town house in Nassau for her honeymoon. Yet, as with Christie, a cloud of suspicion continued to dog Wenner-Gren and – unlike Christie – his postwar ventures amounted to little. He had effectively been sidelined at Electrolux, and though still immensely wealthy he dissipated his energies in fruitless grandiose projects in Rhodesia and British Columbia, as well as in a visionary but frustrating passion for monorail trains.

In 1959, Wenner-Gren sold his estate on Hog Island to Huntington Hartford, the American groceries heir. Two years afterwards he died and was followed a decade later by his wife,

Marguerite. She had spent much of that time in Mexico, almost a
prisoner in her own home, her chief companion a parrot who
uttered over and over the one phrase he knew – 'Don't listen to that
old fool!'

During the next thirty years, Hog Island was turned from a
quiet backwater into one of the most popular destinations in the
world. Renamed Paradise Island, it first became home to celebrities such as Richard Harris and Michael Jordan. Then, in the
1990s, it became the site of the vast Atlantis hotel and theme
park, now Disneyland's principal rival for the dollars of American
holidaymakers. The innocence of oranges on sticks belongs to a
bygone age.

Grim as the post-war routine of the Windsors seems in hindsight –
a ceaseless round of sponging carried on against the backdrop of a
rather loveless marriage – they saw no reason to wish themselves
back in Nassau. The descriptions in the Duchess's memoirs of their
time there has all the warmth of a fixed smile, while her recollection of the events following Oakes's murder is remarkable for its
brevity – and its inaccuracy. She writes only that Melchen was
unable to develop any prints or to find any other clues, and makes
no mention at all of the debacle that was de Marigny's trial.
Embarrassment is never a pleasant memory, and patently it was an
episode that she wished to forget.

By then there was much else that the pair wanted swept under
the carpet, principally the revelation in the mid-1950s that captured
German papers showed that the Nazis had believed early in the war
that they could win over the former king to their cause. Yet for all
his incautious and perhaps even unpatriotic table talk, there is no
credible evidence that the Duke would ever have forsaken his country and his duty. Many of the relevant files, nonetheless, will remain
closed until 2054, proof most likely not of something worth hiding
but of the reverence that British officialdom still has for decisions
made by its predecessors.

In time, the Windsors retreated to Paris. There they saw out their days in games of cards and cultivating their garden, attentively conserving what had become their rather tarnished lustre.

The lawyers involved in the de Marigny trial all prospered. Eric Hallinan first became Chief Justice of Cyprus before returning to the West Indies as its principal judge. In later life, he revealed that from the earliest he had had doubts about Barker's capacities, prompted by the episode in which light was said to have spoiled the film in his camera. He had asked the FBI to intervene, but they had refused on the grounds that another American law-enforcement agency was already involved. Ultimately he had fallen back on the barrister's traditional evasion of his conscience. His task had only been to present Barker's evidence to the jury, and it had been for them to decide whether they believed it. Fortunately for de Marigny, his presentation had not been convincing enough.

Alfred Adderley accomplished even more. Not only was he the first black Bahamian to be nominated to the islands' upper house, the Legislative Council, but when Daly retired he became the country's first black Chief Justice – albeit only for two months, until Sir Oscar's white successor arrived. Full equality would have to wait a few more decades. Nonetheless, in 1953 it was Adderley who was chosen to represent the Bahamas at Queen Elizabeth II's coronation in London. He made the journey even though by then he was suffering from advanced leukaemia. He died on the flight home.

Ernest Callender, whose cross-examination of Melchen had proved so devastating, steadily rose in the profession, and later numbered Errol Flynn among his clients. In 1943 the Nassau Bar had had about a dozen members, half of whom were involved in the de Marigny case. By the time when Callender retired in 1985, aged seventy-six, the law had become one of the islands' principal employers, a reflection of the Bahamas' rise as a centre of international finance.

The tenacious Godfrey Higgs also remained in the law, although he never developed a liking for criminal or even court work. Instead, his handling of the legal side of much of the transformation of Paradise Island made him wealthy, funding his love of sailing and a late-flowering passion for orchids. Exhibit J was given pride of place in the offices of the law firm he founded after the trial. He died in 1986, but his memory is preserved by a plaque in Nassau cathedral.

All these lawyers did rather better than the hapless Colonel Erskine-Lindop, who had so eagerly taken the chance to exchange the Bahamas for Trinidad. He need not have bothered; a Colonial Office assessment in 1945 of his performance in his new posting rated him 'a disaster'. It was not his fault that the Oakes case had been mishandled, but it is legitimate to doubt whether he would have come any closer to solving it had he been left to his own devices.

Although Ray Schindler had not cracked the case either, it did not stop him from assigning it as much prominence in his publicity as any he had. In the foreword to a hagiographic biography of Schindler, *The Complete Detective* (1950), Erle Stanley Gardner wrote that it was a mistake to think that Schindler had been retained to find the killer, when in fact his task had been to secure de Marigny's acquittal. He had done little enough towards that, and then had further angered Nancy by lending his name to several sensational articles after the trial that gave vent to his theories about the murder, chief among which was that the killing had involved voodoo. The last interview that Schindler ever gave, shortly before his death in 1959, was about 'my most famous case'.

His partner Leonarde Keeler had died young in 1949. A year earlier, Edward Melchen had succumbed to a heart attack. He was succeeded as chief of detectives in Miami by James Barker, who was not to remain in the post for long.

When the Miami City Commission altered its requirements so that Barker was the only candidate qualified for the job, the press openly began to ask some long-suppressed questions, such as how he had been able to buy an expensive house in the upmarket retreat of Biscayne Bay. For several years there had been rumours that

Barker was in the pocket of the city's mobsters, rumours even that he was being investigated by the FBI. Under the strain, his handling of cases became increasingly erratic.

Then, in the spring of 1949, Barker's long-running feud with the head of the vice squad, Lieutenant Huttoe, came to a head when Barker beat Huttoe up, breaking his nose so badly that he had to be hospitalised. At the time Huttoe had been investigating corruption claims against Miami's mayor and its city manager, and allegations were now made that Barker had tried to frame the pair in a brothel in order to blackmail them into making him chief of police. As the outcry mounted, Barker was suspended. A year later he retired from the force on medical grounds with a full pension. 'If they force my hand,' he had told reporters, 'I'll go all the way.'

By the next time Barker made it into the newspapers, he was deputy sheriff of Monroe County, down in the Florida Keys, where he was probing the suspicious disappearance of a local beauty queen. The case had a familiar ring to it: the chief suspect claimed that Barker had planted evidence against him. Several months later, in the summer of 1952, Barker disappeared and was seen wandering the Keys, apparently having lost his mind.

At eleven p.m. on Christmas Night of that year, Barker turned up at the house of his son Duane, also a Miami policeman, where he had been living for the past few weeks. Duane and his mother had been out at a party, and on their return had decided that Barker must be told to move out again. The ex-detective and his wife Clarice, Duane's mother, had only recently divorced, as indeed had Duane and his own wife. Reports suggest that the younger Barker had suspected his father of making advances to his daughter-in-law.

When Barker arrived home he was, according to Duane, 'hopped up on drugs'. For more than a year he had been taking morphine, barbiturates, heroin — anything he could get hold of, perhaps to dull the pain of arthritis, a legacy of his motorcycle accident. At about two-fifteen in the morning, he went into Duane's room, where an argument broke out. Barker produced a gun, and he and his son wrestled for it. The gun went off, the bullet hitting the older man in the head and killing him instantly.

'He wanted a father, but he didn't have one,' was all that Clarice Barker could say afterwards about the family tragedy. Her son was released without charge, and a finding of accidental homicide was returned. Shocking as it was, it was not an unfitting end for a life so filled with anger.

With all eyes on the de Marignys as they headed for Havana, Georges de Visdelou took ship for Jamaica. In October 1944 he arrived unobtrusively in Liverpool to arrange his divorce from the wife whom he had had not seen for five years.

Georges did not marry Betty Roberts, however. Her reputation had been hopelessly compromised by the suggestions in court of her intimacy with de Visdelou and, shunned by Nassau, she decided to emigrate. It was then that Nancy came to her aid, repaying Betty's loyalty during the trial by arranging for her to be sent to a private school in America. She emerged two years later a different person, even having changed her name. She subsequently married a Belgian nobleman and then, after his death, remarried into one of America's wealthiest families.

De Visdelou, meanwhile, remained in Britain. Ever the dilettante, he busied himself with his cartographic and historical pursuits, publishing in 1948 his long-cherished account of the discovery of Mauritius. Thereafter he dropped from sight until in 1989 the exotic, enigmatic Maxime Louis Georges, Marquis de Visdelou-Guimbeau, died in the slightly prosaic setting of St Leonards on Sea, East Sussex.

Not everyone found it so easy to escape the shadow of the Oakes case. It cast its pall furthest over the lives — and deaths — of Sir Harry's five children. Their mother scattered the family after the murder and never made a home for them again. The younger children were sent to boarding schools and spent their holidays with friends. Shirley grew up largely in Philadelphia with people she came to regard as her surrogate family, while Harry Philip spent much of his childhood with the Kellys.

Oakes's eldest son Sydney, who had inherited the baronetcy, lived for a time at Oak Hall, the house by Niagara Falls, but in 1959, shortly before a well-publicised divorce from his wife, he sold it; it is now the offices of the Niagara Parks Commission. In 1966, aged thirty-nine, he was killed after losing control of his sports car while driving through Nassau.

By then his brother Pitt was also dead. In his early twenties he had made a spectacular marriage to a well-known model who was said to have turned down a proposal from Orson Welles. By his mid-twenties he had fallen victim to heroin and had begun to lose his mind, running round the house barking like a dog and lifting his leg against the furniture. At twenty-seven he was dead in a New York hospital, the victim of heart and liver failure.

Their younger sister, Shirley, was the brightest of the children, and studied first at Vassar before reading Law at Yale. In middle age, however, she lost many of her assets in a swindle, and then she too had a road accident, one that left her incapacitated for the remaining years of her life.

Crashes are not uncommon in the Bahamas – Charles Hubbard, who had been Oakes's dinner guest on the night of the murder, was also killed in one – but implacable furies seemed to pursue the Oakeses. Only the youngest child, Harry, has lived a relatively peaceful life, as much as one so closely touched by catastrophe can be.

After all that she had endured, Nancy certainly deserved a measure of happiness, but it largely eluded her. Fate, and her own failings, combined to frustrate her at every turn. The first blow was the death of Hans Edsberg, the pilot with whom she was in love, in an air accident in 1946. Fleeing everything that she knew, she entered what friends think of as her Hollywood period, chasing and being chased by film stars. Those who knew her before the trial say that the attendant publicity had turned her head, and that she came to believe herself the poor little rich girl of the press's imagination.

Perhaps she had lived so intensely during the trial that, like a spy no longer undercover, she found real life too humdrum to cope with. She seems never to have lived normally again, to have always been searching for some new thrill. Her trouble was that she needed to be desired, but was not built to defend herself against those who preyed on such delicate nymphs.

It may have been understandable, but the constant breaking of her heart led her to develop a vindictive streak, and its principal target became Freddie de Marigny. 'He would have been good for her,' Marie af Trolle told me. 'He really did love her.' Instead, in her former husband's words, she set out to 'squish me into the gutter.' Her anger took the form of seeking not merely a divorce from de Marigny, but a formal annulment of their marriage, on the grounds that his divorce from Lucie-Alice had been improperly granted.

The Catholic de Marigny jibbed at the idea of the sacrament of marriage being voided in this way, and the matter went to law. Initially he held his own, but in 1949 a Supreme Court judge in New York held that this first divorce had been obtained by false testimony. Nancy was content.

Not long afterwards she gave birth to a daughter, Patricia, born of her liaison with Richard Greene, the actor best remembered as television's definitive Robin Hood. He and Nancy had met on Capri when he was filming one of his many swashbuckling roles. Patricia, who was raised first by her aunt Shirley and then, in an attempt to avoid gossip, 'adopted' by Nancy at the age of four, subsequently married, as his fourth and much younger wife, Franklin Roosevelt, Jr., the late President's son. But her own parents had long since separated.

Instead, in 1952, aged twenty-eight, Nancy had married for a second time. This time her husband was a German aristocrat six years her junior, Baron Ernst Lyssardt von Hoyningen-Huene.

Lyssardt had swum the Elbe to escape Soviet-dominated East Germany and, helped by his uncle, the photographer George von Hoyningen-Huene, he had fetched up at university in Mexico. He fell in love with the beautiful, experienced Nancy, but on the

night of their wedding, he told me, she seemed to change completely, from adoring fiancée to '24-carat bitch'.

It became clear, according to von Hoyningen-Huene, that what
she wanted was a handsome escort on her arm and another noble
title to her name. He detested pretension – including his own title –
and thrived on intelligent conversation. She thrived on parties, and
the marriage soon foundered. The other Oakeses did little to
make him feel welcome, and when Lady Oakes – 'she had all the
warmth of an ice-cube' – grew tired of her daughter's complaints,
she paid von Hoyningen-Huene £500 to agree to a divorce.

He fled to New York, and a career in banking which eventually
took him back to Nassau, while Nancy and their small son soon
moved to Mexico, where she later married Patrick Tritton. Both of
them liked to drink too much, and this union did not last either;
Tritton subsequently married Georgina Ward, previously the wife
of Ali Forbes, the socialite and gossip (and uncle of Senator John
Kerry). Following this third divorce, Nancy reverted to the von
Hoyningen name and style (liking to be known as 'The Baroness')
and lived between London and the Bahamas, where she retained
considerable holdings. Early in 2005, the Bahamas' government
announced that it had finally paid her twenty million dollars for
land it had acquired from her sixteen years previously.

Nancy had admirable qualities, not least a certain generosity, the
stylish way in which she carried herself and the bravery with which
she had submitted to numerous operations on her mouth and face
for years after her initial illness. Yet she could be reckless and self-
ish, although she was always capable of a charming aside, especially
if the recipient were a young man. Nonetheless, her contrariness
and unwillingness to take advice (and her hunger for male company)
lost her the goodwill of many of her oldest friends, and for much
of the 1970s and 1980s her defects of temperament were worsened
by an addiction to prescription drugs. But she remained in touch
with Martha Gellhorn; the two were due to lunch together on the
day that the writer died.

Nancy's increasingly frail old age was perhaps the time to reconcile herself to her past, but she had long since cut her ties with her surviving brother, with whom she had quarrelled over money matters, while her mother had died in 1981. If ever proof were wanted that money cannot guarantee happiness, in Nancy Oakes's life it could be found in abundance.

And what of the debonair Alfred de Marigny, trampled into the gutter? By his own account, he was for a time certainly down and out, unable to get a job because of his notoriety but too proud to change his name in order to do so. Nonetheless, his inability to find employment makes one wonder about his claims that just a few years before he had been a stock-market wizard, with superb contacts on both sides of the Atlantic. Now he was reduced to accepting charity from strangers in the street. One man who recognised a shivering de Marigny on a bitterly cold day in Montreal presented him with a fur coat; in the pocket he found a further gift of two hundred dollars.

Now began an Oresteian period of exile as he vainly attempted to settle first in Haiti, then in Santo Domingo and finally in Jamaica. From each country he was soon ejected. He had little doubt that such action was at the behest of those who still bore malice against him. In 1947 he arrived in New York, flat broke.

De Marigny writes that he had stashed considerable funds there with a lawyer before the war, but the man had died and his papers were in a confusion. To make ends meet he sold his blood to hospitals and walked dogs for society women, a job found for him by his friend Igor Cassini, the gossip columnist 'Cholly Knickerbocker'. It was quite a change from sunning himself on the deck of *Concubine*.

And yet the Count was not all victim. As once he had perhaps been shrewd enough to understand what advantages a title might bring him in America, so now he was sufficiently prepared to trade on his name to accept work with a marriage bureau in Hollywood. There was still a split in his make-up, between a rather shy man within and the external player – too sure of himself and too loud of voice – who lived for the bright lights and easy money.

He was rescued in 1952 by his fourth marriage, to Mary. She was then training as a nurse, but was the niece of Myron Taylor, the steel magnate and America's wartime ambassador to the Vatican. Although she and de Marigny shared the same birthday, he was thirteen years her senior. Yet finally, in his early forties, he had found someone who could give him the stable family life he craved. After spells in Cuba and Mexico, they settled with their sons in Houston, Texas, where de Marigny concentrated on his bridge and tennis.

He proved an attentive, strict father, if one with a weakness for a good yarn about his early days and a penchant for the superficially brilliant argument. In 1975 he became an American citizen, and now without reluctance renounced his title. He died almost as he had come into the world, as plain Alfred Fouquereaux de Marigny, in 1998.

By then he had apparently come to terms with the events that had almost destroyed him over half a century before, but he still bore their scars. Bitterness lingered in a corner of his soul; Nancy would telephone him every March on his birthday, but he would never take her calls.

For others, too, the ties forged during the case remained strong. Years after the trial, Sir James Goldsmith's mother Marcelle gave a dinner party in Paris for those who had lived through it. Georges de Visdelou, Freddie de Marigny, Marie af Trolle, even Betty Roberts came.

In a pause in conversation de Marigny was asked, only half in jest, a question he must long have been expecting: 'So, did you do it?'

'No,' he said coolly. 'But I know who did.'

ELEVEN

Let guilty men remember, their black deeds
Do lean on crutches made of slender reeds

The White Devil, Act V scene vi

Two questions are central to the murder of Sir Harry Oakes. The
first is who killed him, and the second is whether de Marigny was
framed. There is a third, subsidiary, issue: are the answers to the
two questions connected? In other words, if the Count was set up,
does that necessarily point to the identity of the murderer?

The most frequently aired theory about de Marigny's arrest has
been that it was carried out at the behest of the Duke of Windsor.
It was certainly an explanation of which de Marigny himself
seemed convinced. Writing to his family in Mauritius on his
birthday in 1944, he told them that 'this little scoundrel' – the
Duke of Windsor – 'and all his clique' had nearly hanged him,
having organised a trial 'similar to Dreyfus.' In his second memoir,
A Conspiracy of Crowns, published after Edward Windsor's death,
de Marigny directly implicates the former king in a plot to have
him executed.

The Duke's reasons for wanting de Marigny out of the way, as
given by the Count and other writers, can be grouped under
three possibilities. The first turns on money. Either, it is held, the

Duke had borrowed substantial sums from Oakes or, along the lines of Anderson's tale, was involved with him, Christie and Wenner-Gren in an illegal banking scheme in Mexico. In each case, the Duke did not want Oakes's finances too closely investigated after the murder, and needed to find a way of having the case closed quickly. De Marigny fitted the bill as a possible killer and Melchen and Barker obligingly faked evidence against him.

A second motive, it is said, was simply to have the death cleared up as soon as possible before any scandal attached itself to the islands and threatened the Duke's chances of being offered a more congenial post, such as Ambassador in Washington. For this reason the Duke bypassed the Bahamas' perfectly competent CID and turned to the Americans, who responded to his nod and wink.

A third incentive could have been revenge, for de Marigny's insolence to him and his Duchess. Perhaps a combination of all three prompted the Duke to attempt to rid himself of several problems at the same time.

There is, however, a fundamental objection to such ideas, one that their proponents have overlooked for more than half a century. Even if one pushes aside the forceful counter-arguments – the lack of corroborating evidence of money laundering, the difficulty of ensuring the acquiescence of Oakes's bookkeepers, the sheer peril for the Duke of putting his reputation in Melchen and Barker's hands – and accepts that Edward Windsor needed to behave in such a fashion, that still leaves the little matter of when he physically might have done so.

The Windsor theorists have always pointed to his visit to Westbourne some time after lunch on Friday 9 July, just a few hours before de Marigny was arrested. It was then, the scenario goes, that he talked privately to the two American detectives and, explicitly or implicitly, made it clear that de Marigny was the solution to all of their troubles. The Count, it will be remembered, wrote in *More Devil Than Saint* of the strange look that the Duke gave him as he left the house. Even though de Marigny subsequently admitted that he was not in fact there at the time, dubiously relocating the incident to the evening before, that glance has become – symbolically, at least – proof for many of the Duke's guilt.

The trouble is that someone else was also not there that afternoon: James Barker. Not enough attention has been paid to the precise chronology of events that day. Melchen's interview with de Marigny was over shortly after noon, while Barker, as he repeatedly testified, had finished working on the screen by one p.m. As he and Pemberton told the court, by the time the Duke arrived they had already departed, to process photographs of fingerprints at the RAF laboratory. Thus, if the Duke did go to Westbourne prepared to instigate a set-up, he was too late; the Americans had already secured the evidence that they later presented, whether it was taken from a glass or from the screen itself.

It will never be known what the Governor – the Duke – did say to Melchen when just the two of them spoke that afternoon, but any intervention by him would in any case have made no difference. If there was a frame-up, it was already in progress and the Duke was not the driving force behind it. He may well, for reasons of his own, have been pleased that de Marigny was arrested. He may even, though I think it most unlikely, have suggested that course of action to Melchen. But de Marigny was not accused solely on the Duke's whim. He was always going to be fingered for the crime.

It could be argued that the Duke might have made his suggestion the day before, Thursday, in some unrecorded conversation or meeting with the Americans after their arrival. But, again, there is the immovable stumbling block of time. It was not until late that night, when de Marigny was brought in for questioning after the post-mortem on Oakes, that it became apparent to the authorities that he had a far from cast-iron alibi. Given that he would not have known on Thursday that de Marigny did not have a good let-out, the Duke can only have made his wishes clear once he had been informed of that, presumably sometime on Friday morning.

Then he would have had to contact the detectives – but how?
It could only have been by telephoning them, probably at
Westbourne, where they were from nine a.m. Yet a call – with its
dangers of being overheard, not least by the exchange operators –
seems far too risky for such a sensitive matter. It would have
demanded a private, face-to-face meeting, but by the time one
did take place the two detectives had already made their move.
That this was prompted by what they had heard from de Marigny
the previous night seems, on the balance of possibilities, much
more credible than that it was the result of some reckless power
play by the Duke. Of the fact that he could be childishly spiteful,
there is ample proof; that he would knowingly send an innocent
to the gallows, there is not.

A previous writer about the murder suggested to me that sexual
jealousy of de Marigny – whom he believed the Duchess lusted
after – lay behind the Duke's scheme. I think that two other angles
to the conspiracy theory can be just as swiftly dismissed. That the
Duke sidelined the Bahamas police force so as to avail himself of
Melchen is undeniable. But the unprofessional and discreditable
conduct of Pemberton and the police corporals during the case
shows that he was justified in thinking them not up to the job. The
Duke was not merely looking for an excuse to bring in men who
he knew would do his bidding against de Marigny.

Equally, the notion that Erskine-Lindop was deliberately sent
away from the Colony by the Duke so that he could not contradict the Americans' evidence at the trial is not borne out by the
sources. It makes for a better tale – I remember being told on my
first day as a journalist by a more experienced gossip columnist
that I needed to 'change the quote to fit the story' – but the best
tales are rarely true.

Following the publication in December 1942 of the Russell
report, which had strongly criticised his inaction during the riot
earlier that year Erskine-Lindop himself had asked to be seconded
to the Army or transferred to another colony. The Duke had
made a 'strong personal recommendation that his wish be

granted as I consider it unfair that he should be subjected to further bludgeoning by a certain Bay St element which would
undermine his position.' The Colonial Office had approved. The
reality is that the Commissioner's move was sanctioned six months
before Oakes's murder, not as a consequence of it. Moreover, he
was still in Nassau during the earlier hearings in the Magistrates
Court, yet was not called by either side.

Had the Defence thought that the Colonel had something sufficiently important to say – for instance about the lack of burnt
hairs – they could have summoned him then, or indeed brought
him back from Trinidad during the trial itself. That they did not
should perhaps give one pause to wonder what it was they
thought he had seen.

If, therefore, the American detectives were acting on their own
initiative, when did they decide to act? The importance of the
answer to this is that it bears on another well-worn theory about
the case, namely that Oakes's murder was carried out by the
Mafia. Sometimes this supposition has also embraced Christie, the
claim being that it was he who suggested that Melchen and Barker
should be brought in, knowing that they were in the Mafia's pay
and would duly cover up the crime by arresting de Marigny. In
any event, the core of the hypothesis is the notion that by the time
the pair arrived in Nassau the Count had already been selected as
the patsy.

The main support for this idea is that Barker undoubtedly was
in the pocket of Miami's gangsters. The city's police force was particularly corrupt and, as the FBI knew, Barker was among those
on the criminals' payroll. As early as 1940, he had been identified
by agents as passing information about the Bureau's activities to
'local hoodlums'. By 1942, he was 'getting a cut of the gambling
take in Miami' and deliberately losing photographs or refusing to
take fingerprints of suspected con artists. As we have seen, by the
time he succeeded to Melchen's post the newspapers were openly
asking questions about his links to organised crime.

Yet let us again look carefully at the sequence of events on 8 July, after the Duke had made his call to Miami. Even if he'd done so at Christie's suggestion, it was Melchen for whom he asked, a policeman thought by the Bureau to have a 'good reputation' and not one identified as corrupt. Barker was only called on when Melchen requested him because he needed an officer with technical skills.

One can, of course, assume for the sake of argument that Melchen and Barker were both in the mobsters' pocket or that somehow the gangsters were able to give Barker orders during the frantic hour in which he talked to Melchen, packed up his equipment, drove home to collect some clothes and then raced to the airport. Yet the detectives' behaviour that first day in Nassau still seems at odds with the notion that they knew in advance who their target was.

In particular, if Barker already had a plan to trap de Marigny there was no reason for him not to immediately begin to look for fingerprints at the scene. It would have made no difference to his scheme, and we know from O'Neil's testimony that high humidity was not a valid excuse. Instead, he needed to wait for something, to find somebody to accuse. Equally, how could the Mafia have pre-selected de Marigny as a scapegoat without being certain that he would not have a rock-solid alibi?

Given that de Marigny did not come into focus in the investigation until he was quizzed on Thursday night, what is more plausible is that it was then that the American detectives decided (without any prompting) that he was the guilty man and that, although they would undoubtedly find some evidence against him, it would be just as well to have a little insurance. Maybe the routine with the magnifying glass and the burnt hairs had something to do with this. It would have been a ploy that an old hand like Melchen or Barker would have worked many times before. If they had a motive beyond trying to convict a man they thought was a murderer, it must have been a desire to impress the Duke, to justify their having been called in. They would show these toy policemen how good real cops were.

And yet why the plural? It has always been assumed, not least by de Marigny and Nancy, that Melchen and Barker were acting together. There was, for instance, the moment during the interview when Barker put his head around the door to check that all was well – the signal, believed de Marigny, that Melchen had secured the print. But if that is so, how can one explain Melchen's extraordinary revelation at the trial that Barker had not told him about it for almost a week, that he had not known of its existence until Oakes's funeral? Surely he and Barker must have been acting in concert to obtain de Marigny's mark, but if that is true why had they not, in the three and a half months since the murder, got their stories straight?

The answer, I believe, lies in something one might not expect to come across in a murder case: office politics. The two men had joined the police force at the same time, but it was Melchen who had done better. They were technically equals in rank, but as head of the Homicide Squad it was the flabby Melchen who had the more prestigious post, one that the aggressive Barker hankered for as a release from the tepid technicalities of identification work.

Barker and Melchen, it will be recalled, had already fallen out some time earlier over the solving of a quadruple murder, the Vincent Christy case. Despite Barker's 'strenuous protests', Melchen had gone over his head to send evidence found at the scene to the FBI's laboratory, which had led to the arrest of Christy.

Now Barker had seen his chance to get even, and perhaps to do more than that. Just eighteen months before the events in Nassau, he had hoped to achieve his life's ambition by joining the FBI. He had been turned down. As well as noting his formerly heavy drinking, his assessment had pointed to his 'dogged determination to do things his own way without the benefit of advice' and commented that 'under some circumstances, it is believed he would act on impulse to the exclusion of his better judgement.'

That rejection must have rankled. Barker wanted to be a successful officer, one who made the headlines, and the Oakes case offered him precisely that opportunity. He would show the Bureau, and he would get Melchen's job into the bargain. Solving the murder would make his name.

In 1940, an FBI agent who had worked with Barker had noted that he 'expressed a desire to give this case quite a bit of publicity.' As Higgs accurately surmised in court, by 1943 Barker had let his wish for fame go to his head. Yet if he was to get the credit for breaking the case, he must ensure that it was he and not Melchen who found the key piece of evidence. And so, without telling his rival anything about it, Barker quietly lifted de Marigny's print.

The circumstances in which he did so must remain unknown. It seems most likely that, when he looked in on the interview, he noticed the glass and water jug and filed it away for future reference. He might have mentioned something about a fingerprint to a reporter or to Pemberton to cover himself beforehand, but the first that Melchen knew about it was at Oakes's funeral when Barker's impulsive nature again asserted itself and, wanting to make a splash, he blurted out the news of his discovery of the print.

If Barker was playing a lone hand, how can one reconcile that with Melchen's attempts to cover up his colleague's duplicity in court? Certainly, Melchen's lying about the timing of the interview, the suborning of the constables' evidence, and his statement that Barker had not looked in on the interview all suggest that Melchen had been going along with the plot.

The most credible explanation is the simplest, the one that Melchen himself gave in court. The fingerprint was not his and Barker's joint idea. Melchen genuinely had not been told about it by Barker on the train to Maine, for Barker had been waiting for the funeral to announce his triumph. Thereafter, having been called in personally by the Duke, and having brought in Barker himself, Melchen realised that the only way to avoid disgrace was to back up his colleague's story. That Barker was crooked does not mean that Melchen was always honest either.

At the trial, however, Douglas's memory of de Marigny's

movements started to expose the plan, and something inside Melchen snapped. Maybe he was tired or overconfident, maybe Callender wore him down, or maybe he just saw his chance to put paid to the pretender's machinations, and with savage glee deliberately blew Barker's reputation apart.

There is another possibility. That is that de Marigny was not framed at all, and that the print was genuine. This was certainly the view of the International Association for Identification (IAI) and of Quinn Tamm of the FBI who thought that Barker had merely been incompetent rather than dishonest.

It is interesting to note, for instance, that Barker's methods were not in fact as unorthodox as the defence made them seem. Following the trial, the Bureau made for its own purposes a lengthy list of cases in which it had lifted and successfully used latent prints in prosecution.

Barker did know his business. He may have been rather cavalier in the way he went about it: another FBI memo from 1940 disapproves of a new method of recording impressions that he had devised. But that only adds weight to the suggestion that Barker had failed to document properly where he had found de Marigny's print, not that he had never found it at all.

However, even without the benefit of access to the evidence, and working just from photographs of the scene, Exhibit J still strikes modern forensic scientists as suspect. I showed it to three separate experts, and collectively they identified four points of grave doubt. First, the location and direction of the print of the little finger – pointing awkwardly upwards, high on the screen – seems unnatural, although it might have been left there when picking the screen off the floor after it had been knocked over.

Secondly, that just one print was discovered at that spot is unusual, though Barker did maintain that he had found another – from the left hand – elsewhere. Thirdly, his claim to have recognised the print that Friday afternoon after lifting it would have represented a 'remarkable feat of memory', said one expert, given the islands, whorls, bifurcations and mass of other detail on all ten impressions taken from de Marigny. Lastly, and perhaps most obviously, the quality of the print presented is simply too good, too perfect.

In practice, I was told, an officer would be lucky once in a career to find such an unblemished identifying mark. It may in fact not have come from the glass at all, but from the very impressions that Barker had previously obtained of the Count's fingers.

Given what is known of Barker, given the odd behaviour of Melchen, and given the implausible nature of the fingerprint itself, I am certain that the print was used by Barker in an attempt to frame de Marigny. Higgs and Callender too were convinced of this, and ably made it the centre of the Count's defence. But in so doing they also largely diverted the jury's gaze from the other forensic evidence gathered, the burnt hairs on de Marigny's body.

The lack of truthfulness by Melchen and Barker in court entitles one to be sceptical about what the two American detectives claimed to have seen when they examined Freddie on Thursday night. Erskine-Lindop was invited to confirm the signs of burning by looking through a microscope, but one wonders whether he had the expertise – let alone the strength of mind – to have disagreed with their findings. Both Doctors Oberwarth and Huggins, of course, said that they saw no trace of fire when they inspected the Count just thirty-six hours later.

On what basis, then, had Melchen had de Marigny arrested? Naturally, it is arguable that Melchen was as bent as Barker, and that the hairs were part of an earlier joint plan by them to frame the Mauritian, a plan conceived before Barker undertook his lone gambit with the print. Perhaps Melchen was playing a very deep game indeed, and went along with both schemes of Barker's simply so that he could later blow him out of the water.

Two points, however, suggest otherwise. The first is the visit by the two men to the Miami cable censor's office on 10 July, the day after de Marigny was taken into custody. They were looking for a mysterious telegram of which no record was found, yet the real significance of their trip is this: if Melchen knew – because he himself was behind it – that a frame-up was under way, why was he bothering to be so thorough?

The answer is that there was no such intrigue. If Melchen had plotted a deception himself (or with Barker) regarding the burnt hairs, he had no need of extra evidence, no need to waste time chasing down telegrams that might only demonstrate the Count's innocence.

Equally, the visit suggests, since Barker had yet to produce his ace, that at that stage Melchen also knew nothing about the existence of other evidence – the faked print. He had not been in Barker's game from the start. When that card was played, it really did come as a surprise to him. Until then, the only proof he had had been the burnt hairs that he and Barker had seen on de Marigny's arms and face. While that was enough evidence for an arrest, Melchen wanted to bolster it by running down every lead he could.

Afterwards, Melchen found himself with little choice but to collaborate with Barker's scheme and bide his time. Yet one other episode, I think, confirms what Melchen had initially found, and it did not come during his own testimony but in Barker's.

Barker had had to watch Melchen's betrayal of his plan, and then had had to endure humiliation as Higgs dismantled his evidence. It had wounded him, angered him. Now he saw a chance for vengeance. It came when he was asked what had happened to the clippings of scorched hair taken from de Marigny. Barker said that they had been entrusted to Melchen.

At that the older detective had rushed from the courtroom. Schindler had found him vomiting outside, spilling his guts in fear and rage and vowing revenge on Barker. Yet if what Barker had said was true, what Melchen was anticipating, why was his reaction so extreme? It can only be that Barker was lying, and that what he had said had come as a horrible shock to the other detective.

That it was in fact Barker who had been given the packet with the hairs would seem to be borne out by Melchen's testimony that it was Barker who had largely conducted the search. It would thus have been natural for Barker to have kept any evidence that stemmed from it, as he did with any fingerprints that his investigations turned up. Scientific identification, after all, was his speciality.

Melchen had been expecting Barker to produce the hairs and so salvage the case. Now, instead, having already had to lie for him – and having been caught doing it – Melchen had been tarred with the brush of incompetence. He was furious. Not only would both detectives get blamed for the fiasco, but he had lost the chance of convicting de Marigny as well.

And it was all Barker's fault, thought Melchen. If only he hadn't wanted the glory of catching the killer with his stupid print. And Barker had really done a solid job with the hair evidence, hadn't he – pretending to fall into Higgs's trap about de Marigny's hairy arms. As if a cop as experienced as him wouldn't have made notes about what he'd looked at. He'd chosen his moment well, too, knowing that the only person who could contradict him had finished giving evidence. Christ, those lawyers were idiots! It made him sick.

The significance of the hairs is simply this: if they were scorched, de Marigny's explanations for their state do not stand up. Human hair is made of the protein keratin, and only singes when exposed to temperatures above 200° C, such as the flash from a petrol fire. Yachtsmen may suffer some sun bleaching to the hair, but not burning. Proximity to a large bonfire, such as on de Marigny's farm, would also provide insufficient heat, unless he stood so close that he would also have suffered severe skin burns. And lighting candles, as he demonstrated so dramatically in the courtroom itself, would cause at most localised burns to the hands, not to the arms, the head and the beard.

The two doctors said they had seen nothing, but even if one discounts Oberwarth's friendship with de Marigny both admitted to having used the naked eye rather than the lenses that they should have utilised.

Perhaps the two detectives did fake the evidence of de Marigny's guilt. Or perhaps they saw something that Thursday night which encouraged Barker to embark on his own ploy to nail the Count, and which made Melchen think that he had sufficient grounds for an arrest.

One of the curiosities about Oakes's murder is that, for all the evidence of his death, it proved impossible for the police to establish definitively how and where he had been killed. At the trial, the Crown admitted that it could not outline the precise series of events at Westbourne, and its inability to do so has since allowed speculation to flourish.

In particular, the presence of the upward-flowing line of blood on Oakes's face led to suggestions that the corpse had been moved, and even that he had been killed – and tortured with fire – somewhere else before his body was dumped back at Westbourne. The room was then set alight to conceal the manner and real location of his death.

At sixty years' remove, modern forensic science cannot solve all the queries in the case. But taken with a careful analysis of the evidence it can demolish some of the wilder theories that have sprung up.

When Oakes was found, he was wearing pyjamas, while his false teeth were in a glass at his bedside. The tennis clothes he had worn even to dinner are visible in photographs of the murder scene, flung on the other bed in the room. All these facts imply that Oakes never left his bedroom – and certainly not the house – after he had turned in for the night. More than one author has had him meet his death at the hands of the Mafia aboard a boat offshore when a meeting with them turned sour. It stretches credibility even further to see him heading for that midnight appointment in his pyjamas, or to believe that after his death the killers saw some reason to change his clothes or to take out his teeth.

Instead, everything points to Oakes having been murdered in

his sleep. The absence of any sign of struggle – such as the bedside table being upset or defensive wounds to his hands – strongly support this. The forensic pathologist whom I consulted thought it most likely that he had been lying on his right side, as it was on the left side of his head that the killing blows fell. The murderer probably stood between the two beds, which may suggest that he entered from the nearer door, up the stairs from the beach.

It is possible that the body was moved at some stage, as the line of blood suggests, which in itself (because of the weight) would imply that there was more than one killer. If it was de Marigny, then he was not alone. Certainly the blood and the pattern of burns on Oakes is consistent with his having lain more or less face down, his left arm below the trunk, providing it with some protection from the fire. Yet when the police arrived, he was face up, and Christie claimed that he had not moved him.

One macabre theory that would explain these anomalies was, in fact, put forward by Melchen – that Oakes became a human torch. The blows rendered him unconscious, close to death, and he began to burn while face down, blood running along his face and over the nose. Then at some point the flames reawakened him and he rolled over, or even staggered out of bed. One senior fire investigator told me that, if this had happened, it might explain such features of the case as Oakes's face being scorched but not his hair – suggesting that he was in a vertical position at some point – as well as some of the burns on the carpet and smoke patterns on the wall near the door.

It is hard to imagine anyone grappling with Oakes while he was alight, so the flames must have exhausted themselves. If he did then collapse and was put back on a blazing bed, it was face up, the blood now starting to congeal. The bed springs, incidentally, would have allowed sufficient ventilation for the mattress to burn even in the areas under the body, and the notion that the bedding would have been protected by the corpse, and therefore that its burnt state shows that he and it were set aflame at different times, can be discounted.

★

De Marigny always claimed that Oakes had been shot. But the weapon used was never found and is impossible to identify. The Count argued that only a gun could have shattered the thick bone by the ear, and he maintained that the small-calibre bullets had been concealed by the pathologist after the autopsy as part of the plan to incriminate him and aid Christie, who would have found it harder still to explain how he had not heard any gunshots. Yet my medical sources suggest that the four holes made in Oakes's skull could have been caused by any sufficiently substantial metal object. It probably had a broad rectangular edge ending in two sharp points or prongs, and for any killer would have been quieter than a gun.

In murders, the more blows one strikes, the less accurate one tends to become. Because in this killing there are two sets of holes, one deeper than the other, one can infer that Oakes was struck twice rather than four times. That in itself suggests a certain *froideur* in the killer's mentality, and maybe indicates that he was a professional. Oakes was certainly not bludgeoned to death in a hail of frenzied, hate-blinded blows.

A silver cigarette box or the base of a lamp could have done the damage, but there are no reports of anything like that missing from the house. The weapon was brought by the killer: the importance of that is that it is thus much more likely that the murder was premeditated than committed on impulse.

That scotches any scenario in which a hot-headed de Marigny, driving past Westbourne, decided to go in and confront his father-in-law, and the argument then got out of hand. And the likelihood of premeditation also indicates that the killer believed he would find no one else in the house that night who might stand in his way.

It would have been easy enough at the time for a pathologist to have tested for the presence of carbon monoxide in Sir Harry's bloodstream or for smoke in his lungs to establish whether he was alive when the fire was set in his room. But this does not seem to have been done, perhaps because Fitzmaurice wrongly believed from the presence of blisters that Oakes must indeed have been still living at the time.

Accordingly, all that is known for certain about the blaze is that it did not consume the room. The investigating officers seemed to think that it had been put out by the humidity, or by rain from the storm having blown through the open windows of Oakes's bedroom. This last point is transparently nonsense. Even if water had doused any fire near the door, the windows were a good ten feet from the burning bed (which was shielded on one side by the screen), and in any case Oakes would not have regularly slept in a spot where he might get soaked. Nor is there any mention of the carpet being damp.

The question, therefore, is why the fire really was extinguished. Was it a genuine attempt to incinerate the house, or was it meant to go out? In other words, was the killer trying to cover his – or her – tracks, or did they always intend the body to be found? And if the second alternative, then why had they started the fire in the first place?

The physical evidence can be interpreted either way. On one hand, the lack of development of the fire outwards from the bed is surprising. There was comparatively little smoke damage to the room, and though a second fire seems to have been deliberately started on the carpet near the door, it was at a spot some distance from any furniture. It is as if someone started a fire on the bed, waved a torch or brand at the Chinese screen, then let it die down near the door. If that was so, it would imply that they wanted to make it look as if there had been an attempt to destroy the house, but that it had failed.

Yet it is hard to see who would benefit from such a scheme. If Oakes was killed as a warning to others, for example by practitioners of voodoo as one theory has it, then a fire was never part of the plan since the body had to be found. The only explanation would be that Sir Harry was killed by someone who wanted to throw the police off the scent by making it seem as if the house was of no concern to them, but who actually had a vested interest in its value. That would point the finger at Oakes's own family – or perhaps at someone with a frugal mind who also controlled their assets. Someone like Foskett.

On balance, however, it seems more likely that the fire was intended to destroy the house, but that it ran out of fuel. Old materials burn slower than an inexperienced arsonist might realise, and the room was not cluttered with furniture that could easily catch alight. Splashes of accelerant – probably petrol, given the pattern of burns in the carpet – would have produced smoky flames which might have convinced the killer that the room was well ablaze. But in fact these flames would have died down fairly quickly once the petrol itself had burnt away.

The indications are therefore that Oakes's roaring funeral pyre soon became a localised, smouldering barbecue fire. This would explain why items such as the radio and table by the bed were not affected by it. The damage to the corpse, which was partly charred, prompted Melchen to think that there must have been great heat, a raging inferno. He was wrong. The greatest destruction to human bodies actually occurs in a slow fire, when burning material below a cadaver continuously melts subcutaneous fat from the body, which in turn drips down to feed the combustion. This process can consume a corpse, but it takes time: a crematorium furnace, which is a confined and superheated space, can require three-quarters of an hour to do its work on a body.

The time-frame given by the autopsy had first made Melchen suspicious of de Marigny's movements immediately after his party. As the police had learned more, and had been influenced by de Visdelou's hesitancy, the prosecution had come to concentrate on the Count's whereabouts in the middle of the night, at the later end of Fitzmaurice's given window of opportunity.

The nature of the fire, however, suggests that Oakes was killed rather earlier, as it would have taken more than two or three hours for the flames to consume the body. If that is so, then it alters entirely the focus of any case against de Marigny.

For if the crucial time is now around midnight or one o'clock, rather than at about, say, three a.m., any holes in de Marigny's alibi for the middle of the night suddenly become irrelevant. The key issue is what he did after dropping the girls off at a quarter past one, and what his staff saw when he returned to Victoria Avenue. It may be that even 1.15 a.m. is too late, and that by then Oakes was already dead. It certainly throws into sharp relief Christie's exit from Westbourne shortly before midnight.

Several other issues can be quickly resolved. The feathers found clinging to Oakes's body were not a voodoo warning but came from the pillow on his bed, the outer casing of which had burned away, as Christie mentioned. Moreover, for any killer to leave such a sign would be incompatible with a subsequent attempt to burn the room, unless the murderer and the arsonist struck at different times. Such a theory necessitates a leap from plausible conjecture to outright fantasy.

Instead it was the killer himself who brought the fuel. He may have tried to light a trail to the bed from the door, which would explain the line of burns on the carpet. When this failed, he re-entered the room to torch the bed itself, probably tipping petrol directly onto the left side of the body, which was the worst burnt. The pattern of damage in the room is not suggestive of a spray, such as the flit gun. The mysterious handprints, I suspect, were actually the residue of fuel being splashed at the wall. They seem never to have been analysed, and at waist level they were simply too low down to have realistically been left by anyone.

The burns to the stairs in the hallway are consistent with the murderer having gone up or down them carrying a burning, oil-soaked brand; it dripped fire as he walked. His ignition of the petrol vapour would have caused a low-order explosion, but in Christie's favour this could have been mistaken for thunder if he really was half-asleep. Whoever the assassin was, he would have almost certainly incurred flash burns – that is to say singed hairs.

Other questions must remain unanswered. We simply will never know how the intruder entered the house, how he got away, or what the watchmen were doing at the time. Where the room does 'speak', however, it tells us that the manner of Oakes's death and its attempted concealment were planned in advance and not in haste, and that if the fire was meant to seem like an accident the murder itself was not meant to be discovered. That would imply that the killer did not want a police investigation afterwards as he would still be around – and a likely suspect.

Above all, both the murder and the fire indicate inside knowledge. Oakes was a man of irregular habits, who moved frequently between half a dozen homes on the island – The Caves, the penthouse of the British Colonial, the town house in Nassau and Westbourne among them. The killer – or whoever had paid him – had to know that Sir Harry would be at Westbourne that particular evening and had not suddenly changed his mind about where he would sleep. Only a few days previously he had been at The Gatehouse, the property at the entrance to The Caves.

That meant the person behind the murder was someone who knew about Oakes's movements, and who had probably spoken to him or to someone in his household that very day. It was someone who knew the layout of Westbourne. And it was someone who knew that Oakes would be alone; it is a bold man indeed who enters a house confident that he can slay all who might disturb him, however many of them there might be.

As it was, the fire was meant to disguise the fact that there had been foul play and that Sir Harry's executioner knew that the only house guest was absent. Had he been a little more thorough with his pyrotechnics, the secret of Oakes's murder might have remained safe for all time.

Other inferences that can be drawn from Sir Harry's death eliminate some of the more fanciful theories about the killer's identity. Two of the three previous independent histories of the case plumped for the American Mafia as the perpetrators. Both authors believed that the mobsters Meyer Lansky and Lucky Luciano, keen to bring gambling to the islands, had had Oakes

killed (on that yacht anchored offshore) because he had resisted
their plans. Then they had Christie and Barker cover up the
Mob's involvement.

While it is true that the Mafia did take control of casinos in
Havana after the war, and that betting also became a key factor in
Nassau's tourist boom, there is no hard evidence to substantiate
such claims, and there are several awkward objections to them.
First, as mentioned before, gambling was in fact already legal in
the Bahamas, although it had not yet been developed on anything
like the scale that it would be. Secondly, Oakes himself liked a
flutter, and had no moral objections to it or to the growth of
tourism. Thirdly, he had no real political power, so it is hard to see
why the Mafia would have seen him as an obstacle.

Moreover, even if they thought he was exercising some restrain-
ing influence over those who favoured their scheme – Christie, for
instance – it is difficult to know why they should have chosen to
kill Oakes just then. The duration of the war was still uncertain in
the summer of 1943, and it would be the best part of another
decade before the American holiday trade recovered sufficiently for
the Mob to begin realising their plans in Cuba.

That is not to say that Christie, with his bootlegging past, or
even Oakes himself – if one recalls the boxer Greenwood's assertion that Sir Harry had smuggled Chinese workers into the
States – had not had contact with such underworld figures. But
that in itself does not supply a sufficiently convincing motive for
murder.

The Mafia was not the real power in the Bahamas as the islands
began to prosper in the 1950s. Instead, it was a rather more surprising figure. Certainly, Christie was the public face of Nassau,
and he replaced Oakes as its dominant personality. But standing
behind his shoulder was the stout, emollient form of Newell
Kelly.

Kelly had been Oakes's business manager, and was almost the
only person connected to the plutocrat who could demonstrate

that he had been off the island at the time of the murder. Yet that pre-arranged absence in itself raises some questions, not least because one wonders why – with his boss away – Kelly's chauffeur was driving Kelly's station wagon near Westbourne on the fatal night; the af Trolles, it will be remembered, had told the police that he had borrowed a wrench to change a tyre.

For all was not well between Kelly and his employer. Nancy later confided in Marie af Trolle that Sir Harry believed that his manager was cheating him, and he was planning to fire Kelly. Nancy, it must be said, tended to think the worst of the family's advisers, but if this was true it was a humiliation, and a check to his ambitions, that Kelly might not have been able to tolerate.

There may have been a more personal motive too. Rumour had it that Oakes and Kelly's wife, Madeline, who lived in a cottage at the entrance to Westbourne, were having an affair. Certainly Sir Harry was no longer close to his own wife, who had been living a separate existence in Maine for some time. Madeline Kelly was a frail woman, who suffered from a wasting disease, and when she was seen limping at Oakes's funeral it was given out that she had hurt herself stepping from the car. One report, however, places her injury prior to that day, and those who knew her say that her health declined markedly after the killing. Had something traumatic affected her that night? Could she have been struck by a vengeful husband who had secretly returned to Nassau and had caught her with her lover?

Her damaged leg, however, does not seem to have made an impression on those who saw her on the morning when the body was discovered. Any role that Kelly might have had in Oakes's murder remains speculative.

Oakes's death did, however, smooth the way for Kelly's ascent to much greater power. Within a decade of Sir Harry's murder, a small group of men had taken control of most activities – legal and illegal – in the Bahamas. Among them was Stafford Sands, who became the country's chief oiler of wheels until his self-enrichment became so blatant that he was forced into exile in

Italy. The islands had always been a place of moral corruption, but the pretence was that a little adultery, tax evasion and money laundering was not so sinful. Now that their corrosive effects were being revealed the Bahamas became more and more a place of fear.

Several times in the early 1950s, the FBI – and on one occasion the British Embassy in Washington – received complaints from Americans living in Nassau about the atmosphere of lawlessness that prevailed on New Providence. They said that they had been harassed when they tried to do business, and one claimed that he had even been shot at in his own yard. Several murders, they noted, had gone unsolved, while rumour had it that something sinister lay behind the sudden death of the latest Governor. All the letters identified the same clique of culprits, led by Harold Christie and Newell Kelly.

The family adviser of whom Nancy was most suspicious, however, was her father's lawyer, Walter Foskett, whom Zahl had identified as someone he wanted to quiz. Over the course of the several occasions on which I interviewed her, she laid out all her grievances and misgivings about him.

Following Oakes's death, Foskett had moved quickly to take charge of Nancy's father's estate. Arthur Dew, the company accountant, was sacked the same day, and Nancy – to whom money was ever dear – bewailed the fact that no proper reckoning of Oakes's assets was then made. When probate was granted, the comparatively small size of Sir Harry's estate shocked Nancy and convinced her that someone else had got their hands on much of his wealth.

Foskett had already persuaded the Oakeses to alter the terms of their will. For years to come the five boys and girls would be dependent on the annual income that Foskett, as the leading trustee, doled out. Furthermore, his decisions extended to other areas of their lives, for all of them were still, as teenagers or younger, legally minors.

Thus it was Foskett, according to Nancy, who ensured that the boys were taken away from their English public schools and sent to what she termed 'second-rate establishments' in America (in Sydney's case to highly regarded Chote: Nancy tended to think everything about America was second-rate – or at least not very smart – and had difficulty acknowledging that Sir Harry himself was born there). When Sir Sydney, as he had become, married in 1948, Foskett threatened to cut his allowance unless he resigned from the Army.

For Nancy, it was all part of a scheme to ensure that the children never became clever or self-reliant enough to challenge Foskett's hold over them (although it was a pattern she would attempt to repeat with her own children). When her brother Pitt (who had his own theories about his father's killer) died raving in hospital such was her near-paranoia that she thought he had been murdered too, the proof being that the date on his death certificate was a day earlier than it should have been. It was not a slip of the pen, it was no accident, she maintained.

Nancy told me that she did not believe the gossip that Foskett was her mother's lover, but such was his influence over Eunice Oakes that he might as well have been. Nancy was not even allowed to see her mother without his permission. It was this hold over the family, Nancy maintained, that enabled Foskett to swindle the children repeatedly, in particular with regard to valuable land that they owned north of Palm Beach – the city had expanded rapidly in the 1950s.

It became clear to me that Nancy had come to think that Foskett had been behind her father's murder. When I put that to her, we were sitting beside each other on the sofa in her drawing room just off Hyde Park. She could no longer see very well ('Although I can tell you're a handsome young man' – her need to charm was still intact), and she liked to keep the table close to her so that she could easily, and frequently, reach for her glass of rum.

As I made the suggestion, I can remember her turning to me as she was stretching for the tumbler, and glaring at me with her almost sightless eyes. 'Well,' she said indignantly, emotion for once colouring her drawl, 'wouldn't *you* think so?'

Certainly Foskett could behave so as to give one pause for thought. Shirley Oakes trained as a lawyer with the specific intent of solving her father's killing. She had a sharp mind – unlike her mother, described to me as 'devoid of intellect' – and when she qualified she was told by a family friend that she had now done enough law to find the answer she sought: it lay in the record of the trial. Foskett had kept a copy of the proceedings, and when Shirley next went to stay with him – as she did regularly – she announced at breakfast that she was going to spend the day reading the transcript. Her proposal caused Foskett to begin acting so peculiarly that finally she gave up the idea; later, in Nassau, she was threatened by someone if she continued her investigations.

There is little doubt that the dapper, silver-haired Foskett had a sharp mind. That, after all, was why Oakes had taken him on. It might well have been too sharp: even in the late 1930s the FBI was probing the tax shelter that he had set up for Sir Harry's Canadian assets, regarding its legitimacy as 'questionable' – as, indeed, were some of Foskett's Miami-based clients.

Yet this, and some odd behaviour, is hardly proof that he had graduated to murder. There is, however, one intriguing document in the FBI's files, a complaint made in 1959 by a Mr Maloof (or perhaps Malouf) against Foskett, alleging that Maloof had agreed a business deal with Oakes shortly before Sir Harry's death, a deal which the lawyer had conspired to wreck. When challenged by Maloof, Foskett had pulled a gun on him. Maloof goes on to say that he had told Oakes what had happened, and Sir Harry had been irate that he had been double-crossed by Foskett and had promised to have it out with him. Maloof contends that Foskett then arranged for Oakes to be killed to save himself from exposure and to acquire control of Oakes's millions.

The truth of this is simply unknowable. It may merely represent an attempt by Maloof to get even with Foskett for some other reasons, and many of the details he gives to support his story are manifestly wrong. Others, however, seem to ring true and make it probable that he had at least conversed with Oakes; there is mention, for instance, of Sir Harry wanting to bring a particular type of goat to Nassau, which seems like a genuine misremembering of his interest in short-haired sheep.

Nonetheless, as with Nancy's accusations, it is not proof of Foskett's involvement in her father's murder. Her anger at him – which sustained itself over the course of sixty years – was understandable enough, but while his behaviour does suggest that he unscrupulously used his position to take advantage of the family after Oakes's death, there is nothing to show that he actually caused it.

Foskett might well have talked to Sir Harry on the telephone that day from Miami and known his movements. It is possible, too, that he had lost or embezzled part of Oakes's fortune, which would explain in part the diminution of Sir Harry's wealth. Foskett might then have had Oakes killed to prevent his own ruin. There is, however, stronger evidence against less peripheral suspects.

One solution to Oakes's death was almost overlooked in all the hullabaloo: that he had committed suicide. It had been Dr Quackenbush's first assessment on seeing the body – and one that he passed on to the Duke of Windsor. He changed his mind after examining the skull with its four holes during the autopsy, but twenty years later he returned to the idea. Writing to the *Nassau Tribune* in January 1965, he disclosed that both he and the Duke had had reason to believe that Oakes's health and state of mind were such at the time that he might well have taken his own life.

Little has been made of this since, and it is impossible to know now to what motive Quackenbush was alluding, or what private information he might have had. Certainly Oakes must have been worried by the news from Kirkland Lake. Production at the mine, in part because of the increasing frequency of rock-bursts as the shafts were driven ever deeper, had begun to decline drastically.

Between 1938 and 1942, it had dropped off by two-thirds, and had been further hit by the onset of war.

Priority in manpower was being given to munitions and matériel sources such as nickel and copper mines, but Oakes knew the truth was that after thirty years the golden goose had grown tired of laying eggs. Annual profits were down from almost eight million dollars in 1938 to two million dollars (ten million pounds today) in 1942. The shares, which had once stood at eighty dollars, had slumped to sixteen dollars. Lake Shore was almost worked out, and there was nothing that Sir Harry could do about it.

Perhaps Oakes was tired of it all: of the fights with his children and de Marigny, of the failure of his marriage. De Marigny claimed that Oakes had recently taken to the bottle and, although Lady Oakes afterwards denied this, the truth of it was confirmed to me by Lyssardt, Nancy's second husband. Maybe Oakes had or believed that he had some terminal disease, though nothing beyond a fatty heart was revealed by the autopsy.

Oakes, however, could not have made four holes in his own head, or extracted a bullet from it, or hidden a revolver, so some-one else – and it can only have been Christie – must have come across the body and, for motives of their own, decided to make it look as if he had been murdered. Was it to avoid a scandal? To make sure that the family could claim on Oakes's life insurance policy? Or to prevent the police from probing his recent financial dealings – perhaps in Mexico?

Yet why go to the trouble of augmenting the head wound to suggest murder and then set fire to the room with the clear intention of destroying it? As a scenario, it simply doesn't stand up. Nor was Oakes's behaviour that of a man contemplating suicide. He would hardly have troubled to get an exit visa for the following day if he'd had no intention of leaving Nassau alive.

This line of speculation does, however, encourage a closer look at how Sir Harry's family – and in particular his widow – reacted to his unexpected death. Years after the trial, Hallinan revealed that he had always felt they had something to hide, and that they were not being straightforward with him. Did they know more than they were telling?

That Nancy feared that the killer might strike against the family again is borne out by the letter she wrote to her mother three weeks after the murder in which she begs Eunice to see Zahl.

It is not clear whether Nancy had anyone specific in mind at that stage, or was experiencing just a general feeling of menace. By the time that Zahl had finished his own sleuthing, and pointed the figure at Christie, he for one was sure that Lady Oakes's life was still in danger: 'Frankly, I don't think your mother is safe as long as the inciter of this crime is at large.'

And yet Lady Oakes remained, as Zahl noted, 'indifferent' both to the warnings and to her daughter's suffering. Her manner could be ascribed to their estrangement, and to her believing that de Marigny was guilty. She undeniably made a great show of her grief at her loss, both at the funeral and later in court.

Heartfelt sentiments, no doubt, but the tears were shed for a marriage that was no longer a close one, either emotionally or physically. The Oakeses had not seen each other for some months, and they had not been together for their twentieth wedding anniversary at the end of June. Could it be that Eunice's calm stemmed from knowing that the murderer had found his only target – that Oakes had been killed at her instigation? She would certainly have known where Oakes was on the island. Nor is it beyond the bounds of possibility that – as a handsome woman still only in her early forties – she had taken a lover, even if it was not Foskett. After the murder, it was reported several times in the press that she was soon to remarry, although she never did.

Or perhaps Eunice's jealousy had been provoked too often by Oakes's own peccadilloes. The voodoo stories might have had no foundation, but curiously enough their underlying rationale was true. This has not been known before, but Oakes had indeed been fooling around with native girls (if not with Madeline Kelly as well). Furthermore, as I was reliably informed by someone

who knew both men, they had been found for him by none
other than Freddie de Marigny. Sir Harry and his son-in-law
might not have been on the best of terms in the months prior to
the murder, but for the year before that de Marigny would have
done all that he could to get into Oakes's good books. As Hallinan
noticed, everybody really did have something to hide.

There are, of course, difficulties with this theory. It is hard to
imagine Lady Oakes going about finding a contract killer, unless
she was conspiring with someone such as Foskett or Kelly.
Another objection is the circumstances of the fire. In most cases,
a family member who kills another is loath to destroy their own
house to conceal the crime, yet here there had been an attempt
to do so. All that can be said for certain is that the Oakeses, with
their dozen houses, were not like every other family. When I asked
someone who had known Eunice for decades whether she was
capable of murder, the answer was instantaneous, and unequivocal:
'Nothing about her would surprise me.'

Until now, aside from the Mafia speculation, the other main
theory concerning the reason for Oakes's murder has been that it
was a result of his involvement in the supposed money-laundering
scheme. Oakes, it is maintained, either threatened to expose the
plan or discovered that Christie had been embezzling his money,
and so had to be silenced. De Marigny was then used by the Duke
of Windsor and Christie as a convenient scapegoat to divert attention from the truth.

This, by and large, was the explanation of his ordeal that the
Count himself came to assert. Yet while it fits in certain respects –
the need for knowledge of Oakes's whereabouts, the Duke's continued harassment of de Marigny – it bulges awkwardly in others.
It was almost certainly Barker rather than the Governor who ini-
tiated the frame-up, and above all the only evidence for the Banco
Continental connection – the alleged reason for Oakes's murder –
is the tip-off to the FBI from that least trustworthy of informants,
John Anderson.

In fact, though it has never been considered before, Anderson himself is far more plausible a suspect than a conspiracy involving the Duke and Christie. The 'evil little man', as Nancy described him to me – and his brother had got one of her maids 'into trouble', too – was in frequent contact with Oakes about banking business, and was on the island at the time of the murder.

Perhaps he had been given a sum by Sir Harry to invest, or to bring to Foskett or Wenner-Gren. Maybe Anderson had sought to make a turn on it himself, but one of the 'get-rich-quick' schemes that his superiors at the bank had shied away from had gone awry. Sooner or later, Oakes would want to know where his money had gone.

Now Anderson needed to focus the attention of the investigation elsewhere. So began his sly campaign of finger-pointing, first at Wenner-Gren, who was going to leave him 'holding the bag' for Oakes's Mexican cash, and then at de Marigny, helpfully telling the police about the petrol at Victoria Avenue and the huge sum of money that the Count owed to Ruth Fahnestock. And if de Marigny swung, Anderson wouldn't have to pay back the eight hundred pounds (twenty-five thousand today) that he had borrowed from him either. He hadn't meant to harm de Marigny, but now that the police had obligingly picked him out he was going to help him on his way. It was fate. Why, he had even been the first to tell Freddie of Sir Harry's death!

In fact, it is worth considering how it was that Anderson knew so quickly of Oakes's murder. He said in evidence that he had heard by ten o'clock on the Thursday morning – his brother had told him – and that he had confirmed it by telephone with Dr Fitzmaurice. He and his brother must have been almost the first people apart from those at Westbourne to hear of the death. Fitzmaurice himself had not learned of it until ten past nine.

Did Anderson know all along about Sir Harry's killing? And what motive impelled him to start looking for de Marigny? Was it to share the news, or to enjoy the pleasures of secret knowledge as he told him of it? And, when they began driving to The Caves, who really did suggest to whom that Oakes might be staying at Westbourne? Like Anderson himself, each possible answer remains a rather troubling enigma.

Despite its dramatic nature, de Marigny's acquittal made little difference at first to his public reputation. For the remainder of his long life, there were many people who thought that he had got away with murder. Eventually, however, his contention that he had been set up by the police – publicised in his memoirs – became the accepted explanation of the case, and it has been endorsed by all those who have since written about it. The probability is that he was indeed framed by Barker. The difficulty is that that does not mean he was innocent.

Higgs's masterful exposure of Barker's forgery inevitably dominated the jury's thinking, and the poor impression that the detective made contributed decisively to their verdict. Yet even if one accepts that Barker had faked the print, there remains the rest of the evidence against de Marigny: his proximity to Westbourne; the burnt hairs; the shirt that was never produced; de Visdelou's strange behaviour; and de Marigny's 'feeling sick' before even hearing the gruesome details of the murder. Then there was Nancy's inheritance to consider. At the least, it remained a good circumstantial case and, though none ever knew it, the evidence was almost strong enough to bring about a second trial.

In August 1946, three years after the murder, the new Governor, Sir William Murphy, wrote to the Colonial Office to ask them to look again at the evidence against de Marigny. His letter hints that the move was instigated by Lady Oakes, who was still convinced of the Count's guilt - when she and de Marigny found themselves at the same wedding in Mexico, her family only narrowly averted an embarrassing meeting – although Murphy also suggested that Oakes's private and business affairs should be examined. He hoped that this time a motive might be found that 'pointed to someone other than his son-in-law'.

Scotland Yard was asked to conduct a thorough review of the

case. Until now, its 130-page report has been classified, and was not due to be made public before 2022. Its conclusions would have made damning reading for de Marigny.

Writing to the Colonial Office in February 1947, the head of the CID, Assistant Commissioner Ronald Howe, states bluntly 'in our opinion, de Marigny was the murderer and, with great respect, we think the case was mishandled.

'No one seems to have been made responsible for the practical investigation and interrogation of witnesses, while various persons wandered into and out of the scene without proper direction. There should have been a conviction if the facts had been investigated and put before the Court in a proper manner.'

Howe's finding is not, however, surprising when one considers how the review was carried out. Detective Inspector Deighton, who put together the report, worked only from the judge's note of evidence, and did not attempt to collect any fresh interview material. His opinion was that 'if the evidence of the American detectives was true' then de Marigny was guilty. It is a self-evident finding, largely influenced by Daly's pronouncement that there had been no fabrication by Melchen and Barker.

Nonetheless, Deighton did not arrive at his analysis solely on the basis of the problematic fingerprint. He accurately identified the central flaw in the investigation – that there were 'too many senior officers . . . and at times they were taking independent action' – and believed that 'de Marigny was given too much consideration and latitude'. The scrutiny of his property and the interviews with him had been too lax.

'If more time had been devoted to interrogation,' Deighton went on, 'and an early search been personally conducted by the officers at his house, garage, farm etc, it is highly probable that other valuable circumstantial evidence would have been obtained.' He also believed that de Visdelou was probably de Marigny's accomplice.

Deighton was an experienced detective and, unlike those in the Bahamas, was not prejudiced against de Marigny by personal knowledge. He thought that the Mauritian should have been convicted, given the proof available, and his recommendations carried weight. Scotland Yard contemplated reopening the case, but decided that any new evidence they found would only be likely to point to de Marigny, who under the double-jeopardy rule could not be retried for the same crime. That would not prevent them, however, from going after Georges de Visdelou; but on balance they thought that the outcome would be insufficiently certain to be worth proceeding.

Although he did not know it, the Marquis had narrowly escaped charges of perjury and complicity in murder. Governor Murphy wrote to London to say that Lady Oakes was most appreciative of their work. No doubt it confirmed her feelings about Freddie.

Whatever one makes of Deighton's verdict, it is striking that a neutral observer should form such a negative impression of de Marigny. Everyone that I spoke to who had known him well told me that he could not possibly have killed Oakes: he was too charming, too laid-back, too soft. He did not even have the stomach to kill the chickens on his farm himself.

Yet only we ourselves know who we really are, and what we can be driven to. Underneath the *boulevardier*'s façade that de Marigny projected, there are glimpses of something steelier, and darker. There were rumours – unsubstantiated, to be sure, but numerous enough to be noteworthy – of dubious activities less innocent than simple womanising.

One can, of course, dismiss the testimony of the FBI's informant who had been told by Oakes that his son-in-law wanted to see him in his grave before his time. But judging by the Duke's mention of doubts about the death of de Marigny's godfather – information that must have been obtained from the Mauritian police, and that some held was the real reason for the Count's leaving Port Louis – he had begun to make a habit of attracting that kind of suspicion.

Nastier still were the stories of de Marigny and drugs. Not the Mickey Finns that he and de Visdelou might have slipped into girls' drinks from time to time, but the genuine article, the stuff that could make someone seriously rich.

Three days before the trial, it will be remembered, Hallinan had asked the FBI to substantiate information he had received that they had evidence from an earlier investigation that the Count was involved in drug trafficking. As the request came through Melchen, who was in bad odour with the Bureau, Washington did nothing about it.

Less than a year after de Marigny's acquittal, however, the allegations resurfaced in Nassau, and in spectacular fashion. In September 1944, Miami-based narcotics agents broke up what they regarded as the largest drug-smuggling ring in the New York area. They told reporters that they had evidence that between the autumn of 1940 and the autumn of 1941 more than seventy-five thousand dollars' worth of morphine (now worth four hundred thousand pounds) had been shipped from Nassau to the coast of Palm Beach and Broward Counties, Florida, in three consignments. The morphine had originally been brought from Haiti, and it had travelled by yacht.

Seventeen men were indicted by a Federal Grand Jury. They included four Nassauvians, who would be subject to arrest only if they travelled to the United States. Among these was the man the police regarded as 'the kingpin of the traffic in Nassau', Basil McKinney.

McKinney was a close friend of de Marigny's and frequently sailed with him. He had hit a marker buoy in the race on the afternoon before the Count's dinner party, and had been ribbed by de Marigny about his subsequent disqualification shortly before the Count learned of Oakes's death. The Miami police, however, believed that the two men did more than just sail together. The investigating officers had been told several times that the morphine which had come from Haiti had been brought over by de Marigny in *Concubine*.

The police spokesman told the press that there was no evidence that directly linked de Marigny with the alleged dope ring, but it was clear what they intended to be read between the lines. For them McKinney and de Marigny had become the heirs of the rum-runners, using their boats to make the same trips through the islands to Florida, but carrying a deadlier cargo. Only America's entry into the war, and the consequent tightening of shipping restrictions in 1942, had put a stop to their trade.

As a result, perhaps the extravagant de Marigny's money had suddenly dried up. Perhaps Oakes had heard about his son-in-law's activities and had threatened to expose him. Either way, de Marigny would have had a motive, and a premeditated plan, for murder. A slow, quiet stalk up the outside stairs of Westbourne, his footsteps muffled by the rain; a silent approach to the bed; a return to the car for petrol and a brand to light the pyre; the drive back to Nassau, then a quick change of burnt and bloodied clothes in the garage before saying goodnight to the staff.

The only element missing from this scenario is inside knowledge. De Marigny claimed at the trial to have spoken to Christie that day to invite him to dinner, and said that Christie had told him both that Oakes was at Westbourne and that he, Christie, would be sleeping there. Christie himself denied this. Which of them was lying, and for what reason, is a moot point.

Maybe the Count was lucky. Maybe he was bold enough to risk waking Christie, and when he got to the house Sir Harry's friend happened to have left an hour before, giving de Marigny free access to Oakes. Or perhaps Sears's identification was wrong, and Christie was sleeping soundly in his room all along – a sleep deeper than it should have been, and one that de Marigny was counting on. Could he have had help from someone else?

Levi Gibson sits in his office chair like an elderly crocodile, the thin light from the high window behind him doing little to illuminate his thoughts. After he left Christie's employ, the former chauffeur and factotum built his own property empire on New Providence. Yet he retains all the courtesy of his days in service, and kindly affects to remember my grandmother from her teatime visits to Christie. And, perhaps in consequence, he tells me something that he has never made public before.

At about a quarter to two on the Thursday afternoon, the day the body was found, Gibson was in town when he saw a small group of men standing around a car that he recognised as de Marigny's. It was raining, but as well as the Count he could see Georges de Visdelou, Freddie Cerreta, the airfield engineer, and someone else he knew – someone who looked very out of context in that company.

It was a young native Bahamian called Robert Franklin. He had previously worked for de Marigny, and Gibson believed that the two were still in touch for he had sometimes seen them on the street, deep in conversation, when on his way home from work. The Count's easy touch with the black population was well known, and was one of the reasons many of them liked him.

Franklin was now occasionally employed by Christie, and on the night of the murder, since Oakes's butler was off-duty, he had been summoned to Westbourne to help with the dinner party. When Gibson came down to the house to leave Christie's car there, he and his wife, who was a nurse, had given someone a lift to another residence up at The Grove, a fashionable development not far from Westbourne. He thought that it might have been a maid. It was not Franklin.

The next day, Gibson had collected the station wagon from Westbourne and had gone to the airport to pick up Foskett. On his way back, he had seen this small group talking, as he put it, furtively. After that Gibson had seen no more of Franklin. He had heard only that de Marigny had paid for the young man to go to America, where some time later he had died.

What he had seen and learned convinced Gibson that de Marigny had been the murderer, and that Franklin had helped the Count gain access to Westbourne. One might hazard that he had given Christie, and perhaps Oakes as well, a sleeping powder in some late-night drink that had rendered both men unconscious; Gibson told me that in any case Christie was a particularly heavy sleeper. Perhaps, too, Franklin had remained concealed near the house, ready to help de Marigny carry Oakes back to the bed, or to bring the burning brand up the stairs.

The revelation of Franklin's existence undoubtedly provides an appropriately remarkable resolution to a case that has always been steeped in the sensational. There are problems with it, however. A sceptic would point to Gibson's loyalty to Christie, and thus to his bias against de Marigny. But even putting those doubts to one side there is no confirmation of what the Count, Franklin and the others — and that assumes they were also in on the murder — might have been discussing by the car, furtively or not.

Yet, curiously, there *was* an independent witness of that conversation — and it was John Anderson. In court he mentioned having seen the group talking, for it was just before they all went back to de Marigny's for lunch, in time for the delivery of the petrol. He did not refer to Franklin, but that very fact would seem to support the truth of Gibson's claim to have seen them all together in the first place. It would be most odd for him to have otherwise remembered noticing a cluster of white men, or for him to have added Franklin to it for his own reasons. It is more likely that Anderson came across them just after Franklin had left.

There is, however, a more substantial objection to Gibson's theory: Mabel Ellis. The Westbourne maid twice testified in court, and she made no mention at all of Franklin. Ellis said that it was she who had served drinks and dinner to Oakes's guests that night, and the implication was that just she and the cook, Enid Fernander, were on duty that night, as the other maid was noted as being away. Had Franklin been present at the meal, it is inconceivable that the police would not have questioned him. There is no record of their having done so, and it seems probable that he was not in the house that night.

That is not to say that Franklin did not exist, nor that he was not in cahoots with the Mauritian, as Gibson's intuition told him. It may be that, after six decades, Gibson's recollection is not perfect, but that the broad outline is correct. It is possible that

Franklin – promised a ticket to America – did help de Marigny to carry out the murder, which de Visdelou then helped to cover up, but that Franklin was not in the house as their agent that evening.

It is just that for Franklin to have been overlooked all this time, and for him to be the key to Oakes's murder, is the sort of thing that happens only in books.

There is, however, a seemingly insurmountable objection to the notion of de Marigny's guilt: the presence of someone who would appear to clear his name definitively. That person was Harold Christie.

The one fact of that night's events that is best attested to is that Christie was absent from Westbourne. Let us review the evidence: his bed did not appear to have been slept in; he had not heard anything happen in a room just twenty feet from his (heavy sleeper or not – and the rain, he said, had woken him); he reacted peculiarly in court when questioned about his whereabouts; and, above all, he was seen by Sears being driven into Nassau at about midnight.

Christie's friends put it about that he had been going to spend the night with Effie Heneage, and afterwards was protecting her name. But this is simply not credible. Aside from Effie's three young children, their Norland nurse was also living in what was a modestly sized house – her bedroom was across the corridor from Effie's – and so it was hardly the most discreet of places and times to conduct an affair that both parties would have wanted to conceal. There is a reason why Frenchmen visit their mistresses in the late afternoon.

More obviously still, Christie was a passenger in the station wagon seen by Sears, and Gibson confirmed that Christie's own car had not been moved overnight. He had thus travelled in someone else's vehicle. A man does not ask for a lift to his lover's house, certainly not at midnight. He would have taken his own car and gone alone.

There are coincidences and there are coincidences, and this was neither. Christie's absence from Westbourne indicates that he knew that something had happened, or was about to happen. Moreover, his leaving the house ties in with the crucial elements of the crime – the revised time of death in the hours after midnight, the likelihood that the killer knew he would not be disturbed, and the premeditated fire, from which Christie needed to escape.

He had the requisite inside knowledge of where the changeable Oakes would be. And since Christie was involved, is it plausible that the co-conspirator about to arrive at the house was de Marigny? Where would their interests coincide? The same question could be asked of Anderson, whom Christie's part in the matter would seem to acquit – unless both of them really were up to their necks in Mexican bank drafts.

If Christie was complicit in Oakes's death, it is also certain that he was not himself the murderer. Not only was his character decidedly not that of a killer, but if he had just slaughtered Oakes and was fleeing a house that he thought was ablaze, he would surely have taken his own car. He had, after all, asked Gibson to bring it down that very night. No one would have asked any questions if he had attributed his escape to that lucky chance.

Instead, it had been pre-arranged that Christie should be picked up from Westbourne by someone at midnight. He was not making a bolt for it. That can only mean that the house was not yet alight, and that Sir Harry still had an hour or two to live, though perhaps his body was already in thrall to a drug administered during the pair's after-dinner drink; the autopsy only checked for lethal poisons. Oakes slept friendless and Westbourne stood silent, open to the assassin. In the meantime, Christie had an appointment elsewhere, one whose nature was such that he could not later reveal it.

The presence of his car remains a puzzle. As Christie knew that Oakes was going to die, or at least suspected as much, he would hardly have asked Gibson to bring it because he really thought that he was going to inspect farms with Sir Harry the next day. Perhaps he wanted a safety net, a means of flight in case everything went wrong. Or was he contemplating a late change of heart? More likely still is that he did not want to use his own car to travel to the midnight meeting in case it was seen, but as he would soon have to return to Westbourne to find it in ashes he might then need a car to drive into Nassau to raise the alarm.

Gibson was told to park away from the house, towards the Country Club and Cable Beach, maybe to spare the car from the fire, or because – as Christie testified – he genuinely did not want it to be seen by the departing dinner guests and so be asked for a ride into town. A good lie always springs from the truth. Christie had to stay behind and make sure Oakes had his drink.

Assuming that Christie was not double-crossed in some way, the plan – and the fire – unexpectedly went awry. Christie now found himself a suspect, and so did he all he could to encourage first the Duke, and then the police, to look at de Marigny in a most unfavourable light.

'I can assure you,' says Peter Christie, 'that there was no gold in Mexico.' For much of his life, Peter has had to put up with fingers being pointed at his Uncle Harold, a man so different from his own father, Christie's brother Percy, the owner of a shoe store and, in Bahamian terms, a political radical.

Peter was his uncle's executor, and found nothing in Harold Christie's papers to suggest that he had ever been part of some far-fetched scheme involving the Duke, Wenner-Gren and several million dollars. So what could have forced Christie to become involved in murder? He stood to lose much valuable business with the death of his best client. What could he possibly gain?

For de Marigny, the prime mover in theories about Christie's guilt, it was because Oakes was planning to move his home and operations to Central America, as he had once told the Count, and thus was planning to call in loans that he had made to Christie and which Christie could not repay.

That remains a possibility, although the deus ex machina that de Marigny produces in his memoirs as confirmation of his beliefs –

a fortuitous meeting half a century later with the watchman who saw the killers, led by Christie's brother Frank, setting fire to Westbourne – is as preposterous as it sounds. I do not believe, either, the argument that Christie had swindled Oakes, and knew that Sir Harry was preparing to make this public. Being the man he was, with the values that he cherished (and the temper that he had), Oakes would simply not have tolerated Christie a moment longer as a business partner, let alone as a frequent house guest, if this had been the case.

Without knowing whom Christie was going to meet, we cannot guess what his motive was. Nor can we comprehend it without being aware of the circumstances of that rendezvous. Was he going as a principal, as the instigator of the murder? Or do the facts – the pick-up, the killing carried out by others, his own middleman's temperament – point to his being a secondary participant, or even to his acting under duress?

Perhaps there was someone else who wanted Oakes out of the way for their own reasons, someone who promised Christie that he could afterwards keep a slice of the action. Not to mention his life.

Someone, for instance, such as Newell Kelly – perhaps about to be fired, already being cuckolded, and in the years that followed to be identified by some as the man who controlled the island with Christie, and ruled it by violence. The car seen by Sears was a station wagon. There were only five on the island. One was Christie's. Another was his brother Frank's. A third belonged to Kelly, and at about midnight on 8 July, while driving through Cable Beach, his chauffeur had discovered that one of its tyres was flat.

There is no other evidence against Kelly, and it would be irresponsible to accuse him of involvement in Oakes's death without more substantial proof. Of Christie's connection to it, there can be no such doubts.

From the start, Nancy had been sufficiently suspicious to set Zahl and Vaccarelli on Christie's trail, and they had struck gold. 'We think we know who the perpetrator is,' Zahl had written to her. The question is why Nancy then did nothing about it.

We do not have the rest of her correspondence with Zahl, and after I had discovered that letter I was never able to see her again to ask her about it. She had once told me that she believed Christie had not been involved in the murder plot. In the years that followed, did she feel that despite Zahl's endeavours she did not have conclusive proof against Christie, or that he was now too powerful even for her to accuse him? Did she ever feel that she knew the answer?

For decades it was Nancy's policy to let her father's death rest, and only later in life did she call for it to be reinvestigated. By that stage, buffeted by vicissitudes of the heart and enraged by her treatment by Foskett, she may have come to believe that others were responsible. In her final years, certainly, it was difficult to discern whether what she was recalling was really the truth or merely the shape that it had since taken on for her.

There remains one last consideration to take into account, an issue not explored at the time but which for me holds the solution to Sir Harry Oakes's murder. Why was he killed *when* he was?

Everything about Oakes's death points to careful planning and forethought, right down to the monitoring of his movements. Were the motive simple hatred or revenge, merely a desire to have Oakes out of the way at some point, there was no particular reason for the killer to be coordinating his moves with Christie in the way that he was. If Oakes were away, if there were other guests in the house, another occasion would serve just as well. It did not have to be that night – unless time was a factor.

Oakes's assassin could afford to leave nothing to chance, and with good reason. It was no coincidence that Sir Harry was due to leave the island the day after he was killed. The murderer's motive was Oakes's silence.

The explanation that has always been given for Sir Harry's planned departure on 9 July was that he was going to Maine to meet Eunice in time for their wedding anniversary. But, as Nancy herself pointed out to me, her parents had got married on 30 June. The unhappy truth is that such was the state of relations

268
JAMES OWEN

between them that anniversaries were no longer of much consequence to Oakes.

Something else entirely was at the forefront of his mind that
week: corruption. Sir Harry had made his fortune through his
own hard endeavour, and if there was one thing he hated, one
thing he could not stomach, it was people making money without deserving to.

He could be generous to those in need – the sick, the down-
trodden, the underprivileged – but those who just wanted a
handout were knocking at the wrong door. Worse still were governments, who extorted tax like a bunch of robbers, while those
who put their hand in the till or wanted an 'inducement' for a
deal were beyond description.

The sore rubbed all the more painfully when such dishonesty
triumphed at the expense of his own interests. Oakes had bid for
the contract for the greatest cash cow on the island, the construction of the new, US Government-financed airfield, but had
lost out to an American company, Pleasantville.

Now he had learned of the scale of the bribes, backhanders and
profiteering associated with the building of the base, and the
upgrading of his own strip, Oakes Field, and it had incensed him.
In January he had demanded an inquiry from President
Roosevelt, and on 5 July two high-ranking American officers
had arrived in Nassau to begin investigating the sites. Later that
week, Nancy told me, her father had been due to fly to
Washington to present evidence to Truman's committee, which
was inquiring into graft at the project.

Its report, which was published in October 1943 as de
Marigny's trial was getting under way, made it plain that in little
more than a year millions of dollars had been skimmed off the
funding for the airstrip. Seven hundred thousand dollars – now
worth four million pounds – had vanished into the operating
costs of the British Colonial alone, rented from Oakes as accommodation for those working on the base and funded by the
American taxpayer.

Some of the money was traceable and the perpetrators known; the rest was not. It may be recalled that even after Truman became President he retained a keen interest in the affair and wanted to know if the Windsors could shed any light on what Sir Harry had been coming to tell him.

It was what Oakes had discovered about the airfield, and what he was imminently about to reveal, that explains the date of his murder. It also might explain something else – the presence of the fourth figure in the conspiratorial group seen by Gibson: Freddie Cerreta, construction engineer and former employee of Pleasantville.

Like the other person in de Marigny's car, Georges de Visdelou, Cerreta was a close friend of the Count's, and he too had been at his dinner party. He had declined a lift back to the British Colonial with de Marigny afterwards, and the defence had used this to argue that if the Count was planning murder he would not have invited Cerreta along. His refusal had strengthened de Marigny's alibi; yet, as Cerreta testified, he had then subsequently accepted a ride home with Donald McKinney. It is certainly curious that the movements that night of all three men that Gibson saw talking to Robert Franklin – de Visdelou (vouched for by the sleeping Betty Roberts), de Marigny and Cerreta – should seem to be less than straightforward.

There is no evidence that Cerreta was complicit in a scheme to murder Oakes. Yet that he was frequently in de Marigny's company was not a matter of chance, for the Count had deliberately cultivated his friendship for financial reasons. De Marigny himself acknowledged that he had been hoping Cerreta would cut him in on a lucrative sand-and-gravel contract for the airbase, and though there is no proof that Cerreta himself was corrupt, being around him may well have offered de Marigny a way to meet more senior figures at Pleasantville who were.

Within a few weeks of beginning work on New Providence, the company's less scrupulous employees had become notorious for their black-market activities. A newspaper cartoonist at the

time depicts Ajax proceeding at high speed around the walls of
Troy. When the Nassau police stop him, their concern is how he
has so much fuel for his chariot when it is rationed. 'Dat's alright,
officers,' the hero tells them. 'I'se works for Pleasantville.'

Not everything that fell off the back of one of their lorries was
as relatively innocuous as dodgy petrol. John Anderson had seemingly been confident that he could find someone at the base who
could change ten million pounds (three hundred million pounds
today) into dollars. The capabilities and connections of those
striking deals were copious indeed, and presumably stretched ultimately into the underworld. War does not stop criminals making
money: it just offers them different opportunities.

Gibson believes that Cerreta's posture in the huddle suggested
that something untoward was being discussed, but this is intuition
rather than proof. Cerreta himself mentioned the meeting in
court, and might be thought unlikely to have done so if he did
not wish to draw attention to it. Moreover, he said that when he
joined them the Count and the Marquis (and perhaps Franklin)
were already together. That trio may well have had its own
agenda. Perhaps de Marigny only wanted to talk or have Cerreta
give a message to someone at Pleasantville. Beyond a certain
point, the road into the past starts to curve out of sight.

Yet de Marigny's tracks are visible. There is evidence that
strongly connects him to the scene of the killing, while the airbase
connects him with its timing. It is impossible to ascertain whether
he had the assets in his accounts or with de Visdelou that he
claimed. Nonetheless, Ruth's demands had worried him, and an
involvement in the deals at Windsor Field – perhaps a replacement
source of income now that running drugs had become so difficult – would have been exactly the kind of leg-up he needed, one
that showed how a man could use his wits to get ahead. If his
father-in-law was about to sever that last financial lifeline and
bring the police in, it would have supplied the Count not just with
one more motive for murder, but this time with an urgent one.

★

The obvious counter-argument to de Marigny's guilt is again the presence – or rather the absence – of Christie. Since Christie was working with the intruder, can it really be possible that that person was the Count?

At a distance of more than sixty years, with both parties dead and no confession forthcoming, such a scenario must inevitably be – in part, at least – supposition. It is a mosaic whose pattern is now partially obscured. Nonetheless, no other solution so convincingly reconciles all the facts for which we do have evidence: the inside knowledge of Oakes's movements, suggesting coordination between Christie and another; Christie's midnight flight from the house, suggesting the arrival of the killer; de Marigny's being in the area at the approximate time of death; the burns seen by Melchen and perhaps by Erskine-Lindop; the missing shirt; the nervousness of de Visdelou and of Christie himself in court.

We cannot know what the motive was for such an alliance. Perhaps Christie had some interest of his own in the airfield, as he did in virtually every development on the island, that was threatened with exposure. Since he appears to have held no grudge against Oakes, perhaps de Marigny had some hold over him, possibly information about Christie's past picked up from a drug-running contact. Or, as one person suggested to me, it may even have been simple jealously over a woman: Effie Heneage. There is no proof that she was another of Oakes's dalliances, but it would explain why he began to cold-shoulder her after the murder, and why she found giving evidence such a strain.

Since Oakes did not know of Christie's connection to the corruption at the base – for he was still treating him as a friend – it probably was de Marigny who provided the impetus for murder, and who had got wind of what Oakes was planning. It would have been like the baronet to have had it out first with those he suspected at Pleasantville, and to have told them what exactly he meant to do next, though he was probably unaware of de Marigny's involvement as he never made it public.

Now de Marigny has to act, but not being on good terms

with Sir Harry he needs Christie's help with tracking Oakes, and maybe with administering something to ensure that he sleeps all too soundly.

It cannot be the Count himself who then picks up Christie from Westbourne, as he is still at dinner. Christie's task is to confirm Sir Harry's presence and unnatural slumber, but the telephone is too risky. So, as previously agreed, he heads for a rendezvous, maybe driven by Franklin or another party to the conspiracy, perhaps someone from Pleasantville who also fears what Oakes might reveal. Christie has insisted that he will not be present when the killers arrive, nor talk to them outside the house. He wants to keep his hands clean. Information only – that is his line of business.

It will be too obvious if de Marigny absents himself from his own party to meet Christie but no one will miss Georges with that unfortunate cold. If Christie's news demands some change of plan, he is to reappear at the table, now feeling much better, thank you.

The meal over, de Marigny drops Jean Ainsley and Dorothy Clarke home. He cannot take the chance of heading for Westbourne later, long after his guests have left, in case someone sees him on the road. Maybe, too, that sleeping powder administered to Oakes is wearing off. Instead, the two women give the Count an excuse to have been near Westbourne should there be questions afterwards. How lucky that they happen to live at those cottages only a hundred yards from Oakes's house. How convenient that they should have been introduced to him just the day before by Freddie Cerreta. And how charming of the Count to invite the girls to dinner – why, he hardly knew them! And as host he will, of course, see them home.

Perhaps Jean and Dorothy might have been busy. Perhaps their husbands might not have been on duty. But the ability to ride your luck, and the nerve to seize your opportunity, are the hallmarks of every champion sportsman.

Timing is everything in murder, and now it began to go wrong. First de Marigny met any accomplice he might have had, perhaps a native, as Zahl learned, brought in by Christie, or the man from

Pleasantville; the killing demanded knowledge of Westbourne's layout, and the firm happened to have rented the house that spring.

The pair needed to work quickly, and they did. If the dozing Betty Roberts's memory was correct, de Marigny was back at Westbourne within half an hour or so, giving de Visdelou the news (in French, which Betty didn't speak). He had rolled up his sleeves so that they should not be stained by Oakes's blood. He had even worn gloves to avoid leaving any fingerprints. Yet that flash of fire from the petrol had caught him unawares.

Nor had Christie, when he returned a little later, expected to find the house still standing. The flames had not taken hold. The rain was streaming down. And he was near-paralysed with terror. What should he do? Telephone de Marigny to tell him the job was not done – but at that hour, with the operators having no other calls to listen to? Drive over to Victoria Avenue – but that was chancy as well, and he thought Sears might already have seen him. Try to burn down the house himself – but with what? Too anxious to take to his bed, he paced the floor of his room, turning over his options, scrutinising every consideration, making plans.

Now was the time for the cabal to stick together, but there was nothing to bind them – no common aim, no reason to trust each other. The Duke's idea to bring in Melchen was the first rung on the ladder of Christie's salvation. Hallinan remembered him enthusiastically backing the notion. Yes, that American cop wouldn't know anybody in Nassau. That stiff-necked idiot Erskine-Lindop might be a fool, but he might do things too much by the book for comfort. Perhaps this Captain Melchen might be grateful for some background information on a few people.

Christie had naturally hoped that the police would find no clues, but their arresting de Marigny at least took the heat off him. De Marigny couldn't give him up without damning himself, and while there was a chance of saving his neck the Mauritian would have to brazen it out. How stupid of him to have left that print. Still, it wasn't as if he hadn't committed a crime.

Of course, when convicted he might start to blab, but a man about to hang will say anything, and no one of consequence trusts de Marigny anyway. That drop through the trap will solve everything – the hunt for the murderer and de Marigny's blackmailing of Christie. It was just a pity that he hadn't anticipated Higgs's question about his wretched pyjamas.

A forced collaboration between Christie and de Marigny – and one that went sour – accounts for something else: their mutual antagonism in the weeks and years afterwards. It was noticeable at the trial how each tried to turn the spotlight on the other, to the extent that they could without revealing their conspiracy. Thus, for instance, de Marigny maintained that Christie had told him that early in the day he would be sleeping at Westbourne that night, contradicting Christie's nervous insistence that his had been a spontaneous decision.

So great a desire did the Count have to implicate Christie that he even let slip that he knew where Oakes was, in contrast to what he had told Anderson. The episode was lent still more force by it being for once a glimpse of the truth, an echo of the information that Christie had indeed relayed; the imprint of a Judas kiss.

The danger that each man now posed to the other also explains something else that otherwise strikes one as odd – the behaviour of the Executive Council. Of course, the Duke of Windsor was embarrassed by the turn of events and readily supported the jury's proposal to deport the Count. Of course, even were Christie innocent it would still have been in his interests to heap opprobrium on de Marigny to forestall renewed talk about his own movements that night.

But whose idea was it to add de Visdelou's name to the one-way ticket? He certainly was not mentioned in Sands's original rider, and while he figured as de Marigny's sidekick in much Nassau gossip, he had not broken any laws beyond buying a little black-market petrol, much less been tried for murder. Yet someone had speedily got to work on Heape and the Duke – and someone on the Council had sufficient pull with his fellow members – to have Georges forced to leave the island as well, without even time to put his affairs in order. The only person with that degree of influence, and with reason to fear the Marquis, was Christie.

If Georges had helped de Marigny to plan Oakes's death – because he wanted to go on sponging off him or because his chum was genuinely in a tight spot – his loyalty had brought him little reward, and in his memoirs de Marigny takes care to distance himself from, and even deride, a man who since their childhood had been closer to him than any other friend. As close, as he had once reflected, as Jekyll and Hyde.

By making certain that de Marigny and de Visdelou were discredited and no longer near at hand, Christie succeeded in removing the immediate threat to himself. He did not let it lie there. Even if one dismisses de Marigny's stories of the gunmen hired to shoot at him in Cuba, the FBI's records make it plain that for a considerable time afterwards Christie was trying to make life difficult for the Mauritian by marking his card with the authorities. For his part, de Marigny responded by telling all who would listen who had really killed Harry Oakes.

And in time, because a man cannot smile and be a villain, he was believed.

Some weeks after Freddie de Marigny had left the island, an auction of the contents of the house on Victoria Avenue was organised to help pay for his legal costs. One entry on the list of belongings that was distributed around town in advance of the sale caught the eye of a former member of the jury. As he later told his family, it seemed such a peculiar thing to have got wrong.

At the trial, the Count had been asked to account for the burns that Melchen and Barker claimed to have seen on his arms. One explanation he gave was that every morning he had toast for breakfast, and as he liked it very dry he would prepare it himself

in the oven. Perhaps he had got burnt doing that. To some laughter, Hallinan inquired why he had not used the toaster. It was
simple, said de Marigny. He didn't own a toaster, never had done,
nor had it occurred to him to buy such a thing.

The entry on the list of de Marigny's possessions that caught
the juror's eye was for not one but two toasters. He bought them
both as a souvenir.

Few traces remain of the Oakes empire. Kirkland Lake is a forlorn
town that does not much cherish its history. The rock where Bill
Wright first saw traces of gold juts out of the earth, unremarked,
near a municipal bench. The lake is clogged by a grey slime, the
by-blow of billions of tons of milled ore. The shaft of the Lake
Shore mine lies beneath the steel hulk of a hardware store. Teck-
Hughes, just up the road, is the site of a funeral parlour.

After Oakes's death, a slim white obelisk was erected to his
memory on the airstrip that bore his name. The inscription reads:
'A Great Friend And Benefactor Of The Bahamas.' The steps of
the plinth are strewn with couch grass and litter. Around it now
sprawls one of Nassau's less distinguished suburbs.

In a corner of the lobby of what has become the British
Colonial Hilton, there sits a bust of Sir Harry. It is the only other
local monument to him. Dozens of people pass it every day without a glance at the image of the man who first showed faith in the
Bahamas, and whose millions helped make possible their holidays
of a lifetime. Beyond the glass doors the ocean calls them, and the
lone and level sands stretch far away.

AFTERWORD

This is not quite the book that I meant to write. Just before Christmas 2002, two days after I thought I had completed my research, I arrived at Rome station on a bus from the airport. I stood up to wrestle my suitcase off the luggage rack. Down at my feet went my shoulder bag containing my laptop computer and hundreds of pages of notes on the Oakes case, the fruits of three years' work. Then, with my arms above my head, I felt a tug on my sleeve and a man began asking directions to a hotel in broken Italian. I glanced at him, then instinctively down at the floor. The bag had gone and, when I looked up, so had he.

In the backpack was not just the master copy of the book so far, but also the most recent set of back-up disks, which I had had to take out of my coat pocket when it went through the airport scanner. There were also the sole transcripts of several interviews, notes I had made in trips to archives abroad, and scores of scribbled thoughts, theories and corrections, jotted down in the margins of the draft. Much of it was irreplaceable. All of it had disappeared for ever.

Perhaps it really was the curse of Harry Oakes. Maybe some things do not wish to be disturbed. It was not much comfort that I was for once in the company of Hemingway, who had himself lost a manuscript (though at a station in Paris). It took me another two years to re-research the book. On the plus side, it allowed me more time to track down interviewees, while three years after my first request to see it the material from the FBI did eventually begin to arrive. Then again, it also meant I had to go for a second time through the thousands of frankly bizarre documents held by the Bureau on Axel Wenner-Gren, a pilgrimage that involved a week of dawn bus-rides through the suburbs of Washington. Maryland is cold in February.

As I was finally finishing the book, I learned, in the somewhat anti-climactic environment of Stansted Airport, of the death of the last of the principal figures in the case, Nancy Oakes herself, latterly Baroness Nancy von Hoyningen-Huene. I doubt that she would approve of much that I have written, but I am grateful to have had the chance to meet her, and for the insights she gave me.

I should also like to thank my family for their support, especially my sister-in-law Emma Errighi and her parents, my father and my aunt, Mairi Inglis-Jones, and my grandmother, Dorothie Owen, who inadvertently started me on this quest and sustained me along the way with her memories of Nassau. I particularly want to acknowledge, too, the help of Philip Pullman and the Society of Authors of which he was chairman when it made a generous grant towards my travel expenses. Every writer should take advantage of the Society's resources.

For advice, information, introductions and encouragement, my thanks go to: Michael Bloch; Philip Ziegler; Hugo Vickers; Hugh Massingberd; William Hunt at the College of Arms; James Leasor; Atalanta Clifford; His Excellency John Pringle; Teddy Goldsmith; Godfrey Kelly; Levi Gibson; Peter Higgs; Peter Christie; Colin Callender; Eileen Carron; Mario Menocal; Gavin McKinney; Nicola Heneage; Lynn Heneage; Lyssardt von Hoyningen-Huene; Eda Zahl; Marie Gudewill; Patricia Oakes; and Mary de Marigny. I am also indebted to those to whom I talked who did not wish to be named. Their collective time and patience enabled me to avoid many blunders. Those that remain, together with my conclusions, are my responsibility alone.

I also wish to acknowledge the help given me by the staffs of: The London Library; The British Library; The *Daily Telegraph* Library; The Public Record Office; The Family Records Centre; The National Archive, Washington DC; The Bahamas Department of Archives; and The Prime Minister's Office, Civil Status Division, Mauritius. I am grateful as well to: the British Colonial Hilton and The Ocean Club, Nassau; Brent Evitt at the US Department of Justice; the FOIA Section of the FBI; Gay Nemeti at the *Miami Herald*; Lynda Sinclair and Bernie Jaworsky at the Museum of Northern History, Kirkland Lake, Canada; Marissa Harvey, Niagara Parks Commission; David Capus of the Metropolitan Police Service Records Management Branch; and Mel Epstein, who provided valuable material on the Fahnestocks. For their expertise in forensic and pathology matters, I am indebted to: Dr Dick Shepherd; Dr Allan Jamieson; Rodger Ide; and Paul Millen. My thanks also go to those who gave me hospitality along the way in Mexico, Canada, Florida, the Bahamas, Brussels and Washington, notably my cousin Simone Carlier. Kate Gallimore, Andrea Henry and Chantal Noel helped get the book off the ground, while Maria Belivani provided raki and sympathy.

For faith shown and attention lavished, I owe much to my agent Ant Harwood and his henchman James Macdonald-Lockhart. My editor at Little, Brown, Richard Beswick, was much provoked and responded only with fortitude and perceptiveness. I was lucky to have him.

I have made every effort to trace copyright holders but if any have not been traced I will be pleased to make the necessary arrangement at the first opportunity.

This book is dedicated to my wife MariaLuisa, who has had to live with it for much longer than I promised. I would also like it to commemorate Raef Payne, who first encouraged me to write, and my grandmother, Beata Carlier, who did not live to see it published but who taught me that the past is tangible, and that old people are interesting.

Rome
St Valentine's Day, 2005

BIBLIOGRAPHIC NOTE

The letters, manuscripts and official documents that are the source for much of this book are numerous and widely spread. Many papers are to be found in the CO, FO and PREM series in the Public Record Office, notably the Duke of Windsor's correspondence when Governor of the Bahamas, details of Axel Wenner-Gren's dealings with him and the British Government, and records of events in the Colony during the war years. The Deighton report is in MEPO 2/9532.

In Nassau, the Department of Archives' holdings include minutes of Executive Council meetings, confidential dispatches to and from the Secretary of State and the Colonial Annual Reports, as well as Daly's own, voluminous note of evidence given at the trial and the record kept by the Court Registrar in the Criminal Minute Book. The archive's copies of the *Bahamas Handbook* and *Nassau* magazine, and of local newspapers, provide much valuable material on social life in the town at the time.

The FBI's files on Wenner-Gren (particularly NA 800 20211/WG) (for convenience, boxes 135–142) are stored at the National Archives II, in College Park, Maryland. The Bureau's several thousand pages of records on James Barker, Count Alfred de Marigny, Sir Harry Oakes, the Duke of Windsor and Harold Christie are all now available from its FOIA section under the Freedom of Information programme. A number of files on Christie are still kept by the Naval Criminal Investigative Service, Washington.

The Museum of Northern History at the Sir Harry Oakes Chateau, in Kirkland Lake, Canada, is an important repository of both biographical detail about Oakes and the gold-mining history of Ontario.

Selected secondary sources:

Bahamas: Isles of June – H. MacLachlan Bell (Robert M. McBride & Co, 1934)

A History of the Bahamas – Michael Craton (William Collins, 1962)

The Story of the Bahamas – Paul Albury (Macmillan Caribbean, 1975)

Islanders in the Stream, A History of the Bahamian People vol 2 – Michael Craton and Gail Saunders (University of Georgia Press, 1998)

Islands in the Sun – Rosita Forbes (Evans Brothers Ltd, 1949)

A Salute to Friend and Foe – Etienne Dupuch (Nassau Tribune, 1982)

Reminiscing: Memories of Old Nassau – Valeria Moseley Moss (Media Publishing, Nassau, 1999)

The Heart Has Its Reasons – The Duchess of Windsor (Michael Joseph, 1956)

Edward VIII – Frances Donaldson (Weidenfeld & Nicolson, 1974)

The King Over the Water – Michael Pye (Hutchinson, 1981)

The Duke of Windsor's War – Michael Bloch (Weidenfeld & Nicolson, 1982)

The Secret File of the Duke of Windsor – Michael Bloch (Bantam Press, 1988)

King of Fools – John Parker (Futura, 1988)

King Edward VIII – Philip Ziegler (William Collins, 1990)

Proconsul – Bede Clifford (Evans Brothers Ltd, 1964)

American Swastika – Charles Higham (Doubleday, 1985)

More Devil Than Saint – Alfred de Marigny (The Beechhurst Press, 1946)

A Conspiracy of Crowns – Alfred de Marigny with Mickey Herskowitz (Bantam Press, 1990)

The Life and Death of Harry Oakes – Geoffrey Bocca (Weidenfeld & Nicolson, 1959)

The Murder of Sir Harry Oakes, Bt. – The Nassau Daily Tribune (1959)

A Reasonable Doubt – Julian Symons (Cressett Press, 1960)

King's X – Marshall Houts (William Morrow, 1972)

Who Killed Sir Harry Oakes? – James Leasor (Heinemann, 1983)

Sir Harry Oakes 1874–1943: An Accumulation of Notes – Bob Cowan (Highway Book Store, Cobalt, Ontario, 2000)

The Complete Detective – Rupert Hughes (Sheridan House, 1950)

INDEX

correspondence with mother and
appeal for aid, 110–12; death, 224, 278;
deterioration of marriage to de
Marigny and divorce, 209–10, 213,
223; determination to support husband
in public, 74, 77–8, 115, 188, 194–5;
early years, 17; epilogue, 222–4; and
father's will, 112; learns of arrest of
husband, 72–3; and Magistrates Court
hearing, 93; marriage to de Marigny
and relationship with, 49–50, 51, 74–5,
77, 204–5; marriages, 224; rift with
parents, 54, 103, 110, 166, 189–90,
199, 253; testimony and cross-
examination at trial, 188–90;
upbringing, 75–6
de Marigny, Ruth (née Fahnestock)
(second wife), 166, 255; accusatory
letter written to the Oakes, 51, 102,
166; claiming money from de Marigny,
103, 173–4, 194, 255, 270;
deterioration in marriage and divorce,
15, 16–7, 67; marriage to de Marigny,
43–4
de Visdelou, Diana (née North) (wife), 40
de Visdelou, Georges, Marquis, 43, 47,
114, 145, 178, 198, 261; change of
name, 40–1, 172; as de Marigny's alibi,
141, 169, 180–1, 182–4, 192; death,
221; deportation of, 205–6, 208,
274–5; epilogue, 221; relationship with
de Marigny, 40–1, 180; rumours of date
raping, 208; testimony and cross-
examination at trial, 180–4
Deighton, Detective Inspector, 257–8
Dew, Arthur, 70, 248
Dinsha, Edanji, 88
Doubleday, Rhoda, 208
Douglas, Lieutenant John, 55, 69, 101,
102, 138
Drexel, Anthony J., 28
Dufferin, Maureen, 29
Dupuch, Etienne, 7, 117
Dupuch, Eugene, 117
Duveen, Joe, 18

Eccles, David, 60
Edsberg, Hans, 213, 222
Elliott, Maxine, 22
Ellis, Mabel, 93, 122, 123, 262
Erskine-Lindop, Colonel, 3–4, 5, 9–10, 35,

36, 70, 106, 136, 219, 230–1, 236

Fahnestock, Ruth *see* de Marigny, Ruth
Farrington, Hullen, 118
FBI, 92, 94, 114, 163, 248
Fejos, Paul, 83
Fernander, Enid, 262
Field, Frank, 89, 91, 104
Fitzmaurice, Lawrence, 90, 130–1, 242,
255
Floody, Wally, 16
Flynn, Errol, 30
Forbes, Rosita, 45, 67, 79
Foskett, Walter, 19, 21, 70, 102, 189–90,
210, 243, 248–51
Fouquereaux, Charles Chrysostomo, 38
Franklin, Robert, 261–3
Frazier, Brenda, 29, 47
Fulton, Hugh, 213

Gardner, Erle Stanley, xiv, 117, 121, 125,
146, 148, 159, 177, 219
Gellhorn, Martha, 42, 209, 224
Getty, John Paul, 86
Gibson, Levi, 122, 123, 180, 260–3, 270
Goering, Hermann, 82, 216
Goldsmith, Frank, 31
Goldsmith, Marcelle, 35, 79
Gould, Anna, 107
Greene, Richard, 223
Greenwood, Alfred, 92–3
Greig, Louis, 66
Gudewill, Marie, 173

Hallinan, Eric, 63, 114, 119, 132, 252–3;
closing speech at trial, 194, 195–6;
cross-examination of de Marigny,
171–2, 174–6; and de Marigny's
divorce from Ruth, 67; post-trial
career, 218; questioning of witnesses at
trial, 133–4, 149, 185–6; and wage
riots, 35, 63
Heape, Leslie, 35, 63, 67, 206
Hemingway, Ernest, 42, 209
Hemingway, Jack, 209
Heneage, Effie, 31, 125–6, 129, 263
Higgs, Godfrey, 71, 78, 89; background,
78–9; closing speech at trial, 190–3; as
counsel for de Marigny, 78–9; cross-
examination of Barker and exposure of
fingerprint forgery, 150–8, 256;